EARTHRISE

EARTHRISE

HER INSTRUMENTS: BOOK ONE

M. C. A. Hogarth

STUDIO
MCAH

Earthrise
Her Instruments: Book 1

First edition, copyright 2013 by M.C.A. Hogarth

M. Hogarth
PMB 109
4522 West Village Dr.
Tampa, FL 33624

ISBN-13: 978-1484996515
ISBN-10: 1484996518

Cover art by Julie Dillon
http://www.juliedillonart.com/

Designed and typeset by Catspaw DTP Services
http://www.catspawdtp.com/

TABLE OF CONTENTS

PART ONE: CHALK

"Captain—"

Reese's head came into abrupt, unpleasant contact with the bottom of the console. "Ow!"

"Rrrph, I'm sorry!"

Reese pushed back from beneath the environmental controls, leaving the tools beneath the console. Irine was standing behind her with sagging ears, wringing her hands. The felinoid Harat-Shar's breath came in soft visible puffs, and she was wearing socks on both feet and tail.

The *Earthrise* was always in need of repairs, but Reese fled to the engineering deck when she most particularly wanted to be alone. The cold usually deterred the rest of her crew from following. Not that she left it that cold just to convince them to leave her alone; it was honestly good for the electronics.

"I didn't mean to startle you," Irine said as Reese sat up and rubbed her head.

"You didn't startle me," Reese said, then amended, "Much." She scowled. "Well, don't just stand there, Irine

. . . what is it?"

"I'm afraid there's a call for you," Irine said, chafing her arms.

"I thought I told you not to both—"

"Bother you, yes, I know, but this thing's lighting up so many security alarms on my panel I think it's going to blow up."

Reese eyed her. "Security alarms."

The Harat-Shar girl sniffed, her socked tail curling behind her. "Even the handshake is encrypted. Talk about an obscene amount of money . . ."

Reese stood, the beads braided into her black hair clicking against her shoulder-blades as she shook them back. She ignored the clenching in the pit of her stomach with difficulty. "I'll take it. Go see how the loading is going."

"Okay," Irine said, and stepped silently on her socked feet toward the lift.

Reese watched her go, then stalked to the fore of the ship. Built in the Terran solar system, the TMS *Earthrise's* bridge spoke little of the amenities and luxurious waste of space so common to Alliance-built vessels; the human had to wedge herself between a few crates to the forward-facing windows with their communication consoles. As Irine had testified, a real-time comm request flashed on the screen inset on the side wall, the lagged blink of secure traffic.

Not even her curiosity could untie the growing knot in her stomach. Reese could think of few reasons a small-time trader captain might receive such a high priority, highly private signal. She didn't like any of them.

"This is Theresa Eddings of the TMS *Earthrise*. Accept the incoming signal."

The computer chirped its response; Reese rested one brown hand against the console and leaned back to watch the slow blink transform to a handshake screen. The header information stunned her, and then tied the knot in her stomach much, much tighter. Ulcer material. Definitely.

TO: Theresa Eddings
TMS *Earthrise*
Docked: Starbase Fos
FROM:[Scrambled]

Not only a message, but one from someone who refused to identify himself. The last time she'd seen a scrambled source, six years ago, she'd had reason to rejoice. She'd also ended up promising to pay up for the miracle at some future date. At the time, she'd been sure that she'd refit the *Earthrise* and rise above the small freight contracts she'd been able to afford . . . the idea of paying her mysterious benefactor back hadn't worried her.

Somehow, though, her imagined pay-offs never materialized. Bad luck dogged the *Earthrise*, and for every score Reese managed, something needed repair, someone needed repayment early or somewhere interest compounded faster than she could handle it. Six years later, she had just enough for the cargo she could hear being loaded right now—the cargo and enough food to keep them from starving, and that was it. Certainly not enough to pay back someone who'd bought the *Earthrise* back from Reese's creditors, with enough left over to fill her holds with new hope.

Reese's misgivings doubled as the handshake completed and a line of gibberish ran across the bottom of the screen; once the parade reached the other side, it gave the appearance of being completely still save for the twitch of the characters changing. Beneath this line, two numbers popped up in either corner. She knew them, of course—

the right one indicated how many Well satellites this missive was jumping to get to her real-time, and the other, at zero, the amount of identified attacks on the encrypted stream.

A fine sweat popped up on Reese's dark forehead. Every second of a Riggins-encrypted Well transmission cost one thousand *fin*—far more than she could earn back with the *Earthrise* in months. This was also the exact same way her benefactor had last used to contact her. Her time had run out.

On the flat black above the stream, a sentence in amber appeared.

You will remember us, we presume.

"If you are who I think you are, then I could hardly forget," Reese said. Her words appeared one by one in response. There was a long pause. Then:

We told you, long ago, that when we returned we would tell you that we requested your aid in the name of the High Priestess of the Amacrucian Church.

And that took away all Reese's doubts—and hopes— that this was some new obscenely rich person who wanted something from her. With a sigh, she said, "What can I do for you?"

We would that our errand could have waited, for it was not our intention to call in your favor so quickly. Still, Fate does not always allow for wishes. Theresa, you owe our seat a favor. It would please us greatly to call now this favor.

There it was. Reese sighed softly, then said, "I have no money—"

It is not money we need, but aid of a different kind.

The stomach acid that had been busy on her esophagus relented, just a little. "How can I help?"

We sent one of our beloved people to investigate the disappearance of some our own. In the course of his inves-

tigations, he ran afoul of the local law, and is thusly imprisoned. This does not disturb us unduly. What disturbs us is that in the course of his investigations, he may have aroused the ire of powerful foes who may not have had recourse to vengeance had he remained mobile.

"You want us to liberate him," Reese finished. Her nervousness returned full force, and she spared a brief, longing thought for the bottle of chalk tablets in her cabin, wards against the stomach upset that plagued her so often.

Just so. You may return him to us once he is freed, or keep him, or advise him on how best to hide. Naturally, you may want to take his opinions into account, but given his inconveniencing of your goodly ship you may consider his opinions as seriously as you feel the situation warrants.

Reese cleared her throat. "I feel it necessary to point out that my 'goodly ship' isn't exactly a warcruiser."

We trust your ingenuity will provide the way where simple brute force would not.

Reese stared at the amber words, so innocuously presented. She couldn't imagine this going well, but: "I owe you a favor. If this is how you want to call it in . . ."

It is.

"Then I will do my best."

The next words didn't immediately appear. In the small space it gave Reese for breathing, she re-scanned the conversation and managed a breathy chuckle. The whole exchange sounded like something out of one of her romance novels, and while her misgivings still had a grip on her stomach she couldn't help the smallest feeling that she was being cast in some great adventure. Backwards, of course. She was apparently the knight in shining armor.

It is well, and we are pleased. Given the rescue of our unfortunate wayward investigator, you may consider yourself quit of your obligation to us. I will send the relevant information on termination of our contact.

"Thank you."

The real-time stream cut off with the attack counter at seventeen. Reese hadn't been watching the numbers, but the sight of them now made her clench her fists. Encrypted streams usually accumulated a few attacks as a matter of course. People liked to poke at them, just because there were there. But this—what the bleeding soil had this person been investigating to warrant such a concerted effort?

> **NAME:**   Hirianthial Sarel Jisiensire
> **CURRENT LOCATION:**
>   Nurera, Bath-Etu
>   Allied Colony Inu-case
>   Sector Andeka
> **NATURE OF MISSION:**
>   Investigation of cause of missing persons.
>   *Suspected cause:* lost to the slave trade.

Reese stabbed the pads on the console, setting it to trap the information before she squeezed out of the front and ran to the nearest cabinet. A few chalk tablets later, she stared at the ceiling with eyes as vibrant a blue as the seas of Terra at *Earthrise.* The man had been prying into the slave trade, and their mutual benefactor was sending her to fish him out of jail before the slavers caught up with him and sold him off. Paying her benefactor back would have been easier, even if she'd had to take out a thousand loans. She ground on the last of the chalk and warily wound back to the fore to stare again at the screen. The final chunk had loaded in her absence. There was now a picture of her charge on the screen.

He was an Eldritch.

Reese dropped into the console seat and gaped. She'd

never expected to see a real Eldritch in her lifetime. The race's isolationism and xenophobia were so extreme they'd become a stock offering in her yearly romance subscription—Eldritch women learning to love despite their social conditioning! Eldritch men reluctantly learning to touch their alien lovers! Paintings of pale Eldritch in unfathomably silly costumes, drooping artistically in the arms of humans . . . that and the occasional flat photo in the u-banks were Reese's only exposure to the people. The Eldritch didn't leave their planet.

And yet here she was, about to fly off in search of one.

A real picture. Of a real Eldritch! Reese leaned closer.

The elongation Reese had assumed to be artistic license was real. Who would have known? And just like on the book covers, it was unsettling; the Eldritch looked human, so to have them be ever-so-slightly different in proportion was disturbing. Apparently the cream-white skin was real too, and the straight hair that looked like a heavy, silk sheet. He had a long face, a nose a little too straight, and framed in white lashes his eyes were a truly unlikely shade of wine-dark red. He looked fragile, like the distressed damsel. Like too much trouble.

A real Eldritch. In the hands of slavers! Reese sat back, and even in the gear she'd donned to work in the frigid engineering bay she got goosebumps. There were so many rumors about the Eldritch and their powers and their culture it was hard to sort out which might be true . . . but all of them suggested that a slaver would pay a small mint to get his hands on one. And this was her assignment?

Reese pressed a hand against her forehead, fighting anger and worry. Once she had her breath back, she rose and squirmed past the crates, growling an imprecation at them that might have wilted their corners had they had ears. She strode to the lift, down to the lower deck and out the ramp to the starbase's floor.

Three figures labored at the back of the *Earthrise*. The vessel's systems had been engineered to Alliance specs, something that not only included her computers but also her cargo holds. The *Earthrise* had five cat-12 spindles: long cylindrical strength members twelve inches in diameter that could support Type-A and Type-B sized cargo bins. Each spindle could hold twelve, for a total of sixty bins, though the *Earthrise* rarely ran to capacity.

Irine, Sascha and Kis'eh't were tossing bins onto the conveyer belt leading to the loading collars, where the bins would be aligned and shot down the spindles. They had taken on twenty bins of Harat-Shariin rooderberries. While Reese preferred not to cart around anything as sensitive as foodstuffs, they invariably fetched high prices in foreign markets and her coffers were, as always, low.

"Hey!"

The two bipedals, Irine and Sascha, stopped working. Kis'eh't, her stocky centauroid shape barely visible over the slope of the belt, continued pushing the bins.

"What's up, Boss?" Sascha asked, grinning. Unlike his twin sister, he did not wear socks on his tail or his feet.

Reese grabbed a bin and tossed it on the belt. "We have to pack it up and shove off immediately. We've been given a task."

"Ooh!" Irine said, yellow eyes widening. "A contract? Finally?"

"Did I say a contract?" Reese said gruffly. "I said 'a task.'
"

"She means we're not getting paid for it," Sascha said.

Kis'eh't snorted from the other side of the conveyer belt. "Someone must have held a palmer to her head, then," the Glaseahn said in her clipped accent.

"Yeah, what's the deal, Reese?" Irine asked, folding her

striped arms over her chest.

"Work now," Reese said. She grunted as she pushed another bin onto the belt. "We don't have much time to get this done, especially if we don't want these things to rot before we can get them to a useful port."

"Like anything'll rot with the temperatures you keep the ship at," Irine said, rolling her eyes and padding, feline-silent, to the next bin.

"Oh, hush!" Reese said, torn between exasperation and a hint of amusement. The twins were irrepressible, particularly together. The Harat-Shar felinoids raised on colony worlds usually conformed better to the rest of the Alliance's moral norms . . .but a matched set from Harat-Sharii, like Irine and Sascha, were bound to violate every accepted precept of societal behavior. She was fortunate to have Kis'eht and Bryer to balance their outrageousness, or she would probably have beaten them by now. And they would have liked it.

The last of the rooderberry bins rolled up to the collar, spun into position, and sped down the spindle to the retaining clamp. Another clamp followed it, and Reese pressed the pad that levered the belt back into the cargo bay. Twenty bins hung neatly off the spindles in the echoing emptiness. Had Reese had the wherewithal, she would have seen the other forty spaces filled with exotic spices and fabrics and novelty items that would have returned her poor enterprise to some semblance of profitability . . .but because she'd managed to become indebted (almost literally) to a stranger whose name she didn't even know, she was honor-bound to go chasing a wayward alien across two sectors. And then post his bail!

Reese sighed, rubbed her stomach, decided not to ponder her probable ulcers. "Meeting in fifteen. Get moving, people."

"We're doing what?" Irine exclaimed, striped hands twitching on the mess hall table.

Reese leaned back against her chair, letting her silence speak for her. As she expected, Bryer, the Phoenix, had nothing to say; the giant birdlike creature rested against the front of the chair, straddling it so as to give the full length of his metallic plumage unrestricted space.

Kis'eh't, while obviously perturbed, did nothing beyond wrinkle her dark, furry brow and lay back her feathered ears. She had more limbs than all of them: two black arms, four black and white legs, and two stunted leathery wings protruding from her second, horizontal back. And a tail, black with two white stripes running down it, which currently flicked against the cool floor.

The round ball of fluff on the table between the Phoenix and the Glaseahn only ruffled part of its neural fur, turning from ivory to rosy peach in places.

Irine, in her socks and little else, was pouting. "So what . . . we have to ride in like champions and rescue some random spy? For nothing?"

"Not for nothing," Reese said. "In return for the money that this person gave me to save me from bankruptcy before you people came aboard."

"Who is this person, anyway?" Sascha asked.

"Which one?" Reese asked. "The spy or the one with the money?"

"Both," Sascha said.

Reese smothered a small grin. "The spy's an Eldritch."

"A what!"

That came from so many places at once she couldn't tell which of them said it first. Kis'eh't got the first words after: "I hear they can start fires with their minds."

"And read your thoughts," Irine said.

Kis'eh't said, "And sense your feelings. They always know when you're lying."

"That's the *last* thing we need," Irine said.

"I hear they bathe in honey," Sascha said.

Reese stared at him. So did everyone else with eyes— even Bryer. The tigraine shrugged and said, "Something to do with keeping their skin white."

"Honey won't bleach skin," Kis'eh't said. "Moisturize it, maybe. But bleach? Not unless Eldritch honey is actually some other substance entirely . . ."

"What do I know about Eldritch honey?" Sascha said. "They're supposedly all rich, too. And they're all princes or princesses. And they all require servants, because none of them know how to take care of themselves."

"Is this guy in for a slap from the universe!" Irine said, shaking her head.

"He's in jail," Reese said dryly. "I think the slap's already been delivered."

"This is troublesome," Kis'eh't said. "An Eldritch . . . this being may have specialized needs, Reese. No one knows what they eat, what their normal medical profile is like, how to treat one that's sick . . . no one even knows how properly to address them or what social or cultural mores they hold to. How are we supposed to save one of these creatures and make him comfortable?"

"I'm not sure," Reese admitted. "And since the packet I received wasn't exactly forthcoming with any of that kind of material, I'm not sure we'll be expected to do this perfect." She pushed her data tablet to the center of the table with its gleaming pale picture of their charge. "That's him. Hirianthial Sarel Jisiensire."

"Say again?" Sascha said.

Reese repeated it.

Kis'eh't shook her head. "We'll let you address him,"

she said ruefully.

"At least he's handsome for a human," Irine said.

"He's not human," Reese said. "He's Eldritch. And don't forget it, if you don't want him snooping around the inside of your brain. Anyway, there's only one thing I think we can take for certainty . . . you're not supposed to touch an Eldritch. So if all possible, let's try to keep bodily contact to a minimum."

"Awww," Irine said.

Sascha, studying the picture, said, "Angels, boss, I have to agree with her."

"Yeah, well, if you want to come on to him, be my guest," Reese said. "Just don't expect me to put your furry behinds back together if it turns out he can blow things up by looking at them funny. And if we break him, I think our benefactor's going to be very grumpy."

"Speaking of, who's the person with the money?" Sascha asked.

"I don't know," Reese said. "I've never seen her face."

"Her face?" That was Irine.

Reese shrugged. "Just a guess."

"A trap?" Bryer said into the following silence.

"I don't know why she'd bother," Reese said. "Obviously the woman is bleeding rich. If she'd really wanted to sell me, you and the rest of us into slavery, she could have just hired someone to do it long before now."

"I wonder who she is," Kis'eh't murmured. "Who would know an Eldritch? One who left his world? It's most peculiar."

"For all I know she's the Faerie Queen of Eldritches and he's her errant prince," Reese said with exasperation. "Wondering about the assignment is pointless. I owe this person a debt and I'm going to pay it. Since I own this ship and I hired you, you're all coming along. If you don't like it,

I can give you your severance pay in rooderberries."

The silence was refreshing.

"Now," Reese continued, "If you twins would be kind enough to set a course for Inu-Case, I would be much obliged."

The two Harat-Shar, still grumbling, rose and left the mess hall.

"The rooderberries will probably go bad if we keep them longer than it takes to get to Inu-case," Kis'eh't said, her voice quiet.

"We'll have to hope we can sell them to whatever poor sots live there, then," Reese said with a sigh. She stood. "I know it's crazy."

"Honor is the best form of craziness." Bryer said.

Reese eyed him. "This is not about honor. This is just good sense. If someone loans you money, you pay them back."

Bryer canted his head. Of all her crew, he struck her as the most alien. Even Allacazam, with its lack of eyes, mouth or even any obvious personality, seemed less threatening than Bryer with his whiteless eyes and narrow pupils. They made the Phoenix look wild, even though he rarely made a sudden move. "About more than money."

"You're right," Reese said. "Now it's about flying all over the galaxy posting people's bail."

Again, that steady stare. This time Reese ignored it and picked up Allacazam, watching its colors—his colors, she'd never been able to think of him as an it no matter what the u-banks said—flow to a muted lilac. "You'll want to man your respective stations. We'll be casting off in ten minutes."

Kis'eh't rose, stretching her hind legs and wings, then padded past her. Bryer followed. Reese watched them go, then dropped back into her chair with a sigh and cuddled the Flitzbe. She petted the soft neural fibers.

"I wish I was as sure about this as I have to seem to be," she said.

She heard a rising chime, felt a wash of muted lilac, Allacazam's way of asking a question. She'd never questioned how they managed to communicate; few people in the Alliance truly understood the Flitzbe, and those who did weren't exactly writing How-To communication guides for people like Reese. All she knew was that from the moment Allacazam had rolled into her life, things had felt easier. Not necessarily *been* easier, but at least felt that way.

"Of course I have to seem confident," she said to him. "But still . . . an Eldritch? Slavers? I'm just a trader, not a hero. I don't want anything to do with something this dangerous."

The Flitzbe assembled an image of her dressed in plate mail with a shining sword. Reese laughed shakily. "Right. That's not my cup of tea. Speaking of which . . . I could certainly use something for my stomach. And then to go check on the fuzzies to make sure they haven't secretly diverted someplace more pleasant."

The smell of sour yogurt tickled her nostrils and she hugged the Flitzbe. "No, I don't honestly think that badly of them. It's just that this is hard enough without having to explain it to them, too." She sighed, ruffling the top of his fur. "Hopefully it'll be quick and simple and we can drop him off somewhere and that will be the end of that."

She knew better. From the flash of maroon that washed over Allacazam's body, so did he.

Their least time path carried them through Sector Epta and most of Andeka. The engines that their mysterious benefactor had paid to refit six years ago cut the journey from sixteen days to eleven, and Reese spent all of them fretting. Kis'eh't caught her in the cargo hold on the fifth day, walking the spindles in the reduced gravity that reminded her so much of Mars and her happier days climbing the few tall trees there.

"Guarding the bins isn't going to stop the cargo from going bad," the Glaseahn said.

"I know," Reese said, then sighed. "I don't suppose there's anyone who could use twenty bins worth of overripe rooderberries."

"Maybe a maker of rooderberry wine?" Kis'eh't suggested.

"We should be so lucky," Reese said.

"You're worried," Kis'eh't said.

Reese stared down at the centauroid from her perch on the spindle. "Now why would I be worried?" she asked. "We're only about to tangle with slavers."

"Not necessarily," Kis'eh't said. "You borrow too much trouble, if I may, Reese. If you stopped, maybe you could use your money to buy yourself a nice dinner on the town one day, instead of dropping it on multipacks of antacids."

"Dinner out sounds like just the thing," Reese says. "Maybe if we get back in one piece from this debacle."

"*When* we get back," Kis'eh't said. "I'm not planning to die on this mission."

"Right," Reese said. "Neither am I. I'm a survivor."

Kis'eh't only shook her head and left the cargo hold, which suited Reese just fine. She'd hired Kis'eh't three months after the twins, and Bryer a month after . . . that was about three years ago now, when she'd realized she would never do more than break even relying on the ship's automated functions and contractors to do the work. At first, she'd resented their intrusion into her solitude; while she'd had Allacazam for a good seven years, the Flitzbe hardly seemed like a normal person. He didn't require conversation, food, a salary, maintenance. He never complained. He was like a pet, but smarter. Sometimes Reese thought he was smarter than she was.

But she'd learned to love the banter, the silliness, even the nosiness of her crew, and their help had made it possible to keep bread on the table. It was just that lately, they were all more nosy than usual. She wondered what was bothering them.

Reese resisted the urge to tour the entire cargo bay one more time before leaving. Rooderberry wine. She wondered what that would taste like.

The insistent chirp of the intercom roused Reese from a deep sleep several days later. She twisted in her hammock, fumbled for the controls and said, "Yes?"

"We're here, ma'am. Over your stinking colony world. Bet they have nothing to trade us but sheep. How are we going to fit sheep in the cargo—"

"Irine! Enough! Find out where the city of Nurera is and get dressed to go down. Be quick about it, all right? The rooderberries are rotting."

The com cut off the end of Irine's snort. Reese sighed and massaged the bridge of her nose. The gentle rock of the hammock calmed her, reminded her of home, but her stomach still whined. Some part of her had hoped they'd never arrive at this Freedom-cursed world, but here they were. All she had to do now was find the Eldritch and pry him out of jail before anyone noticed her doing it. Then she could deposit him at some Alliance starbase and be done with the whole mess.

Reese rolled out of the hammock, the cocoon of felt blankets unraveling from her body as she raided her bathroom cabinet for chalk tablets, peppermint this time. She rifled through her closet for something unremarkable to wear while grinding up her breakfast. That she didn't have any unremarkable clothes didn't improve her mood. She pulled on a black bodysuit, long-sleeved and high-necked, a pair of soft black boots with flexible, quiet soles, and jerked on her utility vest with its bright blue ribs and orange piping.

She also tapped the intercom. "Irine?"

"Yes?" From the distracted purr, Reese decided it best not to ask what Irine was up to. The cats chose the oddest moments to get amorous, and as long as it wasn't in Reese's face she didn't care.

"Is it cold down there?"

A pause. Then, "Moderately. Colder than the cargo bay but not as cold as engineering."

Reese dragged a cloak off its hanger and slung it over her shoulders. With that, a belt with a sling for her data tablet, a handful of coins and a knife, she was ready. "Put us down outside Nurera, kitties."

"Aye, captain."

"Gentle as a cushion stuffed with feathers," from Sascha.

"I'll be up there in a minute," Reese said. She made one last check of her cabin, then left for the bridge. Sascha was sitting at the pilot's chair wearing the fur that his gods gave him and nothing else. Irine was leaning over his shoulder, eyes fixed on the view through the tiny windows.

"Oh for the love of earth," Reese said, exasperated. "What have I said about piloting naked, Sascha?"

"Don't break my concentration, ma'am," Sascha said, his relaxed drawl at complete odds with his intent stare. "Driving this old crate in and out of a planet's skies takes too much willpower."

Having done it often enough herself, Reese couldn't disagree. And Sascha was good—it was the reason she'd hired him. She'd grown tired of flying the *Earthrise* around herself. Still, she wondered what it was Irine whispered into his ear in their exotic language.

True to his word, their landing sent a bare quiver through Reese's body.

"Good enough?" he asked her with a grin.

"Yeah," Reese said. "Now get dressed."

"Awww!"

Reese poked him in the shoulder. "I don't want us to be noticeable. You nude is noticeable."

"She's got a point there," Irine said, grinning.

Reese rolled her eyes. "Meet me at the airlock." She leaned over and pressed the all-call. "Everyone to the airlock. We have a job to do."

Fresh, warm air, redolent with spices and the scent of fecund soil and sun-warmed incense—Reese shuddered at the first whiff of Inu-case. She'd been born to recirculated air on Mars; from there she'd gone to the *Earthrise*. The freedom of the evening breeze struck her as unnatural and the varied smells alarming.

"And there's where we're headed," Sascha said, pointing out the first of the buildings as they crested the hill.

"How far are we from the jail?" Reese said, choosing the moment to stop for breath. Inu-Case's heavier gravity had sapped much of her energy on the ten-minute walk from the *Earthrise's* position. They hadn't wanted to land too close to town, just in case. Still, she envied Kis'eh't, whom she'd left to guard the ship.

"Once we hit the buildings, we'll be two blocks south of it," Sascha said, studying his data tablet. The tip of his tiger-striped tail peeked from beneath his brown overcoat. "They didn't want it too close to the center of town, I imagine."

Irine squinted. "Looks pretty quiet down there. I guess we picked a good time to come by."

"Let's just hope someone's there to take our credit and let him out," Reese said. "Come on."

Rising past the orange glow of the street lamps, the wooden houses had an ominous cast. What glimpses of the surrounding land Reese could catch between them revealed only a crimped plain drowned in violet shadows and the black smudges of distant mountains. The few trees dotting the lawns proved the source of the odor: their round, waxy leaves reeked so badly that the two felines took to skirting them, and even Bryer seemed to find them discomfiting.

In sunlight, perhaps the rustic building materials and open streets would have seemed inviting. Reese couldn't shake the sense of unease that seeing them in the dark aroused. It didn't help that there was no one outside. No children playing. No people walking home. No one talking, wandering the streets. Reese had never been to a slaver's retreat, but she could only imagine it being this silent, as if everyone was afraid to call attention to herself.

"Doesn't anyone live here?" Irine asked in a whisper.

Bryer glanced into one of the buildings. "Deserted."

"Really well-maintained for someplace deserted," Sascha said, tail lashing.

"I don't like this at all," Irine said. "It looks like a pirate hide-out."

"Try not to look rushed, people," Reese said. "If anyone's watching, we have business here and we're not worried about it."

"Let's just hope they can't hear us talking," Sascha muttered.

At the corner they stopped to allow a single sparrow to zip past . . . a peculiar conveyance in a town, overpowered

for mere hops across blocks and underpowered for any serious spaceflight. Reese watched it streak past and pressed
a hand to her stomach.

"Angels! I can't decide whether to be glad there are actually people living here or not," Irine muttered.

"Never mind the people," Sascha said, pointing at an
unprepossessing one-story building. "That's our stop."

"Let's get this over with," Reese said, and marched to
the door.

"How come there's no gate? You know, with electrified
wire or stunner fields or something?" Irine asked.

"I don't know," Reese said. She tried one of the doors—
it was locked. "I guess all their guards are on the inside."
She scanned for a door announce and found none. "Are
you sure this is the front?"

"I can check around the sides," Sascha said.

"Do that," Reese said. "Take Bryer with you."

"Yes ma'am."

"And in the mean time we just stand here," Irine said.
"While security cameras stare at us."

"We're not doing anything wrong," Reese said.

"Right," Irine said, tail whipping nervously. When
it smacked Reese one too many times on the calf, Reese
hissed, "Stop that."

"Sorry."

They waited. And waited.

"It can't be that big a place, can it?" Irine said.

"No," Reese said, feeling a headache beginning to knot
her brows. "Something's happened."

"Should we go look?" Irine asked.

She wanted to say 'no,' so of course she said, "Yes." And,
"Keep close." Then she set off around the perimeter of the
jail. The nearest buildings were still set far enough away
that they could see anyone coming. No gates or traps star-

tled them.

"I can still smell him," Irine said. She tapped on the wall. "But it stops right here."

Reese glanced at the grass surrounding the featureless wall, then bent and examined it. Irine joined her a moment later. They stared together.

"See anything?"

"No," Reese said.

Irine's ears flipped back. "Would you know it if you saw something?"

"I haven't exactly done much investigative policework in my life," Reese said. She sighed and straightened. "Let's go back around front."

There were no other doors. No lights. Nothing. By the time they wound back up around to the forbidding doors, Reese was beginning to get angry. She pointed at the door. "Do something about that."

For once, Irine did not protest innocence, but began scrutinizing the door frame and feeling along its edge. Reese watched her with growing impatience, but forced herself to remain still until the mysterious actions of the Harat-Shar bore fruit.

"Not bad. But not up to specs," Irine commented as she pocketed her electronic picks and pushed the door in. It complained with a faint creak, then inched into the side-pocket. The girl peeked in through the crack. "Doesn't seem to be manned," she whispered.

Reese glanced behind her shoulder—still nothing. Not a person walking up the dusky streets, no sound of music or laughter or life, just the constant slough of the perfumed breeze. In front of her, a sealed door with no guards and not a breath of a living person, despite Sascha and Bryer having vanished without a clue. There were people here, people far more dangerous than she was.

"Maybe we should go," Reese said.

"But my brother!" Irine whispered. "And Bryer!"

"We need reinforcements," Reese said, tense.

"What, Kis'eh't and Allacazam? Sure, they'll help," Irine said, scowling.

"I was thinking more like Fleet," Reese said. "We're not up to this, Irine."

"Think what you want," Irine said. "I'm not leaving Sascha in there."

"Irine—!"

But the girl had already slipped inside. Reese lunged after her, trying to catch her tail, but Irine had ghosted past the empty front desk to the row of cells. No halo shield arced across the wall leading to them; no guards stood rigidly before them. Reese fought a renewed foreboding as she hurried after the Harat-Shar. The warmth of the stone floor communicated to her toes through the soft material of her boots.

"No sign of Sascha or Bryer," Irine called back, "but at least here's our expensive Eldritch!"

Reese sprinted after the girl, a cold sweat erupting on her brow. As she pushed Irine aside, her throat closed for a precious second at the sight of the body. Then, strangled, "That's not him!" She flung herself around, preparing to flee—

And met the business end of a metal pipe. She didn't even remember going down.

"Stand away from the door."

Hirianthial judged that a joke, since he was currently wedged into a corner of the cell.

"You have guests," the ruddy guard said. He leaned on the wall as his tow-haired fellow dropped two bodies onto the straw. Hirianthial watched them without lifting his

face, and the fall of his pale hair masked his alarm at the
boneless flop of the first and the slack feathered limbs of
the second. Were they even alive?

"Don't worry. They'll be awake soon enough, and then
you can spend the rest of your visit trying to avoid them,"
the ruddy guard said with a grin.

The second guard withdrew and re-armed the halo
field. They paused at the bars, waiting for some reaction
for him as they had the first few times they'd surprised him
with some ploy. By now they should have grown used to
his stoic withdrawal. Hirianthial closed his eyes and waited for them to leave.

They didn't. Instead they talked in low mutters. Blond
smothered a chortle. No doubt Red was telling Blond the
point of crowding one cell with all their prisoners when
the cells lining the corridor remained empty. Red knew far
too much about what made Eldritch uncomfortable, and
after a few months of investigation Hirianthial had a good
idea why. The Queen would not be pleased to have her
theory proven. One needed only two hands to count the
members of his race who'd ventured beyond their world
. . . and only a few fingers to number those who'd returned.
Liolesa had traced some of the missing to legitimate enter-
prises—there was a Galare studying psychology on one of
the Alliance's core worlds, for instance—but a good part of
them had simply vanished without trace.

Hirianthial himself had been one of those sojourners
when Liolesa enlisted his aid. He hadn't wanted to help,
but one did not refuse Liolesa, and not just because she
was queen. He'd been drifting for several months anyway;
the hospital on Tam-Ley had lost the funding for its xeno-
critical care and been forced to contract those duties to a
nearby emergency center, which hadn't been hiring doctors who'd taken the Kelienne oath. He'd had a choice to

take a different ethical oath every year since completing
his schooling, but even if he'd been able to bring himself to
do so nothing he'd seen in the wards had convinced him to
change his mind. Jobless, he'd left Tam-Ley and taken up
travel for its own sake, unwilling to return home, uncertain what to do next.

It wasn't that he hadn't wanted to help the queen. He
was a passable spy. He was just a better doctor, and that by
accident.

When Hirianthial could detect no more talk at the cell
bars, he extended a feather of intent outward, searching
for the mental presence of his guards: nothing.

Opening his eyes, he approached the two bodies. Both
auras rested flat against their skins, gray and heavy as
mercury. Hirianthial didn't have to look hard to find the
bruises and the discoloration of the palmer burn near their
heads. He unlaced his sleeves and pushed them up his pale
forearms before rolling the first body, the Harat-Shar, onto
his side to look for any extended burns or swelling. Some
people had adverse reactions to being struck with a palmer, and these two were too deeply unconscious for him to
measure that without a visual inspection.

The first frissons of the Harat-Shar's mind traveled up
Hirianthial's fingers, rising through the thin layer of clothing and fur. The Eldritch sensed the dull stupor of the
subconscious struggling against the body, the quick red
flashes of dreams and disconnected thoughts. He ignored
them, seeking any other signs of damage, and found none.

"You'll be fine," he murmured to the Harat-Shar before turning to the Phoenix. A similar inspection brought
him the susurrus of the Phoenix's alien thoughts but no
cause for worry. As he examined the second being, Hirianthial reluctantly admired the precision of the palmer
shot. Something about the metallic iridescence of Phoe-

nix feathers diffused palmer fire—to take down a Phoenix required a shot at the head, hands or feet where feathers thinned to down or skin. Since Phoenixae had fearsome taloned fingers and toes, felling one at a distance was a wise idea.

Aside from the palmer burns, neither patient showed any signs of his guards' attentions; Red had a particularly hard backhand, difficult to miss. He set them both on their backs with enough straw to keep them from sore heads and spines. Sitting back on his heels, Hirianthial managed a wry smile. If Red had planned these two to discomfit him, he should have used a lower setting on the palmer.

Still, he couldn't resist wondering: who were they? And what were they doing here? Hirianthial frowned at the newcomers while unrolling his sleeves and tightening the laces again. Perhaps when they woke they'd be amenable to conversation. He wouldn't be surprised if they'd been caught unawares and had no idea what this place was or why they'd been imprisoned. So it went with pirates and slavers.

Hirianthial retreated to his corner and resumed his silent vigil. He extended a thread of attention toward his two charges before allowing the rest of his mind to drift into trance. His ability to sense others without having to touch them was rare among Eldritch and had always been both boon and bane. Against the unpleasant over-sensitivity it gave him to touching a waking person, he could favorably weigh this ability to monitor patients without machinery. It lacked specificity, but he'd used it countless times while working to track the general health of his patients. It had also proven useful in this ancillary mission for Liolesa. Not useful enough to keep him out of his present situation, but one could not fault the talent for the mistakes of its user.

Neither of his patients woke before Red and Blond returned with another two bodies. Hirianthial didn't open his eyes, watching their auras instead: hot yellow violence with spurts of green for Red, Blond with similar yellows but with flashes of sizzling brown resentment, and in their arms another pair of dull grey auras.

"More guests for you," Red said. "Getting fairly crowded in here, isn't it?"

Hirianthial didn't reply.

"Set them there."

"There" was near enough to him that their physical presence crimped his own aura. Hirianthial sucked it in until he felt well and truly trapped in his corner. He was not a claustrophobic man but even he had his moments of Eldritch xenophobia. Had they been awake and mobile, he would have been forced to sink into meditation to combat the urge to flee.

They were not awake. They were not well. They were patients, not threats.

Hirianthial held himself still until the guards lost their patience and left, taking their spurts of sick green humor with them. Then he unfolded first one leg and then the next and opened his eyes.

The nearest body belonged to another Harat-Shar, female this time, and similar enough to the first that Hirianthial wondered at their relation. He gently turned her face, reading her body's louder complaints over her mind's unconscious murmurs through his fingers. He found the burn on her jaw that had put her down and verified the lack of any secondary effect before pulling her over to rest against the male. Lying beside one another their similarities were so marked Hirianthial judged them closer than mere kin. Twins, perhaps. Even the stripe patterns on their brows mimicked one another.

That left one more person. Hirianthial returned to the

other end of the cell, retying one of the laces that had come undone while dragging the tigraine. The glimpse he caught through his fingers made the laces slip back down, forgotten. The Eldritch went to one knee next to the woman on the floor.

He wasn't sure what arrested his attention first—her body or her health. He'd seen countless humans in his studies and rotations, enough to recognize her light-boned limbs as an indication of a low gravity origin . . . space-born, or one of the Moon or Mars colonies. Probably the latter, given her short stature. Nor would he have called her beautiful, though he found the chocolate honey hue of her skin exotic, and her braided and beaded hair reminded him of a noblewoman's coif. It was her mien despite unconsciousness that fascinated him. Her limbs were clenched. Her fingers still had a hint of a curl, as if they were trying to remain fisted. Even her brow was furrowed.

Her state was so grievous a collection of pre-existing conditions that he warred over touching her. Just running his hands over her aura scored him with lances of pain, irritation and swelling. The area over her stomach made him want to check his palm for blood. The spikes that pierced her aura despite its weighted unconsciousness matched her tense posture for stubbornness. If she was so obstinate in her sleep, it beggared the imagination to picture her awake.

Hirianthial craned his head over hers, seeking the burn that had put her down and finding a lump instead. Unlike the others, this woman had been struck, and it behooved him to ensure the blow had done no lasting damage. He didn't look forward to touching her to check. He tried without grazing her skin first, trailing his fingertips along her aura near the lump. Thankfully, he could sense no danger.

Why he felt compelled to touch her, just to double-check, he didn't know. Hirianthial stretched his fingers, steeled himself and trailed them along her cheek. The storm of emotions that clashed beneath their tips warned him that her struggle toward consciousness had almost been won, and still she surprised him when her lashes fluttered, revealing a crack of brilliant blue.

Nevertheless courtesy required that he remove his hands and help her orient herself.

"Ah, good morning. Early morning, that would be."

Reese didn't recognize the voice, male and baritone with an indescribable, open-throated accent, one that didn't linger long on consonants. She forced her eyelids apart and found herself staring straight into hair like poured milk and eyes the color of an expensive merlot.

She groaned, though whether from the throbbing at her temple or the situation was debatable. Both, probably. "You!" she croaked.

"Hush. You'll wake the others." Hirianthial glanced to the side, giving her an excellent view of his profile. There was a purple bruise marring the hard line of his cheekbone. "They are roughly in your condition or better, but they are all still unconscious."

"The others? Sascha? Bryer? Irine?"

"I count two Harat-Shar and one Phoenix. Is that sufficient?"

Reese scowled, then closed her eyes when the bump on her head sent another lance of pain through her temple. "Curse it all. I knew something was going on with this place. Where are the guards?" She tried to look to the side but one of her pupils was vying for independence. She closed that one and tried to focus.

The Eldritch held a finger up over her lips, not touching. "Hush. They'll hear you, lady. We're underground, where they keep prisoners."

"Underground! Then the jail upstairs—"

"—is a falsehood."

"They did a rotten job of hiding their tracks then," Reese said. "We knew something was wrong the moment we couldn't find a real door."

"You misunderstand, my lady," the Eldritch said. "The jail is not intended as a cover. It is meant to intimidate. On that count it is quite the succes . . . the pirates have driven everyone who isn't part of their operation completely out of this part of town, and the rest of it they own in fact if not in name."

"Great," Reese said, losing what little energy she had. She imagined it bleeding into the ground beneath her tailbone and shoulders. "You were supposed to be in a jail cell we could get you out of for money, not underground in a place pirates hide people they want to make disappear."

The Eldritch canted his head, hair hissing against one shoulder. "I'm sorry for the inconvenience."

"Yeah, well, I'll send you a bill," Reese said, trying to get a hand under herself so she could sit up.

A hand appeared over her chest, not touching but not moving either. "Ah! Don't. You're still gray."

"Gray?" Reese asked.

He frowned. His expressions seemed formed only by the faintest of tugs at his lips or eyes; Reese wondered if all Eldritch were so subtle. "The color of your aura, you might say. Gray's not an auspicious color to be."

His accent was so distractingly pretty that she didn't actually hear what he said until a few moments later. Or maybe that was her headache, making it too hard to hear past the pounding in her ears. "What the bleeding soil do you know about auras?"

"I'm Eldritch," he said, as if that alone explained it. As an afterthought, he added, "I'm also a doctor."

"Someone decided a *doctor* would make a good spy?" Her stomach started burning. Reese fought the desire to laugh, suspecting she would sound hysterical. "Oh, that's a good one. Whoever sent me on this job . . . this was not worth the money they gave me six years ago. A doctor!"

"If you must have your moment of derisive laughter, at very least keep it quieter," Hirianthial said. "As to my being her choice . . . I have . . . talents that made me suitable for the job. But that matter begs me to ask: what are you doing here, looking for me? Who sent you?"

"As if I know," Reese said. "Some woman with more money than sense who never gives me her name when she calls and speaks like some fairy princess. I owed her a favor. She said you'd been jailed here and sent me to go get you. I was hoping to just post your bail."

Hirianthial laughed, a sound both quiet and despairing. It sent goosebumps down Reese's arms. "Ah, lady. That is funny. The pirates found me two weeks ago, and for two weeks I have been here in this cell while they wait for the slavers to pick me up. I was as good as sold the moment I was put in irons. They even wash me periodically so I'll look my best for my future masters. I had to try to earn the few bruises they dealt me . . . God forfend I look less than pristine for my auction."

Reese groaned and closed her eyes, letting her head loll back. "I didn't sign up for this."

"Again, I'm sorry, my lady."

"Stop calling me that!" Reese exclaimed. "I'm no lady, and I'm certainly not yours. And as for sorry . . . sorry! My cargo's fermenting while we lie here, and it might be vinegar by the time we get out of this. I'm no match for slavers! We have to get out of here before they come for you, or we're all going to end up some Chatcaavan's sex-toys in a month. Bending my neck to a dragon wasn't in my life plan."

"I can't say the thought appeals to me either," Hirianthial said.

"You don't say." Reese would have rolled her eyes, but the attendant nausea made that a bad idea. "You're a doctor?"

"I did say so."

"Well then see if the rest are ready to wake up. If we're lucky we can make it out of here with our bleeding cargo still fresh. If, that is, you'll let me sit up?"

The Eldritch's eyes lost their focus, drifting over her forehead and temples. "Yes," he said after a moment, then held up a finger. His wine-colored eyes refocused on her face. "But as I tell you."

"Fine," Reese said. "Make it quick."

He talked her through it, but it wasn't quick; just rolling onto her side made her want to vomit up what little there was in her stomach. Still, she made it upright, noticing the hand he'd had hovering behind her back only when he withdrew it. If she'd started to waver, would he have caught her, or would his Eldritch instincts have let her fall? She wanted to spit at the look on his face when they were done, and had no idea what made her angrier . . . that he looked concerned when he had no right to be concerned as the person responsible for this mess, or that his concern wasn't obvious enough, since she was the one who was going to drag his sugar-pale backside out of his mess. Blood and freedom, but she hated doctors.

"Good?" he asked after a moment, eyes resting too directly on her for her comfort.

"Fine," Reese said. "Check the others."

He studied her for a moment longer, then backed away,

leaving her to take stock. Aside from a few scrapes and bruises to complement the mother blooming near her temple, she'd taken no additional harm. Her suit had been slashed across her midriff and upper arms. Her knife was missing as well as her belt; she felt the loss of both coins and chalk tablets. She could have used a chalk tablet right now, in fact . . . but she could have fared worse.

Reese watched Hirianthial as he bent over Irine. He drew closer to her than she was accustomed to doctors coming, but he never touched her. After a few moments, he spread his hands above her ribs, as if setting them on a barrier that hovered a few inches above her skin. Though she couldn't tell whether the Harat-Shar was conscious, the Eldritch was talking, and his soft words were so gently spoken they felt like blankets. It made her want to trust him—no doubt one of his Eldritch mind tricks.

Reese gritted her teeth and directed her attention to their jail. The ground was packed earth strewn with yellow straw; there were no windows, and a wall of thick metal lattice faced the corridor. In addition to the lattice, she spotted red lights lining their door, indicating an operating halo field . . . not something she wanted to touch, but something Irine could possibly disarm since it didn't encompass the entire wall. The air was stale and warm, tinted here and there with earthier scents. Their cell formed the end of the hall; all the other cells were empty. She thought of the cell she'd seen upstairs and the figure lying in the back.

"Hirianthial," she said—slowly. The consonants in the name seemed to exist only to add a lilt to the vowels.

The sound of his hair against his back announced him. She wondered how he could walk without making any other noise. She didn't like it. "There was a man upstairs."

"Dead," he replied. For once the accent, the blanket-soft baritone fell flat. "Bait for me."

"They knew you were rooting for information."

"Of course. It was foolish to think otherwise."

Reese frowned at him. "And you stuck around?"

"I had a duty." A wry smile ran to the corner of his lips. "Granted, I should have remembered that part of that duty included returning to the queen with the information she sought, but even Eldritch make mistakes."

"Mistakes," Reese repeated, eyeing him. "With so much at stake."

He shrugged, a tiny motion involving the ends of his shoulders. Had she not been watching him, she would have missed it. "I became angry."

"Angry?"

He was staring out through the bars, but even in profile she could see his face change. Harden. The red of his eyes seemed less like wine and more like blood, like the color Reese saw on the inside of her eyelids when she wanted to explode. The doctor, the alien, the inconvenient object of an unwanted mission, those faces became masks, and something darker looked out. "I found a man whose tastes were repellant, even for a slaver."

For some reason Reese didn't want to ask what those tastes were. She didn't even want to ask, "What did you do to him?" but by the time she realized that she didn't want to hear the answer the question had already escaped her.

"I set his house on fire. With him in it." He didn't look at her, but even in profile his lack of expression terrified her.

"REESE!"

Irine's wail dragged her attention away, and she crawled to the Harat-Shar. The tigraine had Sascha's head cradled in her arms and she was rocking, her ears flat and eyes wide. "Reese, what's wrong with him? Why won't he wake up?"

"He's not ready to wake," said a steady voice behind Reese's shoulder.

Reese jumped. "Stop doing that!"

"Doing what?" the Eldritch asked absently as he slid past her to Sascha's other side, running a hand above the tigraine's face.

"Sneaking up on me," Reese said. "At least have the grace to make a little more noise."

"Grace and noise aren't usually associated with one another," Hirianthial murmured.

"What's wrong with him?" Irine asked the Eldritch. Reese could hear none of her typical skepticism in her quivering voice and she wondered at this instant trust. Was he influencing her mind?

"There's nothing wrong with him," Hirianthial said, his voice gentle. "He isn't ready to wake, that's all."

"But this burn—"

"Just a palmer, *alet*. He took no greater harm from it. He'll wake soon."

Only then did Irine look at Reese, still holding onto her brother's body. "Captain?"

"He's a doctor," Reese said. "He'd know better than me."

"What about Bryer?" Irine asked after a moment. "Is he okay?"

"Everyone's okay," Reese said. "We're just in a bit of a fix."

Irine's gold eyes flicked to the walls of the cell. "Yeah, I see that." She looked back at the Eldritch. "This is him, isn't it? Our spy?"

"At your service," Hirianthial said.

"I guess you already have been," Irine said, stroking Sascha's mane.

Reese sighed and turned back to the bars. She prodded

the back of her molars with her tongue, searching in vain for any minuscule deposit of chalk that might have stubbornly clung to her gums. Her stomach was going to kill her. "So how many people are guarding us?"

"I've counted six," Hirianthial said. "Two personal guards and four up the corridor."

"Six," Reese repeated, musing.

"There are five of us," Irine said from behind them.

Reese said, "They have palmers. And the keys."

Irine shrugged and didn't reply.

"The ship's coming tomorrow to pick them up," Hirianthial said after a moment. "Presumably we'll be going with them."

"So we have . . . what, twenty-four hours to break out of here, overwhelm six people, get to the *Earthrise* and flee far enough to lose a slaver-ship?"

"Twenty-two," Hirianthial said. "Days here are shorter than Alliance mean."

"Wonderful," Reese muttered, rubbing the bridge of her nose.

Hirianthial's voice sounded quietly behind her. "You need only secure your escape from this cell, lady. You were captured and put here only to inconvenience me. If you disappear, they will not bother to track you. It's me they want."

"I can't leave you behind," Reese said, irritated. "You're the debt I have to pay. If you rot here, I'll have to do something else and I bet it won't be any easier."

"The Queen isn't expecting you to save me if the odds are overwhelming," Hirianthial said.

"Well, six guards isn't overwhelming," Reese said, then stopped. "Did you say . . . the Queen?"

His voice was quizzical. "Of course. I thought from our talk that you'd concluded she was your mysterious benefactor."

Reese turned, setting her back against the bars. The Eldritch's face remained composed, but somehow she could still sense his confusion. A polite confusion. She couldn't quite mesh this courteous facade with the darkness revealed by the memory of the slaver. "Are you trying to tell me that the Queen of the Eldritch saved me from bankruptcy?"

Another one of those miniscule shrugs. "It seems that way."

"Damn," Irine said in wonder.

"That makes no sense!" Reese exclaimed. "What would a queen want with me? How did she even find me? Why would she bother?"

"Why did she bother with me?" the Eldritch said. "But she chose you and she cares what becomes of me and here we are. Why question it, lady?"

"I'm not your—"

"—lady, so you say," Hirianthial said. "But you are an instrument of a queen, so what shall I call you instead?"

"My name is Theresa Eddings," Reese said. "I am the captain of the TMS *Earthrise*. And you will call me 'Reese' because that's what people call me. Not 'lady' and not 'madam' and not 'princess' or whatever else you can come up with. Just "Reese." Or 'captain' if you insist."

"As you say," he said.

Such polite words, such courtesy, and yet she couldn't shake the feeling that he was going to call her whatever he wanted, and damned what she thought of it. Reese pursed her lips and eyed him skeptically, but his expression never changed. With a sigh, she steadied herself against the bars and rubbed her temple. "These guards. Do they ever check on us?"

"They check about every hour. They don't always come

within eyeshot, but I can sense them."

She glanced at him, then back at her crew. Irine had curled up around Sascha, her striped tail wrapped around his so tightly she could barely tell which inserted into which spine. Bryer remained unconscious. This was what she had to work with. Reese sighed and looked back at the Eldritch. "Can you set the guard on fire when he comes? Then we can grab for the field key and make a run for it."

The Eldritch stared at her, white brows lifting. "Lady— Captain—do I look like a magician to you?" he asked.

"You did say you set someone's house on fire. How much harder is a person's clothes? If you were sent for your special talents. . . ."

He laughed then, a breathy, quiet thing. Reese had never seen someone laugh without relaxing; it seemed unnatural. Did all Eldritch have this extreme control over their bodies?

"Good God! I can't break the laws of physics at a whim, I'm sorry to say. The Queen sent me because I'm one of the few non-touch telepaths, not because I can set things on fire by staring at them, or teleport or anything equally preposterous."

The hairs on the nape of Reese's neck bristled beneath the tangle of her beaded braids. "How was I supposed to know? Your world is so cloistered it makes a monastery look positively cosmopolitan! I didn't even know it was your Queen who sent me to rescue you . . . how do you expect anyone to know *anything* about you under circumstances like those?"

His cheeks colored a faint blue-tinged peach. "Your point is taken, lady. Pardon me."

Reese snorted and looked away, clenching her hands on the bars. No knives, no data tablets, no pyrokinetic Eldritch, no peppermint chalk, and a hold full of rotting rooderberries. She stared at her dirty, broken fingernails. By the time she found another port she'd have to do some fast talking to get someone to buy the things—

Reese's chin jerked up. She smiled, feral, and turned to face Hirianthial again. "But what if they *thought* you could set them on fire?"

The Eldritch lifted a brow.

"I mean, why don't we set things up so that it looks like you're doing some sort of magic with our help, and use that to scare the guard into letting us go?"

"Do you truly believe we can talk our way out of this cell?"

Oh, he sounded so certain. Reese folded her arms over her chest. "I've talked my way out of worse situations."

His face remained maddeningly smooth. She wanted him to sneer or roll his eyes or something. "Have you?"

"Look, Hirianthial," she said, "I'm sure I can do this. I know my people can. It's you I'm not sure of. Can you act? Because if you can't pull this one off, then it won't matter that I can do it and the twins and Bryer can do it."

"What exactly would you have me pretend?"

Was it her or was he actually uncomfortable with the idea of lying? Trust her to find the one Eldritch in all the worlds who actually believed in personal honor. In the books she'd read they'd never had a problem abandoning their beliefs to serve the story. "You'd have to pretend to be what everyone believes Eldritch to be. And don't tell me you don't know what that is. If you're out here playing spy, mingling with pirates and slavers, you know very well what Eldritch are supposed to be like."

"Supposed to be like," Hirianthial repeated, and for the first time she heard what she was expecting. Bitterness, maybe. Fatigue. Except he wasn't looking at her, but at something on the inside of his own eyes. "As if we are expected to fill some void in the universe."

In the face of uncertainty, Reese did as she always did. "Look, are you up for this or not? Because unless you have some better idea how to get us out of this hole in the ground, we're going with my plan."

"Had I had a better plan, we would not have met," the Eldritch said at last.

"Then let's get Sascha up. This is how it's going to go."

Hirianthial rested his hands on his knees, feeling the guards mill against the edges of his awareness. He could just—just—pick them out past the flares of the people sitting in a semi-circle around him. Where Reese had obtained her ideas about ritual magic he had no clue, but try as he might he couldn't complain that they lacked dramatics. There was no real magic outside of wild stories of ancient Eldritch mind-mages, of course, and his mental talents couldn't be intensified by any outside aid, but the concept sounded good and he supposed that was all that counted.

He'd been many things on Liolesa's little mission. He'd played instruments he barely remembered learning at a tutor's side for dinner. He'd washed dishes, scrubbed decks, even bandaged a wound or two. He had not yet played the charlatan. All of it galled. That he'd taken on this role to free himself made it only a hint less bitter. Always, his people wanted something of him he wasn't made to give; his attempts to fulfill those expectations usually ended in failure. While he wasn't expecting this to be any different, he hoped for the sake of the aliens grouped around him that it would be.

The guard pierced his circle of awareness, heading for their cell. "He's on his way."

"All right, people, look calm," Reese said.

Irine giggled. "This is too silly."

"It'll work," Reese said. "Just remember your lines."

The Harat-Shar giggled again. Hirianthial opened his eyes and found them all in position facing him. Reese and the two Harat-Shar had copied his stance, palms up on their knees with eyes closed. Bryer, who couldn't sit cross-legged, kneeled with his hands pressed together at his breast, the feathers splayed from his arms in a decorative fan. One could argue they had the hard part: to remain composed and to seem as if they were concentrating when they knew the farce they were engaged in. Still, Hirianthial hated lying. Obfuscation he could do. Lying wounded him.

The heavy thump of boots on stone pulled him out of his reverie. Hirianthial set his face. As he'd hoped, Blond stood in front of their cage, staring at their group and playing with the key ring. Spikes of sweaty uncertainty jumped around his aura. He cleared his throat of thick phlegm and said, "What are you people doing?"

"What does it look like?" Hirianthial asked with just a hint of contempt.

The guard's aura flared red. "Don't you mess with me, pastehead. You'll be dancing a different set when they put you in real chains."

"Oh, I don't think they'll be doing that. Not with my new . . . friends . . . to help me."

The guard's left boot creaked, then the right. Nervousness gave his colors a green sheen. "Ummm . . . look, I don't know what they're doing, but they should stop it." He stared at Reese and the others. "What *are* they doing?"

Now for the lies. The premise had sounded so ridiculous Hirianthial couldn't imagine anyone believing it, but Reese had convinced him. He thought of the last time he'd been angry from pit to fingers and summoned up that voice, the deep soft one with the hard edges, the one that made a lie out of his cultured accent. "Channeling power to me . . . so I can set this building on fire. Or didn't you hear about the last time?"

On cue, Sascha began to hum.

"What the—"

"The power is flowing to me. I might spare you afterwards. Unlock the door."

"I don't, I . . ."

Irine added her mezzosoprano to her brother's tenor. They started out in harmony and then Sascha dropped his voice until they were only an octave and a quarter tone off. Hirianthial wondered if they realized what they were doing or if they were just tone-deaf. He focused on the man. "Unlock the door. If you do, I'll give you time to run before I start."

Reese added her contralto, filling part of the lower register.

Blond shifted from foot to foot, books creaking. His fingers played almost spasmodically with the keys. Hirianthial stared him in the eye, willing him to do it.

"Unlock the door."

"I—"

"Unlock the door."

"It's not—"

"*Unlock the door.*"

Bryer broke in with a shrill ululation that skidded up the scale of comfortable human hearing. Blond's fear shot his aura with actinic sparkles, and the man lunged forward, keying first the field and then the door. The latter beeped its processing tone. A few seconds later, the door opened. Blond stood paralyzed before it, as if unable to believe his actions.

Gently, Hirianthial said, "Run. Now."

Blond stared wildly at him; his eyes flicked to Bryer's

feathers. Then he turned tail and fled.

"All right!" Reese said, jumping to her feet. "Quick, be-fore it's too late!"

The two Harat-Shar dashed out first, striped tails sway-ing. Bryer loped after. Reese pointed. "Out. I'll be behind you."

Hirianthial rose, and she darted around him, closing the door behind him.

"Which way!" Sascha yelled back.

"Left!" Hirianthial called.

The two tigraines vanished around the corner, and then Irine yowled. He could just see two more people in front of them. "Guards," he warned.

"I think they already found them," Reese said dry-ly, running up the hall. They turned into the corridor to find Bryer leaping on one of the guards, his bronze claws muted by the red flash of blood. Disoriented, Hirianthial turned toward the smell—blood required two kinds of attention—but a hand grabbed the back of his tunic and yanked. He felt concern and pain and fear and adrenaline like a punch to the spine.

"This way!" Reese said, pulling him past the two Pelted and the Phoenix, who were doing more than distracting the guards.

"They'll die," Hirianthial said, transfixed by the defla-tion of the auras under Sascha and Bryer. Old instincts warred with new oaths.

"Have your crisis of conscience later!" Reese said. "Or have you forgotten what these people have done? Do you want to live your life in chains?"

He still couldn't force himself forward. It had been so long since he'd seen blood spilled in violence. It woke demons.

"Blood on the dust, Hirianthial, MOVE!"

He moved. He couldn't not move beneath the force of that command. He couldn't decide if they were wounded or enemies and in the face of that ambivalence he could turn his back on them and leave them to die. Even if he'd wanted to turn back, Reese was at his heels, riding him, herding him. He didn't want to have to push past her and her cut-glass aura.

Sascha pushed past him, blood streaking his fur. "Are there more?"

"Two more ahead," Hirianthial said. "They know we're coming."

"Stop!" Reese said. "They're going to have weapons—"

"Yeah well, now so do we," Irine said, holding up three palmers.

Reese crowed. "Excellent, fuzzy! Just be—"

Sascha and Bryer had already taken one of the palmers and run ahead.

"—careful," Reese finished to the sound of palmer fire. She winced.

Irine shrugged, then ambled up the corridor. "It's clear, boss."

And just like that, they'd taken care of everyone in the prison that had held him for so long. Dazed, Hirianthial followed Reese up the corridor, paused to stare at the bodies. These two, at least, weren't dead. Memories tangled with reality in his eyes, blurring the edges of the room.

"Come on," Reese said. "No time to sight-see. The moment someone wakes up and realizes we're gone our lives are worthless. Or at least, to us. I love my old crate, but she's not going to outrun a pirate."

"The tumbleweeds await!" Sascha said, pushing open the door. He threw a telegem to Reese. "Might as well use this. They're going to find out about us anyway."

Reese tossed it aside. "I don't want to alert them any

sooner. Let's just run and hope Kis'eh't can get the *Earth-rise* ready fast enough without warning. You. Prince Charming. You go in the middle where we can—"

"—guard me?" Hirianthial asked, a brief sense of amusement blowing away the numbness.

"Just go."

He went. Bryer ran alongside, wings and tail a flutter of bronze and muted crimson. Sascha took lead, with Irine at the side. Reese ran behind. They sprinted out into a purple twilight and onto the empty streets, avoiding the street lamps. There were no lights puddled in the windows, but the breeze that sloughed through his hair—Hirianthial had felt nothing finer.

"I assume," he said once they reached the edge of town, "that we're going somewhere."

"Yeah. To the *Earthrise*. She's parked a few minutes out of town," Reese said. She stopped to pant, propping her hands on her knees. "Our ride out."

"And then?" Hirianthial asked.

The beads on the end of her hair clicked as she whipped her head up to glare at him. "Providing we get out of here alive, I'm dropping you off at the nearest starbase. You're way too much trouble for me."

Hirianthial laughed. "Alas, lady. I hope it's that simple."

"Yeah, me too." She straightened. "On we go!"

They ran. Leaving the town pleased Hirianthial greatly. He could almost forget they were fleeing and enjoy the run. He hadn't been able to stretch his legs for days, and the expanse of the world around him, rolling away to the horizon in every direction, restored some of his tattered equilibrium. Enough of it, in fact, that when he saw their ride off-world he didn't immediately fall into despair. The squat ovoid balanced on its landing stilts looked as much like the sleek Alliance ships Hirianthial had seen as an axe resembled a laser scalpel. He couldn't imagine it outrunning a barge, much less a slaver's ship.

Reese hobbled the last few yards to one of the stilts and whacked a panel with the heel of her hand.

"Kis'eh't! Get us out of this system, and now!"

A ramp descended from the belly of the ship, too slowly for the twins who jumped onto it before it had fully extended. They scampered up it, followed by Bryer.

"Up," Reese said.

Hirianthial stared up into the dark and wondered just what kind of future the Queen had planned for him to tangle him up with this human and her strange people.

But he went up the ramp. He was, he thought, short on choices.

The engines changed pitch. Reese didn't hear it as much as feel it through the soles of her feet in the rattle of the deck-plates.

"Where to, Captain?" Sascha'd made it to the pilot's chair already.

"The nearest starbase in civilized space. And move it, Stripes."

"Starbase Kappa it is, boss!"

The floor beneath her jumped as the *Earthrise* lifted. Reese steadied herself against the wall and felt the faintest relief from the churn in her stomach. Maybe they'd get out of this one unscathed. She toggled the comm to all-hands. "Irine? Where are you?"

A striped head popped into view from up-corridor. "Err . . . right here?"

Reese jerked a thumb at Hirianthial, who hadn't moved since coming up the ramp. "See that he finds a place to sleep."

"Right, Captain. You there, you're with me."

Reese watched them long enough for them to turn the corner, the solid and curvy tigraine girl and the willowy man. She wondered how he kept so much hair so healthy . . . nearly two weeks in captivity and he still looked like he belonged on the cover of a novel. It boggled the mind.

Reese jogged to the bridge, swaying as the ship rose through a few bumpy winds and rocking as the stabilizers balanced. The pressure exacerbated her headache; she'd never gotten used to gravities higher than Mars's, and high accelerations always made things worse. When the lift ejected her onto the cramped bridge, she was only too glad to slide into a chair and buckle on the safety harness. Kis'eh't was at the exterior sensor control panel, her own harness binding her centauroid lower body to the floor and Allacazam cradled between her forelegs. Sascha was in the pilot's seat.

"Did we succeed?" the Glaseahn asked, glancing at Reese.

"We got him, yes," Reese said.

"We're clear of the atmosphere," Sascha interrupted.

Reese slid her hand over the engineering display, scrutinizing the stress analyses as they scrolled past with a grim face. The ride smoothed out as the *Earthrise* rose, the transition from atmospheric night to the void-black of space invisible save for the glowing blue sensor data and the steadying of the starlight. Reese breathed a sigh of relief as the internal gravity evened to something approaching normal.

"We might even make it to Kappa in time to save the rooderberries," Kis'eh't said.

Most Pelted revealed their skin and its flushes at their ears. Humans, of course, suffered from whole-body blushes—most of them anyway. Reese had been blessed with skin dark enough to keep her embarrassment or upsets to herself, most of the time. But only a tiny corner of skin around Kis'eh't's eyelids was exposed. Reese was nevertheless startled by how stark a gray it turned.

"Uh . . . we've got a ship up our tail."

"I see it," Sascha said, voice distracted.

Reese twisted, staring at the sensor data. Her eyes rose to the aft windows where a gray splotch occluded part of the planet, growing even as she watched. "ID?" she asked hoarsely.

"It isn't running a beacon," Kis'eh't said, bending over her panel.

Reese's stomach screamed for chalk.

"What's going on?" Irine asked, popping out of the lift with Hirianthial.

"We've got a tail, and it's heading straight for us," Reese said, fingers playing hopscotch over the keypad. "And it's pulling a higher acceleration than we are."

"They'll overhaul us in fifteen minutes," Kis'eh't reported.

"Not if I can help it," Sascha said.

"I thought I told you to put him in a room?" Reese said to Irine.

The tigraine shrugged. "You said to find him a place to sleep, not trap him there. He wanted to come with me, so I said 'sure.'"

"We'll talk about this later," Reese said. Providing there was a later. "Buckle up if you're going to stay."

Irine wedged herself into the space next to the pilot's chair and tied on a spare harness, then clamped herself to her brother's leg. Hirianthial stayed in the back. Smart man.

"Reese, they aren't exceeding our maximum limit," Kis'eh't said.

"She's right," Sascha said, "but we can't go our max unless we—"

"Dump the berries," Reese said, covering her eyes. "Blood and Freedom."

"Captain, that boat is crammed with weapons. Half of them look like they're going to fall off, but our one laser isn't going to do much good," Kis'eh't said, still punching buttons.

Reese stared at the oncoming pirate: obviously jury-rigged, operating with only shoddy, low-level navigational shields, but with engines well a match for theirs and weapons all out of proportion to its size. It required effort to move her hand to the comm panel and twitch it.

"Lowerdeck."

"Bryer, I want you to jettison the cargo. And make sure the clamps don't go this time."

The silence was eloquent.

"Just do it," Reese said. She pressed a hand to her stomach, massaging it. "Damn rooderberries," she said. "Last time I'm ever taking on any fruit. You guys are my witnesses."

"Heard and witnessed," Kis'eh't said with a laugh.

"Here, here!" Irine added. Then said, "Does this mean we get to have rooderberry sorbet tonight?"

"This is not funny," Reese said, glaring at the pirate ship. It seemed like a better idea than glaring at Hirianthial, who'd been the indirect cause of all this. Bad enough that he was responsible for the loss of her investment, but did he have to actually be on the bridge where he could remind her of just how much she didn't want to be here?

The floor shivered and a muffled series of clunks followed as the bay doors opened. The loading collars sucking the pins from the spindles and ejecting the cargo bins resulted in much louder clangs, one for each bin. Reese counted them, flinching at each one, until the first bin tumbled end over end into view on the aft windows.

"Look at them go!" Sascha said.

Kis'eh't said, "They're gaining on us."

"Do something about that, Sascha," Reese said.

"Maximum power on all engines," the tigraine said. "We're opening the distance."

"How long before we shake them loose entirely?" Reese asked.

"I don't know. Ten, fifteen minutes maybe."

Fifteen minutes of staring at each of those bins, trying not to count how many fin each represented as they fell down the drain of the planet's gravity well. Reese rubbed her burning throat as the long minutes hobbled on. The tension was interminable, and yet she was as bored as she was edgy. Her stomach did not approve. Her throbbing temple agreed, reminding her that she hadn't even stopped to look for any medicaments before rushing to the bridge. No chalk tablets, no headache elixir, nothing. She regretted the lack of both.

Hirianthial's baritone interrupted her reverie. "Do they always burn that way?"

Reese straightened, stared at the windows where tiny flares of fire erupted like miniature bombs. "What . . . ?"

Kis'eh't was already checking the sensors. "I . . ." The Glaseahn's head dropped onto the console, her shoulders shaking. Between her forelegs, Allacazam turned a lurid shade of plum purple.

"Kis'eh't?" Reese asked.

"Yeah, manylegs, give us the score here," Sascha said. "Some of us are too busy to look for ourselves."

The Glaseahn lifted her head, her demi-muzzle parted in laughter so intense she couldn't even squeak.

Irine unbuckled her harness and straddled Kis'eh't's second back in front of her wings. The tigraine looked over

Kis'eh't's shoulders and choked on a laugh. "Captain, it's the rooderberries."

"I *know* it's the rooderberries! What's going on with them? Are they hitting atmosphere?"

"No . . . they're hitting the slaver."

With her mouth already open to speak, Reese found herself abruptly deprived of words to say.

"Do you mean to say that the bins are striking the pirate vessel?" Hirianthial asked Irine politely.

"That's exactly it."

"Like . . . say, a grenade. Or a torpedo."

"Exactly like that," Irine said around her giggle.

"And . . . the odds of this?"

Sascha interrupted, "Well, if they're right on our tails, and the bins are falling along our trajectory—"

Reese couldn't handle any more. "What are you saying? That some of the cargo bins are—"

"There goes number four!" Irine crowed. "Ke-poom! Look at that!"

In the rear windows the pirate ship bucked beneath a brief, blinding splotch of fire; cheap cargo containers were only partially air-tight, but this evidence of just how partially left Reese with the absent thought that perhaps she should invest in better cargo bins.

"Captain, they're . . . they're decelerating."

"They're *what*?" Reese wheeled from the window to gawk at the sensor display as the pirate vessel dropped speed. "Blood! I think they're *damaged*!"

"I'd confirm that," Kis'eh't said. "They're definitely losing speed. And—yes, I'm seeing life pods."

Sascha grinned, displaying white fangs. "Guess they're not much for jam."

"Life pods?"

Hirianthial's question doused the wildfire merriment

on the bridge. Reese barely heard it, staring at the pirate, trying to convince herself that all this was happening.

Kis'eh't cleared her throat. "Captain? Reese?"

She shook herself. "No. Keep going." And before Hiri-anthial could say another word, she said, "No. Not only are they floating above a pirate safehouse which can very well rescue its own maniacs, but those people want us dead. We're not out of the woods yet."

"They're not going to catch us now," Sascha said.

"No, but—"

And then the ship bucked and the soothing hum beneath the deck-plates faltered. "What the?"

"They just shot us!" Kis'eh't exclaimed.

"Are they still coming for us?" Reese asked. "Can we still get away?"

"Engines are at half power," Sascha said with a growl. He punched the comm. "Bryer!"

"Can't talk. Much repair-work."

"What did they get?"

"In-systems. Also Well drive."

"We can't get out of here?" Irine squeaked.

"You can coast but you can't ride," Bryer said. "Bother me later. Or come down and help."

"Damn," Sascha said, unstrapping himself. "I'll be below-decks with Bryer. If we can't use the Well Drive we're slavebait. They'll send someone new after us while we limp out of here."

"And here we're out of rooderberries to fire at them," Kis'eh't said as Irine slid into her brother's place.

"Where now?" Irine asked.

"There's an asteroid belt," Kis'eh't offered, studying her display. "We could hide there while we do repairs."

"Do it," Reese said. "How long do you think it'll take?"

"I'll give you an estimate once I get down there," Sascha

said, and vanished into the lift.

"This is not our lucky day," Irine muttered.

Reese stood up. "Don't say that until it's over, unless you really want to jinx us."

"Sorry. Say, Boss?"

"What?"

"My ability to concentrate on keeping us hidden would greatly improve if you went somewhere else. It's not like anything's going to happen in the next hour or so."

"How can you be sure?"

Kis'eh't said, "I'll call you if something happens."

Reese looked from one to the other, torn.

"I wouldn't mind seeing what passes for a clinic on this ship," Hirianthial said from behind her.

She wasn't sure what infuriated her more, his assumption that she could afford a ship with a clinic or his assumption that the one she could afford could only "pass" for a clinic. Her stomach churned as she stared at him, trying to decide what to say.

"We don't have much of a ship's clinic," Kis'eh't said, interrupting her thoughts. "There's a combination clinic-lab that I converted next to my room . . . I use it for experiments sometimes. Reese knows where it is."

Of course she did! It was her ship! She'd approved the change!

"And you could take Allacazam," the Glaseahn continued. "I think he wants to be with you." The woman offered her the Flitzbe, and Reese took it by reflex. Instantly she felt a touch of sparkling concern at the edge of her mind, and she sighed, holding him against her stomach.

"Is that a real Flitzbe?" Hirianthial asked, and even Reese could read the wonder in his voice.

"It is," Kis'eh't answered for Reese. "Why don't the two of you talk about it somewhere else?"

Reese opened her mouth to complain, but Allacazam's sad violin trill distracted her. She sighed. "All right. I'm leaving. But if anything changes—"

"—we'll tell you right then," Irine said.

"We're going to talk about this gross insubordination later," Reese added, heading for the lift.

"Yes, ma'am," said Kis'eh't.

"Just so long as you whip me good," Irine added.

Reese rolled her eyes. "Come on, Prince Charming. Into the lift with us, before Irine starts whining about how I never let her have any fun."

"You don't!"

The lift door closed.

"A real Flitzbe," Hirianthial prompted again.

"Would you like to hold him?" Reese asked, wondering why she was offering.

"May I?" he said.

Reese held Allacazam out to him, wondering if Hirianthial would take him directly from her hands and risk touching her, or if she'd have to set the Flitzbe on the floor and let him roll to the man's boots. But no, the Eldritch didn't flinch at the transfer, though his hands never touched hers.

"You've never seen one?" Reese asked.

"In textbooks," Hirianthial replied. He set Allacazam against his ribs, tucked against his elbow, and rested his opposite hand on top of the Flitzbe. It was a tender hold, and in it Allacazam blossomed all sorts of calming colors. Pastel purple. Shimmery silver. Touches of rose and peach and blue. Reese stared, mesmerized, until the lift door opened.

"I didn't think you'd want to touch him," she said. "He emotes a lot."

"I didn't think I would either," Hirianthial said. "But it

seems rude not to, given he can't communicate any other way."

"The clinic's this way," Reese said, glancing one more time at the supreme contentment of the Flitzbe before heading down the hall. She heard the soft whisper of the Eldritch behind her, wished that the *Earthrise* would at least oblige her by sounding noisy under the man's feet. Naturally, the ship wouldn't. Did anyone dislike an Eldritch? Except her? She'd liked them fine as mythical characters, but meeting one in person . . . no one had told her how infuriatingly perfect they'd be.

Reese opened the door on the small room Kis'eh't used as a lab. The Glaseahn had studied some sort of fancy chemistry and with Reese's permission installed some enigmatic lab equipment. Since she occasionally donated money to the ship when her articles earned any, Reese didn't complain. The things took power, but they were Kis'eh't's romance novels, her escape to something else. Somewhere better. Why the Glaseahn didn't do her chemistry as a formal job Reese didn't understand; Kis'eh't had only ever said that she and academia had had a difference of opinion.

"Larger than I expected," Hirianthial said, sitting on a stool. He was petting Allacazam now. They seemed well-suited. Reese wondered if the Flitzbe would take to sleeping with him from now on.

"Captain?"

Reese tapped the comm, glad for the distraction. "Go ahead, Sascha."

"We're looking at at least three hours of repair. Maybe four."

"Four hours!" Reese said.

"Just be glad we've got the parts on hand."

Reese sighed. "All right. Get us out of this, Sascha, and

I'll buy you and Bryer dinner at Starbase Kappa."

"Yeah, right. With what money, boss?" A chuckle. "Still, thanks for the thought. I'll give you an update when we've got one."

"Thanks," Reese said, and switched channels. "You guys hear that?"

"Three or four hours to hide in the rocks. Can do, Captain." In the background, Kis'eh't added, "Didn't we tell you to stop worrying?"

"Not going to happen," Reese said. "Tell me if we get visitors."

"We will. Bridge out."

"They seem like good people," Hirianthial said.

"They are good people," Reese replied testily. "Just a little less formal than your average Fleet crew."

"I wouldn't know."

Reese sighed and sat on the low bench Kis'eh't used for herself.

"As long as we're here," Hirianthial said and trailed off.

Reese eyed him. "I don't like the sound of that."

"If you have a first aid kit I could do something about that digestive problem. Or your head."

"I don't need you to mess with my head, or my stomach. They're fine," Reese said.

His calm gaze on hers only infuriated her more. She looked away, blushing. "I've done fine on my own."

"You have. But you could do better," he said.

"I'm not interested in you fixing me," Reese said, and when he looked about to object she said, "And that's final. Get it? I've got chalk and I've got elixir and I've got pills. That's enough."

He looked down at Allacazam, but not fast enough to hide the irritation that pulled ever-so-slightly at his mouth. Reese hid her satisfaction. At least he could get angry.

A memory flashed in her mind of his face when talking about the slavers.

Okay. Maybe not that angry. Pettily angry, like normal people.

"So," and she couldn't hear any of that anger in his voice, "how did you meet a real Flitzbe?"

"On a space station near Earth," Reese said. "I was docked there for licensing and repair and he just . . . well, started following me. We seemed to get along, and he didn't like the idea of me leaving him behind, so I didn't."

"You can talk to him?" Hirianthial asked.

"Can't you?"

The Eldritch shrugged, that hitch of one shoulder that was so easy to miss. "I'm an esper. They say it's supposed to be easier for us to talk to them."

"Do they?" Reese warred between agitation and curiosity. "I've read about them but there's not much available in the u-banks. The usual stuff . . . some biological information about how they eat and reproduce, and historical information about how we ran into them. But nothing more than that."

"Probably because there's not much more than that to be said." In the Eldritch's arms, Allacazam turned an amused goldenrod yellow. "We had some additional information in medical school but not much more. I never saw a Flitzbe anywhere I worked. If they get sick, they've never done it where someone could record evidence of it."

"Never?" Reese asked.

"Not that we know of," Hirianthial replied. "Even seeing one is fairly unusual. You're a lucky woman."

Reese said nothing to that, only watched the colors on Allacazam as they changed. All happy colors. "He likes you."

"You sound surprised," Hirianthial said and laughed. "I

suppose you can't imagine anyone liking me right now."

"I'll thank you to stop reading my mind," Reese said, bristling.

"I'll thank you to stop assuming I'm some sort of magician," Hirianthial replied. He leaned down and set the Flitzbe on the floor. "The only thing I can sense from you is your emotional state, and trust me, any number of factors can cause a single emotion. Guessing at which of the many things in your life is currently causing you distress isn't as easy as you would presume. I am making an educated guess from your tone of voice and the things you've said, lady. Not plucking my wisdom out of your frontal lobes."

"Are all Eldritch this infuriating?" Reese finally said, unable to help herself.

"No," Hirianthial replied. Then, glancing at the ceiling. "Most of them are worse."

Allacazam bumped up against Reese's toe. She pulled him into her arms and was surprised at how quickly he soothed her. She sighed over his round body, feeling the thrum of the engines in the deck and wondering how soon they'd be able to escape this particular nightmare. Allacazam slipped a tendril of curiosity into her mind, like a shoot of green trying to push up through soil. She imagined packing it back into the earth. She wasn't ready to deal with the alternatives to their venture if they failed.

The ship chose that moment to shudder hard and jink to one side. Reese clutched Allacazam with one arm and the bench with the the other. The moment it passed she was on the intercom. "What in Freedom's name are you people doing up there?"

"Sorry," came Kis'eh't's terse reply. "We got dinged by a small rock. We're not going to get out of this without dents, Reese."

"I'm coming up there," Reese said, and cut off Irine's

protest.

"Lady," Hirianthial said.

"Not now." Reese set Allacazam down and headed for the door.

"I would sit down—"

Her stomach felt like a burst fuel-line. Even her throat was burning. She kept going.

"Captain Eddings," Hirianthial said, standing, and that almost made her stop but Irine and Kis'eh't were going to get her ship completely bent out of shape and she was the only one who could possibly stop it—

An ominous taste in her mouth gave her pause. Was she queasy? She hated being queasy. The corridor suddenly seemed a lot longer.

"Maybe you should come back in here and sit." His baritone was so soft she almost couldn't disobey. But no doctor, no *Eldritch* doctor was going to tell her what to do. She kept walking.

Her stomach lurched. The burning in her mouth intensified. Reese licked her lips and swayed beneath a wave of hot unease. She reached out and braced herself against the wall, no longer caring if he saw her. What was he going to do . . . come out here and pick her up? Not likely!

"Since kind suggestion doesn't work on you," Hirianthial said with what sounded like a hint of asperity, "I'll simply be blunt. If you don't walk back in here under your own power and let me treat you for the ulcer you've been nursing for what looks like several years, you're going to fall and vomit up what remains of your last meal, which I am wagering was a pack of antacids. Then you'll be forced to accept the help you're currently refusing, which will only make you angrier. So save us both your future frustration and come in here now."

Reese stared at the lift at the end of the hall as waves

of sickness flooded her, each one making her hunch just a little more. Every word made her clench her teeth harder. When he finished his speech she felt crushed between her body's impending crisis and her obstinacy.

"Treat me out here, because I'm not moving," she said, and fell forward onto her knees.

Hirianthial swept forward but not in time to catch her. The moment her palms hit the floor plates, Reese gagged. He didn't even pause to steel himself before pulling her up by an arm, and when she didn't support herself on her wobbling legs he caught those up and heaved her into his arms for the short trip from the corridor to the bench in Kis'eht's lab. He didn't have time to organize the impressions he got through their brief contact but all of them hurt. The moment he laid her down, she groaned and said, "I'm going to throw up."

"I know," he said, and found a waste container in time. He held her steady as she retched bile and blood.

"Oogh," she said, hanging onto the edge of the pail.

"Done?" Hirianthial asked, but gentler. He hadn't expected to be able to see such a radical change in her skin, but the brown had lost most of its warmth in the short minutes between the collapse in the corridor and her transport to the bench. Seeing her so wrung out made him realize just how small she was. It wasn't a thing one noticed while she was biting someone's nose off with her words.

"I . . . I don't know," Reese said.

"That usually means 'no,'" Hirianthial said, keeping his grip.

She rolled a dull blue eye back at his hand. "Doesn't that hurt?"

"Not as much as—" he stopped as she dropped her head back into the container and paid attention to her aura this time, feeling his way over the spikes and static hiss. When she lifted her head, he said, "Now you're done," and helped her lie back on the bench.

The ship shook under them again and Reese tried to rise. He pressed her down with fingertips on her collarbone. "No."

"Got to drive," she said.

"No," Hirianthial said again. "Where's your first aid kit?"

"Don't need—"

"Captain Eddings," he said, using his sternest tone. "Every ship is supposed to have one. Where's yours?"

She sighed. "Above the blue thing."

The "blue thing" must refer to the chemical analysis machine, though the only blue on it was a stripe down the side. Hirianthial looked in the cabinet above it and found the kit along with a couple of blankets. He took them both down, covering her with one and folding the other into a makeshift pillow. "Now, how about the nearest source of water?"

"Water?" Reese asked weakly.

"Water," Hirianthial agreed.

"Bathroom. Further down the hall. Turn left."

"Right," Hirianthial said. He lifted Allacazam from the floor and tucked him in next to Reese's arm. "Neither of you move."

In the cramped bathroom, Hirianthial washed his hands and avoided looking at himself in the tiny mirror. He hadn't questioned his desire to become a doctor on fleeing his homeworld; whatever his original motive one could hardly find fault with the healing professions, and once he'd begun he'd found he loved the work. But moments like this, where he realized that taking care of someone provided a useful distraction from the wider view, he wondered just how noble it was to be a doctor. So much easier to think of the patient than wonder whether they'd be slaves in a few hours. So much more satisfying to treat someone's sickness than to serve as their executioner. So much better to run to a good cause than to admit why one started running.

He chanced a look at himself and saw only a bland mask learned among the Eldritch and refined by the school of medicine. He could hide in it for the rest of his life and no one would ever guess. Not even irascible young human women with riding crop tongues.

Hirianthial returned to the clinic to find both patient and palliative alien where he'd left them. He sat next to Reese and slid his hand through her braids. He knew from sight they would be wiry and light, but somehow he still expected them to slide as smoothly as satin and as heavily as rope. The memories were still raw.

"I can lift my head without your help," she said, dispelling the ghost.

"Hush and drink."

She slurped at the cup, swished out her mouth and spat into the waste container three times before actually swallowing.

"That's enough. You're not ready for much more."

She eyed him rebelliously, but he pressed her back onto the bench.

"Are you going to force me to keep pushing you down or will I have to tie you there?" he asked.

"If you keep touching me, will you eventually faint?" Reese asked.

"That would make me fairly useless as a doctor, don't you think?" Hirianthial asked. Some of the notions Alliance citizens had cobbled together about his people would have been amusing had he not had to work past them so often in the past. He knew the reasons for the Veil of Secrecy decreed by Jerisa, the first Eldritch queen, but even he chafed at them sometimes and he considered himself a private man.

Hirianthial turned his back on Reese and opened the kit. Standard kits were packed with supplies sufficient to solve typical problems—bone breaks, bites, cuts, scrapes, basic infections—but didn't contain any of the things he'd need for a solution to her problem. With his own kit in a Sendaine storage locker, he'd have to pray the quick fixes he had access to would tide her over until they reached Starbase Kappa. If they reached Starbase Kappa. Hirianthial prepared an ampoule of mellifleurin and said, "This will see you to the starbase if you follow my instructions about what you eat and when. Will you do that?"

"What's the alternative?" Reese asked, watching him with a gloss of gray skepticism as he pressed the AAP to her side. She eyed the paper tab he offered her, but let him swab her tongue with it anyway.

"You vomit more and more often until I have to operate on you with—" he checked the kit, "—medical tape, paper cut-grade antiseptic and my boot knife."

Her eyes lost their anger, though her gaze remained as intent. "You're kidding, right?"

He ran a hand over her aura, feeling the tight wad of wrongness around the middle of her esophagus. "No." He left his hand there, feeling the extent of the pressure on her chest as he slid the tab into the analysis unit. He was not surprised to find a large concentration of keliobacteria. Humanity's determined march into space had inspired several thousand new variations on old microbiological foes, most of them more virulent than their Terran ancestors. He'd sewn up a few esophaguses as an intern, but never without surgeon's tools . . . and while he couldn't tell exactly when Reese's esophagus would rupture the pressure under his hand suggested it would be soon.

If it did before they reached the starbase, she would die.

"Don't make me do this with a knife," he said. "I'd rather knock you unconscious and keep you that way until we get to Starbase Kappa than have to cut you open with something I use to trim my meat at supper."

Reese blanched. "You're serious."

"Yes."

The ship shivered beneath them again. Reese rolled her full lower lip between her teeth, then said, "At least find out what's going on. I promise not to go anywhere, but if I don't know what's happening I'll gnaw a hole through my arm."

"That I can do, as long as you promise not to get up," Hirianthial said. He leaned over and rested a hand on the comm but didn't activate it. Her belligerence returned, flaring orange.

"You're actually going to make me promise?"

"I have the feeling you keep your promises," Hirianthial said.

She rolled her eyes. "Don't tell me you actually believe in personal honor and all that."

Hirianthial said nothing. Personal honor had driven him to unpleasant ends, and discussing it wasn't one of his favorite pass-times.

"Fine, fine, I promise. Now call!"

He depressed the button. "Clinic to the bridge."

"Nice try, doc, but this is lowerdeck," Sascha said. "What can I do for you?"

"The captain wants to know what's going on."

"And she's not asking? Did someone tie her down?"

Hirianthial eyed Reese, who looked about to vault to her

feet. "In a manner of speaking. She can hear you, though, so I wouldn't indulge in too much flippant language."

Sascha's laugh sounded tinny, as if he'd moved away from the pick-up. "Right. You don't know anything about how things work here yet, I see. You'll learn fast enough. Repairs on the inside are doing okay. What the rocks are doing to the hull is outside our purview. Ask the bridge about that."

Another shudder ran through the floor, the walls. Reese said, "What, are they *aiming* for the things?"

"I'd ask them," Sascha said. "Lowerdeck out."

"I need to drive," Reese said again, though this time she didn't try to get up. "We can't make it out of here if they punch a hole in the hull."

"I'm presuming you hired them for more than company," Hirianthial said while studying the panel for clues on how to switch channels.

"Yeah, well, I can't be everywhere at once. That doesn't mean I'm not better at everything than they are," she said. "Hit it three times."

"Are you really better at everything than they are?" Hirianthial asked as he did so.

Reese sighed. Muttered, "No. But I care more."

"Bridge, this is Kis'eh't. We're sorry about the ride there, Captain."

"The captain is resting," Hirianthial said. "But she'd like to know how we're doing."

"Resting!" Kis'eh't said. "Maybe we should keep you around. We're lucky if we can get her to sleep once a week."

"That's not true," Reese said sourly.

"The ride?" Hirianthial prompted.

"We're cruising just inside the sunward edge of the belt, looking for a clear path to the opposite side. We figure if we can shimmy over to the outside we can sneak out of here without blowing our cover."

"What!"

"The captain is wondering how you propose to do that," Hirianthial said, hiding the smallest of smiles.

"It actually gets easier the further in we get. The interior of the belt is more sparsely populated. It's just that the rocks are bigger, so running into them is a worse idea than it is with these smaller ones."

"I knew they were aiming for the things," Reese muttered.

"Larger rocks should mean you can see them coming more easily, correct?" Hirianthial asked.

"That's right. So tell the captain to catch a nap. The further in we go the smoother the ride."

"I didn't authorize this kind of risk," Reese said. The gray tinge to her skin was now accompanied by a worried black wrinkle in her aura.

"Are you sure this is the only way out?" Hirianthial asked.

There was a pause. Then Irine said, "It's this or fly out there free and loud where they can hear us. This is the only sneaky way we can think of to get out of here. Unless you installed a duster on this boat that you didn't tell us about, captain."

"Thank you, Irine," Hirianthial said. "I'll see that the lady rests."

"You do that, pretty. Bridge away."

Reese surprised him by remaining silent. She petted Allacazam's fur and the Flitzbe wiggled beneath her brown-and-pink fingers before turning a soothing dark blue. After a moment, she said with obvious resignation, "If I'm going to rest, can I at least do it on a proper bed?"

"There's a proper bed on this vessel?" Hirianthial asked, surprising himself. He didn't usually feel the need to tease.

"A more proper one, anyway," Reese said. "The bench doesn't qualify."

Settling himself, Hirianthial said, "A more comfortable place is a good idea. You should be able to move around now that you're done with this episode."

"This episode?" Reese grimaced. "There are going to be more?"

He cocked a brow at her. "Unless you're planning on reducing your stress level?"

That prompted the acerbic response he'd been expecting. She lifted a hand and pointed at each finger in turn. "I am letting my crew fly me through an asteroid belt. My ship needs repairs. I am now dirt poor because I used my cargo as makeshift torpedoes to hobble a ship I could have stayed behind to salvage. And I now have an irritating addition to my crew that I didn't ask for and who hasn't left yet."

"I can escort myself to the nearest airlock," Hirianthial said, barely keeping the edges of his mouth from twitching. He gathered the kit and stood. "Can you get up on your own?"

"Yes!" Reese said with a grumble. "And unless you have some superpower involving breathing without atmosphere, you're not going anywhere unless we get to Starbase Kappa."

"Until."

"Right," Reese said.

"This is my room. I promise to rest," Reese said, stopping at the door.

The Eldritch was standing a more-than-polite distance away, hands folded behind his back. Though he'd never come closer than five or six feet on their way here, he'd still somehow managed to give her the impression that he was breathing down her neck. More creepy mind-tricks, maybe . . . or that six-ton personal space he was projecting around himself like some sort of halo field.

He also wasn't moving.

"You do have a room, right?" Reese asked, struggling with her irritation. "Irine showed it to you?"

"Forgive me my impudence, lady," he said. "I would like to see you settled in before I leave."

She stared at him but he didn't move. Usually her glares sent everyone in the crew running unless the matter was too important to ignore. Which, she suddenly realized, described all the issues her crew brought her, even the insignificant ones. Maybe it was time to work on her glaring.

"Look, Hirianthial," she said, trying to find the words that would make him go away. He just watched her struggles with that courtly calm like someone out of her monthly romance squirt—ah! "Look, Hirianthial, I appreciate your concern but we've only just met and it would hardly be . . . uh, appropriate for you to see me in my bedchambers."

"Your bedchambers?" Hirianthial asked, lifting that infuriating white brow again.

"Yes, you know. The lady bit? Me in a nightgown? You're supposed to be a gentleman about this and not chase me into my room."

He laughed, the cad. Reese wanted to deck him. "My apologies, lady. You are correct. Under normal circumstances I would ask permission to enter and respect your wishes if you turned me away. But I'm also a doctor and I am still concerned about your status. Let me see you to your sleep and I promise I'll away with none the wiser about our indiscretion."

Reese scowled. "Nothing I say is going to make you leave."

"I beg a thousand apologies, lady. No."

She threw up her free hand and let herself into her room, too angry to even regret the mess of it. Setting Allacazam in her hammock, she went to the washroom to rinse off her face. The adjacent bathroom was the one luxury of her personal cabin; otherwise it was the same as everyone else's. On the *Earthrise*, getting your own bathroom was about the most you could hope for in the captain's quarters.

"You're from Mars, then," he said from the main room.

Reese eyed him, her hands still dripping. She toweled off her face and leaned against the door frame, arms folded. "And you figured that out . . . "

"From your body shape and weight. And the hammock is telling," Hirianthial said.

"I hope the "doctor" approves, because there's no way I'm sleeping on a bunk."

"No, this is even better," Hirianthial said. "You won't feel the jolts in the ship quite as much and you'll be able to sit more upright."

He looked completely ridiculous investigating her plain pouch hammock with its worn pillows and mess of tangled blankets. He was too tall and too alien to be standing next to something so normal. The entire room was too normal to hold him, with her scattered clothes and the data tablets and her small handful of decorations. Reese said, "It won't be too much longer and we can get you back to what you were doing. What were you doing, anyway?"

"Spying on slavers," Hirianthial said dryly.

"I meant before that," Reese said. "Doctoring or something, I guess, right?"

"Yes," Hirianthial said. Was she imagining the grimace? No, his face had become more set and his eyes less focused. He smiled at her, suddenly affable again. "I'm between jobs at the moment."

"No kidding," Reese said and shook off her boots. He stepped away as she approached the hammock and didn't help her as she wormed her way into it. Allacazam rolled onto her side.

"Are you sure you want to sleep in your clothing?" the Eldritch asked.

"I am *not* changing into something more comfortable with you hovering over my shoulder. You being a healer might make your forced entry all proper but there's no way I need to get naked around you."

"I can turn my back," he said.

She searched his face for any sign of the joke that was certain to be . . . but no, he was serious. Sascha and Irine would have run with a statement like that, but her Eldritch prince-doctor-spy actually meant it. How did she end up meeting all the weirdest people in the Alliance?

"I'll pass," Reese said, not quite able to give it the vinegar she'd wanted to. "I should be dressed in case something comes up with the ship anyway."

"Reasonable," he said. "Don't eat anything until I see you next."

"There's going to be a next?" Reese asked.

"Yes." No arguing with the firmness of that one. He continued. "Try to sleep. I'll come by in a brace of hours. There should be news by then."

"Sleep! I couldn't possibly—"

"I think you'll be surprised," he said.

Reese picked at the corner of one of the blankets, then asked, "You're not going to . . . help me fall asleep. The way you threatened. Right?"

That startled one of the first unguarded expressions out of him she'd seen. Maybe the first, for all she knew. She almost didn't recognize it; as with all his other expressions, he erred on the side of minimalism.

She'd hurt his feelings.

And curse it all, she felt bad about it.

He set both hands on the edge of her hammock so carefully it didn't even rock. Looking into her eyes, he said, "I would never. Never. Abuse my oath."

"I didn't mean to suggest it," Reese said after she caught her breath. "I just thought if you thought it was in my best interests you might—"

"Never," Hirianthial said in a voice so soft and so intense she stopped talking and just believed him.

Reese swallowed and huddled back into her blankets.

"Now, good sleep, Captain Eddings. I'll be back later." He held her eyes a few moments longer then left. In the dark, Reese held onto Allacazam and muttered, "Blood in the soil! He's not a little intense at all, is he."

Allacazam painted a muted purple sparkle across the inside of her eyes. She wasn't sure if he was laughing or not.

Outside in the corridor, Hirianthial trailed his fingers against the wall and let out a long breath. Forty years he'd spent practicing the skills taught to him by Alliance doctors, forty years that had felt like four hundred thanks to the density of experiences in every day. And in all those forty years he'd never been accused of anything as underhanded as drugging a patient without her consent. For all he knew, Reese hadn't even thought he'd use a drug, but assumed he'd somehow knock her out with his mind alone! Was it him that inspired so much vitriol and distrust, or was it normal for her? The Queen had chosen Reese from all the bankrupt traders in space, had indubitably put her under surveillance since. What about this human spitfire had inspired Liolesa's interest? It couldn't solely be the woman's suspicious ways . . . there were Eldritch who would make

Reese look naive. Most of them, even; he didn't think she'd last a single week at Ontine amid the predators in their so-smooth masks.

No, there was something else at work here. He would have to ask as soon as he found a comm line he could secure. The starbase, then.

Still, Reese's assumptions about him didn't relieve him of his responsibility to see her back to health, no matter how unlikely it was that she'd remain healthy after treatment. He'd come back in the promised hour and a half and hopefully find her sleeping with Allacazam in her arms. The intervening time he might as well use to restore his own equilibrium. A little meditation in the small room he'd been assigned wouldn't be unwelcome.

He had just settled into a comfortable pose and begun the ordering of his mind when the comm panel in his room hissed awake.

"Doctor."

Hirianthial stretched up from his crouch far enough to hit the button. "Yes, Bryer?"

"Can you set bones?"

His body tensed. "Yes."

"Please you to come to the lowerdeck, then. There is an accident."

Hirianthial rose. "Do you have a medical kit there?"

"None."

"Give me directions and I'll be there as soon as I pick up the kit from the clinic."

The *Earthrise* surprised him by being larger than he'd expected, but he found his way to the lowerdeck and a cramped corner of a large and empty bay. He'd never seen the inside of a cargo vessel and as modest as Reese made the ship sound the sight of the thick spindles hanging so far above his head filled him with both wonder and unease.

Bryer waved him over to a prone figure.

"Fix," the Phoenix said, pointing at Sascha's leg.

"Right," Sascha hissed. "Just like that." The tigraine rolled yellow eyes up to Hirianthial's face. "You can do magic, right?"

Hirianthial popped the lid and had an ampoule in the tigraine before he finished his sentence. Sascha sighed, quivering.

"Better?"

"As long as I don't look down," the tigraine said meekly.

Hirianthial studied the injury and judged it average: very little mess compared to some breaks he'd witnessed in emergency room rounds. He started undoing the laces at his wrists. "Sharp, heavy object directly on your shin, corner first, yes?"

"The offender's over there," Sascha said with a jerk of his chin. Hirianthial spared it a glance but had no idea what it was other than capable of doing the damage.

"Can I go back to work?" Bryer asked.

"Yes, we're fine," Hirianthial said.

"Are you sure?" Sascha asked.

"You are the proud owner of a compound fracture of both the bones in your lower leg," Hirianthial said, pushing back his sleeves and tightening the laces to anchor them at his elbows. He dragged the medical kit to his side and found the bone kit. "Providing you don't take up marathon running while it's healing, you should be fine once we're done."

"Are you sure I can't be unconscious for this?" Sascha asked.

Hirianthial glanced at him, noted the gray skin inside the ears. "If you want a sedative I can give you one, *alet.*"

The tigraine licked his nose and stared up at the ceiling. "I guess as long as I don't look at it."

"Blood bothers a lot of people," Hirianthial said. "There's no shame in taking the sedative."

"If it were only the blood," Sascha said. "I can deal with injuries in just about anyone else, even Irine who might as well be another me. But my own body? I want my own body to stay in one piece."

"This won't take long," Hirianthial said, opening the bone kit. Most treatment modalities taught in the Alliance core emphasized allowing the body to heal at its own pace despite the availability of technology that accelerated tissue replacement. There were exceptions and broken bones obtained. The Eldritch disinfected the break.

"Please tell me you're not actually swabbing my bones with something," Sascha said, his aura frizzing violently green.

"Tell me about your employer," Hirianthial said.

"What, Reese? Reese's all right. A little wound up, maybe."

"So it's not me in particular that she finds annoying."

"Oh no, she finds you very very more annoying than the rest of us," Sascha said, his laugh trailing to a hiss as Hirianthial began to move the bones.

"You shouldn't be feeling any pain," Hirianthial said, stopping.

"I'm not, but I can still feel pressure. Just do it and get it over with." The tigraine's tail lashed. "Anyway, it's because you weren't part of the plan. She'll get used to you though, presuming you stay around. You are staying around, right?"

"I hadn't thought about it overmuch," Hirianthial said. Talking smoothed out the tigraine's aura, so as he placed the setting clamp around the calf he continued, "Why, do you think I should?"

"You don't seem like you have someplace else to go,"

Sascha said. "And Reese pays pretty well. If you're not afraid of hard work she's a fair boss."

"And what would I do on a merchant ship?" Hirianthial asked. "Unless you have a habit of dropping large metal objects on your body?"

"No, but as I'm sure you've noticed the only reason Reese still has any of her digestive system's because it hasn't found an organ bank to defect to."

A laugh surprised its way out of Hirianthial. He sealed the clamp. "Yes, I noticed. And we're done here. How do you feel?"

"Like I don't trust my body," Sascha said, pushing himself up on his palms. "Is it safe to walk around?"

"Walk but not run. Be gentle with it. Have you had a bone set this way before?" When Sascha shook his head, Hirianthial said, "Don't expect to sleep much. You're going to be hungry often enough to wake in the middle of the night, probably several times. That's normal: your body is burning through your stores generating new cells at several times the usual speed. Eat until you're sated whenever you're hungry and we should be able to take the clamp off in two days, maybe three."

"Right," Sascha said. "Look, doc, let me give you a tip. In the next few days Reese is going to try everything she can think of to get you to go away. Just ignore her and she'll make you an offer."

Hirianthial stared at him. "Why would I ever stay if she wants me to leave?"

"Because she doesn't really want you to leave," Sascha said. He chuckled. "Look, you're exotic and you fascinate her, just like the rest of us. Who doesn't want to know more about a real Eldritch? But you arrived in her life in a way that makes her feel like she's lost control, which means she has to get it back even if she ends up forcing the decision in a direction she doesn't want. Let her feel like she's in charge and she'll let you stay."

"You keep presuming that there's some reason for me to stay beyond ministering to your captain's stress-taxed biology," Hirianthial said. He no longer made the pretense of putting away the medical kit but looked at the tigraine directly.

"Well, like I said, it's not like you have some other place to go," Sascha replied.

"And how do you divine that?" Hirianthial asked, careful to project only curiosity and not his alarm.

The other chuckled. "Look, *arii*, I've been around a while. I've been through times where there's been no place to go. Not because there wasn't, but because I just couldn't, wouldn't go to the places that were left. I know your patience. It's the kind you get when there's nothing pressing pulling you on."

Though appalled, Hirianthial showed only polite interest. Still, something in his face must have changed enough for the tigraine to see.

"Hey, it's not like it's some terrible crime!" Sascha said. "We've all been there, most of us. Certainly all of us on this berth. And like I said, this isn't all that terrible a place to work. We see a lot of interesting places, hauling cargo. Some of them are good and some of them are bad and all of them are new. It's something to do."

"I really need to get back to work," Hirianthial said, finding his voice at last and tapping the kit. "This is what I do."

"For now, anyway," Sascha said. "Correct me if I'm wrong, but you don't look too old and your people live longer than tortoises, right? What's a couple of years . . . a couple of decades, even! To someone who lives that long?"

"Time is always precious," Hirianthial said softly.

"Only if you fill it with something," Sascha said. "Otherwise it's marking the hours." He gingerly rolled onto his knees. "Speaking of marking hour, I need to get back to repairs."

"Don't let something else fall on you, ah?"

"No," Sascha said. "Definitely not in my plan. Thanks, *arii.*"

Reese surprised herself by falling asleep, rocking in her hammock with Allacazam burbling the white noise of a brook. She wasn't sure if that was his way of lulling her or his version of snoring, but she liked it either way. She woke feeling better, if not completely hale, and decided that was healthy enough to go keep an eye on things. On her way off the hammock, she saw a crow form in her mind's eye, sitting on the top of a dark building and staring at her.

"I'm just going to the bridge. It's not like I'm going to take over," Reese said.

The crow kept watching her.

She sighed. "Look, I'm not going back to sleep. I want to know what's going on and I'm tired of acting like an invalid. I promise not to strain myself, okay?"

The Flitzbe's sending transformed into a muted wash of silver and the sound and smell of rain. She took that for resigned agreement and petted his wiggling neural fur. "Thanks. If that busybody Eldritch comes around tell him where I am, okay?"

More wiggling. A picture of Hirianthial rose in her mind, surprisingly clear: as far as Reese knew the Flitzbe didn't see the same way she did, so this was either Reese's image of the Eldritch or Hirianthial's. Since she couldn't possibly imagine that she thought of him in such bright and pleasant colors and with squiggles of gold and deep scarlet around him like a brocade halo, it must be his.

"Right, him," Reese said. The image of the Eldritch began to glower comically. "Yeah, I know he won't be happy. But he's got to learn he doesn't run things around here. So just tell him where I am, okay? I have things to do."

Before the Flitzbe could reply, Reese swung herself out of the hammock and headed for the bridge. Halfway there she detoured to the galley and picked up food for the girls. They probably hadn't stopped to eat. There was nothing appetizing in the larder, but she grabbed a couple of yogurt-coated protein bars and a jug of water and brought them with her.

Kis'eh't and Irine were still sitting where she'd left them, though both of them had unstrapped their safety harnesses and were relaxed in their chairs. Reese squeezed past the crates of spare parts and said, "Lunch is here. Dinner. Whatever."

Irine's ears perked. "Did someone say food?"

"Not great food, but yeah," Reese said, handing over a bar. She gave the second to Kis'eh't and found a place between them to sit. "How's it going?"

"We're in good shape coasting with the rocks," Irine said. "Getting in here was a bit of an adventure, but we made it." She pointed through the small windows at the asteroids in the distance. "We should be fine here until the repairs are done. Bryer tells me our in-systems are ready . . . that was the easy part. They're working on the Well Drive now."

Reese looked at Kis'eh't. "Sensors say anything?"

"Can't see anything past the rock noise," Kis'eh't said. "We're hoping if we can't see anything, they can't either. It's not like pirates have Fleet-grade sensor arrays."

"Hopefully," Reese said. "Thanks, guys. You did great."

"Thank us when we get to Starbase Kappa in one piece," Irine said, but she purred between bites of the bar.

"Did you have a nice nap?" Kis'eh't asked.

"Surprisingly," Reese said. "Though now that I'm awake again I wish I was still in bed. I have no idea what we're going to do now. I spent almost everything I had on the rooderberries."

"I guess we'll just hang out and hope for another assignment, then," Irine said. "That's worked before, once or twice."

"And in the meantime, protein bars," Kis'eh't said, eyeing hers with distaste.

"Hey, pass it over if you don't want it," Irine said. "I'm hungry."

The Glaseahn grumbled and unpeeled the wrapper.

"What about you?" Irine asked. "Hungry?"

"Nah. I'm not allowed to eat until Lord High-and-Mighty says I can."

"—or?" Irine asked.

"Or he'll cut open my stomach with sandpaper and a boot knife."

"What boot knife?" the tigraine asked. "He doesn't have any weapons on him thanks to his keepers."

"I'm sure he'll improvise with something," Reese said. "A nail clipper. A butter knife."

"We haven't had any butter in ages," Kis'eh't said.

"We'll have butter again," Reese said and sighed. "I really meant to take better care of you all."

"It's not your fault we can't seem to keep out of disaster's way long enough to turn a fin," Irine said. "We'll get out of this one, boss, and then you'll write a book: "Rooderberry Torpedoes and Other Strategies for Outrunning Slavers." And then you'll get rich and we'll all retire."

Reese laughed. "A nice story—" and the ship shivered. She sat up. "What was that?"

Kis'eh't frowned. "Not sure. A stray asteroidlet from

the outer bands? We shouldn't be getting those right now." Her fingers drummed the board as Reese watched, and then they stopped and that unsavory gray color returned to the skin around her eyes. "Aksivaht'h! They've followed us in!"

"The pirates?" Reese said, rising to her knees and propping herself on the board to look for herself. Two hazy red blips were showing up in the muted gray and black dapple that represented the asteroid belt. "*Two* of them?"

Irine strapped herself back in. "Were they shooting at us, Kis'eh't, or just trying their luck? If they're guessing I don't want to light up their arrays by firing the thrusters."

"I can't tell," Kis'eh't said. "They're not gunning for us, though. They seem to be drifting through the outer bands."

"Don't these people give up?" Reese asked. "What could they want so badly to send two ships into an asteroid belt? That's crazy!"

"It's not that crazy," Irine said. "We're in here, after all. And we've got their pet Eldritch. Angels know how much an Eldritch is worth on the slave market."

"If they even want to keep him," Kis'eh't said. "If he was spying, they might just want to kill him."

The thought of Hirianthial's body robbed of its grace, sprawled on the floor at odd angles with all that white hair tangled and bloody, bothered Reese more than she wanted to admit. "The guy's annoying, but not annoying enough to let someone else kill him," she said. "Let's see if these two get any closer or if they're just hoping for a lucky shot. And finish eating, Kis'eh't. It might be a while before you have the chance again."

The Glaseahn went back to chewing on the bar. When Reese passed her the water jug, the other woman said, "You're taking this well."

"No, I'm not," Reese said. "I'm just hiding it better." She

grinned, but privately wondered. Kis'eh't was right . . . she was calmer about this than she expected. Maybe she was just tired of worrying about everything herself? Or maybe the Eldritch had drugged her on the way out after all—

—no, that was unfair. He hadn't done anything to her except make her admit she needed the rest.

The lift opened then for Sascha. "Did someone call for me?"

"I'm always calling for you," Irine said, purring.

"Is the Well Drive ready?" Reese asked, hoping.

Sascha shook his head. "No, but only one of us can get at it at this point and Bryer's the better mechanic. He sent me away before I dropped another crate on my other leg."

"Your leg!" Irine exclaimed. "What happened?"

"I'm fine. The doctor patched me up and I should be good as new in a couple of days. Though I'm famished. Anyone got any food?"

"Here, take mine," Kis'eh't said, offering her half-eaten bar.

While crunching it, Sascha sat next to the pilot's chair. "So what's cooking?"

"Two ships followed us into the belt and are looking for us," Reese said.

"Can you drive?" Irine asked.

"As long as my arms are fine I can fly," Sascha said. "Want me to take over?"

"Please," Reese and Irine said in unison. The latter blushed. "I'm really good, but not as good."

"No problem," Sascha said, sliding into the vacant chair. "We drifting until we have evidence they've actually seen us?"

"Yeah," Reese said.

"Good plan. I can finish eating."

Which he did. In the ensuing silence, Reese looked

over the twins and Kis'eh't. She wondered if this would be the last run they flew together. What would pirates do with her ship? Convert it into a slaver? She couldn't imagine it decorated with poorly-mounted weapon additions and used as a pirate ship. The notion of her battered old freighter threatening much larger vessels made her want to laugh out loud. She didn't, though.

"I could seriously use a vacation," Sascha said after a while.

"Mmm," Irine said.

"Someplace warm," Kis'eh't offered. When Reese eyed her, the Glaseahn shrugged her wing arms. "You do keep it cold around here, Reese. Even for me."

"Home is warm," Irine said.

"Home is hot," Sascha amended.

"But there are wonderful open houses with stone tiles warm beneath your feet," Irine said. "And with fluttering scarves to filter the hardest sunlight and turn it colors. And there's always fruit, the juiciest melons, all cool and crisp and fit to put streams down your chin."

"Sounds good to me," Kis'eh't said.

"And water," Irine said. Reese handed her the jug, which the tigraine looked at, puzzled, then drank from. "Water splashing in fountains, really soft. And birds at the fountains, bright birds with curious eyes that will eat berries from your fingers."

"Sounds like a nice place," Reese said.

"You wouldn't like it, boss," Sascha said, grinning. "It's full of Harat-Shar."

Reese laughed. "Oh, maybe you two have grown on me." She sobered. "A vacation sounds nice. We'd just have to win the most improbable gambling streak to be able to afford one. Besides, as nice as your warm paradise sounds, Irine, I think I'd prefer something cooler. Snow, maybe."

"Snow!" Irine said and shuddered.

"Not the entire year," Reese said. "Just for a month or two. Enough so you could appreciate a fireplace and hot coffee and bread fresh from the oven. And a blanket."

"Reese, I think they're heading for us."

She looked over Kis'eh't's arm. "At least, they're heading deeper into the belt."

"Doesn't change that at that angle of approach they're going to have to be blind to miss that we're in their sensor cone. We're in trouble."

"Irine, man our laser please."

The tigraine scampered to the corner of the bridge. The laser that had come with the *Earthrise* had been intended to clear debris, not to provide much by way of protection from pirates. Reese doubted it would prove at all useful but one never knew. "Sascha, can you outfly these people?"

"Normally? No, I don't think so," Sascha said, tail flicking. "These two are beefier than the last pirate they sent after us. But in here, gambling with rocks the size of small moons? Yeah, I think we're crazier than they are. Just say the word."

Reese watched the blip of the first pirate, strangely distanced from it. She couldn't quite believe it was in here. She had never carried cargo valuable enough to warrant interest from pirates. The idea that she was dodging two of them in an asteroid belt like some kind of 3deo action star was ludicrous and simply couldn't be happening.

"Do it."

Sascha fired the engines and the *Earthrise* lurched to one side.

"Are you heading for that asteroid?" Reese asked.

"Boss if you can't handle the view, get off the obdeck."

"Right," Reese said, and clutched at side of the station. Now she was getting worried.

"They've seen us!" Kis'eh't said. "They're both changing course to follow."

"Let them," Sascha said. "We're heading for the mid-belt, where the asteroids are small enough to cluster and big enough to kill us."

"Joy," Reese muttered. "I hope you know what you're doing."

"As long as I know just a little more than they do we're in business."

"Just try to keep our repair bill manageable," Reese said, clenching her teeth as a rock flew past, narrowly missing.

The intercom chimed and Kis'eh't flicked it on.

"Lowerdeck. Am not getting much done with you sending me shooting across the deck on feathers."

"Sorry about that," Kis'eh't said. "We're trying to out-fly two raiders they've sent for us. I recommend strapping down."

"Thanks for the not-warning. Will get back to work." The comm shut down.

"At least he doesn't have the screaming shakes," Reese said.

"Kis'eh't, find me the densest bit of this band."

"Head further sunward. There's a pack of asteroids ahead."

"Thanks."

Irine sidled over until her side was pressed against Reese's. For once, Reese didn't care; usually she discouraged the twins from coming near since their hugs tended to turn into cuddling. It seemed like a crime to die without having a good cuddle though, at least with someone who wasn't practically a plant, like Allacazam.

"Are we going to die?" Irine whispered.

"Don't think things like that," Reese said.

"Seriously," Irine said. "Because I think I'd rather live as someone's pleasure slave than die free."

Reese glanced at her, was just a little surprised to discover the tigraine was serious. Homeworld-bred Harat-
Shar could be very strange. From experience, Reese knew
better than to try to explain that she and Kis'eh't and Bryer
and certainly Hirianthial would probably have a much
more difficult time spending their lives in captivity, so instead she said, "What if you don't wind up a pleasure slave?
What if they put you to work mining ore or something?"

"No one forces slaves to do manual labor," Irine whispered. "Machines are faster and last longer."

"What if they send you to the Chatcaavan Empire? I
hear they torture their slaves."

"A little pain is a good thing," Irine said. Added, "Sometimes a lot of pain."

Which was more than Reese wanted to know. She
winced as an asteroid whacked the side of the ship, sending
a quiver through the deck plates. Finally she said, "What if
they don't want another Harat-Shar slave? What if they kill
you and use your pelt as a throw rug?"

That paled the skin inside Irine's ears. "Do you really
believe there's a sapient fur trade?"

"I didn't believe there was a slave trade either," Reese
said.

Irine wrapped her arms around Reese's waist and
shuddered. "I don't want to be someone's rug!"

"And I don't want to be someone's harem girl, so let's
just hope your brother knows what he's doing."

The ship shivered again. "You'll want to avoid the
rocks, Sascha."

"That wasn't a rock," Kis'eh't said. "They're firing at us.
Ranging shots, looks like."

"Let them try to keep a bead on us," Sascha growled.
"Hang on, *ariisen*."

The *Earthrise* banked so sharply to the side an alarm went off. Reese slapped a hand against one ear and crawled to the other side of the bridge to find the source. One of her panels had gone red and was flashing 'Structural Stress Overload' and 'Gantry Separation Imminent.' "Blood and Freedom, Sascha, there are things threatening to separate from this ship I didn't even know were on it!"

"Not now, boss," Sascha said tightly.

Reese chanced a look out the rear windows and froze. She'd spent an appreciable amount of her adulthood in space and was accustomed to the distances—"near" in spacer terms wasn't eyeshot, which meant she should not, under any circumstances, be able to see that pirate there that was flying around the asteroid that Sascha must have been swerving to miss. Now was not the time to vomit, but her stomach flexed in her middle anyway.

The second raider appeared on the first one's heels and the *Earthrise* bucked so violently Reese lost her hold on the board and smacked sideways into a crate.

"They missed us!" Kis'eh't cried.

"That was a miss?" Irine asked.

"Rocks separated from the asteroid they nicked instead," Kis'eh't said. "Hurt us but just cosmetically."

Just as Reese righted herself, the *Earthrise* dove to the other side, introducing her upper back to the corner of the station. Acceleration pressed her into it hard enough that she couldn't find a way to get up. "Saaascha!"

"Almost done—GOT 'EM!"

In the corner of her eye, Reese could see a rock swooping into view behind them and the raider not turning fast enough to avoid it. The explosions that rippled from its side seemed to happen in slow motion.

"That one is definitely out of the game," Kis'eh't said. "The other one's still coming, though."

The alarms from Reese's board were still whooping. Now that she could turn she did to find new problems bordering the old ones, which were now flashing their distress. "If I lose some part of this ship because of this—"

"I'm just working on getting the oxygenated part out of this in one piece," Sascha said. "The rest of it can be replaced." The ship began leaning to one side again.

"They're still tailing us," Kis'eh't said.

"Not after this they won't be," Sascha said, and dropped the bridge out from under them. Reese's mouth filled with burning fluid but she swallowed it back down before it could have any other ideas. Her palms were sweating more than usual. Was the room spinning?

One of the alarms stopped abruptly. 'Gantry Separation Imminent' became 'Gantry Has Separated. Please check for leaks.' "Leaks!" Reese exclaimed.

"I'm not seeing any leaks," Kis'eh't said. "What happened?"

"I think one of the cargo cranes just came off," Reese said weakly.

"Dodge that, friend," Sascha said, and pulled them out of their dive so quickly Reese gave up her watch on the board and dropped onto the floor to fight with her stomach full-time.

"And—he's skidded to a stop!" Kis'eh't said. The Glaseahn squinted at her board, then added, "He's venting, Sascha. You did something!"

Sascha hit the intercom button. "Bryer, now would be a good time to tell me we can get the hells out of this system."

"Can do. Vector away."

Sascha crowed. "We're out of here!"

Irine and Kis'eh't cheered. Reese would have joined them but wasn't sure opening her mouth would have been a good idea.

From the lift, a baritone said, "So is it safe to come out now?"

"Hey, Hirianthial! Looks like we made it out alive!"

"Good to hear. And here is my runaway."

Reese stared at the man's gray leather boots and hated them. Did they have to be so finely polished? They weren't even scuffed. Even the pewter buckles were unmarred. The Eldritch crouched over her and the open concern in his eyes irritated her as much as it worried her.

"I hope you don't mind if I take you back to your hammock," Hirianthial said so softly he must have intended only her to hear.

"Preparing to Well away," Sascha said.

Reese licked her upper lip and chanced a few words. "Think I could handle that."

The *Earthrise* shook so hard Reese flew forward into Hirianthial, who caught her before sliding back against the lift.

"What was that!" Kis'eh't shouted.

"A parting blow," Sascha said. "Their weapons still work, I guess. Doesn't matter because . . . three, two, one, we're gone!"

The smooth hum beneath her thinned away until the Well Drive's nigh silence took over. Reese waited long enough to ensure they'd made it into folded-space before vomiting onto Hirianthial's brocade tunic and fainting completely away.

"How far are we from Starbase Kappa?" Hirianthial asked, running a hand over Reese's chest. The black knot over her had become so thorny sensing it brought tears to the corners of his eyes. He wished fervently for a real medical scanner, one capable of penetrating to the tissue level he needed. It could be that she was worsening but not in danger yet . . . or she could be dying. Reading her aura wouldn't give him the specifics he needed to make surgical decisions.

Of course, he had no operating room to fix any surgical problems, so perhaps it was for the best.

"We're about six hours out," Sascha said.

"Can we get there faster?"

Irine unharnessed herself and crawled over. "What's wrong?"

"She needs medical attention," Hirianthial said. "Soon."

"Aren't you medical attention?" Irine asked. Her brother glanced over the back of his chair and added, "How soon?"

"Now would be best," Hirianthial said. "And while I appreciate your confidence, a doctor without tools isn't much use in a situation like this."

"Well, we're not going to be able to get there now," Sascha said. "The best I can do is shave an hour or two off the total."

Hirianthial said, "That would not be a poor idea. In the mean, I'll try to keep her stable until we arrive."

"Try?" Sascha asked, eyes round.

"This isn't a broken bone," Hirianthial said, slipping an arm beneath Reese's shoulders . . . carefully, so very carefully. Her entire body was a tangle so taut he feared aggravating it.

"We can push the drive," Sascha said. "Cut it down to four hours."

"That might also blow out the drive," Kis'eh't said. "Bad enough that we lost the cargo crane and probably something else in that last shot. But to lose the Well Drive? It won't matter if Reese survives whatever's wrong with her, she'll blow up from new stress the moment she finds out."

Hirianthial put his other arm beneath Reese's knees

and lifted her into his arms. He hadn't paid much attention to the bouncing and jerking of the ride, but it had taken a toll. Getting to one knee made him realize his joints were not those of a youth's anymore.

It didn't hurt as much as Reese's body was hurting.

"Look, how serious is this?" Kis'eh't asked, feathered ears fanned closed. "I thought she just had some sort of ulcer."

"She does," Hirianthial said. "The problem is she has more ulcer than esophagus, and it might be rupturing."

"Might?" Kis'eh't said.

"Without a real scanner I can't be sure," Hirianthial said. "But I would guess that if it's not rupturing it's very close."

"That sounds serious," Irine said, her eyes as wide as her brother's.

"It is serious," Hirianthial said. He couldn't quite bring himself to frighten them beyond that. "I'd appreciate being able to deliver her to appropriate facilities as quickly as possible."

Sascha searched his face, then turned in his seat. "Right. We're pushing the drive."

"Sascha—"

"Kis'eh't, if she eats me for lunch when she wakes up at least she'll be awake to do it. Bryer? You awake down there?"

"Awake, yes. Astounded also."

"Reese is sick. We're redlining the drive to Kappa."

"I will pamper it like a colicky child."

"Thanks," Sascha said.

Hirianthial turned to the lift and was surprised to find Irine in his way.

"Can I help?" the tigraine asked, squeezing the end of her tail. Her aura pulsed in rhythm with her accelerated heart rate.

"Of course," Hirianthial said.

He carried her to her quarters with Irine silent at his heels. The tigraine keyed the door open for him and he laid Reese in her hammock with Allacazam, who turned an alarmed orange once he bumped Reese's side.

"I know," Hirianthial murmured, petting the Flitzbe. "Irine, would you be so good as to fetch the kit that's in the clinic?"

"Right," Irine said and scampered away.

In the silence and the dark, Hirianthial filled a small bowl with lukewarm water and began removing Reese's soiled vest. The lead gray of her aura, choked with black knots, promised she'd stay unconscious long enough for him to take the equally soiled pants off as well, but knowing how she'd react if she discovered he'd unclothed her kept him from doing more. That and the comment about impropriety, a claim so unusual in the multicultural Alliance that it both charmed and discomfited him. He'd become accustomed to the libertine—by Eldritch standards—mores of the outworlders, and anything more conservative reminded him strongly of home.

"You're getting the nasty stuff off?" Irine asked as she entered. "Why don't you let me do it? At least that way when she asks who put her in her nightgown you can honestly say it was me."

"A fine idea," Hirianthial said, taking the kit from her. He turned his back as the tigraine began pulling off Reese's pants. The inadequacy of the kit proved a useful if unfortunate distraction. What he wanted was a complete medical scanner and the tools to act on its findings; first aid kits were not equipped to handle Reese's problem. If her esophagus ruptured, nothing short of surgery could save her, and no drug in this kit could retard the process. . . .

Except . . . what had the charge doctor on Tam-ley said once? Something to do with mucus? Hirianthial rubbed a temple. "What's in your larder, Irine?"

"Our—what? Our galley? I don't know, what do you want to eat?"

"Not food," Hirianthial said, trying to pin down the memory. He'd started losing track of things by the time he hit three hundred despite the mental disciplines he'd learned to prevent it . . . remembering things now so long removed from his young adulthood was a challenge. He tapped a finger on the edge of the kit, trying to remember. Not cream, but . . . ah! "Do you have powdered milk?"

"Everyone carries powdered milk," Irine said, mystified. "Do you want some?"

"Please. Bring it in the package."

Irine left, taking her perplexed aura with her. Hirianthial hoped they had what he needed and returned to the drug stock. Like every kit, it held the red vial in the corner mold, more than enough for several score emergency doses. Even with his stopgap measure, using the vial's contents would better Reese's chances. He doubted she would like it, and he absolutely wouldn't apply it without her consent.

He'd have to wake her for the makeshift palliative, anyway.

Irine had gotten Reese into her nightgown, a lace-edged affair sewn of ivory cotton so fine it neared translucence and long enough to tangle at her ankles. It suited her, which made little sense to Hirianthial; she'd also suited her brightly-colored vests and jumpsuits. He sat beside the hammock on a stool, monitoring her through her aura's hissing crawl until Irine arrived with a single-serving box in hand.

"You look confused," she said.

"Do I?" Hirianthial asked, taking the box.

Irine nodded. "If it's about the nightgown, you're not the only one who thinks it's funny. She reads romance novels too."

"We all have to pass the time somehow," Hirianthial said, reading the ingredient list. He allowed himself the smallest breath of relief and noticed his shoulders losing their tension. "Thank you, Irine. I think you found your captain her four hours."

"You mean . . . it . . . she could . . . "

"She's in a bad way," Hirianthial said. "This will tide her over."

"Powdered *milk*?"

Hirianthial fetched a bowl and filled it with a shallow puddle of water, then poured the entire box into it. He gloved a hand and swirled the result with his fingers, praying that it would work as well as the charge doctor had claimed. The man had been excellent at finding unusual solutions to problems; Hirianthial had watched him pioneer countless peculiar methods but hadn't actually witnessed this one in action. "The milk from one of the herdbeasts used commonly in powdered milk isn't all that different from mucus. It should coat Reese's esophagus long enough to get her to Kappa."

"We just have to wake her up," Irine said.

He nodded. "There's something in the kit for that." The solution in the bowl began to resist his stirring. "I think we're ready. Hold this, please."

Irine grimaced at the bowl. "She's going to have to drink this?"

"Eat it, more like," Hirianthial said.

"I thought it was supposed to have more water in it."

"We don't want it too dilute," Hirianthial said, loading the AAP. He smoothed back some of Reese's errant braids, then gave her the smallest possible dose to bring her back to consciousness. He waited, monitoring her colors as they began to flicker through the black and gray of her aura.

Finally—"Ohhh."

"Boss, it's us," Irine whispered on the other side of the hammock. In the dark, the tigraine's pupils were swollen and flashed green when she blinked.

"Don't talk," Hirianthial added. "We're going to give you something we want you to swallow and some water to wash it down. It'll make you feel better."

Reese tipped her head down once. He brought the bowl to her lips and slid his fingers through her braids again. This time he was expecting their texture. Her skull seemed small in his hand, though. He'd lost enough patients to trust his instincts and his perception of her frailty worried him. "Here. Drink."

Reese sputtered on the first swallow.

"Come on, boss, do it for us," Irine said. "How are you going to yell at us if you can't talk?"

That bought them a third of the bowl. Hirianthial let her have water and watched with concern as she let her eyes flutter shut. After a few breaths, she resumed drinking. Her aura remained a knotted black and as she drank he sensed it worsening. Consciousness would not serve her. Reese finished off the bowl and Hirianthial let her have a few more sips of water before putting them aside.

"I have some questions I must ask you," Hirianthial said. "I want you to save your strength, so if you have anything to say make it simple."

"What's wrong with me?" Reese whispered.

"You're very unwell," Hirianthial said. "When we reach Starbase Kappa you need to go into surgery to repair the ulcer in your esophagus."

She didn't speak but a flame of yellow alarm made it through her aura's thorns.

"Your condition is serious," Hirianthial said. "The solution you just drank will help keep you from getting worse, but remaining conscious is an invitation to trouble. I would like your permission to dose you with slowsleep."

Fear jumped through the crevices of her pain. "It's only for four or five hours," Hirianthial said. "The dose will be low and I'll be monitoring your condition continually. You'll feel as if you're drifting off to a sleep full of vivid dreams. When you wake up, you'll be done with the operation and your body will be better than new."

"Don't like slowsleep," Reese said, eyes wide.

"Please, boss. We won't let anything happen to you," Irine said, taking Reese's hand.

"She's right," Hirianthial said. "I won't let anything happen to you. This is just a precaution to make the operation go more smoothly once we reach the base."

"I'll be okay?" Reese whispered.

"You'll be okay," Hirianthial said, softening his voice.

Reese bit her lip, then nodded once.

Hirianthial leaned back and pulled out the vial and the syringe. As he loaded it, he said, "As a matter of formality I need to ask if you have a healthcare proxy. Understand that I'm required to ask whenever administering a dose of slowsleep."

Her anxiety level spiked, thorns spitting black sparks off her aura. He rested a hand on the edge of the hammock and said, "A five-hour dose of slowsleep isn't dangerous. Trust me, Theresa. You won't come to any harm."

She swallowed, then said, "Don't have a proxy. You're the doctor. You decide for me."

He nodded. "Very well. I'm going to give you the slowsleep now. When you wake up, you'll be out of danger. Allacazam and Irine and I will take care of you, we'll be right here. All right?"

She swallowed again and nodded.

He set the syringe against her arm. A low hiss, and it was done. Irine squeezed Reese's hand and whispered, "Do you think I should sing to her?"

"It couldn't hurt," Hirianthial said, putting away the vial and AAP.

Irine sang in a surprisingly sweet furry soprano. He recognized parts of the language as Meridan but peppered with enough foreign words that he couldn't fully understand the song, something about wind and light. He put the kit away and watched the colors in Reese's aura drain away, leaving only the black and gray tangle. By the time Irine finished her lullaby, Reese had succumbed to the dose.

"Now what?" Irine asked in a soft voice.

"Now I watch her," Hirianthial said. "It's rare for anything to happen during slowsleep, but most people report remembering the presence of others under the influence."

"Then I'll stay too, like you said," Irine said, and curled up on the floor. "Um, Hirianthial . . . will you please . . . I mean, you have been very cagey about Reese. Could this kill her?"

A direct question about the health of a friend Hirianthial couldn't dodge. So he didn't. "Yes, it could."

Irine shivered. "But it's just a stomach thing!"

"It's not just a stomach thing," Hirianthial said. "It's a bacterial infection that she's been ignoring which has been intensified by stress to the point of rupturing her esophagus. Once that occurs, fluid can enter the chest cavity and that can kill. But we're going to get Reese to Kappa long before then."

Irine was silent. Hirianthial composed himself on the stool, hooking his boot heels on the bottom rung. After a while, the tigraine said, "Have you lost a lot of patients?"

"One is too many," Hirianthial replied, "So the concept of 'a lot' is difficult to take seriously. Yes, I've lost people under my care."

"Even in the Alliance," Irine said, ears flattening.

"For all its technological wonders, and they are many, the Alliance is not the same everywhere," Hirianthial said. "A woman in Terracentrus is going to get better care than a woman on a freighter in the middle of no-space. Location matters. Access to facilities matters. Money matters. Up-to-date kits matter."

"I guess some things don't change," Irine said.

Hirianthial rested his gaze on Reese's slack face. "Not easily, no."

The many shifts Hirianthial had spent on patient watch had taught him how to relax so deeply he encroached on sleep's soft threshold without crossing it. In such a state he not only maintained his emotional equilibrium but could track the auras of any people in his care. Reese was close enough that her presence intruded on his, but even Irine's registered, a sparkly, healthy gold muted now by a gray veil of worry. The colors paled as she fell asleep, coiled into a ball beneath Reese. The hammock's webbed shadow fell over her body, cast from the dimmed overhead lights.

Allacazam's body created no aura, a fact Hirianthial found fascinating and enigmatic in the extreme. But the rest of the crew he could sense even through the bulk-heads—not with enough granularity to assess their health and mental state, but strongly enough for him to sense their distance and that they lived. In busy hospitals he'd been overwhelmed by the amount of data his abilities had brought him without asking, and he'd learned not so much to ignore the people around him as to allow their auras to blur into one undifferentiated mass. His workplaces had developed auras of their own, the combination of thousands of patients and personnel on their business, and though he never paid attention to it he always knew in the back of his mind the "health" of his workplace.

There were days that death and suffering had blackened the entrance to the hospital so that he hated to enter, and days when miracles sent white ripples through a floor to lighten the mood of the entire workplace. But it had been long and long again since he'd been somewhere small enough that each person cast a distinct emotional, without the blur created by his cultivated psychic myopia. He found it pleasant and drifted, a lagan tethered to those distant auras as to buoys in the darkness.

The flare of Reese's pain doubling brought him to the surface immediately. He slid a hand above her chest and felt the tear as if it were in his palm. With his free hand, Hirianthial punched the intercom's bridge combination. "Sascha. Tell me we're close."

"We're just coming out of Well. Half an hour at the most, depending on how quickly they dock us."

Hirianthial glanced at Reese. She was breathing too quickly for slowsleep. "When you connect with the docking authority, put me through. I'll get us a space."

"You're the boss, doc. Stand by."

Irine uncurled and rubbed her eye. "Are we there?" Then, "What's wrong?"

"We're running out of time," Hirianthial said.

Irine's tail lashed. "The insystems just fired. We must be on final approach."

Hirianthial said nothing, leaning against the wall in an effort to seem less concerned than he was. He left his hand over Reese's chest, trying to gauge the extent of the trauma. He'd always taken for granted the vague knowledge he'd gained through his abilities and had used them in tandem with his clinical experience and observation of physical symptoms to make his diagnoses . . . but he'd always confirmed and refined those findings with diagnostic equipment. Having no scanner to track the extent of Reese's danger frustrated him.

"Docking authority is pinging me, doc."

"Can I talk to them from here?"

"Yeah, hang on. Okay, you're live!"

"Starbase Kappa, this is Doctor Sarel Jisiensire of the TMS *Earthrise*. We have a medical emergency requiring immediate surgery. Do you have an emergency deck berth?"

"*Earthrise*, this is Kappa Docking. We are transmitting a vector and docking assignment now. Please advise as to the nature of the emergency so we can prepare for your arrival."

"I have one human female suffering from rupture of the esophagus with possible pleural effusion, currently coming out of slowsleep. Vital statistics are fluctuating."

"Thank you. We'll have a team waiting for you. Kappa away."

Sascha's voice returned, now hard with tension. "I've got the assignment. We'll be there in under ten minutes."

"Now what?" Irine asked.

"Now we go wait at the exit," Hirianthial said. He gathered Reese into his arms though he felt as if he was embracing an armful of naked swords and said, "Show me the way out, Irine."

"Yes, sir," Irine said and darted out the door. Hirianthial followed. With Reese pressed against his chest he could feel the hard and irregular thump of her heart.

"You are not allowed to go this way," he told her. "I simply won't have it. I know you can hear me, Theresa Eddings. You are ten minutes away from the medical care that will save your life so you simply cannot, will not, are not allowed to falter now."

A flicker of gold against the knife-sharp black. With Irine so far ahead of him, he leaned down and whispered into one ear, "You cannot die yet, Theresa. What other human woman has been held in the arms of an Eldritch? Surely that's too good a story not to live to tell."

The ship shivered before he reached the exit. And again when he caught up with Irine at the edge of the vast docking bay with its ominous spindles and their long shadows on the cold ground. It seemed to take too long before the thunderous groan of the dock doors sliding into their pockets sounded. Hirianthial didn't wait but squeezed through them sideways and delivered Reese into the arms of the medical team waiting there. As they put her on the stretcher he said, "I'm certified. I'm coming with you. Don't try to stop me."

The orderly glanced at him and shrugged before heading back toward the corridor.

On one side, the smell of antiseptic . . . on the other, a field of waving flowers. Reese tried to choose the flowers, but the harder she reached for the field the further it receded. Exasperated, she put her hands on her hips and tried commanding the field to stay put, but it was no use. Come to think of it, she'd never been in a field of flowers. The image had come off a calendar some repair shop had given her, and the smell of the flowers . . . that was one of Irine's perfumes. She couldn't even have original dreams. Reese gave up and decided to see if waking was any better.

Waking was worse. She was under a halo-arch in an unfamiliar Medplex. Not just a clinic, a small place that supported only routine medical visits, but a real Medplex, a space hospital. She'd seen the inside of a Medplex only three times and hated every memory involving one. That she was trapped not just in a Medplex but also apparently as a patient horrified her.

How had she gotten here? The last thing she remembered was throwing up on the bridge.

"She's awake!"

The twins' faces appeared above her. They made no move to hug her, and their unwonted caution scared Reese even more than the halo-arch. She swallowed and discovered she could talk, though her assumption that talking would hurt puzzled her. "Where am I?"

"Starbase Kappa," Sascha said. "In the Medplex."

"I figured that part out," Reese said. "Why am I here?"

The two exchanged glances. "You don't remember?" Irine asked.

"Remember what? Throwing up on the bridge? I got that part," Reese said. "I hope Hirianthial wasn't too upset about his clothes."

"His clothes!" Irine shook her head. "Reese, you almost died!"

Reese laughed. "I did not."

They didn't laugh. The halo-arch beeped into the silence, doing whatever it was halo-arches did to monitor the condition of their occupants.

"I didn't," Reese said again. "It was just stress."

They continued to not say anything. Reese started to worry. "Guys?"

"You've been unconscious for a day since they operated," Sascha said.

"Operated!"

"I'll go get Hirianthial," Irine said and vanished.

"Sascha, what is going on here? This is crazy talk."

"Boss, just relax, okay? Hirianthial will explain it."

"Right," Reese said, rolling her eyes. "The Eldritch

doctor."

She expected a chuckle, but instead Sascha's gaze hardened with disapproval and his ears flattened. "'The Eldritch doctor' saved your life, Reese. The surgeon said so. You would have died on the way to Starbase Kappa without him."

Reese stared at him. "You're not kidding me."

"No."

Reese flushed. "Well how was I supposed to know that? I was unconscious!"

His expression didn't change. "Well, now you do."

"I still don't understand how I can have been that sick," Reese said. "I feel fine now!"

Sascha managed half a grin. "You'll understand well enough when you get the Medplex services bill."

"The bill!" Reese exclaimed, trying to sit up. The field from the halo-arch repulsed her and she squirmed, trying to find a way around it. "What bill?"

"There is no bill." Hirianthial's hair preceded him into view, swishing over the edge of the field. The lines beneath his eyes were far more pronounced, and his baritone had deeper tones, rough edges. "Welcome back, lady."

"What is going on here? Let me out of this so I can see you all at once."

"If you promise not to leave the bed," Hirianthial said.

"Yes, yes, I promise, let me up!"

He tapped a few notes on the edge of the arch. "All right."

Reese struggled to sit up and surprised herself by feeling too weak. The twins caught her before she could wobble and propped her up. "Just a touch of vertigo."

"Right," Sascha said dryly.

"Now," Reese said, staring at Hirianthial. "Explain."

He remained composed. She had expected him to look

ridiculous against the backdrop of a modern medical establishment with his anachronistic clothes and princely demeanor, but for some reason this was the one place he seemed to suit. He wasn't wearing the doublet she'd thrown up on, though. Her cheeks warmed at that memory. She hoped he'd been able to clean it up . . . the camellias had been pretty.

"We sealed your esophagus and used a resurfacing agent to encourage the regeneration of the mucosal layers," he said after a moment. "You're on antibiotics until we've cleared your system of the infection that started this problem, and to ward off any infection that might have thought about colonizing your chest cavity."

"You make it sound like it I was some sort of road that needed repaving," Reese said, rubbing her throat. She didn't feel like she'd had one of her body parts sewn up.

"It was only like a road that needed repaving if part of the road had collapsed and the rest of it was nearing the same state."

Reese swallowed, waiting for the customary jolt of heat and nervousness that accompanied unpleasant news. Instead her stomach tightened. That was it. Nothing more. No burning, no sour tastes, no convulsive need for chalk tablets. That finally convinced her. "Blood and Freedom, you replaced my esophagus!"

"More or less," Hirianthial said.

Reese leaned forward and covered her eyes. "What did I owe?"

"You didn't hear him before?" Irine asked, poking Reese gently in the ribs. "There is no bill."

"No bill?" Reese said. "How is that possible? You didn't pay it, did you?"

"If by pay you mean handing over coins, then no, I didn't," Hirianthial said. "If by pay you mean work here for a few shifts until the value of your operation had been re-couped by the Medplex, then I suppose I did."

Reese pointed a finger at him. "I didn't ask for your help!"

"I owed you a debt," Hirianthial said. "You saved my life."

"I didn't want you to pay me back," Reese said. "I wanted you to get the hell off my ship and take your slaving pursuers with you!"

"Regardless, I'm a doctor," the Eldritch said. "If someone starts dying in my presence, it's my duty to stop it."

"I didn't ask for your help—"

"Actually, you did," Irine said.

Reese glared at her. This time she noticed just how poorly her glare worked. Irine didn't even wilt.

"You did," the tigraine said. "You made him your proxy and told him to make all the relevant medical decisions to save your life. I was there, I heard you."

"I don't remember saying that," Reese said.

"I'm not sure what you're so upset about," Sascha said. "You're here, you're healthy, and you don't have to pay for the medical procedure that saved you. What have you got to complain about?"

"I don't want to owe anyone anything," Reese said.

"Too late," Sascha said. "You owed that woman something for her help in bailing you out. Now you're going to owe our creditors for our repairs. And you certainly owe the doctor there for taking care of you despite being so rude about the whole thing."

"He and I are *even*," Reese said, clenching her fists.

"She's correct," Hirianthial said. "And since I came with nothing to your ship, there's nothing I need to retrieve." He bowed, a formality she thought would look silly and instead looked far too serious, too final. "I thank you for your help in effecting my escape, and I wish you well. Good day, madam."

And then he was gone.

"What did you do that for!" Irine said. "You sent him away!"

"Of course I sent him away!" Reese exclaimed. "Haven't you noticed he's got slavers and pirates after him? We can't afford another episode like the one we just got out of. You haven't even told me what the damage was from the whole thing!"

"He's nice to have around," Sascha said. "And he's a good doctor."

"He's an *Eldritch*," Reese said. "What good is a doctor who can't handle you?"

"For a doctor who can't handle you, he did a lot of carrying you around," Irine said. "Or did you forget those parts too?"

They were angry at her. The twins had never been angry at her. Reese looked from one furry face to the other and felt the world drop from beneath her. Then she got a tight rein on her sense of desolation and said, "Look guys, I appreciate your opinions, but if you hadn't noticed we barely keep enough money in our pockets to feed the people we have. We don't have room for another deck-swabber. I'm glad the man made a good impression and I'm glad he was around to re-pave my esophagus but we've got to move on, okay? Can we start with someone telling me when I'm going to get released, and how bad the repair bill on the ship's going to be?"

They exchanged glances. Irine sat on the bench next to the bed and Sascha left.

"What was that about?" Reese asked.

"Nothing important to you," Irine said. "So let's get down to the stuff that is."

Reese grabbed her wrist. "Irine, stop it. I don't need your disapproval." She sucked in a breath and forced the word out. "Please."

The tigraine looked at her hand, then hesitantly petted it. The underside of her fingers were smooth. "Can I say something you might take badly, Reese?"

Last time Irine had said something similar, Reese had learned things about the twins' intimate life she hadn't really wanted to know. Still it didn't seem like the time to refuse. "Sure."

"I don't know how you're ever going to catch a mate and have kidlings at the rate you're going."

Yes, definitely a place she didn't want to go. Still, she wanted Irine to stop with the evil eye routine, so she gave the question the serious response she would otherwise have avoided. "You're assuming I want a mate and a family. That's not even the way it works on Harat-Sharii, so I'm not sure where you got the idea that I'd want it for myself."

"Even on Harat-Sharii we choose someone to have children with and have them," Irine said. "Sascha and I will get to that when we're older."

Reese chuckled. "I don't have a father, Irine. Why would I want a husband?"

"I might be wrong about this, but don't humans still need both sexes to reproduce?" Irine asked, canting her head.

"Yeah, well, my family found a way around that a few generations ago," Reese said.

"That doesn't sound right," Irine said, mouth twisting.

"And your harems and sibling intimacy does?" Reese asked. "You of all people should know these things are relative."

"So you haven't had a father in your life ever? Or a grandfather?"

Reese shook her head and managed a faint smile. "My grandma thought it was best that way. Men meddled, she said."

"No, women meddle," Irine said. "Men just go after what they want. It's part of their charm."

"Not all women are like that," Reese said. "Some just go after what they want, too."

"And some men meddle," Irine agreed. "At least now I know why you sent the doctor away."

Reese frowned. "That being . . . what, some orbit trash about me not knowing how to handle men because I didn't grow up with one?"

"Well, you've got two girls on your crew, me and Kis'eh't. Allacazam is neuter and Bryer might as well be . . . I don't think I could sex a Phoenix unless I tied one down and hunted for parts. The only guy on your crew is Sascha and you've got me to keep him in check. So what's a girl supposed to think?"

"I do not have issues," Reese said.

"If you say so, boss."

Reese sighed, but didn't argue. At least Irine wasn't glowering at her anymore.

She wasn't sure that this was an improvement.

"When can I get out of here, Irine?"

"They say you should be fine within a day. They want to keep you under observation until then. You're paid up for the full time anyway, so you might as well enjoy it."

"Enjoy my stay in a Medplex," Reese said. "Right. Tell me about the repair bill."

Irine caught her tail and started picking at the fur at the tip. "Well . . . we lost the main cargo gantry. The hull's dented all over the place, but we've identified the six places that the dents are more than cosmetic and have to be fixed. The last pirate laser destroyed the starboard sensor array

. . . and the Well Drive's gone cranky since Sascha redlined it to get you here. The bill is pretty sizable."

Reese's eyes had already glazed over. "How minor are the bumps in the hull we have to fix?" she asked, trying to concentrate on the least serious sounding item in the litany.

"Four of them are preventing the port cargo doors from opening," Irine said. "The other two have twisted up waste vents."

Reese lowered herself back onto the bed, which did not yield beneath her shoulder-blades. Her entire back refused to relax onto the cushions.

"It's a lot of money," Irine said, ears drooping.

"I know," Reese said. She'd collected estimates for repairs too often not to know. The Well Drive alone . . . she could be grounded for months trying to convince creditors to give her that much money.

"Miss Eddings?"

Reese sat up on her elbows and found a Tam-illee dressed in Fleet blue-and-black standing at the door nearest her bed. She couldn't read the collection of pins and stars and braids Fleet used for rank but suspected from the air of authority that the man was in charge of something.

"I'm Reese Eddings," she said.

The Tam-illee joined Irine at her bedside. He had a stern and craggy face, almost completely human in seeming save for the shadow of a nose-pad traced around his nostrils . . . and of course, the large pointed ears on his head. "My name is Jonah NotAgain. I'm captain of the UAV *StarCounter*. I was wondering if I could ask you a few questions."

"Oh great," Reese said. "Don't tell me the pirates followed us here."

"Good news, ma'am. They didn't. We wouldn't mind

any details you could give us about them, though."

"Right," Reese said, and launched into an account with Irine's help. The Fleet captain nodded through the story, taking notes on a tiny data tablet she hadn't even noticed holstered at his hip.

"Would you mind terribly passing us the sensor data?" NotAgain said when she finished.

"No," Reese said. "You're welcome to it if it means you'll have a chance to get rid of them."

"We've been trying for most of a year to chase down all the hide-outs nearby," the Tam-illee said. "This should give us enough data to shut down Inu-Case. The bad news is that they got a good look at you, ma'am, and they tend not to like the last few people who got away before Fleet comes down on them."

"You mean to tell me that my data is going to incriminate them, you're going to arrest them, and their pals are going to remember me and hold a grudge?" Reese asked, aghast.

"That's about the size of it," the Tam-illee said. "Most of the time they get distracted easily, though. If you lay low for a while they tend not to bother with revenge."

"It's not like we're going to be running cargo any time soon anyway," Irine said. "We've got a lot of repair work to do."

"I can't believe this," Reese said. "Can't you do something about it?"

"If we had enough manpower to assign a convoy to every freighter working the shipping lanes we'd do it in a heartbeat's pause," NotAgain said. "Unfortunately we're spread a bit thin for that. All I can advise you is to head further into the Core and stay out of sight for a while. Take a vacation, if you like."

"A vacation!" Reese exclaimed. She closed her eyes.

"How long a vacation?"

"Certainly no longer than a year—"

"A year!"

"But at least two months," NotAgain continued. "Three or four to be safe. I'm sorry, ma'am. It's just a recommendation."

"Thanks," Irine said. "We appreciate the advice. We'll send the reel to you later today."

The Tam-illee smiled. "Thanks, ma'am. If there's any question we can answer we'll be glad to help. I'm border patrol liaison for Frontier Three . . . just use the Fleet broadband and we'll be glad to help."

"Thanks, we will," Irine said. Once the man had gone, the tigraine leaned over. "You okay, Reese?"

"Four months to a year!" Reese said.

"Two to four months," Irine said. "We have to make repairs anyway. We can do them in the Core just as well as we could out here."

"But the Core is more expensive," Reese said. "Besides, I thought if we got rid of Hirianthial the pirates wouldn't care about us anymore!"

"They probably wouldn't have if our escape hadn't seemed to lead to their arrest," Irine said. "But would you rather them not get arrested?"

"Of course not," Reese said. She sighed and covered her eyes with a hand.

"It'll be okay, Reese. You'll see."

"I hope you're right," Reese said.

Most of the time Hirianthial did not envy his cousin's talent for pattern-sensing for he'd never observed it to bring her happiness. Satisfaction, occasionally, but never joy. It had shaped her as inevitably a carver's knife did wood, transforming her from a mercurial child into a planner of great effectiveness with an escape route in every muff pocket and a raft of cushions against contingency. She never worried, but she never rested either. Her power continually warned her of the changing currents in the world and the situations those currents might inspire. Most people accused her of manipulation. She didn't deign to answer such accusations and had acquired the many enemies one might have expected of someone in power with power. No, he rarely wanted her talent.

Today he wanted it. He wanted to know where the pattern was moving him and where he should position himself to give it better access to his tired body, to sweep him away to a place where he no longer had to think or act. After six hundred years, a man grew tired of living with the thousands of consequences of his thoughts and actions.

A starbase was a busy place, no matter how far from civilization one traveled. Exiting the Medplex, Hirianthial merged into the stream of aliens heading further in from the docks. He didn't question the direction the stream took him but contented himself with following it. He had no other place to go, no pressing business, no work to report to. He supposed at some point he would have to make arrangements for the release of his luggage; he'd had it placed in storage here before embarking on Liolesa's little mission. . . .

Liolesa's mission. He'd survived it and been sprung from his prison with the information she wanted. He still had duties, then. A secure comm facility first, then he could find someplace to eat and try to decide what to do now. If he was lucky, Liolesa would have some other ridiculous task for him.

Perhaps she would ask him to come home. He wondered if he would acquiesce.

Hirianthial walked toward the residential areas,

where shops and services would be interspersed with smaller gardens and restaurants. As he entered the more populated areas he spotted several of the stranger species among the first and second generation engineered races that composed most of the Alliance: here and there a Phoenix like Reese's engineer, trailing metallic feathers on the ground, or one of the great horned Akubi, head ducked to talk to smaller companions. For the most part the crowd was Pelted: humanoid but with the marks of the animals from which they'd been designed, fox and feline, wolf and any number of other influences. He'd found occasional humor in the realization that humanity had spawned more than one prodigal child in the galaxy. The Pelted had run away and eventually invited their parents to join them.

The Eldritch hadn't even told their parents they were related.

No doubt people wondered as they did about every species that looked suspiciously like humanity, but no Eldritch would ever confirm such a rumor. It was part of the Veil, the same Veil that drove Hirianthial to the high-security facilities closer to the short-term hotels for the well-heeled. He paid the solemn man at the silver gate enough to feed Reese's crew for a week and passed into the intimately lit foyer that led to several dark chambers. His was number six. He walked in, closed the door and checked the seal; he didn't have the tools for more a sophisticated check and would have to trust his coin had bought him privacy.

It hadn't bought him a Riggins-encrypted stream, but he laid out the money for one on the outgoing call and waited as it went through its complex security routines on the way to the Queen. He wondered what time it was at home.

Delairenenard answered the call in formal midnight

blue dinner coat sparkling with silver embroidery; as always he was the picture of poise, his face smooth of any emotion despite how long it had been since Hirianthial had been seen or heard from on the homeworld. "My lord Hirianthial! How good to see you."

"Chancellor," Hirianthial said. "I regret interrupting your supper. May I have the Queen's ear?"

"A moment, if you would. I shall inform her of your call."

Not just a formal dinner, but one with enemies, then. If she'd been dining with allies Delairenenard would have promised her presence. Hirianthial wondered how much more knotted the political situation had become in his absence. It had never much interested him despite the influence bequeathed by his inheritance, but it had been hard to avoid the consequences of the poor decisions made by successive generations of Eldritch. Halting the decline of their species was the Queen's priority, but all the solutions she'd suggested had not been well received by a species deeply in love with its own cultural pride. He had not envied her the resulting mess.

Hirianthial waited a good fifteen minutes before the Chancellor returned. "The Queen, my lord."

The man bowed away and Liolesa sat across from him. She had dressed for dinner with political opponents, and as always she looked her best when girded for battle. Something about it gave her back the flush of youth. He could practically smell her perfume, the aggressive bouquet of ambergris and thorn marten musk she wore only to disarm her enemies. Her pale, cool eyes, her aristocratic face with its lines sharp as swords, her throat and white breast with their deceptively feminine promises, all of it he remembered too well. He loved his Queen but the world she lived in exhausted him.

And it hurt to see again a noblewoman's gown, embroidered in pearls, and to see the long braided coil of a woman's hair, threaded through with opals and electrum chains.

"You have survived our task, cousin."

"You sent an able rescue," Hirianthial said. "I have what you want."

Her gaze sharpened. "Who is it?"

He drew in a deep breath. For all her ability to sense patterns, Liolesa could not pull names for unseen aggressors out of the air. She'd known a power moved behind the abduction of their people off-world despite the otherwise loosely-connected organizations in the slave trade, had nursed suspicions, but hadn't known a name.

"The Empire," Hirianthial said, and released her from the prison of uncertainty.

"The Chatcaava," Liolesa breathed. They shared the silence together. He didn't have to guess her thoughts; they were following the same line his had when he'd found out. Being abducted by petty villains was a bad enough fate. Knowing that the shapechangers were behind it . . . he'd spent not an inconsiderable time grieving the fate of those who'd gone into their taloned embrace . . . grieving, and fighting the anger that was no longer his to wield in the name of throne and deity.

She didn't ask him if he was certain. She didn't question how he'd done it. All she did was meet his eyes and say, "Thank you."

And like that, she would have concluded their call had he not cleared his throat. "There's no other task which requires my service, my liege?"

"You have already done enough," Liolesa said. "What comes next is not for you."

Just like that, she'd freed him. "This woman, my lady.

The human."

"Theresa?" Liolesa said, then chuckled. "Quite a treasure, is she not? Stay with her if you can. She'll take care of you."

"I don't need a woman to take care of me," Hirianthial said.

"Nonsense, cousin," Liolesa said. "It's just what you need and well you know it. Do you need a command? Very well. Go to her. She won't lead you astray."

"My lady—"

"We will talk to you soon enough. Give me some report of your doings when you have time. Until then, good evening, cousin."

The stream terminated, leaving him with a blank screen. After a moment it flashed his final total and debited his account. He sighed and rubbed his forehead. When he'd hoped for Liolesa to tell him how to fit back into the pattern, he'd been anticipating a new task he could start with a glad heart, not the injunction to return to a woman who'd already sent him away. He sometimes suspected Liolesa believed all his problems would dissipate once he resolved his grief over his role in the death of the last woman in his life. Sometimes he remembered growing up with Liolesa the fierce and irreverent child, and that intimacy made him long, briefly, to shake her.

Standing outside the comm facility, Hirianthial decided he'd worry about whether or not to follow the Queen's directive after lunch; Reese couldn't leave the Medplex for another day anyway. That meant having his luggage delivered could also wait. Consulting the base directory brought up a list of well-reviewed restaurants. He chose the most likely one near him and headed that way.

While standing next to the fountain leading into the restaurant and waiting for a table, Hirianthial sensed a muted yellow aura gliding against his. A moment later, Sascha stepped up beside him.

"Mind if I join you?"

"Only if I'm buying," Hirianthial said.

"Deal."

"And if you tell me how long you've been following me."

The tigraine folded his hands behind his back. "Since you left the Medplex." He glanced up at Hirianthial. "I was sitting outside the comm station long enough to read half a magazine. Did that go well?"

"You *are* curious," Hirianthial said. The maitre'd noted his party's addition without so much as a change in expression and brought them to a table outside in the patio. The yellow stone tiles and the plain wooden beams had been shrouded with blooming tropical flowers. Hirianthial had passed through enough starbases not to be surprised by the simulation of nightfall, but the candles on the table were still a welcome touch.

"It's not curiosity," Sascha said, once they'd unfolded their napkins and requested something to drink. "I was hoping you weren't about to get sent off somewhere else."

"Why does this worry you?" Hirianthial asked. "Your mistress has made it clear that my business isn't of any concern to her or her people any longer."

"Well, that's where she's wrong and you're wrong." Sascha set his menu down with a wrinkled nose. "I hate menus without prices. You order for me."

Hirianthial cocked a brow at him, but did as requested. With no more distractions, he folded his hands on the table and waited for the tigraine to elaborate.

"Look, we're no challenge for Reese."

"And she needs a challenge," Hirianthial said.

Sascha nodded, cupping his hands around his cup of kerinne. Hirianthial had never developed a taste for the

hot cinnamon drink, though he suspected it would be favorably received on his homeworld.

"Because . . . ?" Hirianthial prompted.

"She's not happy," Sascha said simply.

"She's not happy."

"No," the tigraine said. "She's been doing this freighter
thing for a while, and she'll have you believe that she's doing it for the money. And it's true that she's easier to be
around when we're not in debt . . . but then, who isn't? But
this thing with the *Earthrise* . . . it doesn't make her happy.
And we aren't enough of a distraction from that."

"And this role you want me to fill? Wouldn't it be easier
to suggest that she find another line of work?"

Sascha laughed. "You've known her long enough. You
tell me if that would fly."

Hirianthial considered it and smiled. "I suppose not.
I'm still not certain where I come into this picture. My arrival wasn't exactly auspicious."

"Well, she was going to have that problem with her
esophagus sooner or later, right?"

"Sooner, most probably," Hirianthial said.

"So it's not like you not being around could have prevented that. As it was you kept her alive. Not only that,
but you kept her kicking." The tigraine traced the rim of
his cup. "This is kind of hard to explain. It's more a feeling
than anything I can point to directly. But it's like having
you around draws her out of herself. She's more of everything on the outside, and less of it on the inside, where she
can bottle it up."

Which was the finest description of a common cause of
physical ailment-inducing stress as Hirianthial had heard
from a layman. "Granted that I make a good distraction,
which I suppose I shan't argue . . . there's still the small
matter of your captain not wanting me on her ship."

"Oh, she didn't mean that," Sascha said with a wave of a hand. "She might have said it then but it was anger talking. If you come back she'll still be angry but she'll be more likely to keep you around. She's fascinated by people who don't go away. Besides, when you tell her that you don't need her to pay you, she'll have to relent." The tigraine eyed him. "You don't need to be paid, do you? You seem wealthy enough."

"I can take care of my own needs," Hirianthial said.

"So she won't be able to object on those grounds," Sascha said. "Plus we wouldn't mind having a doctor around."

"You're certain you can convince your mistress to take me aboard?"

Sascha shook his head. "It's not about me convincing her, me or anyone else. She didn't really want to send you away. She never wants to do most of the things she forces herself to do by deciding them when she's upset. It's just that she feels trapped into following through on her promises. Even the stupid ones."

The silent waiters arrived bearing a plate with a duck stuffed with rice, mushrooms and white broccoli in a blush wine sauce with cream and shallots. One of them carved the duck into pieces onto smaller dishes as the other poured Hirianthial his wine. They left after setting the plates before them, and though Hirianthial believed in Reese's poverty he noted with interest that Sascha did not seem at all unaccustomed to being served.

"So you think she'll change her mind," Hirianthial said when they were alone. "You haven't told me why I should do this."

"I didn't think I had to, Healer," Sascha said. His yellow eyes flicked up to meet Hirianthial's, and then demurely lowered again to his plate.

For a moment Hirianthial couldn't move. Then he relented and laughed, low. "Why does she need me when she has you?"

"I may see clearly sometimes, but I'm still Harat-Shari-in in my heart," Sascha says. "I can't see why she won't do the things she should to make her happy because . . . well, I would in her place. I can't help her. I can't offer her solutions that she'd be willing to do." He smiled without humor. "The humans wanted to create aliens when they made the Pelted and for the most part they failed . . . but I think the Harat-Shar actually are different enough from the rest of the Alliance to cause problems. We don't love the way you love."

"And you know something about how Eldritch love," Hirianthial said.

"No, but I can guess," Sascha said. "And I imagine a society that doesn't even look fondly on doctors touching their patients isn't all that conducive to the kind of love I would espouse."

Hirianthial let that pass. "You've been with the *Earthrise* for some time now. Tell me how the days are spent there."

Sascha spoke at length about the adventures of trading cargo and playing special courier to the occasional client; about the games Reese played with the thermostat to keep him and Irine from surprising her with their amorous interludes and their secret (if rather cramped) solution to that problem; how Kis'eh't and Bryer's arrival had changed the tenor of their workplace; and most of all about Reese, about Reese's stubborn determination in the face of debt and disaster, her tendency to worry, her unexpected and clumsy displays of affection. It made a fine counterpoint to the meal. Hirianthial wasn't certain when between stories Sascha found time to eat but the tigraine finished his meal around the same time Hirianthial set down his own fork.

As they waited for the server to return with the final bill, Sascha leaned forward. "So, did it work?"

Hirianthial finished the wine and printed the okay on the bill. He folded his napkin and set it on the table. "Let's go talk to your mistress."

Sascha beamed and scrambled to his feet.

Though the data tablet Irine had left her was supposed to have the information Reese had requested several times throughout their conversation about repairs, it was well over three hours before Reese could bring herself to pick it up and spread the file. Even after opening it, she didn't look at the totals. Instead, she scanned the itemized list of things broken, things broken off, and things burned to bits with a growing sense of horror.

Then she glanced at the total.

Reese put the data tablet aside with a shaking hand and lay back on the bed. The ceiling above her had spiral patterns, lighter blue on cobalt. She traced them with her eyes, wondering who'd had the notion of painting the things there. Or was it a wallpaper? On the ceiling? Ceilingpaper? Maybe this was what insanity was like . . . a constant need to stare at inconsequential things and worry at their significance.

No, this was what denial was like.

Reese sighed and rubbed her forehead, dragged her hand over her nose and lips. The last time she'd been in debt this badly she'd had to accept a stranger's money or admit that her venture had failed. She simply couldn't accept that she could fail. No evidence would convince her that she wasn't any good at merchanting . . . especially if it meant limping back home to her mother and grandmother and enduring their censure for using up her inheritance on her misguided determination to break free of the pat-

tern of their lives. Their plan for her had involved her staying on Mars and continuing the Eddings clan with another
anonymously-donated batch of sperm. That she'd had other plans had broken her mother's heart and angered her
grandmother, her aunts . . . even her nieces had found her
outrageous.

She couldn't go back. She'd have to find a way to pay for
the repairs. Reese linked to her existing funds, scanning
for the cheapest repair she could afford that would get her
hobbling out of dock.

The Well Drive. She could repair that—

The Well Drive? Last she'd checked, she'd had enough
money to buy protein bars and chalk tablets, not fin for
one of the more expensive repairs on her list. Where had
the money come from? Perplexed, Reese tagged the deposit and spread the note attached to it.

Glowing blue letters: *Wire from account 0002178942 at
station Terra Firma. Amount, 7500 fin.*

The same account from the same place as the first
anonymous donation she'd received.

She stared at the screen, struggling to throttle a growing indignation. The man who appeared in the corner of
her eye proved a distraction she couldn't decide whether
to be thankful for or send away.

"How are you feeling, Ms. Eddings? I'm Rick Barringer,
the ward doctor."

Reese looked up at him: human, blocky build, silvering
hair at his temples on a honey-yellow complexion and a
mild and pleasant face. She curbed her irritation and managed, "I've been better, thanks."

Immediate concern tempered the doctor's voice. "Any
pain? Burning? Nausea?"

"No, no," Reese said, waving a hand. "Money troubles,
not bodily ones."

"Your visit here's been paid for—"

"It's not about this visit," Reese said. She forced a smile. "So are you the doctor I have to thank for the new highway down my throat?"

"The new—oh!" He laughed. "No, not at all. Your personal physician took care of it. You're lucky to have such a talented surgeon for a doctor. That's rather rare."

"Are you trying to tell me Hirianthial literally did the surgery?" Reese said, staring at him. "I thought he brought me here and gave me to you people. You let some random man do your job for you?"

Barringer chuckled. "You make it sound like you don't know the credentials your doctor's carrying around." When Reese didn't stop staring at him, he said, "You don't? You actually have a doctor you didn't check out?"

"He's a guest, not an employee," Reese said. "I haven't exactly read up on his medical records."

The man whistled. "Well, I'd encourage you to do that. Suffice to say he was more than qualified to stitch you back together. In fact, the Head of Surgery's been wooing him since they tucked you into the halo-arch to recover. He'd never seen a defter hand on a Medimage platform."

"He fixed me? His own hands?" Reese asked, unsure whether to feel used or relieved.

"With more care than a maid embroidering her wedding gown," the man said. "It was almost as if he could tell when he was hurting you." A flash of a grin. "Though I guess if the stories are right, maybe he could, eh?"

Reese stared at him.

"Whatever the case, we'll release you tomorrow morning. Until then, try to relax, Ms. Eddings. Your body's been through a lot, even if you feel fine."

"I'll try."

"And hey, here he is!" Barringer said, and then respectfully, "Lord Sarel Jisiensire . . . good to see you back. Does this mean you'll be staying or are you visiting Ms. Eddings here?"

"Just visiting, I'm afraid. Thank you, *alet*," Hirianthial said. Sascha was standing just behind him, and Reese could just guess what part the tigraine had in the reappearance of her unwanted guest.

"I'll leave you alone, then," Barringer said. "Feel better soon, Ms. Eddings."

As soon as the human doctor left, Reese grabbed her data tablet and threw it at Hirianthial. The Eldritch caught it but from the whack of it against his fingers it must have stung. She was glad. "What the hell is going on with your Queen? I'm not some mercenary to be bought in installments!"

"My pardon, lady?" Hirianthial asked, and she thought she saw surprise in his eyes.

"She sent me money. More money! I am not going to be indebted to her again. What, does she want to send me racing around after every little lost Eldritch she's got? Or is this an allowance for keeping you around?"

"I have no idea," Hirianthial said, glancing down at the data tablet. Reese wished she'd shut off the link. She didn't like him knowing just how poor she was. "Are you certain it's from her?"

"It's from the exact same place as it was last time."

"But without any note? Any request?"

He actually sounded puzzled. She frowned. "Nothing. Just the money. It's not as much as it was last time. Just enough to cover the Well Drive repair."

Hirianthial was reading the figures. She sighed. Damned nosy Eldritch. No, damned nosy men . . . she could tell Sascha was eyeballing it from behind Hirianthial. While they studied the columns, she picked at some fuzz on the blanket. It reminded her of Allacazam; she hoped someone was taking care of the Flitzbe in her absence, that someone had told him she was okay. He'd be worried.

The data tablet slid onto the bench beside her bed with more noise than Hirianthial'd made getting there to place it. "Never fear, my lady. That was no earnest against future services."

"No?" Reese asked, suspicious. "What is it, then?"

A faint smile crossed his lips. "A patron gift."

"A what?" Reese exclaimed. "Like . . . like in books, when a duke gives his vassal a bag of coins for good work?"

"You're acquainted with the concept?" Hirianthial asked, brows lifted a little. "Yes, just so. You've pleased her and she is showing her appreciation."

Reese blinked.

"Wow," Sascha said. "Her way of saying thank you is dropping enough money on us to fix the Well Drive? Angels, Reese! Make her thank you more!"

"I don't think so," Reese said. "I had to work too hard for that first thank-you. Besides, there's still all the rest of the ship to fix and I don't know where we're going to get the money for that. Particularly at Core prices."

"Core prices?" Sascha asked.

"Oh, yeah, you missed that part," Reese said, rubbing her forehead. "A Fleet captain came by for our data on the pirate hide-out. Apparently slavers get grumpy with ships last seen fleeing them if Fleet comes down on them afterwards. It's been suggested we find a nice cozy place to wait for a season or two."

"Wow," Sascha said again. "Where are we going?"

"I'm not sure yet," Reese said. "We'll talk it over when I get out of here."

"I'd like to come with you," Hirianthial said.

Reese eyed him. "I thought I told you to leave."

He rested his hands on the edge of the bench and leaned on them. "Your health is of great concern to me, lady."

"Particularly after you stuck your fingers in my throat and stitched things up yourself?" Reese asked. "Since when are you a surgeon, anyway?"

"Since I was licensed to be one in two different specialties," Hirianthial said.

"And you just happened to have one in esophageal surgery," Reese said.

"No," Hirianthial said. "Just in human surgery."

She waved her hands, exasperated. "Fine, okay. I can see that. But I absolutely can't afford to feed you—"

"—he's got money, boss," Sascha said.

Reese pointed a finger at him. "You stay out of this. In fact, you go back to the ship right now and start asking people where we should go for four months to hide from slavers. Right now!"

"Okay," Sascha said, then added, "But I'm voting for him to stick around."

"This is not a democracy!"

"If you say so, boss."

Turning from his disappearing tail, Reese glowered at Hirianthial, arms folded over her chest. His face remained serene, almost unreadable.

Almost. She thought she saw a trace of sorrow in his merlot eyes. How many years had it taken to incise the lines beneath them? When he laughed she could see wrinkles framing his cheeks that made it seem as if he'd laughed often, but she couldn't find those lines now. How long had it been since he'd been that merry youth? Were those hidden lines what made him seem so sad?

"Let me guess," Reese said. "You've got no other place to go."

A flicker of a smile, then. It didn't reach his eyes.

"Fine," Reese said. "Just don't make too much of this, okay? I'm giving you a place to stay until you figure out where you're going next."

"As you say, lady."

"And it's not lady, it's captain."

He bowed. "As you will."

"I'm going to regret this," Reese said, though she hadn't planned on saying it out loud.

"I humbly hope not," he said, and added, "Captain."

"And don't you forget it," Reese said.

PART TWO: SUN

"We've discussed our next stop," Sascha said.

"Just like you told us to," Irine added.

Reese paused on the threshold of the mess hall to eye them both. Bryer and Kis'eh't seemed far more innocent, sitting in their usual corners. Someone had turned on the sun lamp for Allacazam.

Hirianthial was behind her, shadowing her steps. Sometime between their discussion and her release he'd had his camellia tunic cleaned and was once again wearing it.

"And no doubt you've come to some conclusion I won't like," Reese said.

"We want to go someplace warm," Kis'eh't said.

"Paradisiacal," said Irine.

"With good access to the parts needed to fix things," Bryer said.

"And this magical place is?" Reese asked, wary.

The twins looked at one another, then at the others. It was Sascha who spoke with a shrug. "Harat-Sharii."

Reese laughed. "You're jesting."

"No!" Irine said. "No, our family's always asking about the people we work with. They'd be glad to put you up, and then you wouldn't have to pay for lodging. There's enough land nearby to set the *Earthrise* down. I'm sure our train will cook for you, and there's a city nearby to scrounge up assignments or work or what will you. And it *is* warm, and it is paradise and I know you'd like it, Reese."

"It's full of Harat-Shar!" Reese exclaimed. "Two of you are bad enough. A planetful of you? I might choke."

"Actually the city near home has a sizable offworlder population," Sascha said. "It's one of the few places that serves tourists and non-native residents, so it's not quite as outrageous as the rest of the world."

"Not quite as outrageous," Reese repeated.

"It's as close to wading into the shallow end of the pool as you can get on the planet," Sascha said. "But Irine's right, boss. If we want to cut costs, being able to get free housing and a few free meals a day is going to win over just about any other scenario. Any we could come up with anyway. Maybe you or Prince Charming have some insights we don't."

Except that Reese didn't, something she'd been mulling while staring at the patterned ceiling in the Medplex. She glanced at Hirianthial, but the Eldritch said only, "I've never been to Harat-Sharii. I admit to curiosity."

"They'll love you there," Irine said.

"I'm not sure he'll enjoy that," Reese said. "Look, Sascha, Irine . . . I admit the free bed and board is very enticing, but it's a little presumptuous to assume that your family's going to want to sleep and feed six people, plus Allacazam."

"I already called," Irine said. "Mamer said you must all come immediately. And Mamari agrees."

Taken aback, Reese said, "Well, then. Umm . . ."

"We have an invitation," Hirianthial said. "Can it hurt to take it?"

Reese eyed him. "Have you seriously lived with home-world-bred Harat-Shar?"

He smiled. "I can't say I've had that particular pleasure. I have worked with them."

"We're much more fun the longer you keep us around!" Irine said.

"No doubt," Hirianthial said.

Reese tried to imagine the Eldritch surrounded by striped and spotted Harat-Shar in various states of undress, that unfathomable dignity assaulted by their eager offers. The picture was delightful. "Free room and board it is," Reese said.

Irine squealed and leaped over to crush Reese in an arm-and-tail hug. "You'll love it, Reese, I promise!"

"Right," Reese said. "Let's just get there before Fleet does their number on Inu-Case."

"And for that we need the Well Drive fixed," Sascha said.

"I've gotten some people to come do the work," Reese said. "It shouldn't take them long. They're used to overhauling Fleet ships ten times our size, so squeezing us in wasn't a problem. We should be out of here in a week."

"A week?" Kis'eh't said. "That's luck!"

"That's not all of our luck," Reese said. "They did it for five hundred fin less than I thought they would . . . which means all of you have a hundred and twenty-five each to go shopping."

All of them cheered. Even Bryer let out a trill.

"It's not much, but enjoy it," Reese said. "And make sure you're here when we're done with the refits. The sooner we flee the scene of the crime, the happier I'll be."

"That makes six of us, I'm sure," Kis'eh't said, already up and lightly bouncing on her foot-pads.

"What are you waiting for?" Reese said. "Shoo!"

Hirianthial stepped aside as the four of them made for the door. He paused there. "Would you like lunch, lady?"

"You mean to go out to lunch?" Reese asked.

"There are good places nearby."

It was tempting; how long had it been since she'd had other people prepare her food, serve it to her, do the dishes? But she wasn't sure she wanted to spend that much time with Hirianthial, not before she'd had a chance to sort out her thoughts about him dropping into her life, changing it completely and then sewing up her bursting innards as an encore. Bad enough that she'd be stuck on the ship with him for the several weeks it would take to get back into the heart of Alliance space. Reese said, "Food sounds good, but I should really stay and oversee repairs."

He nodded and left without another word, without trying to convince her to change her mind. She thought about being miffed. Then she realized she was hungry and she wasn't sure if she had any dietary restrictions.

"Hirianthial?"

The man wasn't in the hall.

"Curse it, how does he move so fast?" Reese muttered. "I guess it can wait." She stopped by the sun lamp and crouched, running a hand along the shadowed lower half of Allacazam. "You full yet?"

The Flitzbe sent a contented, drowsy sensation, like napping in a pool of sunlight.

Reese grinned and snapped the light off. "I think that's enough."

A mournful bleat sounded in her head, like a broken set of bagpipes. "Oh, don't be greedy," Reese said, gathering him into her arms. "You can have more later. I need you with me while I wait for the contractors. You know how mind-numbing it is to sit at an airlock waiting for their version of "being on time."

Drooping trees and gray skies. "Yes, that boring," Reese said as she carried him toward the airlock. "Boring enough to kill trees." A few leaves fell off the branches in the mental image. "Just like that."

The small foyer outside their airlock was empty. Reese wondered how quickly her crew had rushed through it in their urge to enjoy the starbase's amenities and grinned. "Well, at least they're having fun," she said.

"Is this the TMS *Earthrise*?"

Reese glanced up from Allacazam to find a young man in a tailored courier's suit. A bag and a long case had been set at his feet. "I'm Captain Eddings of the *Earthrise*?"

"I'm delivering two pieces of luggage in care of your ship. Will you sign here for me?"

"I . . . sure," Reese said, shifting Allacazam to her other arm and scribbling on the man's tablet.

"Thanks," he said and left.

Reese bent to examine the luggage and wasn't even within range to touch them before she smelled the wisp of cologne. "I guess these are his," she said, and Allacazam sent a trickle of blue and green agreement. The smaller bag looked like standard luggage for an Alliance citizen, a soft dark blue embroidered in bronze. The case, on the other hand . . . "Looks like an instrument case," Reese said. "I wonder if he plays an instrument? I guess you would if you had centuries to develop new hobbies. I wonder what kind of instrument? Can you see him with a trumpet?" Allacazam painted a sparkling orange and gold amusement at the thought. "Nah, I don't think so either. Should we look?"

The Flitzbe's fur ruffled, turning dark gray.

"I guess that's a no," Reese said. "Ah well. We might as

well deposit it in his room. You just roll along with me, okay?" The Flitzbe turned pink and she set him down before turning to the luggage. The bag's strap she slung over one shoulder before turning to the case, thinking it looked unwieldy but otherwise not a problem. That was before she actually lifted it. "Blood and Freedom! If it's a trumpet, it's made of lead!"

Shaking her head, Reese climbed through the airlock and started down the hall. Halfway to the lift she switched hands on the case. That got her to the lift.

By the time she was outside Hirianthial's new room she was dragging the case and both her arms hated her. She had no idea how Allacazam had managed to stay out of her way as she stumbled, tripped and pulled the weight of the case here. Getting the thing into his room took the last of her energy. Manhandling it onto his bunk was out of the question. Reese collapsed with her back to the wall and panted as Allacazam rolled in between her legs and bumped up against her stomach. The Flitzbe was bright orange with alarm.

"Okay, so maybe that was more exertion than I should have been doing fresh out of the Medplex," she said, petting him. "But I got it here and I'm no worse for the wear."

An image of a bent-up trumpet flashed in her mind and she winced. "Right. Let's hope I did no damage."

The thought entered her mind then, that she should check: not Allacazam, but her own rebellious curiosity. She honestly did want to make sure she hadn't destroyed whatever important thing Hirianthial was carrying with him, but the curiosity remained foremost. She leaned forward over Allacazam's body and examined the catches on the case. There were no locks; no adornment save for the tag from the luggage company. Reese flipped it over and paled at the name and shield stamped on it. She'd heard of the company, but never had anything valuable enough to warrant their prices for storage.

"Okay. Maybe I shouldn't look," she said.

Allacazam was silent.

But something Hirianthial cared enough about to have stored in secure and guarded lockers was important enough for her to ensure she hadn't damaged it. Before she could talk herself out of it, Reese reached out and flipped one of the catches open.

No locks. No stops. If he cared so much about it, why didn't he lock the case? Would she ever understand the man?

"All right," Reese said. "Let's just get it over with. A quick peek, just to make sure it's okay."

Allacazam turned a soft silvery gray. Reese ignored the reproach and flipped the second and third catches. She opened the lid and dropped it at the sight of the contents, rattling them. Of all the things she'd been expecting Hirianthial to be toting, weapons were not among them. Embarrassed, Reese said, "Well, at least they're okay."

The Flitzbe sounded a few bells in her mind. Reese couldn't resist another look. This time she didn't fumble the lid.

Not just any weapon, but bladed weapons. And not just one but four. She remembered pictures from her reading. The smallest one was a dagger, polished steel with a bronze hilt wrapped in burgundy cords. It had inset opals, winking like blue fire. The two pieces above it were too long to be daggers but too short to be swords; Reese had no idea what she'd call them, but she spent several minutes staring at her hazy reflection in the steel.

The blade above them was responsible for the unwieldy length of the case and most of its weight. Reese had never actually seen a sword in person; the cover illustrations she'd seen had made them look big, but she'd expected them to be exaggerations, like the extravagant length of hair they put on the maidens. This one had a wider tongue and a longer hilt, too . . . she could fit two of her hands on the hilt with room to spare. She couldn't imagine lifting the thing.

But it wasn't just that it was a sword, and the first sword she'd ever seen in person. It was the sense of *use* to the thing. She trailed her fingers over the wine-colored cords wrapping the hilt and they chafed . . . age had frayed them into patterns that suggested the grasp of a man's hand. And the designs on the hilt and worked into the crossguards had worn away in places, making it unclear exactly what they were—ivy leaves? Random designs? Was that blue-tinged bronze a facing on something harder, or was the hilt actually made of it? And the opals . . . she'd never seen an opal quite the size of the one below the sword's cross-guards, and the setting holding it had been mashed where it met the cords.

"Blood above," Reese whispered. "Real swords. Swords that someone *uses*."

Allacazam's gray-lilac agreement was so muted she almost didn't sense it.

The crushed velvet that cushioned the weapons was a beautiful wine color, like Hirianthial's eyes, and shiny in places where it had been pressed against the grain and flattened there. The inside of the lid had some sort of crest: a rearing hippogriff with forked tongue in bronze and burgundy, and below it a smaller mark, a unicorn in blue and silver.

"Not my business," Reese said, closing the lid and securing the catches again. "Definitely not my business."

Allacazam's fur ruffled purple with worry, but in her mind she heard the tingle-chimes of his agreement.

"Now let's see if we can't get this thing on his bunk now that I've had a chance to rest."

It was easier to fit into life on the *Earthrise* than Hirianthial expected. The crew quarters comprised a tiny fraction of the ship's actual volume and everyone seemed to have perfected methods for keeping out of each other's way. How they did it with such ease the Eldritch couldn't imagine, given that none of them had his ability to sense where each of them was at a given moment. Certain areas had been designated communal spaces according to a set of rules Hirianthial had not yet guessed; while the mess was a communal space, the galley wasn't, and interrupting whomever was cooking was the fastest way to earn a cold retort. The bathroom was private despite it being shared among everyone but Reese. The bridge, a workspace, was communal but the cargo holds and the engineering decks weren't. Hirianthial avoided several faux pas by reading the auras off the people in a compartment, but he wondered how well others had integrated in the past.

His small room had become more comfortable with the addition of his luggage, which he'd found in his quarters a few days previously. The swords he slid beneath his bed as was customary; the sheath in his boot he'd filled on the starbase with a dagger of good quality but less lineage than the one beneath his bunk. While he misliked the feel of a foreign weapon at his knee, he would not carry the House blades again unless he returned home. They were not weapons to be casually worn, not with the memories that attended them.

The remainder of his luggage consisted of several changes of clothing, both Alliance standard and relics from his Jisiensire wardrobe; toiletries he'd missed but could have replaced; and the items that he usually ended up setting on a shelf in an altar-like display of his past. The incense holder could have come from anywhere, though had anyone analyzed the wood they would not have found it in the Alliance specimen library. The Woman's Book of Hours, however, was written in Eldritch, splendidly illuminated with hand-ground pigments, some of them toxic. His mother had given it to his wife, for this particular version of the Book of Hours covered only three seasons of the year and terminated with prayers appropriate to a woman holding her first child in her arms.

It was hard still not to grieve.

The wooden box incised with its relief trim of horses running he set last on the table. Opening it revealed the ring he'd put off to attend to Liolesa's mission. It was no longer his ring to wear but the habit of it had proved difficult to break. Running his thumb over the cloisonné hippogriff, Hirianthial thought about leaving it in the box, but the spaces alongside the ring cushion seemed too empty with the ring there to mark them. He pulled it from the box and slid it back onto the finger where his mother had set it decades ago.

The book, the incense holder, the jewelry box: they'd always served as a focus for meditation, a frame to lend meaning to solitude. Before he'd left Jisiensire, he'd cherished solitude and the time it gave him to center himself. It was only after his loss that he'd begun to need the distraction of people, and so badly it had driven him to the outworld with its gaudy streams of alien life. Even the *Earthrise's* narrow confines gave him too much time to himself, and while it did not upset him he recognized the growth of his melancholy and did what he could to contain it.

Still he had duties, and the air that had made him into someone's confidant at so many of his workplaces followed him to the *Earthrise*. He found Sascha in the mess alone several days into their cruise, aura a flattened blue-gray with spikes of black depression.

"Leaves for the doctor, huh?" the Harat-Shar said, glancing at Hirianthial's salad and summoning up a passable cheer. It appeared in his halo as a flicker of gold that drowned moments later.

"For dinner at least," Hirianthial said. "I find eating lightly before bed makes for easier sleep."

"Maybe I should try that," Sascha said, poking his dinner across the plate half-heartedly. It looked like some kind of small bird in a sauce that smelled fragrantly of orange and cinnamon. No one on the *Earthrise* ate foods Hirianthial found offensive but some of them were better cooks than others; Sascha's cooking won over everyone else's.

"So do you want to tell me why you hate the idea of going home so much?" Hirianthial said, spearing a fork-full of lacy greens.

"How did you—" Sascha stopped. "I guess I'm not the only one who has the right to make cutting observations, ah?"

Hirianthial only smiled.

"It'll sound stupid."

"I doubt that," Hirianthial said.

Sascha prodded his meal a few more times, then put his fork down. "I hate the land."

"Do you mean that literally?" Hirianthial asked.

The tigraine's brow furrowed. "That's not what you were supposed to say."

"I'm sorry?"

"You were supposed to say, 'but you're Harat-Shar! How could you hate your own culture?' or 'But it's your homeworld!' or 'But you seem pretty typical Harat-Shariin.' You know, missing the point."

"Which is that you hate the land itself, not the culture

or the people?" Hirianthial said. "It seems sensical to me."

Sascha growled. "Yeah, well, you're the first to say so. I've never been able to explain it. It's not just the land underneath the house of my family. It's not just the city. It's not the band of climate next to my place of living. It's the whole planet. When I try to explain that, the whippy-tails will always say, 'But oh, Sascha, you know a planet doesn't have a planetary climate. If you don't like the land where you live, just move!' As if a planet can't have a feel to it, you know?"

The observation was strangely astute of him, but Hirianthial didn't say so. The theoreticians of his world would have complimented Sascha on his sensitivity to the land's aura . . . if they would have been willing to talk to a Harat-Shar at all. And capable of understanding that worlds, too, gave off an energy all their own, and not just kingdoms on them. The first time he'd felt the aura of an alien world singing through his nerves he'd gotten chills. "I think it's perfectly reasonable," Hirianthial said.

"It's almost as if the place repels me," Sascha mumbled. Louder, then, "As if it hates me. Well, I don't like it all that much either, and explaining that to my family and friends . . . Angels, not a memory I want to relive." He sighed. "At least we're not going back to stay. Though the moment we touch down my parents will be at me about it. Do you know how hard it is to fend off seven people?"

"Not in that capacity," Hirianthial said. "I don't envy you the duty."

"Yeah. Me neither," Sascha said. He began tracing lines through the sauce on the rim of the plate.

"Have you ever found a place you liked?" Hirianthial asked. "A place that called you?"

"I found a few I liked and a lot more than that I would be content to settle on," Sascha said. "One of the nice parts of being a pilot was just how many worlds I got to visit. I'm not looking for perfection, you understand? Just a place that doesn't hate me. That doesn't seem too much to ask."

"Not at all," Hirianthial said. "I wouldn't settle in a place that hated me either."

"It's not fair, either, that the place where so many people I care about live isn't the place I feel comfortable living," Sascha said. "It's one of the few things Irine and I used to fight about—she wants to have babies on Harat-Sharii where the train can help raise them. I want to go somewhere else. Now that we're going back we've started arguing about it again."

"Parting from her would be too painful," Hirianthial guessed.

"I couldn't do it," Sascha said. "She's my twin. It would be like cutting out one of my lungs. I could survive, but for the rest of my life I'd feel crippled." He shook his head. "No, I just couldn't. I love her too much. But I'm all for her choosing a mate or two and starting her family somewhere else. If we get enough good people around it won't matter as much that our blood train is on Harat-Sharii. It's one of the unadulterated good things about being brought up homeworld Harat-Shar. We can choose family and it's just as real to us as blood."

"Is it?" Hirianthial asked.

"Yes," Sascha said. "That kind of attitude happens when you have multiple adults acting as your parents, most of whom had no genetic material to contribute to your birth."

"How soon do you think your sister will want a family? And what about you? Do you want a mate of your own?"

"Only one?" Sascha asked with a chuckle. "Having spouses of my own's not as important to me as Irine having her own kidlets. I'm guessing she'll want a few more years before she settles. She finds this whole 'flying around the Alliance' thing exciting, but her excitement will wear off and when it does she'll want to find a nest. I never feel the depth of excitement she does, but once I'm committed I focus a lot more easily than she does. We make a good team that way. She keeps me enthused and I keep her determined."

"No wonder you feel her like a part of yourself," Hirianthial said. "I wish there was some way I could relieve some of your burden."

"You have," Sascha said after a moment. "Funny, you're the first person I've ever mentioned this to who understood what I was talking about without me having to explain it. That makes me feel worlds away better about it."

"Then I'm glad to have helped," Hirianthial said.

"Well, don't get too comfortable on your laurels there," Sascha said. "Once we get to Harat-Sharii I won't be the only wreck you'll have to deal with. I bet even Bryer and Kis'eh't will leave problems for you to clean up . . . if they reject too many people, you might have kitties crying on your lap."

"I hope not!" Hirianthial said with a laugh. "I'll hardly be much comfort to them if they're seeking balm for forlorn hearts."

Sascha eyed him. "It really doesn't bother you? The notion of being on Harat-Sharii. I would have assumed that your strictures against touching would make the prospect of staying with us uncomfortable."

"Many things bother me," Hirianthial said. "People who offer inadvertent discomfort out of a desire to be friendly are far from that list."

"So what's on the list?" Sascha asked.

Hirianthial touched the lip of his cup of tea. "Slavery. Suffering. Unnatural death. Cruelty." He picked up the cup and drank, feeling the wash of Sascha's brown sobriety, so quick a transition it felt almost embarrassed. He looked up but did not speak.

"I guess it seems like a silly question now," Sascha said.

"Perspective," Hirianthial said. "All the matter wants is perspective."

Sascha stared at his plate for several moments, then said, "I think I'm done with this. Do you want the rest?"

"I'm fine," Hirianthial said. "But save it for Kis'eh't. She hasn't eaten yet and she often waxes poetic about your cooking."

Sascha laughed. "I'll do that." He stood. "I'd thank you, but I won't. You did what you had to for me. I'll do the same for you when we get home."

"Thank you," Hirianthial said, and wondered.

"Here we are, Captain . . . home!" Irine bounced on her heels. "Isn't it beautiful?"

"Most planets are," Reese said, but even she had to admit there was something enticing about the blazing brightness of Harat-Sharii. Its turquoise oceans set off its rust-red continents with their belts of shimmering gold desert and yellow-green forests. Even its clouds made her eyes water with their brilliance.

"Aww, come on," Irine said. "You have to admit this one is special!"

"All right, fine, it's special," Reese said, then relented at the girl's wounded look. "It is beautiful, Irine. It just . . . well, it's so bright it's like a punch in the eyes."

Sascha laughed. "You have no idea, boss."

"I don't like the sound of that," Reese said and leaned past him to hit the broadcast comm. "Hello, hello! This is the TMS *Earthrise*, Captain Theresa Eddings commanding. Our destination is the city of Zhedeem. Any landing or approach protocols?"

"*Earthrise*, this is Systems Outpost Three. Welcome to our wonderful system! Is this your first visit?"

"This is," Reese said, "though I have two hires who call this place home."

"Excellent. Please proceed to upper orbit and synchronize over Zhedeem. Once you're in place you can call them for landing instructions."

"Thanks, Systems Outpost."

"You're welcome, madam. Anyone ever tell you that you have a very enticing voice?"

"Only my pet Harat-Shar and no, I'm not looking for more."

"Curses! Send them my regards, and my envy."

"I'll do that," Reese said. "*Earthrise* away." She shook her head. "Am I going to have to deal with that all the way in-system?"

"Not only will you have to, but it'll get worse," Sascha said.

"Freedom preserve me," Reese said. "You handle the landing, then."

"Consider it done."

"I hope you've packed your suitcase," Irine added.

"Suitcase!"

"Well, of course! You don't think the train will let you sleep in the ship, do you?"

"I admit I hadn't thought that far ahead," Reese said. She lifted a hand when Irine opened her mouth. "No, I won't object. As long as we're on a planet's surface I might as well run maintenance on the air-scrubbers. It's been a while since I bought us fresh air and we could use a recharge."

"Fresh air from home to carry with us when we leave? That's so romantic," Irine said, bouncing again.

"It's just common sense," Reese said. "What's our time-to-landing, Sascha?"

"Five hours, about."

"Right. See you fluffies at the airlock."

Five hours sounded like a comfortable span but by the time Reese had found the rest of the crew and advised them to prepare, chased down Allacazam, packed her own goods and finished another session of staring at her finances wondering where to find all the money she needed for the remaining repairs, the in-systems were firing against atmosphere. Reese gave up on the data tablet and instead smoothed down her vest and examined herself in the bathroom mirror. She didn't look prepared to tangle with a city full of Harat-Shar. Then again, she never did, even on good days. Shaking her head she shouldered her duffle and headed to the airlock. The rest of the crew was already there, standing with their backs (or in Kis'eh't's case, side) to the wall.

"Well, Sascha . . . will you do the honors?"

"My pleasure," he said, and keyed the airlock open. He shoved his shoulder into the door and forced its reluctant hinges.

The air that rushed in smelled of incense, exotic spices, burgeoning plant-life waxy with green life over an arid heat. Reese blinked several times, overwhelmed by the charge of it. She'd grown up in domes of carefully maintained, recycled air and graduated to ships with even less assertive supplies. She'd touched down on her share of planets and found them all complex to smell, but nothing so far could compete with this.

"Come on!" Irine said, and dashed outside. Sascha followed at a more casual pace. One by one they filed from the lock and Reese walked down last, shutting the door behind her.

Zhedeem looked the way it smelled but not the way

Reese had imagined it. She'd envisioned a bustling metropolis full of the high-rises and parks of a typical Alliance city. Instead, the *Earthrise* had settled beside a town so low some of the buildings weren't even a single story high. Hissing fountains and extensive gardens dominated the edges of the town, and past them Reese could see very little save more palms, more trees and the occasional edge of another low building.

The series of buildings they were standing next to were the tallest Reese could see: several half-story buildings and two with very small first stories. The gardens and fountains were a fortress of cool color against the burnished red sands upon which they stood. Even their shadows seemed hot. The house looked welcoming but also unreachable from the edge of the airlock. The sky was so very, very tall and the sand so very empty.

"Where's the city?" Reese asked finally. Irascibility had always helped bar panic from the forefront of her mind, and if she looked too long at the vista her agoraphobia would send her straight back into the ship. "I thought this place was supposed to have several thousand people living in it."

"It does," Sascha said. "They're mostly underground." He hiked his bag higher on his shoulder and started down the hill toward the nearest buildings. Irine skipped after him, followed by Bryer and Kis'eh't.

"I guess we can't show up and not at least say 'hi' to everyone," Reese said, watching their figures dwindle.

"I doubt the inhabitants of the household have noticed us yet," Hirianthial said. He stood a comfortable distance away, holding Allacazam in his arms and looking supremely unruffled in his long-sleeved blouse, breeches and boots despite a heat that was already inspiring sweat on Reese. "The twins would be disappointed, though."

"Yeah," Reese said. "I guess they would be." Still, she couldn't bring herself to move. She waited for Hirianthial to say something about it, but surprisingly he remained silent. Nor did he fidget as she struggled with her fear that the sky would fall on her—or worse, never end.

It seemed to take forever to decide to make the first step. She wondered if the moment lasted as long for Hirianthial as it seemed to for her. Maybe living forever gave a person a different perspective on what a "long time" was. With a sigh, Reese trudged after the rest of the crew. By the time she reached the base of the hill her ankles and shins ached from walking over the unsteady sand and her body was so slick with sweat she no longer feared unsolicited hugs from Irine and Sascha's family . . . no doubt she stank so fragrantly of hot human now that no one in her right mind would come near until she bathed.

Hirianthial, curse his eyes, looked remarkably fresh. On closer, surreptitious examination he was sweating, but it simply made him look glossy and vibrant rather than exhausted and untidy. She wondered where she could buy that trick.

The delineation between desert and garden was as sharp as the first brick beneath the gate that stood half-open. Reese passed into this wonderland of green and imagined that it felt cooler.

"Wonderful," Hirianthial said behind her. "You can smell the water."

"Is that what that is?" she asked, surprised, and sniffed. "I thought I was imagining it."

"No," he said. "The very plants sing of it."

She glanced at him, decided to say nothing and moved on. The paths showed signs of meticulous care, pruned and swept, bordered by shining plants with new but not yet open blooms. The deeper into it Reese walked, the

more she felt the change in the air, how it softened, became almost a caress. The best part was definitely how the
plants shielded her from the panoramic view.

A trickling fountain proved to be the first in a set,
each one growing larger and larger as they came closer to
the house. The first was only big enough for a desultory
plaque. The final depicted a woman with an infant at her
breast, a tumbled urn at her feet dispensing the water into
the basin.

"Reese!" Irine stood at the arch into the first of the
buildings, built below the gardens and accessible from a
set of five steps. "Come on, get out of the heat!"

"Do I look like I'm lingering?" Reese said. She joined
the Harat-Shar, hoping for an enclosed space and air conditioning but the hall she entered was lined with windows
set over the ground level. The fans on the ceilings whispered a soft *whuff-whuff* as they sent their breezes across
the floor mosaics, but the place felt very exposed.

"Is the whole town like this?" Reese asked.

"Most of it," Irine said. "Come on, I'll introduce you to
Father's first wife."

"Your mother?" Reese asked, following Irine with Hirianthial at her heels like a second shadow. A white shadow.
She wished he wouldn't do whatever it was he did that
made her feel stalked, but also felt ridiculous telling someone who wouldn't come within six feet of her that he was
walking too close.

"Yes," Irine said, then added, "One of them. If you mean
my birth-mother, no. But she nursed me, as did a few of
Father's other wives."

Reese touched her forehead. "Just be gentle with the
culture shocks, okay?"

"I'll try," Irine said, laughing. "Look, here she is! Mazer,
here is Reese, my captain!"

Beyond the entry hall was a smaller room . . . no less a chamber than the first, but with a circular couch in the center of it and several sideboards. Reese couldn't imagine what use the room would be, since its size did not invite intimacy. Her crew proved that by being scattered around the room, uncertain of where to stand or sit. Only Sascha seemed to have found a place to settle, though the tense cant of his ears belied his slouch.

None of that mattered, though, because the woman sitting on one of the couch's cushions made her want to turn and march right back to the *Earthrise*. She'd even risk Hirianthial's curious gaze to do it, except the woman was already rising and offering her hands and it seemed too impolite to run now. With a sigh, Reese gave hers to the woman and said, "You're the kind who knows everyone's secrets within a few minutes of meeting them, aren't you?"

The woman blinked several times, then grinned lazily. "Yes, but until this very day no one's had the eggs to up and say it the moment they noticed."

"Don't try to make my life any harder, please," Reese said. "I really appreciate being able to stay here, but if it means I'm going to have Harat-Shar crawling in my brain I have no problems going back to the ship and sleeping in my hammock."

"Captain!" Irine exclaimed.

"Oh, hush, Irine," the woman said. "Your mother can handle straight talking." To Reese she said, "It's never my intention to make people's lives harder. I will do my best not to drive you away."

"Good," Reese said. "As Irine said, I'm Theresa Eddings, Captain of the *Earthrise*. You've met my crew?"

"Everyone but the fine fellow standing behind you, and the gentlecreature in his arms."

"That would be Hirianthial Sarel Jisiensire and Allacazam," Reese said.

"My name is Zhemala," the woman said. "I am the first among Mascher's wives and it will be my duty to see to your welfare. Though I may delegate that duty to my co-wives or children if the rest of the household demands me. If it pleases you, I'll bring them out of the zenana for you to meet?"

"The zenana?" Reese asked, perplexed.

"Harem," Hirianthial said from behind her.

"How do you know another word for a harem?" she asked him, irritated.

Zhemala laughed. "Obviously he is a well-read man. Or he's worked with Harat-Shar before?"

"Intimately, Lady," Hirianthial said with a dip of his head, "Though not, perhaps, in all the meanings of that word those coworkers would have liked."

Reese wasn't sure what annoyed her more, the fact that he was lady-ing someone besides her or that she was offended by it. If it got him off her back, well and good!

"Is this a literal harem?" Reese asked finally.

"What other kind is there?" Zhemala asked, her mouth widening in a grin. "Or do you think the costume is for show?"

"Why don't we get them something to eat and drink and show them someplace they can relax while we figure out where to put them?" Sascha said from the floor. "They're probably hot, Mazer."

"Would you like to change into something more comfortable?" Zhemala asked.

"No," Reese said. The last thing she needed was to let Irine dress her up in some version of her mother's crazy outfit. She didn't need to bare most of her belly, stomach, ribs and arms in front of anyone. "But the food and drink sounds very nice."

Zhemala nodded. "Children, why don't you take them to the Moon Patio? I'll send some slaves with food and drink."

"You must be kidding me," Reese said.

"Not at all," Zhemala said. "It is my pleasure to see you properly served. I will join you have arranging accommodations . . . all separate rooms, I presume?"

"Yes, please."

She nodded and left at a pace both brisk and graceful. Reese stared after her for several minutes.

"Umm, Captain? Food is this way," Sascha said, tugging on her arm.

"She was kidding about the slaves, right?" Reese asked.

"Of course not," Irine said. "We buy slaves all the time."

Reese said, "Slavery's illegal."

"Not here. We get special dispensation," Irine said. "Just wait until you've had our marzipan pastries!"

"You guys walk ahead," Reese said. "I need to take it slow. The heat, you know."

Irine eyed her, then shrugged and skipped forward, pulling Kis'eh't by an arm. Sascha followed her, with Bryer alongside.

"You're not going to set them on fire, are you?" Reese asked the Eldritch, her voice hushed.

"What?" He blinked several times, then looked down at her. "Gracious Lady, no. Why would I do that?"

"Slaves!" Reese exclaimed.

Hirianthial laughed, a few soft puffs of breath. "Ask Irine more about Harat-Shariin slavery once we get to the table. It's not a sin of the same magnitude as the illegal trade I was pursuing."

She thought for certain he must be jesting, but he seemed at ease and in his arms Allacazam remained a contented blue-peach.

"Never fear, my lady . . . I shan't feel compelled to take justice into my hands on behalf of the slaves of Harat-Sharii." He bowed, ever-so-slightly, never removing his eyes from her face, and gestured up the hall. "After you."

Unsettled, Reese followed the twins.

The Moon Garden was not a garden of night-blooming flowers, as Reese had expected from the name. Instead all of the carefully manicured plants, from the glossy dark shrubs lining the half-height stucco walls to the delicate ivy trained up the trellises, bloomed in shades of white and ivory and a blush-tinted cream. Their perfume was so dense it was not dispelled by the ceiling fan hung from the bottom of a balcony that projected from the roof, far over their heads. Between that far-away ceiling and the profusion of flowers and plants, the patio managed to feel far more enclosed than it actually was.

As with most of the rooms and gardens they'd passed through to reach this one, Reese could hear the far-off trickle of water. She was so busy trying to find the source of the sound that she didn't notice the naked people until she was halfway into the patio. Her abrupt stop nearly made Hirianthial bump into her.

"Ack, Irine!" Reese said. "You didn't tell me they'd be *naked*!"

Irine waved a hand. "They're slaves. Did you expect them to be dressed?"

Reese couldn't bring herself to move. Something about the two women with their serving platters, their nudity accentuated by the jewelry they wore, disconcerted her more than any of the more extreme things she'd read about Harat-Shar.

From behind her, Hirianthial's voice sounded gentle, calming. "Go ahead. Sit with your people."

She glanced over her shoulder at him, trying to hide how rattled she was. Then she sighed and plunked herself on one of the stone benches. Hirianthial followed her and lit on one of the nearby stone columns, this one cut half-height.

Reese said, "All right. Explain this right now before I go crazy. How come this planet gets slaves?"

"They enslaved themselves voluntarily," Sascha said. "They sign up for a period of time, at the end of which they either renew their contracts or go back to being free. When they sign up they specify what they're willing to do or undergo."

"And they get paid for this?" Reese asked, mystified.

"Of course not," Irine said. "That's not slavery, that's employment."

"When they sign up, they can get a special kind of high-interest account at any bank," Sascha said. "While they're "unemployed" their savings accrue much higher dividends, plus they get a host of other protections under the law." He scratched his nose. "Actually, depending on how long you want to stay, Captain, that might not be a bad way to deal with our cash deficits."

"You must be kidding," Reese said.

"Not at all," Sascha said. "We get a lot of our workforce this way. That and the indentured servitude." Before Reese could interject, he said, "Convicts, captain. They work a term of service, unpaid and unprotected, for petty crimes."

"Do all of them wander around naked?" Reese asked.

Irine giggled. "Only if their masters want them to."

"House and pleasure servants typically do," Sascha said. "Slaves choosing other means of service wear whatever's appropriate to the task they signed up for." He glanced at Hirianthial. "The medical profession is almost entirely slave labor. The law doesn't allow a person to sue slaves for damages, so it's the cheapest and safest way for doctors to practice."

"Now you really must be kidding," Reese said. "All your doctors are *slaves*?"

"Servants," Hirianthial murmured. "All doctors are servants, no matter how they're compensated."

"I did not cross the Alliance to save you from slavers so you could meekly offer yourself to a city full of insane cats," Reese said.

"He can practice as a free-man," Sascha said. "It's just a different balance of money and risk." He grinned. "Besides, Captain, he can't enslave himself without your permission. None of us can take any form of employment or contract without your say-so, in fact."

Reese tapped her fingers on the table. "I told Irine one culture shock at a time, Sascha."

Kis'eh't offered, "Maybe it's better just to get as many of them over with as possible, Reese . . . while in the presence of people you trust."

"I trust you people?" Reese said. When they laughed, she said, "All right, Sascha. Tell me why people need my permission to do anything."

"Under the law here," Sascha said, "Visiting crews are considered owned by their employer. They can't be employed without permission from the captain of the vessel."

"I don't run a Fleet ship," Reese said. "You people are my employees, not in service to me."

Out of the corner of her eye, she saw Hirianthial look at her, suddenly.

"It's the law, Captain. It doesn't matter if you're a merchant or military."

Another slave appeared at the entrance to the house. "Mistress, if it pleases you may we speak with the Phoenix and the Glaseah? We believe we have comfortable accommodations for them, but we would be pleased if they would examine them for suitability."

"Just when the conversation was getting exciting," Kis'eh't said with a lopsided smile.

Bryer stood, saying, "The conversation lacks focus. We go."

Irine popped to her feet. "I'll come too."

"What, you don't want to take part in the unfocused conversation?" Reese asked.

Irine grinned. "Oh, I'm sure you won't let the matter drop quickly. I'll have plenty of time to hear you complain about it later."

Sascha stared after them for longer than Reese expected, after they left. She said, "Something wrong?"

Sascha shook his head. "She's just very happy to be home."

"And you're not," Reese guessed. "I might have a chance to keep sane after all."

She expected him to disagree, but instead the Harat-Shar chuckled and looked at Hirianthial. "So, are you going to work as a doctor here?"

"If I can," Hirianthial said. "I have licenses in several specialties. Most Core worlds accept those wherever you travel."

"I am not going to give you over to slavery," Reese said, folding her arms.

"It is service, Lady, not slavery," Hirianthial said, petting Allacazam. Beneath his hands the Flitzbe turned a deep, contented purple-blue, and those long white fingers sprang into sharp relief. Those hands had opened up her body and knitted her back together. They looked like a surgeon's hands.

"I'd be careful about your assumptions," Sascha said. "We call it slavery and it is slavery. You don't have any choices once you sign the contract."

Those long hands stopped moving. "So your master could beat you?"

"Sure, if you needed to be punished," Sascha said.

"To death?" Hirianthial asked.

"of course not!" Sascha said.

"And abuse?"

The Harat-Shar fidgeted. "Not unless you sign up for abuse."

"Starvation? Medical procedures without consent? Sterilization?" Hirianthial said. His voice remained calm and evenly paced, but Reese couldn't shake the feeling he was pressing.

"Of course not," Sascha said. "You have to find a very special segment of society to sign away that much of yourself."

"What a genteel existence," Hirianthial said. "Enough food to eat, enough to drink, a place to sleep, masters who dare not abuse you or torture you beyond what you have yourself allowed on a piece of paper you have signed." He resumed petting Allacazam, who began to turn a very unpleasant orange. "Call this slavery if you like, Sascha. It bears as much resemblance to it as wine to poison."

Reese stared at him. He looked as serene as always, but something about his face had changed. Beside her, Sascha sat stiffly transfixed, even his tail unmoving.

"Besides," Hirianthial said after a moment, "I haven't said whether I would take a slave-doctor's contract. Even I am leery of giving Harat-Sharii that much of me." A flicker of a smile.

Reese let out a long breath. "Thank the blood in the dust. The man has a sense of self-preservation."

"He'll need it," Sascha said and stood with a tail-lash. "I'll check on your rooms."

Reese nodded, but the tigraine was gone before she could finish the gesture. She glanced at Hirianthial. "This is going to be harder than I thought."

"Is it?" Hirianthial asked.

"You're not nervous about this?"

He continued stroking Allacazam, who slowly turned a lovely turquoise green—what that meant, Reese hadn't the slightest idea. "Worrying about what has not yet come to pass was never my duty, lady."

It was such a bizarre thing to say she wasn't sure how to respond. Finally, she came up with, "What is your duty, then?"

"To go where I'm sent," he said. "To do as I'm asked."

"To think as you're told to think?" Reese asked with a trace of acid. "Doesn't sound like the life of a responsible adult."

"And your way is better, lady?" Hirianthial asked. Allacazam had bloomed several splotches of alarmed red. "To cast off all the threads that would connect you to others? To deny your responsibility to them? To mistake destructive stubbornness for individual choice?"

Reese gaped at him.

"Even a short life is no excuse for such selfishness," he said, standing.

"W-what?" Reese managed. "Hey, wait! You can't say that kind of thing to me! What gives you the right to judge me? You barely know me!"

"And you me," Hirianthial said at the door. "Keep this in mind, captain," heavily touched with irony, the title, "Harat-Sharii's laws have made you the lord of your ship and we your liegemen. Take care with the role."

"I didn't ask to be in charge!"

"Few people do," he said.

"Wait!" she said, but he was already through the door.

Blood and spit! He had no right!

It had not been his plan to wander, but the alternative had not been palatable. So with Allacazam slowly calming in his arms, Hirianthial drifted through the gracious halls of the twins' family estate. The subsequent rooms had been built on the same model as the first few he'd seen: large windows at ground level, high ceilings and fans. Lovingly tended plants lined the corridors, some reaching from outside to coil tendrils along the inside walls. Broad-mouthed pots proved to be water gardens, sporting exotic lilies and populations of tiny fish and other less familiar creatures. Each hall seemed to branch into a shaded terrace, a sheltered alcove, a perfumed garden. Occasionally he caught sight of stairs leading into the ground and up to the earth.

Slaves passed him, their auras dense and lazy with pleasure. How could he explain how easily he could discern their contentment? He'd run his mental fingers over the distant auras of true slaves before, felt the spikes of pain so long suppressed the barbs had turned inward, sinking into the person's mind with the cruelty of despair. He would never have willingly given himself to the work these slaves had signed themselves to, but their willingness was real. There was no menace in this household.

In time, Hirianthial found a garden so charming he couldn't leave it. He perched on a crumbled stone wall among flowers so tiny their blossoms seemed more like lilac spatters off a paint brush. They smelled spicy, like sandalwood and ember bark. Half a dozen orange butterflies floated among the bushes, and at his feet black lizards raced from one end of the patio to the other. With Allacazam drowsily eating sunlight at his side, Hirianthial relaxed.

"Did my son release you so quickly, then?"

"He seemed eager to arrange our rooms," Hirianthial said, turning to look at Zhemala.

"You are overdressed for the weather," she said. The crumbling wall had once framed a gate, and she sat on the gate's opposite side, her gaze resting on his.

"If that was an invitation, lady, I'm afraid I shall ignore it," he said.

She laughed, her teeth and red mouth obscured by the filmy veil that fell from the level of her cheeks. "No, old alien. It was an invitation to have water. You will need more water than you are accustomed to drinking on a dry, cold ship."

"Water would be welcome," Hirianthial said.

She called for the attention of a servant and sent him away for a pitcher, then turned back to the Eldritch. "Will you forgive my staring? Most people expect Harat-Shar to stare, but your people are not rumored to know much of the Pelted."

"As you will, lady," Hirianthial said. "Your eyes will not harm me."

And with amusement, he observed the frankness of her appraisal and how it did not lift until the servant returned with a sweating silver pitcher and two goblets. She did not pass him his after pouring it, but set it on the edge of his side of the gate with all the practiced etiquette of an Eldritch courtier.

"I have lived long and hard and never regretted it," Zhemala said. "But I never thought I'd see an Eldritch in the real. I would greatly love to see more of you, but if this is all I ever see then I am satisfied."

"Are we worth so much?" Hirianthial asked with a lifted brow.

"Oh, anything rare enough is worth so much," the Harat-Shar said. "But this . . . yes, this even more. Your captain is a lucky girl. But come, there is business to discuss."

The water was cold enough to shock, cold enough to numb his mouth. He could feel it traveling all the way down his throat and into his stomach. "Business, lady?"

"My children tell me you're a doctor, and I happen to have a particular need for a doctor at this time. If you show interest, I would offer your captain a contract for a few hours of your time a day."

"And my duties?" Hirianthial asked, setting the goblet down.

"One of my husband's wives is expecting and this is her first," Zhemala said. "She is suffering from anxiety over her physical condition. A doctor would be a welcome addition to her midwife."

He was glad he'd put the goblet down as it gave him ample reason to fold his hands together in his lap where they could not shake. He was similarly glad that Allacazam was too far and too somnolent from gorging to react to the panic that had gripped his chest. "I do not have a specialty in obstetrics, lady," he said.

"I didn't imagine so," Zhemala said and took a long sip from her goblet. "I won't require your help in delivering her baby—she's not close to her time—only in reminding her to care for herself, to eat the right foods and take the right supplements, and to ease her anxieties about being a mother. I will talk bluntly, sir. I do not require a doctor. I require a babysitter whose degrees in medicine will lend him a lulling air of authority. I will pay your captain well for you to deal with her histrionics, for all of us are beginning to find them tiresome."

"I can play the nursemaid," Hirianthial said, forcing his discomfort aside. "But I must point out that I am no woman. How can your co-wife believe me if I have no direct experience with what she will soon undergo?"

"The midwife has not calmed her, despite her many successes and her own long line of children," Zhemala said. "So perhaps the girl's habit of obedience to men will shut her up in your presence." She sighed. "I would have brought in someone from the city, but you are close, you are convenient, and you'll be leaving . . . so I need not worry about alienating a neighbor." She managed a faint smile, one that didn't rise far enough above her veil to touch her eyes. "Her mother died giving birth to her second sister. The girl is convinced the baby will kill her. We're tired of telling her otherwise. Perhaps you will have better luck."

The irony of the situation was heavy-handed enough to off-set the reminder of his grief. Hirianthial said, "You'll have to check with Captain Eddings—"

"—of course."

"But if she approves, I will do my best," Hirianthial said.

Zhemala smiled and left him with the pitcher. He poured himself another serving and watched the butterflies.

"Reese!"

She paused at the entrance to the hall to find the twins trotting toward her. She'd almost escaped without anyone seeing her, which would have suited her fine . . . her talk with Hirianthial had left her angry and unsettled.

Sascha stopped first. "I was going to show you and Hirianthial to your rooms, but I get back to the Moon Patio and find you both gone! Where are you going? And where's Hirianthial?"

"I'm heading into town," Reese said. "I don't know where Hirianthial is."

"Town already?" Sascha asked. "You're not even settled!"

"In case you haven't noticed, the ship's in need of repair," Reese said, clipping her data tablet onto her belt.

"Can't it wait a single day?" Irine asked. "Mamer's preparing a glorious dinner!"

"Dinner's not for another five or six hours, unless you people call lunch dinner," Reese said.

"We can't lift off for an entire season, though," Sascha said. "What's the point of rushing?"

"The point of rushing is that the faster I get this done, the more relaxed I'll be. I hate having things hanging over my head. So tell me which way, fuzzies, or I'll have to figure it out on my own and you know how cranky *that* will make me."

Irine sighed. "Go down Market Avenue. The port's at the end of it."

"That's it?" Reese asked, lifting a brow.

"Hey, that's just how Hirianthial looks sometimes," Irine crowed, tail waving.

"What are you talking about?"

"The thing with the brow," Irine said.

As if sensing Reese's forthcoming tantrum, Sascha hastily said, "Market Avenue's the largest street in town. You won't miss it. It's in the middle of everything."

"Right," Reese said. And added, "I do not look like him."

"Of course you don't," Sascha said, pushing Irine deeper into the hall. "Enjoy your walk."

Reese eyed them both, then shrugged and headed toward the nearest exit. Finding it wasn't as easy as she'd hoped, but she managed to navigate out without having to ask one of the naked people how to get to the street. Blood and Freedom, but a little clothing wouldn't have hurt them, would it? Except that she had to admit that it was hot, so hot that it distracted her from staring at the size of the sky. She was used to climate-controlled environments, not places where the light was accompanied by heat dense enough she bet it could melt plastic. By the time she reached the edge of town, Reese regretted her black jumpsuit more than she could describe.

Market Avenue was indeed easy to find, though not needing directions didn't save her from the flirtatious calls from a few bystanders. Reese fumbled her responses and escaped while they laughed. Blushing only made her feel hotter, so she found the first grocer and jumped down the stairs to buy something to drink. It was a little strange at first to be halfway underground while inside, but if the Harat-Shar claimed it made it easier to cool their buildings she wasn't going to argue. Especially when arguing prolonged conversations that inevitably involved a proposition.

Back up on the street Reese began the long walk to the end of town, grateful that the profusion of stores and people made it easier to ignore the vastness of the world around her. Sascha's claim about Zhedeem being off-worlder-friendly seemed true; for every five Harat-Shar strolling the street in veils and flowing pants there was one alien. Humans, Seersa, Karaka'An, Asanii, the occasional Ciracaana flowing past on four feet . . . quite a selection. With the crowd so dense and so many people intent on errands, no Harat-Shar pounced the off-worlders either, which went a long way toward making Reese relax.

No, it was entirely unfair that she was enjoying the shade of the palms and the vibrancy of the passersby and the jabber of different languages amid the more common use of Universal. It was also entirely unfair that there were so many fascinating and exotic shops, from restaurants smelling of unfamiliar but enticing spices to vendors of luxury items Reese had never been able to afford. Expensive cloth. Boutiques selling haute couture so bizarre she couldn't figure out how it stayed on the solidigraphs. Art in blazing colors appropriate to the planet. Personal hardware that made her battered old data tablet look positively prehistoric. Cosmetics appropriate for whatever kind of face you had, whether covered with skin, fur or scales.

She managed to ignore it all with only the faintest pangs of longing. Her account simply couldn't clothe her in hand-woven brocade or buy her jeweled sandals. She was, in fact, feeling proud of her own willpower when it failed.

Her feet took her down the stairs and her hand pushed the glass door before her, and she was standing inside a real bookstore before she realized where she was. And oh, the smell of paper!

"May I help you?" a cheerful woman asked. She had spots . . . leopard spots? Something like that. What little Reese knew about Terran cats she'd learned because of Harat-Shar patterning. The woman also had a veil draped over her nose and chin and throat.

"Books," Reese managed. "These are real books?"

"Of every kind," the woman agreed. "From the electronic sort you can order in squirts to hand-made, hand-painted, hand-lettered curiosities from around the Alliance."

"Oh my," Reese said around a tight throat. "I've never held a real book in my hands."

"Never?" the woman said, eyes round. "Virgin hands! We should remedy that at once! Come along."

In the coldest, driest section of the store near the back, Reese found herself holding a real book with a leather cover, leaves of raw silk that chafed beneath her fingers and glossy ink she could still smell, pungent and rich. Her reverence inspired the woman to hand her yet another, and another, each one more glorious than the next until finally Reese sat on a bench and said, "I can't possibly see any more. I'll die of wonder."

"You could take one home," the woman said.

Reese laughed. "There's no way I could afford any of these treasures. I can buy a soft copy of something . . . I should, anyway, I've run out of my monthlies . . . but those? Those are far, far beyond my reach."

"You never know," the woman said. "But tell me what you'd like to look at and we'll see if we can't set you up with something."

"A romance novel," Reese said. "Preferably something new." Against her better judgment she added, "And with Eldritch in it."

"Eldritch!" the woman said with a laugh.

"I know," Reese said. "It's silly. Especially since I've got one of my own and I realize they're not the way they're written, not at all."

"You've got an Eldritch of your own to play with?" the woman asked, eyeing her as she replaced one of the treasures on the shelf.

"I don't . . . er . . . ," Reese stopped and sighed. "The Eldritch's not someone I'd play with, but yes, I've got one. They're as much trouble as they are in the books, but about six times more obstinate. In the books if you push them with a finger, they fall over. In real life you could ram them with a wrecking ball and they'd stay put just to spite you."

The Harat-Shar laughed. "It sounds like you're having quite an experience with her!"

"Him," Reese said.

"Even worse," the woman said. "I'll show you where the romances are. The best romances."

"That sounds like just what I need," Reese said and stood.

On the other side of the shelving, the leopard-spotted woman plucked a book down and handed it to her. The cover was absolutely scandalous: not just one Harat-Shar, but two Harat-Shar men and an Eldritch woman.

"Are you sure about this?" Reese said. "It looks pornographic."

"I think you'll be surprised," the woman said. "You can trust this author."

It was so glibly said Reese didn't know what prompted her to look up at the Harat-Shar and see the utter sobriety in the woman's coffee-colored eyes. It was such an unexpected expression that she said, "I'll take it."

The woman smiled.

Outside the store with the soft copy of the novel in her data tablet, Reese wondered what she'd just missed. Shaking herself, she headed back down the avenue for the port and reached it an hour later without being tempted by any of the other stores in her way. There she began collecting quotes for her repair work, keeping alert for any rumors about which shops did better quality work than others. By the time she made it to the end of the port her feet ached and her skin felt stretched taut from the heat. She found a bench to rest and watched the passersby.

While she'd been working she hadn't taken much notice of the balance of aliens and Harat-Shar in the port; now that she looked, she found far more aliens than natives. A lot of humans, not all of them someone she would have trusted to shake her hand. She began to wonder how safe the port was. Sascha had said something about Zhedeem being one of the few cities with a healthy mix of off-worlders and natives . . . maybe that wasn't the advantage she'd been hoping for.

Reese rubbed her forehead. She was being ridiculous. Surely the pirates wouldn't bother to follow her here. She would have trouble enough with the crew and her crazy Harat-Shariin pair without borrowing more about pirate vendettas.

At least her stomach didn't burn up anymore. It still

twisted, but it no longer burned. It was a spare blessing, but Reese counted it anyway. With a long breath she heaved herself to her feet and headed back into the port to do a few more errands.

By the time Reese let herself back into the gardens around the estate the world had turned purple after an astonishingly clear, high sunset. Irine greeted her as she let herself into one of the halls.

"You missed dinner," Irine said.

Reese flushed. "Sorry. I got caught up in what I was doing."

Irine shrugged. "There will be other dinners, I guess. If you want to come."

"I do," Reese said. "I just . . . I'm sorry, Irine. I'm just overwhelmed."

"Are we that scary?" Irine asked, ears drooping.

"It's not you," Reese said, then sighed. "It's not *just* you," she amended. "It's everything. It's having so many bills and not knowing where the money's going to come from. It's worrying about slavers. It's being dirtside—you know I hate the way planets smell. It's being in an unfamiliar place. And curse it all, it's Hirianthial."

Irine glanced at her, catching the glow of a lantern in one mischievous eye. "So that's it. He *did* say something to you."

"He's always saying something to me," Reese muttered. "I thought Eldritch were supposed to be quiet and mysterious, not high-handed and insufferable."

Irine grasped her by the elbow, pulling her down the hall. "You don't think he's quiet and mysterious? He's not exactly chatty, you know."

"Chatty would have been forgivable," Reese said. "What he actually does is far more annoying."

"Sascha and Kis'eh't and I had a bet about whether he

said something to annoy you," Irine said with a chortle. "I knew I'd win! What did he say?"

"That I'd better start taking care of you people now that we'd landed here and Harat-Sharii's laws had put you in my care," Reese said. "Have you ever heard anything more ridiculous?"

"Of course I have," Irine said. "But you're talking about our laws, so what else would I think? Here's your room."

Reese paused in the threshold, had a sense of walls, windows, and gauze curtains. Something outside was chirping . . . no, several somethings. Insects? Amphibians? Who knew? The fan and the night's breeze intersected somewhere around the window, and someone had hung a hammock for her there.

"Are those seriously supposed to stay open?" Reese asked.

"How else will you stay cool?" Irine said reasonably. "You'll get used to it."

"And the noise?"

"Greerhorns," Irine said. "Sort of like crickets, if you know what those are." At Reese's look, the tigraine shrugged and said, "Imagine long-legged insects."

"Ugh," Reese said. "I hope they don't get in."

"Don't worry about it, you're off the ground," Irine said. "Now tell me more about your being annoyed."

Reese eyed her.

"This is more than prurient curiosity, I promise," Irine said with a grin.

With a sigh, Reese rumpled her braids and sat on the edge of the hammock. To her surprise, Allacazam rolled out from beneath her blankets and bumped into her thigh, blending a chime of welcome with a sleepy blue-violet veil. Without thinking about it, Reese started petting him. "I'm just not comfortable with dictating other people's fates."

"Why not?" Irine asked.

Reese stared at her.

"Really," Irine said. "If they give you permission, why not?"

"Because you can't make someone else's choices for them," Reese said. "It's not right."

"What if they want you to?"

"It's not right," Reese said again. "We're all individuals. We all have to make our own choices. We all have to take responsibility for our actions. No one can do that for anyone else."

"If you really feel that way, why do you read all these romances about princes and kings?" Irine asked.

Reese gawked at her.

"We don't read your mail," Irine said. "But everyone sees the squirts in the communication logs. It's not exactly a big ship." She grinned. "I like a good romance novel myself . . . but you seem to have a theme to your choices."

"Well maybe I do like the princes and kings," Reese said. "But they're fantasies. They're escapes."

"They must touch something in people, otherwise why would they endure?" Irine said.

In the back of her mind Allacazam shrouded her frustrations with draping black willows that rustled in an evening breeze. Reese let the sound muffle her angry response until something more reasonable came up. "Maybe we wish we could have that much faith in people, that we could trust them to keep our hearts and lives in the forefronts of their minds. But the truth is that no one can do that . . . not fairly, not all the time. That's why they're escapes. They're not real. And I resent having to treat you people like vassals when you're my employees, who came to me out of free will and who should be free to make your own choices."

Irine shrugged. "If it bothers you that much, when we bring you our temporary contracts sign them without reviewing them. Think of it as a formality if it makes you more comfortable."

"I guess I can do that," Reese said.

Irine stood and stretched. "I think I'll go find a cuddle-pile. Do you want anything from the kitchen? There's a water pitcher in the bathroom, but no food."

"I'm fine, I think."

"All right. Good night, then."

"Good night," Reese said.

At the door, Irine said, "You know I'd trust you to make my decisions for me any day."

"Oh, shoo," Reese said and Irine scampered out, laughing. But sitting in the hammock, Reese felt such a confused mess of emotions she couldn't sort them out. Allacazam touched the edge of her mind with a rising note, and to his question Reese could only murmur, "I wish I knew myself."

There was indeed a pitcher of water in the bathroom, and Reese availed herself of it several times before finishing her preparations for sleep. Her body ached so much she decided to wait until morning for a bath. Yet when she clambered into the hammock with Allacazam, she tossed and turned, twisting herself into the netting until finally she sat up. The smell of the breeze, deep and dry, the rustling it made, the crickets, the very openness of the chamber . . . all of it was so unsettling she couldn't compose herself. Allacazam sent a faint candle into her mind, questioning.

"I don't know," she said and sighed. "Maybe I'll just read until I fall asleep."

The candle trembled for a moment, then receded again. The Flitzbe's presence in her mind faded to what sometimes felt like a distant white noise. Reese reached for her data tablet and brought up the cover with the two Harat-Shar and the Eldritch.

"Still looks pornographic," she muttered and began to read.

⇒ ◆ ⇐

"I am Karya Midwife," the old woman said when the servant deposited Hirianthial at the chamber door. "And this is your charge, Salaena."

Salaena looked up from her nest of cushions in the corner of the room. "Karya, I feel strange. Something's wrong."

"You're probably hungry," the old woman said dryly. "Now, girl . . . see, Zhemala has sent for a doctor for you. He'll make sure you're healthy."

"A doctor?" The girl's restless eyes fastened on Hirianthial's face then slid away again. "So I am in trouble."

"No, nothing like that," Karya said. "He's here to help you have the healthiest baby possible by telling you what to eat and when to rest. You're already fine, girl. The doctor is just here to answer your questions."

"What's wrong with me?" Salaena asked.

Hirianthial restrained the urge to say, "You're pregnant." Instead he sat on a bench next to one of the broad windows and said, "There's nothing wrong with you."

"How do you know? You haven't even checked!"

"I've seen sick people before, lady," Hirianthial said, gentling his voice. "They don't look the way you do." Which was only truth: even the briefest brush with his mental fingers had brought him nothing but a glowing aura and the contented nestled sendings of a still-unaware infant.

"Sometimes people look completely fine and then they just die," Salaena said. "My mother died that way."

"Your mother died in childbirth after hours of agonizing labor," Karya said. "It's not as if there wasn't warning."

The girl burst into tears. Karya sighed.

Hirianthial settled in for a long three hours. Salaena paced when she should have been resting, sat when she should have been enjoying the respite from the day's heat, constantly ran her hands over her belly, searching for what Hirianthial knew not. She never ceased to tremble, and her gaze when she managed to look at anything for very long had the poor focus of panic. The Eldritch did what he could to calm her, everything from soporific, pregnancy-safe teas to examining her with Alliance equipment and explaining the positive results, but nothing seemed to allay her concerns.

"I'll be back tomorrow morning," he said when the servants began bringing lunch.

"Did you choose my lunch?" Salaena asked. "Should I eat? I can't tell if I'm hungry. Isn't it a bad sign if you have no appetite?"

"You're fine, dear," Karya said.

"Just eat what you seem to crave," Hirianthial said and stepped out.

Karya joined him in the corridor. "Thank you. You were good with her."

"She is beyond any of our help," Hirianthial said. "If she doesn't calm down she'll hurt herself."

"Don't I know it," the midwife said, exasperated. She offered him a card. "I imagine you'll be looking for work for the rest of your hours? If you're interested, try this hospital. I have an off-season contract with them and they're always interested in people who can calm others."

Mindful of the woman's fingers, Hirianthial took the card and glanced at it. "A children's hospital? Lady, I would rather work with adults."

"Not here you wouldn't," the old woman said with a huff. When he glanced at her, she said, "Whether you wish to or not, your pretty white skin and lovely long face will get you more attention than you want. Salaena's too self-absorbed to notice you, but no one else will be. Even I notice you, and I'm a bit far gone in these old bones to care as much about such things."

"All the Harat-Shar I've worked with have been very understanding," Hirianthial said.

"Yes, yes. You're on Harat-Sharii now, young man. And don't you quirk your brow at me like that. You're probably four times my age but I'm going to die centuries before you and as far as I'm concerned that makes you a young man. Now listen to me . . . the first proposition might be easy to shrug off and the second, but you're going to get tired of fending off all comers. Our babies aren't born libertines . . . you may not think you like children, but you'll far prefer our kittens to our adults. Trust me."

He glanced at the card again.

"Besides, you have a gentle hand," Karya said. "There are young ones who could use it."

"Thank you," Hirianthial said. "I'll go see if they have openings."

"You do that."

She left him in the corridor to struggle with his thoughts. He hadn't honestly thought much of children since leaving home. He didn't really want to think of children.

Or did he?

He'd thought being around a pregnant woman would be pain enough, but Salaena's hypochondria had been so demanding he'd barely noticed anything else about her. Perhaps the children would be similarly distracting.

"I need another one," Reese said, standing inside the bookshop.

The leopardine looked up, brows rising. "You're back

already?"

"I stayed up all night reading," Reese said. "I want another one by her. She got it *right!*"

"Right in what way?" the leopardine said, gesturing back toward the shelves.

Reese followed her. "The Eldritch. She got it just right. The way they talk. The way they act." And the author had . . . from the moment the Eldritch character in the novel had stepped onto the stage, Reese had been captivated. She hadn't turned out her lights until far too late in the night, and waking up had been difficult. She'd engage a shop today to begin the *Earthrise's* repairs, but she'd known she had to stop here first.

"It didn't disappoint you, then?"

"Disappoint me! Why would it have?"

The Harat-Shar grinned. "There's a little less action in it than typical romances."

Reese paused. "I hadn't thought of that. But then again, I guess I wouldn't have. It was about an Eldritch. I'm beginning to think they reproduce like Flitzbes, by budding."

The woman laughed and handed her another volume. This one had a single couple on the cover, male Eldritch, female Harat-Shariin woman. "Try this one. There's some heavy breathing in it. And it's believable."

"Ha!" Reese said. "I'll take the soft-copy. Let's see how it goes."

"And if you like it, come back in a couple of days," the woman said. She debited Reese's account and transferred the copy to the data tablet, then tapped a flier on the counter. "She's doing a book signing here."

Reese glanced at it, expecting to see the author's face and instead seeing a different cover: this one had a despondent-looking Eldritch male wilting over the arm of a couch while a human man looked on. "I'll do that. She's written a lot, I see."

"Twenty-two novels so far. And all of them have Eldritch."

Reese started laughing. "Is she obsessed?"

The leopardine grinned at her. "Who wouldn't be? They make such useful mysterious lovers. Some of the stories get even hotter than the one you're holding."

"I'll give you my review next time I come by," Reese promised and left the store. She looked at the cover on her data tablet and shook her head. It would be something to do while waiting in line at the repair shop, she supposed. She thought of Irine and the comm logs and sighed. At least the twins wouldn't notice these purchases—she'd never hear the end of it.

Finding a single shop that covered all her necessary repairs, did them well and offered them at a reasonable price had turned out to be impossible. Instead, Reese decided to spread the tasks across several different outfits. Arranging the schedules and haggling over the prices took her most of the afternoon and by the time she was done she realized she was going to miss another of Irine's family dinners, but given the totals on her data tablet she couldn't bring herself to care. The numbers shone so brilliant a red Reese thought of new blood and wondered if the person who'd chosen to display negative amounts in red had made the association on purpose. Repairing the *Earthrise* would put her in debt again. Substantial debt. Substantial enough that she might have to borrow money from the people she least wanted to borrow it from.

They wouldn't just wire her the money. She'd have to visit. It wasn't far if she took a shuttle . . . but she really, really didn't want to go.

Reese rubbed her forehead. She wasn't in trouble yet—wouldn't be until the first two major repairs were done.

That would take a month or so. A month was long enough to bolster her courage.

A month would be long enough to figure out what to say to her mother and grandmother when she came home for the first time in years . . . to ask for money.

The children's hospital was in a pleasant part of town a short walk from the twins' house, shrouded in the spiked shade of palm trees and abutted by several emerald ponds full of paddling geese. Hirianthial couldn't help but think as he walked past them that there should be children enjoying them, but he could spot none in the gardens. Come to that he saw no adults, either, and the building when he approached had such a distinct aura of abandonment that he half-expected the corners to sag.

He entered the silent lobby and proceeded past it and its murals of spaceships with child astronauts to a waiting room, which also proved to be empty. Straining his ears brought him no sounds of habitation: no shoes scuffing on tile or muffled by carpet, no quiet talk. He was beginning to wonder if the hospital was even operational when the door to the room opened for a harried-looking Harat-Shariin man, his arms full.

"Visiting hours are over," he said, obviously startled. "We're a little busy."

"I'm here to ask about work," Hirianthial said.

"Oh." The man blinked a few times, then said, "Hold this baby. I'll be with you in a few minutes."

Startled, Hirianthial cradled the infant to his chest and watched the Harat-Shar dash away. "Well then," he said to the closing door before turning his attention to the child. "Good afternoon, little one."

The baby did not open her eyes. Her aura fluttered like a candle in a draft, and cheeks that should have been plump and soft with felt-fine fur were instead taut and gray. She didn't respond to the warmth of Hirianthial's arms even though the Eldritch body temperature ran hotter than most of the Alliance's races, so Hirianthial tucked the blanket more carefully around the tiny body and began to drift from one end of the waiting room to the other. Humming didn't seem to help but he found that the more he concentrated on the infant's unsteady aura, the more it seemed to stabilize . . . so he cleared his mind and focused on the task.

"How about that," came a very soft voice. "She's sleeping easier. How did you do that?"

"I don't know," Hirianthial admitted, releasing the child back to the man who'd left him in the waiting room. The Eldritch barely felt the flare of concern and distraction of the Harat-Shar when they brushed hands, exchanging the baby.

"You said you were looking for work?"

Hirianthial said, "A midwife suggested I try here. I have several certifications, though none of them are pediatric or obstetric."

"You seem to have a way with them, though," the man said. "What specialties do you have?"

"Mostly surgical," Hirianthial said. "But one in general internal medicine."

"We can always use more people in the ward. Are you interested in learning neonatal surgery? We desperately need more people in that area."

Surprised, Hirianthial said, "I'm not sure I'll be on-planet long enough to develop the expertise."

"Ah well. Do you have your credentials? How long are you staying?"

Hirianthial offered the man a thin card. "Three months. Maybe four."

"Pity that," the man said. "We'll barely have time to get to know you, if we hire you." He smiled weakly. "And that wasn't a salacious invitation . . . I don't have the energy for those anymore. We're so understaffed I'm developing a split personality; I send people home to rest while yearning to keep them on-duty for two or three shifts."

"What happened?" Hirianthial asked.

The man sighed. "It's a long story," he said. "But the short of it would be that half of our staff was on free-man contracts and we had a string of very bad luck. They got in trouble and lost their licenses." He grimaced. "Not their fault . . . but parents are especially bad about litigation."

"I see," Hirianthial said.

"I'll get back to you tomorrow on whether we want you," the man continued. "I'm desperate to say 'yes,' though, so don't be surprised if I do. By the way, what's your name? And what's an Eldritch doing here? You don't have problems touching people do you? Although if you do I still might take you. Having someone watching monitors would be better than what we've got now."

"I'm Hirianthial Sarel Jisisensire. I'm here because my employer's set down here for repairs . . . and I have no problem touching patients."

"Good, good," the man said. "I'm Jarysh, train Kharite. And I'll drop you a message tomorrow morning."

"Thank you," Hirianthial said, and was alone again in the waiting room before he could offer a cordial farewell; the man's habit of abrupt departures and harried air did not bode well for the hospital. The Eldritch wondered if it working here was a good idea at all. Perhaps there were other establishments in town he could investigate: someplace near the port that served the out-worlders, perhaps. He turned to go.

A shriek of pain erupted against his shields, so strident, so *real* he couldn't tell whether it had been voiced or sent. He could no more ignore it than he could have stopped breathing; his body was already turning from the lobby back toward the waiting room. The cry led him into the hall where it was joined by a physical wail. He followed it to a ward where Jarysh and two harried healers-assist were leaning over a bed.

"It's his neck," Hirianthial said from the door.

"His what?" Jarysh said as the monitor began to sound.

"His neck hurts," Hirianthial said, coming closer to the bed, then added, "And his back."

"He's running a little hotter than normal," one of the healers-assist said.

"Angels, spare me another spinal infection," Jarysh said with a moan.

"If that's what it is," one of the assistants said.

"We just had a bout of it," the other said.

"Too soon to tell," the first said.

Hirianthial glanced at the monitors, eyes snagging on temperature, blood pressure, pulse, respiration rate. It had been long enough since he'd done a pediatric round that while he could sense the levels were off he couldn't remember what normal levels were for Pelted children that age. "What kind of spinal infection have you been having lately?"

"We just had a strain of Ackman's off Karaka'Ana, one we've never seen before" Jarysh said, ears flattened. "The port here brings a lot of offworld mutations, and a lot of them latch onto vectors we haven't blocked off yet."

Hirianthial reached for the child's foot and hesitated over it, then grasped it firmly, skin to fur. "You took a tap?" he asked past the sudden feeling that his neck was too stiff to move.

"This morning. Negative for virus or bacteria," Jarysh

said. "But—"

"It might be too early to tell," one of the assists said.

"It's not too early for him to tell," Hirianthial said. "Take another one."

"But—"

"Do what he says," Jarysh said.

"It won't be wasted," Hirianthial said.

The assist shrugged and left. The baby continued to wail. Jarysh sighed and pulled a stool over, sat. "You might as well get one for yourself," he said.

Hirianthial nodded and did so, watching the monitors. "One of your bad luck runs?" he asked.

"Yeah," Jarysh said, shoulders slumped. "It's virulent like Chatcaava have talons. I thought we'd seen the last of it two days ago. Our best antibiotics seem useless against it, and we've wasted a lot of drugs on trying to keep these kids alive. It hasn't been working. The stuff just eats into the pia mater like it's going through sponge cake. The arachnoid webs swell up with the byproducts and eventually shut down the nerves."

Hirianthial glanced at the child. "You have no pharmacologists to run up a new drug strain?"

"We've never had any on staff," Jarysh said. "We send samples to off-site labs, but none of our regulars have been able to get back to us with a specific."

Hirianthial watched the vitals fluctuate. The Harat-Shar followed his gaze and let out a long breath. Then, "This is the earliest we've ever caught one. Maybe it'll be enough. If he's got it, of course."

The assist returned with a pump and needle for the spinal tap. Some tests could be done by sensitive enough halo-arches, but this hospital didn't appear to have any at all. He didn't bother to ask why not: it didn't matter why a facility didn't have the best equipment. What mattered was the sample the healer-assist drew and the infection Hirianthial knew would be lurking in it.

During the following twenty minutes, Jarysh fidgeted and Hirianthial waited, eyes half-closed. The assist returned and said, "It's positive. But it's not as bad as the last cases. Yet."

"Damn thing," Jarysh said, jumping to his feet. "Get the antibiotics."

"Right."

The Harat-Shar began to pace. "We caught the vector . . . can you believe it was a honey shipment that ended up in candy? We stopped the spread and finished all the cases. This was supposed to be over."

"I suppose you don't have a Medimage platform," Hirianthial said. A platform of sufficient complexity would allow them to pinpoint the infection and treat it cell-by-cell, if necessary.

"Not anymore," Jarysh said, tail lashing.

All the years of his life began to drag on his joints. Hirianthial asked, "Anymore?"

"Our service contract ran out," Jarysh said. "And of course, with no surgeons there was no point repairing the thing. Surgery was never our specialty anyhow . . . that's what the acute care center in Kherdiwen's for." The man stopped pacing to stare as the assist arrived with the AAP and injected the child's stiff neck with it. "Damn."

The pain beating against his shields was already beginning to ebb—not because it had retreated, but because the child was losing the strength to project it.

Jarysh returned to the stool, drooping. "You don't have to stay."

"I know," Hirianthial said. "How many more of these do you have?"

"We're not sure. It wasn't something we were equipped

to handle. We usually only work with chronic diseases. This was just so unexpected."

"Why not move them to the Kherdiwen center, then?" Hirianthial asked.

Jarysh shrugged. "No beds for it." He sighed. "It's complicated."

"Explain it to me, then," Hirianthial said. When the Harat-Shar glanced at the monitors, the Eldritch gentled his voice. "We'll be here a while."

"All right," Jarysh said, tail twitching. "It's like this. . . ."

"A mechanic?" Reese asked, eyeing the contract. "You're going to be a mechanic?"

"A very junior one, and only for the time we're here," Sascha said. "If I had the time I'd be studying engineering, but since I don't I'll settle for the hands-on stuff."

"Huh," Reese said. "That's practical." She read the fine print, trying to catch anything that might twist Sascha up into knots. "This is for a lot of hours!"

Sascha shrugged. "It'll get me out of the house."

Reese glanced at him and decided not to ask. She returned to reading and said, "I didn't know you were interested in engineering."

The Harat-Shar chuckled. "Neither did I until I actually started flying. It's good to fly. It's also good to be able to fix something you're flying when it stops."

Reese leaned back in her chair to peer at the Harat-Shar. She'd come home exhausted and tried to slip into her room without anyone noticing only to find Sascha already there. Happily he didn't harangue her about missing dinner again; instead, he'd presented a stack of paperwork for her to sign along with a small covered plate.

"Engineering," she said again. "You know, you could take remote classes."

"I guess," Sascha said. "I hadn't really thought about it until we touched down here."

"Well, think about it," Reese said.

"Classes take money, boss."

"Yeah, well, we'll find the money," Reese said, hiding her frustration. "Looks like Bryer's got dock-work. That seems harmless enough." She signed it along with Sascha's. "Where's Kis'eh't?"

"Kis'eh't's taking the time off," Sascha said. "She wants to learn to cook from my mother."

Reese laughed. "Well, more than one cook's always good. That leaves Irine and Hirianthial."

"Don't look at Irine's," Sascha said. "Just sign it."

"That bad, huh," Reese said, hand hovering over the data tablet.

"That good," Sascha said, but the smile on his face didn't touch his voice. "She'll have fun. But you don't want to know."

Of course, now that he put it that way, she did. But she flipped to the bottom of the contract and set her stylus on the line.

And couldn't sign.

"Just do it," Sascha said. "I read through it. It's fine."

She wanted to, but she couldn't. What if there was something in the contract that would tie Irine down? Her name would be on it, okaying it. Reese scrolled back up and started to read. Sascha pulled a chair up beside her with a sigh.

"Well," Reese said by the time she got to the end of it. "I guess this sort of thing is typical here."

"Yes," Sascha said.

"You're right that I didn't want to know about it," Reese said, signing the bottom.

"Yes," Sascha agreed, this time with a hint of a grin.

"I had no idea contracts like this could be so . . . detailed."

He shrugged. "It's one thing to roll in the sheets for love and entertainment," he said. "When you're doing it for profit with strangers, you have to be very specific about what you will and won't do."

"I guess so," Reese said. "You're sure she'll have fun?"

"Yes, captain. Really," Sascha said. "And she'll earn more than the rest of us combined, I'll bet."

Reese sighed. "That just leaves—"

"A moment of your time," came Hirianthial's baritone from the threshold.

Reese stared at him, wondering if the exhaustion she heard in his voice was her imagination or not. "Uh, sure."

"I have a contract for you to sign."

"I have one here for you already . . . something with Irine and Sascha's mother?"

"This is an additional contract."

"Not too much more additional I hope," Reese said. "This one's already going to take up three hours of your day. You don't want to run yourself ragged."

"No," he said. She realized then part of her foreboding: his speech lacked its 'my lady' adornments and its indistinct evasions. What had stripped him down to bare words? He even handed her his data tablet without any of his courtly gestures, without bothering to set it down somewhere so they wouldn't accidentally touch. Reese took it gingerly and started scanning. Her eyes caught first on the "mandatory dormitory stay," lingered over the multiple shifts and glazed at the parts about acceptable punishments for unacceptable results.

"Oh, no," she said. "I'm not signing this."

Sascha cleared his throat. "What did he do?"

"I'm not giving you over as a slave to any hospital," Reese said, ignoring Sascha. "I thought you said you didn't trust the Harat-Shar with that much of yourself?"

"I had the alternative explained to me," Hirianthial said. "They're having a healthcare crisis, one set off by too many free-man workers."

"We're just visiting, Hirianthial. We're not here to save the Harat-Shar. Even if we were, you're one man and one man alone won't be able to fix whatever social problems they've gotten involved in," Reese said.

"They're children."

"Yeah, well, so am I from your perspective, but they're adult enough for the rest of the Alliance—"

Something about his eyes stopped her mid-sentence. "The patients," he said, his voice very careful. "They're children. Infants."

Reese blushed, torn between anger and embarrassment. "I don't care if they're saints and martyrs," she said. "If I sign this, I'm giving you away completely."

"It's my choice to make, is it not?" Hirianthial said. "Or have you now decided you really are in charge?"

That stung. Reese said, "Hirianthial—"

"I'm not yours to give away," the Eldritch said. "Or isn't that your philosophy? Besides, it will take me out of your sight, which should please you."

Reese snatched the tablet and signed it with several angry jerks before tossing it to the end of the table. "There you go. Enjoy. Don't come crying to me if it's more than you can handle."

He didn't speak—only faded from her door so quickly she wondered how someone with such pale skin and hair could vanish into the blue-violet dusk of the hallways.

"You could have handled that better," Sascha said, picking up the tablet and flipping through the dumped contract copies.

"Hell with handling it better," Reese said. "He got what he wanted. Isn't that the point?"

"This is . . . really intense," Sascha said, skimming the text. "I hope this place isn't abusive."

"It's a hospital," Reese said. "If they abuse him, they can just patch him back up afterwards."

The Harat-Shar's ears flipped backward. "Boss, what's with you? I'd swear you had bed-fleas, but you're sleeping in a hammock."

"There's nothing with me," Reese said. Then sighed and added, "Nothing new, curse it all. Now get out of my sight, fluffy."

Sascha said, "It's too late to rip that thing up, but you could at least apologize to him."

"I was just thinking he should apologize to me," Reese said.

Sascha paused at the door. "Well, check up on him, then. Make sure he's not taking this whole 'multiple shift' thing too seriously."

"Why don't you do that?"

"Because I'm not the one who signed the papers," he said. "Like it or not, you're in charge."

"Then I get the right to delegate," Reese said. "I hereby delegate the duty of making sure Hirianthial doesn't work his sugar-white skin to rags to you."

The Harat-Shar shook his head. At least he left her alone with her bills and her questions: foremost being, what was she going to do for the next month or so? Everyone else had found something to occupy themselves. The only duties she had to occupy herself with were her worries.

Jarysh didn't ask him if he was sure about working at the hospital, which suited Hirianthial. He gave his bed in the dormitory a cursory glance, tossed his bag on it and went to the bathroom to change into the durable and shapeless synthetic tunic and pants that were the medical industry's uniform throughout the Core.

The explanation Jarysh had given him for the state of healthcare in the region had required most of two hours, but by the end of it Hirianthial had distilled it to the same premise that ruled all modern medicine: people left behind with nothing but sorrow and a body tended to want to balance the scales. If they could find no solace in family or faith, they found enough in money. Harat-Sharii's answer to medical litigation had, not surprisingly for Harat-Shar, involved voluntary enslavement. But a wave of specialists trained by off-worlders with a more mercenary bent had produced a generation of highly-paid free-man doctors . . . creating an industry once again vulnerable to law suits and medical claims.

That the medical industry had a sociology of its own had intrigued Hirianthial when he'd come to the Alliance to study. Medicine on his home world could barely be called that, and doctors were so few they hardly had an effect on the population, the economy or the social order at all. Sick Eldritch died. Weak Eldritch died. Old Eldritch died. Eldritch babies died of diseases that the Pelted had cured so long ago they were taught only in historical classes. The Eldritch had no vaccines. No surgeons. Women still died in childbed at a rate the Pelted would have found horrifying.

Every society in the Alliance dealt differently with the social issues raised by the marriage of high technology and biology. Zhedeem's healthcare crisis was only one of a hundred thousand examples of what could go wrong.

Hirianthial could not regret the contract. He was also old enough to dispense with the self-denials he might have indulged in as a youth about why he was here. He'd been at a loss when everything had fallen apart with Laiselin and then the executions, and it had led him to the Alliance. He was at a loss again. Better to drown himself in the work than to think about what he would do with the remainder of his still-too-many years. Better to think about Pelted children than about the daughter he'd almost had and the wife who, unlike Salaena the pard, had been certain that everything would work out for the best.

Hirianthial began to braid his hair back in preparation for work. He could hear a child weeping through the open door. His contract would expire, or it wouldn't. Reese would come for him, or she wouldn't. The work here would be worth doing even if he remained here for centuries.

The classifieds in Zhedeem almost inspired Reese to pack up the *Earthrise* and head right back out into the Core, pirates or no pirates. She figured out how to sort the listings so that nothing offensive would pop up on her screen, but by that time the pickings were so slim she didn't really want any of them. She hadn't bought the *Earthrise* so she could spend her layovers as a waitress or a cashier in a clothing store.

Then again, she hadn't bought the *Earthrise* intending to spend ninety percent of the year hemorrhaging money like blood. Any job would do if it reduced the amount she'd have to plead for from her mother.

Reese applied at several places until a port-side cafe offered her a contract pouring coffee and serving dessert cakes so dense she could have used them for weight-training. The view out the large windows offered a disconcerting mix of high-tech landing pads and waving palm fronds, but the cafe itself was cozy enough to lull her agoraphobia. She even got used to the dusty breeze.

She hadn't had the heart to read the book she'd bought since her fight with Hirianthial . . . or at least, what had felt like a fight. But frustration and boredom drew her back to it the following day and sucked her straight into the pages. Despite her mixed feelings about Eldritch and the fact that she had no physical copy to bring, Reese planned her lunch break so she could attend the book signing.

"Oh good, you came!" the leopardine said. "She's in the back. Here, take this."

Reese glanced down at the brightly colored reproduction of one of the covers. This one was an unlikely illustration of a Harat-Shar man torn between a ghost-pale Eldritch woman and a demure Tam-illee foxine. "Err, thank you."

The woman sitting behind the table in the back of the bookstore looked nothing like Reese had imagined: no young and sensual woman this, but an older woman with spots on her fading fur. Her head hair had also run to white, and there were wrinkles in the finely felted skin beneath her eyes. In front of her on her desk was a sign that read: "Natalie Felger: Writer of Exotic Alien Romance." A younger woman kept her company, but other than her the room was empty, its many chairs abandoned.

"Am I the only one here?" Reese asked, bewildered. "You should have more fans."

"So far," the older woman said, her grin flashing yellowed fangs and arching whiskers. "But it's nice to be told otherwise. I assume you're here to have something signed?"

"I guess," Reese said, looking at the paper in her hands. "I hadn't planned on it, but the bookseller gave me this."

"You look a bit perplexed," the writer said.

Reese sat on the nearest stool and said, "You got them so perfectly you have to know how infuriating they are. How can you fight with someone who barely talks?"

The two at the table exchanged glances, then the elder said, "Sounds like you have a story of your own."

And since the Harat-Shar seemed so disposed to listening, Reese found herself telling the whole crazy tale from the Queen of the Eldritch giving her money to Hirianthial vanishing into some hospital to give up his freedom for little children. Or to avoid her. Or both.

"You need advice," the older woman said. She handed Reese a card. "This will be of far more value to you than any signed flat, though I'll sign that too if you want."

"What is this?" Reese asked, trying to make sense of the numbers on it.

"My address," the Harat-Shariin said. "Stop by tonight for dinner and we'll talk."

Just what she needed: another missed dinner with Irine. Reese looked up into the other woman's face, though, and saw something there: not just kindness, but something alert, something shrewd.

"Later tonight, then," she said.

After her shift released, Reese headed for the address on the card. She had to ask for directions several times, which proved irritating since every adult who helped her had to invite her to his or her home instead before pointing her down the next lane. A pale violet twilight finally found her on the doorstep of a modest house that showed only its glazed tile roof and a few feet of wall before submerging amid a collection of flowerbeds. Reese took the earthen steps to the dark blue door and rung the bell; while waiting for someone to answer she reflected that she felt safer here, cocooned in the earth, than she did under the open sky. She might not like everything about Zhedeem, but this part she liked a great deal.

Natalie's younger companion opened the door. "Ah!

You did come. We're eating in the garden, come with me."

Reese followed her through a central corridor that opened onto several other rooms, none of which she saw more of than the dusky lanterns illumined. She had an impression of warmth and close walls, though, as the girl led her back up a set of stairs on the opposite end of the house, up to a circular patio set into the ground. Its walls ended somewhere at ground level, which hit Reese around her shoulders. Spicy-scented flowers draped into the enclosure, where a round table had already been set with ceramic plates glazed a beautiful deep blue.

Natalie was pouring water from a pitcher as they entered. "Ah, here she is. Did you have trouble finding the house?"

"A little," Reese said. "I've never been off Market Avenue."

"Probably wise," the younger woman said with a grin. "We haven't met. I'm Shelya, Natalie's niece."

"She keeps my house for me, Angels preserve her," Natalie said. "I'd forget to eat if she didn't remind me. Sit, sit! And tell me how you find Harat-Sharii, if this is your first visit, and how long you're staying."

Reese sat and obediently took a warm yeast-scented roll from the basket Shelya passed her. Natalie's questions proved so easy to answer that she didn't notice the second course: sweet green spears with a tangy glaze. The main course proved to be some sort of tiny bird, still bird-shaped, and Reese was wondering how to eat it when Natalie said, "Now tell me why you dislike your Eldritch so."

Reese jerked her gaze from the fowl to her hostess. "I don't actually dislike him."

"Are you sure?" Natalie asked. "You seemed very unsettled by him."

"Being unsettled is different," Reese said. She tried

stabbing one of the tiny birds with her fork to see if she could peel the meat off the bone; her hostesses were eating with their fingers, which looked messy. "He's hard not to be unsettled by."

"You wanted something more like the books other writers write," Shelya said. "Instead you got what Aunt Natalie writes."

Reese paused.

The girl laughed. "Don't think we haven't read the competition! They make the Eldritch sound like fragile, forlorn creatures, easily led astray, broken or changed. Not like that at all, are they?"

"No," Reese admitted.

"But they are as mysterious," Natalie said. "Imagine it, though. If you live as long as they do, why bother getting to the point of anything?" She wrinkled her nose. "It makes writing the sex scenes hard. That's why I never write a book about two Eldritch. We'd be dead before the triumphant part with the birth of the heir."

Reese almost choked. As Shelya patted her back, Reese wiped her watering eyes with the edge of her napkin and said, "You seemed to do well enough with the one I just read."

"That was a little more of a fantasy than I usually write," the older woman said agreeably. "And if you keep at it with the fork you'll shred the meat. We won't mind if you eat it with your hands."

So Reese did, and it was messy but also delicious. "Why Eldritch?" she asked over the second bird. "You could have picked any number of other races."

"Oh, I've done others," Natalie said. "Under a different name, I write rather shocking books about humans falling in love with Ciracaana that involve quite a bit of physics, if not in the way most physicists imagine."

"You've made her blush," Shelya said. "I can smell it."

Reese said, "Well, the Ciracaana are nine feet tall and centauroid. If you were human, you'd have the sense to blush about it yourself."

"No wonder she and the Eldritch don't get along!" Shelya said with a laugh. "Do you talk this way to him?"

"Maybe," Reese said. "Sometimes." She sighed. "Okay, maybe all the time."

Shelya snickered and cleared away the dishes.

"Why Eldritch, you asked," Natalie said. "Why not? I'd say. Except that would be an unfair answer. The reason is because my family's always been interested in them, and it seemed appropriate to uphold the tradition."

"That seems like a weird thing for a Harat-Shar family to be interested in," Reese said.

"Not at all!" Natalie said, laughing. "We are the Alliance's libertines, aren't we? Pleasure for its own sake. If it feels good, how can it be wrong? And naturally we would gravitate toward our opposites, yes? What could be more diametrically opposed to a Harat-Shar than an Eldritch?"

"Nothing, I guess," Reese said. "Still, that seems like a good reason to stay away from them. Opposites might attract, but they also cause friction."

"Perhaps," Natalie said. "Are you so unlike your Eldritch, then?"

Reese sighed. "He's not mine. As I keep telling him, or he keeps telling me, or which I can't remember anymore because he's so stubborn I can't tell when he's disagreeing with me or doing what I want him to do." She turned her glass in her fingers, leaving greasy prints on it. "I just want him to leave me alone. Things were better without him."

"Were they?" Natalie asked.

"Yes!" Reese exclaimed. "I feel like he's always judging me according to some standard I'll never meet. Like he's seen everything and I'm nothing special. I hate that he only answers the questions he wants to answer. I hate feeling like he's part of some world that only barely touches ours. Why does he get to live so much better than we do?" She stopped abruptly, wondering when her voice had risen.

"Didn't quite realize how much you were holding in, did you," Natalie observed.

"I guess not," Reese said, then straightened. "It's still true, though."

"Wash your fingers," Natalie said, nodding to a bowl with a hot towel at Reese's side. "Then come with me. I have something to show you while Shelya prepares dessert."

Scraping the grease from her fingers with the pebbly surface of the hot towel left her hands feeling surprisingly clean, almost raw. Reese set it aside and followed Natalie into the lantern-lit warmth of the house, through the shadowed corridor in its center and into an intimately lit room, one almost too small to be called a room . . . in a groundsider's house, anyway. There was a single cushioned bench in it facing a dark wooden bureau, and this Natalie opened with a thin brass key she withdrew from her vest. When she opened the bureau's doors, the pungent smell of paper, ink and paint rushed out, tickling Reese's nose.

"This folio never leaves this room," Natalie said, turning from the bureau with a leather folder in her arms. "But you have plenty of time. Enjoy it, and when you're done set it back and join us for coffee."

"I couldn't possibly—it's so old—"

One of the woman's brow ridges quirked. "And only young things need to be touched?"

Reese blushed but couldn't come up with a response before Natalie abandoned her with the folio in her lap.

It was larger than she'd thought—longer than her forearm, but narrow. The leather wasn't stiff, as she expected, but supple, dyed a dark blue. Hesitant, Reese untied the cords holding it shut and spread it open.

. . .and gasped at the parchment inside, a painting in vibrant hues, so jewel-rich she had to restrain herself from touching it. The smell of oil rose from the page and with it a sense of age.

It was only barely less staggering than the subject matter: a Harat-Shar jaguar? Leopard? reclining on a day bed beside a young Eldritch woman in sumptuous garb. The Eldritch had a book in hand and appeared to be reading out loud. The Harat-Shar was listening.

They looked so real. And they continued to look real in all the paintings that followed: twenty-two in all, each more unbelievable than the one before. It wasn't what Reese had expected from a folio of paintings in a Harat-Shar's bureau—there was nothing salacious about it—but despite the two never touching, never being undressed, never doing anything at all inappropriate, there was an unbearable sense of intimacy in each scene, so pointed Reese touched her cheek and realized it was warm from blushing.

She looked through the whole series of pastoral scenes twice, trying to decide what about it made them so hard to look at, and for the life of her couldn't decide. And despite her embarrassment, she found her fingers reluctant to tie the folio shut and put it away.

The two women were back in the garden, sipping coffee and nibbling on a white cake thick with a frosting made especially rich by the yellow candlelight. Reese resumed her seat, blinked at the slice handed to her by Shelya, and sipped the coffee, bitter and dark.

"Well?" Natalie asked.

"Who were those two?" Reese asked.

"Sellelvi and Fasianyl," Natalie said.

"Were they real?" Reese asked.

"Ah!" Natalie said with a laugh. "Does it matter?"

Reese focused on the cake, then looked up at the Harat-Shar. "Of course it matters."

"Does it make the paintings any less special?"

"No, of course not," Reese said. "But it could make them more special."

"Eat the cake," Shelya whispered. "You look like you could use it."

Dazed, Reese parted a corner of the cake with her fork and tried it. The frosting was lemon.

"Maybe they were real. Maybe they weren't. Even if they were real, some secrets aren't mine to give away," Natalie said. "That's the first thing you should have figured out about Eldritch. It's not just that they keep secrets . . . it's that the secrets keep them, fast as prisons." At Reese's expression, she grinned and continued, "Those paintings have been in my family for over a hundred years . . . and whosoever made them didn't do us the kindness of telling us about their inspiration. She had a fine hand with a brush, and maybe painting them was all she could say. Or maybe it was all she had to say."

"They're priceless," Reese said. "Reproductions of them would make you a rich woman."

"You saying that as a trader?" Natalie asked. "Or as a woman who wishes she had a copy?"

"A little of both, maybe," Reese said, realizing the cake was good. She gave it more of her attention, and the more she ate the less vague she felt.

"There's more than one way to be rich," Natalie said. "I have no use for more money."

Reese hesitated over the cake.

"You're thinking something awkward, I'm sure," Natalie said. "Say it, say it. We're not oh-so-polite Eldritch ourselves."

"It seems wrong to keep something so beautiful hidden, when so many people could see and enjoy it," Reese said slowly. "Those pieces could hang in a museum."

"They could," Natalie agreed. "But not everyone could enjoy them as you have."

"What makes me so special?" Reese asked.

The old woman grinned. "You have an Eldritch of your own. That makes you special . . . very special. I hoped that seeing the pictures would keep you from wasting him."

"He's not mine to waste!" Reese exclaimed.

"Of course he is. Haven't you figured it out yet?"

"Figured what out?" Reese asked, gripping her fork harder.

Natalie only shook her head. "Read more carefully, girl. And finish your coffee there, before it gets cold."

Try as she could, Reese got no more information out of the writer than that, and though she ate more cake than she intended in her pursuit, Natalie cheerfully offered no more insight. Standing outside the Harat-Shariin's house and staring at the stars, Reese reflected that while dinner had been pleasant, she'd gotten even less information out of Natalie than she'd ever gotten out of Hirianthial. . . .

Except for the paintings. The beautiful paintings.

With a shiver, Reese headed back to her hammock.

After the child survived, Jarysh showed active reluctance whenever Hirianthial left to discharge his duties to Irine and Sascha's mother. Had he not already promised those hours, he would have gladly given them to the hospital. Where once thirty doctors worked, including five surgeons, now only ten reported . . . and of those ten, only Hirianthial and Jarysh had residential contracts. The hospital was a permanent home for forty children with diseases crippling and chronic enough to require full-time care, and the ward offered beds to those who needed only occasional check-ups. Two doctors alone weren't sufficient to the task. Without enough full-time employees to keep track of the residents, Hirianthial often found them trailing him through the halls when he did his rounds on the transients or draping across nearby furniture while he attempted to repair the single Medimage platform the hospital owned.

He was no mechanic but the set-up had come with a basic repair manual; it had contained a long block of explanation on how the Pad technology had made the Medimage platforms possible and then a smaller set of pages instructing Pad technicians on the differences and similarities between the two. He'd glanced through them, picking up several bits of trivia about lights and quantum tunnel disruption before flipping to the troubleshooting sections. Lying flat on his back beneath the raised floor of the operating room he could just see the solidigraphic diagrams projected by the manual; if necessary, he could turn the projector with a foot to examine it from a different angle and continue work.

When the children used his midriff as a pillow he didn't complain. Their thoughts were so thin and tired they barely sank past his shields. More than the discomfort of stiff muscles or the ache that drove him to bed, those tiny flickers of thought made him feel his age.

"We really shouldn't let them do this," Jarysh said from the door one day, voice thick with too little sleep. "If they separate they might have a seizure in some corner and we'd never know it."

"I can feel them," Hirianthial said shortly, squinting into a mass of conflicting circuitry and wondering which relay needed replacement. He felt along their seams.

"Feel them . . . even without touching?" Jarysh asked.

"I wouldn't mention it otherwise," Hirianthial said.

"And you know where they are? And how to get to them?"

"Yes," Hirianthial said.

"Even when you're sleeping? Would it wake you up?"

Beneath the platform, Hirianthial paused to consider. "I don't know."

"Because . . . well, maybe we both could sleep more if that was the case." The Harat-Shar rubbed his forehead. "They climb over the bed rails and go wandering sometimes. Gives me nightmares."

Hirianthial had shared them, but didn't say so. The place felt abandoned and desperate and listless, a disorienting combination that left him feeling anchorless in a deep melancholy. He wasn't sure if his daily excursions out of the hospital exacerbated the problem or blunted its edge, but he kept the feelings tightly reined. Espers were rare among the Pelted outside of the Glaseahn race, but some individuals still developed the talent and children were especially sensitive to emotional pollution.

"I think we need to replace this card," Hirianthial said. "That might be all we have to do to have the platform work again."

"Sounds worth a try," Jarysh said. After a moment, he said, "Can you get up? There's a girl on your stomach."

"I'm not sure," Hirianthial said. "She's asleep." When one of Jarysh's footsteps sounded close, the Eldritch said, "No . . . let her be. She was very tired and if you try to move her she might wake."

"I can't just leave you on the floor," Jarysh said, exasperated.

Remembering the insistent throb of pain that had sent the girl on her wanders, Hirianthial said, "I'll get up later, after she rises."

"At least let me bring you a pillow. You've only got a couple of hours before you have to head to your other job."

"Is it that late already?"

"Or that early, depending on your skew."

"A pillow would be welcome," Hirianthial said.

He didn't expect to sleep, but once he'd resigned himself to the floor he surprised himself by dropping unconscious as soon as he'd settled the pillow beneath his head. He woke to a dense, thin finger of worry tapping him near his foot.

"You need to go," Jarysh said. Clearing his throat, he added, "I'm sorry about touching you. I thought the boot would be least offensive."

"Thank you," Hirianthial said. The girl was drowsing on Jarysh's shoulder and did not radiate the frustration that had driven her to follow him, and that was the best he could ask given her condition. He brushed himself off and headed to the estate.

He'd thought when he took the hospital contract that it would prove the more difficult of the tasks. It was significantly more grueling, physically; emotionally he found it depressing, but depression concerning patients who would never recover and would die long before their time was at least a phenomenon he was familiar with.

Salaena, on the other hand, drove him to distraction. She would have been perfectly at home in the courts he'd left behind. Her anxiety was so extreme she refused to be comforted; she would not allow him the medical tests he could have used to diagnose the precise chemical imbalance that threatened her mind's brittle well-being. His only success involved mildly sedative teas, and he prepared her one before even entering the chamber to see how she was.

"Good morning, lady," he said. "I have your tea."

"I don't want tea," Salaena said, arms crossed over her

chest.

"Don't sulk," Karya said. "If the doctor says you must have tea, then you must have tea."

"I don't want it. The stuff you bring smells like grass," she said.

"I also brought a selection of fruits, cookies and cheeses," Hirianthial said. "Let us break our fast."

"I've already eaten," Salaena said. "You eat, if you're hungry."

"Surely you'd enjoy a little cup of tea?" Karya said. "Sit with us, enjoy the day."

"I don't have time to enjoy the day," she said. "I have to plan."

"What for?" Karya asked, though Hirianthial had an idea of the answer.

"For my baby. Just in case something happens," Salaena said, eyes drifting out the window. "You can't be too careful."

"For the last time, girl, you're not dying. Now come here and drink your tea or I'll pour it down your throat."

Salaena shivered. "I'm not thirsty."

"We'll take the tea, then," Hirianthial said. "Join us if you like."

She didn't like. He and Karya ate, the latter with forced enthusiasm. In a whisper, the midwife said, "Maybe music would calm her."

"I don't sing," Hirianthial said.

The old woman laughed. "No, I wouldn't think so. I can bring some people in."

"It may help."

But it didn't. Salaena couldn't concentrate on the musicians. The energy required for worry simply failed to be available for Hirianthial, but her behavior was abnormal and demanded repair. He edged the tisane closer to her elbow until in her distraction she began to drink it and calm.

"There now, wasn't that delightful?" Karya asked.

"No," Salaena said. "They were too loud."

"Babies can hear through the walls of the womb," Karya said. "If you didn't enjoy it perhaps your son did."

"A son," Salaena murmured. "Or a daughter."

"Or twins," Karya said, ears flicking forward. "Wouldn't that be lovely?"

"Twins would kill me," Salaena said listlessly. She tilted the tea cup. "I guess I was thirsty."

"The tea is good for you," Karya said. "It calms the soul."

Salaena drew herself upright with a quivering tension that set off alarms in Hirianthial. "You mean it's *medicine*?"

Perhaps alerted by the same signs, Karya did not reply.

"It is medicine, isn't it!" Salaena said.

"Yes," Hirianthial finally said. "A very mild kind. Nothing harmful to you or your baby. Do you not feel better after drinking it?"

"Yes . . . but it's medicine," Salaena said. "What if . . . what if something changes, and it does harm me? Or I drink too much? Or not enough?"

"I wouldn't allow that," Hirianthial said.

"You're not here all the time!" Salaena threw the cup aside. "I won't drink it again. Only water from now on! Water can't hurt me. Unless . . . no. The water is fine."

Karya sighed.

"Water then," Hirianthial said, and wondered how he'd keep the girl calm enough to carry to term.

As if only just noticing the long-suffering of her caretakers, Salaena blinked several times, very slowly. Then she said, "What? I'm in terrible danger."

"No," Hirianthial said. "You are in the best of circumstances. You are young and in fine health. Your body was built to bear children."

"No it wasn't," Salaena said. "Everyone says so. My hips are too small."

"The breadth of your hips is immaterial in a civilization where your baby can be lifted out of your abdomen in half an hour with no effort on your part," Hirianthial said. "You should be thankful you live in a modern city with excellent medical facilities and an excess of caregivers and that you aren't forced to give birth in a cold, damp hovel, straining for days because no one has the expertise to save you."

Salaena gaped at him. She turned to Karya to find the midwife nodding her head. "Just so, girl."

"But I could die!" Salaena said.

"You *will* die," Hirianthial said. "Everyone dies. Whatever gave you the notion that you'd live forever?"

The girl gasped.

"Even him," Karya said. "Even the likes of him."

Hirianthial poured a new cup of tea, set it on the warmer in front of Salaena and said, "Drink." When she made no move toward it, he said in a crisper voice, "Drink and be glad to be under the care of two professionals."

She drank, but by that time Hirianthial didn't care.

Waitress-work didn't agree with Reese, particularly for clientele that half the time was more determined to invite her home than to order cake and coffee. She left the cafe for her mid-day breaks, struggling with her foul mood, and returned only because she didn't like any of her alternatives. If she lingered too long with the twins, they might feel compelled to introduce her to the rest of their family and she wasn't sure she could handle the culture shear. Nor did she want to trap herself in her room, staring at a list of bills that her paltry tips did little to reduce. Living here was cheaper than any other choice she could have come up with, but nothing would be cheap enough to make the repairs go faster.

Every other day she stopped at the port to see how the first set of mechanics were handling the *Earthrise*. She'd just finished one of those inspections when the sky let loose a wall of rain. Cursing, Reese darted under the awning of a pastry-seller's cart.

"I didn't think it rained here!" she said.

The man laughed. "You spacers are so funny. Of course it rains."

Reese glowered at the sky. Why did planets have to have weather along with all their other unsavory characteristics? "But there were no clouds when I went inside!"

"There were clouds," the man said. "They just weren't rain clouds yet. We're just touching the rainy season now. In few weeks we'll have storms all the time. I hope you like being wet."

Reese glared at him. He chuckled. "Guess not. Why don't you wait it out at an ale house?"

"I don't drink," Reese said.

"They have food," he said. "Or do you also not need to eat?" When she didn't reply, he went on. "It's going to last a good half hour, forty minutes. You're a pretty girl, but if you're not going to buy anything I'd prefer you moved on. Unless you want to pass the time some other way?"

"An ale house sounds good," Reese said. "Thanks."

His laughter rang in her ears as she darted into the shifting gray veils. They looked sort of pretty when you weren't in them . . . as if they'd be soft and cool to the touch, not at all wet. Naturally she was drenched almost instantly. Rain drops smacked her face and eyelids. She felt trapped between the steam rising from the ground and the falling water, and she was sure she'd never smelled anything as nasty as hot rain on pavement.

The first dim shape she rushed for turned out to be a

parts store. The second smelled like fried fish and Reese traded the rain for an entry that worked like an airlock, releasing her into a tiny antechamber that gave her a chance to shake herself off and wring her braids. Even so as she stepped into the crowded room she started shivering. She took the only seat left in the place, squeezing between two taller men at the bar, and ordered hot coffee.

She'd barely had time to dilute the stuff with cream before the Harat-Shar on one side of her said, "There are rooms upstairs."

"That's nice," Reese said.

He canted his ears. "Is that a brush-off?"

"Yes," Reese said. "Thanks for asking."

The human on the other side of her laughed. She glared at him, but he said nothing.

The coffee had little power to warm her while her clothes remained wet. Reese resigned herself to shivering. It wasn't even good coffee. She could have gotten better from the cafe she'd abandoned.

The Harat-Shar beside her forced his way back into the crowd and another man took his place. Reese was just beginning to notice that the clientele was a little rougher than she liked to deal with when the newcomer said, "You look shoved out."

Reese shrugged.

"Come here often?"

"I'm not interested," Reese said, disgruntled.

"I wasn't asking."

"Oh," Reese said. "Good."

"You must not be from around here," he went on.

"What gave you that idea?" Reese asked.

His turn to shrug, a hitch of one shoulder. "You have the spacer look. You got a crate here?"

"Yeah," Reese said.

"Hauling freight or people?"

"Why do you want to know?" Reese asked, a scowl forming despite her best efforts. The man had a craggy face, but he kept it shaved and his rough clothing seemed clean enough. She had no reason for her wariness except that she was wary of everyone and so far paranoia had kept her out of trouble.

"I'm looking for freight haulers. Got a job for someone with grit." He eyed her. "You got grit."

"Yeah, well," Reese said. "I don't just do jobs I pick up in a bar."

He glanced at the coffee, then shrugged again. "Pays a lot. We'd make it worth your while."

"We?" Reese asked.

"I'm agenting. My boss's off-world. Always looking for reliable merchants."

Her wariness ripened into a nice, juicy suspicion. "I don't work with go-betweens."

"I can arrange a meeting, if you're interested." He smiled. "It would be worth it."

"Oh? How worth it?"

He dunked a finger in her coffee before she could object and scrawled a figure on the bar, dark liquid on dark wood. Reese gaped at it as he wiped it away. She said, "I don't run illegal cargo."

"It's not illegal," he said. "It's just way far out in the frontier and getting it requires some legwork. Most people don't want to bother."

"Nothing in the frontier is worth that kind of money," Reese said, hardening herself against hope. The amount the man had written would take care of the repairs and then some. She wouldn't have to ask for the loan.

"Money's where you make it," the man said with a shrug. "If you're interested—"

"—I'd need more details," Reese said.

"No," the man said. "You sign the contract. You find out what the boss wants. You get paid half. The other half on delivery. Those are the terms."

"You want me to agree to do something without telling me what it is?" Reese asked, staring at him.

He grinned. "We pay enough for it. And it's not illegal."

She wondered if its legality was due to some convoluted loophole. The chill in her bones was not solely her clammy clothing. "I'll think about it," she said.

He handed her a card. "If you decide, give us a call."

"Right," Reese said. The man slid off the stool and was replaced by a Tam-illee pilot who drooped so far over his beer Reese wondered if he would dunk his muzzle in it. She ordered a fresh cup of coffee and drank it black, but instead of warming her it just made her feel wet on the inside to match her skin.

The rain let up and she headed back to the cafe. The money was tempting, but Reese knew better. As embarrassing as her trip home would prove, a known quantity won over anything as potentially risky as entangling herself with nameless merchants who had too much money and required too much secrecy.

"Do they bother you?" Jarysh asked.

Hirianthial lay with eyes closed in the playroom adjacent to the ward. Two Harat-Shar children were using his long torso as a pillow; another sat near his foot, puzzling at a series of colored rings that had been interlocked a moment before. The sleepers dreamt in fragile washes of color, such delicate constructs they barely held the two minds unconscious; the pressure of their heads on his ribs seemed too heavy for the frailty of their slumber. "They're children," he said after a moment, keeping his voice too low to disturb the dreams.

"And that means they're exceptions to the rule for you?" Jarysh asked.

Hirianthial didn't reply. Even worked to exhaustion he'd been trained too well to accidentally tear the Veil Jerisa had decreed for the Eldritch. When he did not answer the direct question, Jarysh assumed agreement and said, "Here too. Children are very special for us. I think people think we don't love our children because we treat them so differently."

"Perhaps," Hirianthial said.

The man poured himself onto the ground, boneless in his own exhaustion. Hirianthial thought he had spots beneath his shapeless tunic and pants, but he'd never seen Jarysh out of hospital scrubs. He knew very little about his coworker beyond the Harat-Shar's medical competence . . . which was fine. Jarysh probably knew even less about him.

Staring at the ceiling, the Harat-Shar continued, "My wives are very angry with me. This is a change."

Hirianthial could not muster a response to that, but his silence must have seemed receptive, for Jarysh said, "They're usually too busy being angry at one another to be angry with me. It's because I have two. One wife is bearable. Three work together well. With only two there's no peace in the house. They rival for my attentions. I have very few attentions to spare." His sigh whistled through his nose. "They want me home more often. They want babies. They want my time. I told them that the residential contract was a temporary thing . . . but the longer I'm here, the more I realize I like it better than being home."

"You do not love your wives?" Hirianthial asked after a moment.

"Better to ask whether I loved my life," Jarysh said. "The

wives are only incidental." He sighed. "Do you ever get the feeling that you got knocked off a nice, simple life path, but that once you got off it you couldn't figure out how to get back? Or even if you wanted to?"

Hirianthial forced a curl of a smile, though why he had no idea. Perhaps he felt compelled to at least make an effort to appreciate the many ironies of his life. "I am acquainted with the situation."

"Now that I'm here," Jarysh said, "now that I'm working like this . . . I don't want the wives. The babies. These patients are my babies. What am I supposed to do now?"

"The honorable thing," Hirianthial suggested.

The Harat-Shar snorted. "Honorable. For whom? Me? Them? By what standards?"

"Perhaps then the just thing," Hirianthial said.

Jarysh rubbed his temples. "Kajentarel shield me. The 'just' thing. As if I knew what that was. I should probably divorce them, let them seek a husband who cares better for them." After a while, he said, "You don't talk much."

"You ask counsel on a topic for which I have no adequate advice," Hirianthial said.

"Is that because you have no wives, or because you're an Eldritch?"

"Neither," Hirianthial said. "It's because I'm not Harat-Shariin. I may know enough to keep from making any egregious errors, but I cannot begin to guess what would be fair or just for you or your family. Your customs are too different."

"Probably," Jarysh said and rubbed the bridge of his nose, his temples. "Still, I wish I had the wisdom of your years." He managed a grin. "You probably have children older than my grandparents."

"No," Hirianthial said, surprising himself with the admission. "I have no children."

"None?" Jarysh asked, eyes widening. "But you're so good with them."

"Children ask very little and what they need is simple," Hirianthial said. "To be good with them is easier than to be good with adults."

The Harat-Shar snorted. "You'd be surprised. Too many people grow up embarrassed at their own naiveté. They think to be sophisticated they have to cut themselves off from anything that seems simple. There are plenty of people who are bad with kits."

"I suppose that might be true," Hirianthial said.

"You should have children before you die," Jarysh said. "It would be a waste for you not to be a father."

As stunned as he was by the assertion, he was saved by habits cultivated to shield against the venomous barbs of bored courtiers. He answered before he knew he'd formulated a reply. "As it would be a waste for you to not be a father?"

The Harat-Shar's voice lowered. "Well. I guess when you put it that way, it makes me sound a little hypocritical."

A soft beep sounded from near the ceiling: not a monitor, but the hospital comm line. Jarysh answered.

"Soft Fields Hospital."

"Yes, I'm looking for an Eldritch doctor. . . ."

Hirianthial nearly sat up. "Sascha?"

"Doc, come quick, will you? Mom says there's something wrong with Miri Salaena."

He almost asked if it was Salaena's imagination, but Sascha sounded frightened. With gentle hands, Hirianthial lifted his two sleepers onto Jarysh's lap, shattering their fragile dreams. He hoped the fragments reassembled after he'd gone.

"Hopefully nothing too serious," Jarysh said.

"I'll be back," Hirianthial said, answering the question

Jarysh had wanted to ask and failed to.

Sascha was waiting for him at the garden gate when he arrived at the house. "The midwife won't let anyone in," he said. "She said to get you immediately, but wouldn't say what's wrong."

"Thank you," Hirianthial said absently and passed the Harat-Shar, heading toward Salaena's resting room. He'd wondered when he first arrived what a closed door would look like in a Harat-Shariin home . . . now he knew. He knocked.

"Who is it?"

"The doctor," Hirianthial said.

Karya opened the door, and with it came a long wail and a smell that struck Hirianthial deep in the gut, like a knife there, like a memory.

"I think she'll be fine, though I want you to check," the midwife said. "I suspect she did it to herself somehow, though I can't find any evidence." After a pause, she added, "I haven't had time to clean up."

She looked clean enough. He didn't understand until he reached the blood-drenched bathroom. In the middle of the stench and the mess, Salaena kneeled, rocking and sobbing into her knotted night-dress. A swift sweep revealed a pebbly red aura, already smoothing as the cramps faded: her emotional distress was surprisingly mild, a bare wobble of gray and orange. The sense of the peaceful infant was, of course, gone. It hadn't developed enough to offer any more information to his mental touch and now it never would. If she'd had to miscarry, doing it early was at least less traumatic.

Somewhat less traumatic.

Hirianthial stepped into the bathroom, preparing to unpack the more sensitive, technological diagnostic tools. As he moved, Salaen stopped crying and lifted her tear and blood-streaked face. Her eyes glittered, and the sudden spear of violent crimson in her aura twisted her words into fierce, lethal things.

"You weren't there."

The words entered his mind, which filled with white noise. He knew there were sounds outside his head, but they seemed very distant.

You weren't there.

It wasn't the first time.

Very carefully, Hirianthial shut the door on Salaena. He walked, unsure of his footsteps, back into the outer chamber and past a puzzled Karya. He closed the second door on the chamber and stood in the hallway. He had no idea how long he remained there. Staring. Tracing the lines in the stone walls with dry eyes. Sensing from very far away the breeze against the side of his neck and jaw. Perhaps the fan made noise as its blades cut the air, endless toil.

". . . ial? Hirianthial?"

He blinked to clear his eyes and looked down and to one side. Sascha was standing there, ears flat against his skull. "Are you okay? You—there's blood—what happened?"

He should move. Leave. Go someplace where no one would happen on him. This sounded like the best course. The gentlest wisdom. Hirianthial forced his stiff joints to bend and walked, one foot before the next, toward where muscle memory dictated.

Did Sascha follow? He thought he heard someone talking. Best not to listen to people talking. People spoke without thinking. Short-lived people in particular.

One foot before the next. And the next. He thought of the pond with the geese, the one that children—*stop*—the one that would make a pleasant meditative retreat. He would go there.

"Boss, I need your—what are you doing?"

"Packing," Reese said. "I need to take a trip."

Sascha stood at the door into her chambers, one ear pointed up and the other out. His expression was a fine example of astonishment. Reese ignored it to toss another shirt onto the unused bed.

"You can't leave!" he exclaimed.

"Actually, you have that backwards," Reese said. "I can't stay. If we're going to get the money to get off this rock, I need to go arrange for our finances. I won't be gone long. I should be back in a week."

"No, you don't understand, you can't leave," Sascha said. "Hirianthial's breaking. You have to take care of it."

Reese paused, her nightgown over her arm. "What?"

"Hirianthial. You need to dissolve his contracts and put him back together. Better yet, take him with you. Get him away from here."

"I'm not taking him with me!" Reese said. "I don't need more trouble where I'm going."

"He won't make trouble," Sascha said. "He'll barely make noise, the way he looked just now. Take him with you, Reese, please."

Her irritation mounded into something more extreme. "I don't have time to babysit."

"If you don't do something you won't have anything to babysit, period," Sascha said. "Look, if being alone with him's what's frightening you I'll come along. Or ask Kis'eh't. Whatever it takes, just . . . just do something."

For the first time since he appeared, Reese took her time and looked at Sascha. Noticed the white rims around his banded irises. The fur standing on end at his shoulder-tips. The way he flexed his fingers, and the switching tail. With a frown, Reese said, "You're really upset."

"Yes!" Sascha said. "I haven't seen him look this bad

ever! Call that hospital, recall him. I've already told my mother to expect your message."

Uneasy, Reese turned to her data tablet and searched for the hospital address. "Where is he now?"

"I don't know," Sascha said, balling his hands into fists. "I should have followed him but I wasn't brave enough."

"He's not exactly scary," Reese said.

"He doesn't have to be scary to give off "don't come near me" waves," Sascha said. "Those are forbidding enough." He stood at her shoulder as she connected with the hospital. "He wouldn't answer me when I called. I'm not sure he even heard me."

The man on the other end of the hospital line was obviously loath to terminate the contract, but Reese reminded him of her prerogatives as Hirianthial's original employer and he signed the release. It bothered her that she could make decisions like this for all her crew on Harat-Sharii—simply choose to end whatever job they were working on. For a few moments after the call ended, Reese stared at her reflection in the data tablet's finish; she was chewing on her own lip.

With a sigh, she had Sascha build the call for his mother and informed her that she wished to terminate Hirianthial's contract with her.

"I'm happy to do so," Zhemala said. "We won't be requiring his services any longer and I was planning to discuss it with you anyway."

"Did something happen?" Reese asked.

The woman waved a hand. "I asked him to oversee the pregnancy of a sister-wife, but she miscarried. We have no more need of a doctor."

"That sounds unpleasant," Reese said.

"She would have been a troublesome mother," Zhemala said. "The Angels took care of it."

"I see," Reese said. "Do you have any idea where he is?"

"Not here, if the blood he tracked out of the house is any marker," Zhemala said. "He went out by way of the Lizard Garden."

"Blood!"

The woman shrugged. "Miscarriages are messy. I wish you luck finding him."

"Thanks," Reese said to the ending call. She turned to Sascha. "Sounds like he had a bad time."

"The Lizard Garden's the way he goes to the hospital," Sascha said. When Reese eyed him, he said, "You told me to watch him for you, so I did."

She sighed. "I didn't mean it literally."

"I know you didn't," Sascha said. "Let's go check the hospital grounds."

"I need to finish packing!" Reese said.

"You can do that later," Sascha said. "I'm not going to go looking for him alone. You're his employer . . . you come with me."

"His employer," Reese said. "That sounds so formal."

"Yeah," Sascha said. "Not at all the person you want to comfort you over something bad that's happened. For that you want friends."

"Oh, hush," Reese said. "I'll come with you. Isn't that enough?"

Sascha snorted and flowed out the door. She followed, looking in vain for the bloody footsteps Zhemala had mentioned; she supposed they'd already been wiped up. Past the Lizard Garden, it was a twenty minute walk to the hospital, where Sascha plunged into the grounds with a grim determination that did more to unsettle Reese's stomach than anything he'd said. They pushed through overgrown bushes, investigated secluded copses, trudged through flower gardens and over ornamental bridges. Reese had no idea how much time had elapsed since they began their hunt, but by the time it ended she was sticky, thirsty, and completely unprepared for the sight of Hirianthial.

They'd been apart for weeks, she reasoned. Doing separate duties. He'd been rooming somewhere else; she'd had no opportunities to see him, not easily . . . all a rationalization. Had she made the effort to check up on him, she would have seen this deterioration.

Reese stood in front of him, struggling to keep her uncertainty from transforming into anger. Sascha stood well behind her, nearer to the pond than to the bench where Hirianthial rested. He was too long for it; one leg rested against the ground, the other curled on top of it. His arms were furled against his breast. She wasn't sure if he was sleeping and she wasn't glad of the chance it gave her to see he'd lost weight, that there were real hollows in his cheeks. It made him look half-dead. It was terrifying.

"Hirianthial," Reese said. She stopped when her voice fluttered and rubbed her throat. "Are you awake?"

He didn't stir. She didn't want to touch him. Instead, she crouched across from him and addressed him face to face. "Hirianthial?" She thought of her romance novels. "Lord Hirianthial, awake."

His eye opened. Behind her, Sascha said, "Damnfeathers! That worked?"

She ignored the tigraine. "I need your help."

That opened both eyes. He didn't blink or look away. He usually let her go after a few minutes. Maybe he knew his gaze made her uncomfortable.

"Please," Reese said. "I need you to come with me to run an errand off-world. To get us some money."

"I—" He stopped, licked his lips. This time the words had volume. "I have duties."

"I've canceled your contracts," Reese said. "This was

more important."

He stared at her.

"Will you do it?" she asked. On a hunch, she added, "It has to be you. You and Sascha. One of you to drive me insane and the other one to keep me from joining him."

He didn't answer immediately. Reese tried not to fidget, but her heart was beginning to hammer when he finally said, "Which one for which role?"

"I'll let the two of you figure it out on the shuttle," Reese said. "Go to the hospital and pack your things, then meet me at the port in a couple of hours. No, one hour, in front of the Long Bird. We'll eat before we leave." She took a long breath. "Please."

"Yes, lady."

She didn't have the heart to take offense at the title. Sascha joined her as she retreated from the pond, and together they walked off the hospital grounds.

"You handled that better than I thought you would," the tigraine said once they'd started down the path back to the house.

"Yeah, well, I'm not all bad," Reese said. She sighed. "Thanks for doing what I told you to."

"I'm all over the delegation, boss," Sascha said, grinning.

"Right. Well, Mister Delegation, you go pack. I'm going to tell the rest of the crew where we're off to."

"Sounds good," he said. "Where are we off to, anyway?"

"Home," Reese said. "To Mars."

⇒ ◆ ⇐

Hirianthial ate because arguing with Reese about not eating took more energy than doing what she wanted. He followed her off-world because following her constituted a course of action, and he had no energy to formulate one of his own. The beginning of the trip involved several shuttle transfers that kept him tracking wayward baggage and investigating new quarters often enough to drive all other thoughts from his mind.

It was a form of meditation, in the end. He concentrated on the minutia of the trip, moment by moment. New flight numbers glowing on a board. The musk and sweat of a busy space station. The tinny sound of poorly-insulated insystem drives. Cheap carpet, barely soft enough to cushion metal floors. Beds too short for his body; ceilings too low for his height. Reese and Sascha arguing, out of affection, out of exhaustion. Their auras, tingling bright and dimming after too long cooped in a tiny shuttle.

The second-to-last leg was scheduled to bring them to Pluto's welcome station, a trip of two days. It was the longest of their rides and the most confining. There were passenger liners that connected there that would have brought them in lush comfort, but the best Reese could afford for their passage involved a single dormitory with bunk-beds and a passenger mess that doubled as a recreation room. Hirianthial avoided it, but Sascha and Reese took turns hiding there.

"The closer we get, the more irritable she is," Sascha said as he entered the dorm. "Angels on the fields! Even I want to throttle her. What on Mars could possibly be so scary?"

Hirianthial turned onto his side to look at the tigraine.

"And you're not helping," Sascha said. "You've said maybe two words this entire time. You want me to handle her alone? The least you could do is distract her from me on occasion so I don't have to deal with the brunt of it all the time."

That pang in his chest . . . guilt. Yes, he recognized guilt. "You seem to do well enough."

"Of course I do. If I stop talking, she'll brood and the longer she broods, the more explosive she is when she snaps out of it. My only hope is to keep her from getting too introspective." The Harat-Shar stopped across from their bunks and folded his arms, ears flattening. "Don't tell me I have to do the same thing with you."

"No," Hirianthial said after a moment. "I don't explode."

"No," Sascha said. "You dwindle. You implode. That's no good either. I wanted this trip to get away from this kind of behavior, not get socked in the face with it again."

That sparked something in him. "There was trouble?"

The tigraine wavered, eyeing him. Then with a sigh he dropped onto the floor and pressed his back against the bunk frame. "Ah, Angels. My siblings are going to drive me crazy."

"So it was as you feared," Hirianthial said.

"And worse. They want me to stay, and playing with them again has reminded both Irine and me about how nice family is." Sascha stared at his folded hands, resting on his knees. "Nice becomes cloying. And then smothering."

He could have sensed the shape of the wound in Sascha's words even if he hadn't felt the dull red shimmer under the flat gray in the man's aura. When Sascha didn't volunteer more, Hirianthial said, "I didn't know you had other siblings."

"With my father having seven wives?" Sascha laughed. "He'd have to be chaste. There are seventeen kits in the family, not counting me and Irine. Most of them are nice enough. It's just there's . . . well, there's some politicking. Even if we don't like to admit it, a woman wants her children to have the best of everything. Six other women with children makes it a competitive field."

"Your family seems prosperous," Hirianthial said.

"Oh, they are," Sascha said. "Thank the Angels for that." He scratched his ear. "It's so hard to say 'no' to family. You know?"

A wave of cold anger and mingled regret washed to the forefront of Hirianthial's mind. He remembered steel and brown blood. "Yes, I know."

Sascha sighed. "Sometimes you just have to get away. I didn't want to do anything I'd regret."

"Wise," Hirianthial said. "Of course, we'll be back in less than a week."

"Hopefully with the money to cut short our visit," Sascha said. "I can't imagine you'll be sorry to leave either. And don't go all silent on me. I'm not going to get offended if you tell me you hate Harat-Sharii."

"There are very few things I hate," Hirianthial said. "Your homeworld is not among them."

"But?"

"None of us belong there," Hirianthial said.

"Except Irine," Sascha said. "And I'm going to have to drag her away. She'll forgive me for it and the excitement of traveling will distract her, but I'll know in my heart that I took her away from her family. I don't like that. I don't like deciding for her, even though she won't mind."

"Perhaps Harat-Sharii isn't the best place for her," Hirianthial said.

"How do I know?" Sascha said; his aura had flattened to a morose black, sticky as tar.

"You don't," Hirianthial said. "But she'll choose to go with you and that's all that matters. It is her choice, *alet.*"

"Right. Follow me or get left behind."

"No. To choose the love of her brother or the safety and familiarity of home. Do not belittle her by diminishing the choice just because you know what she will choose. Instead be honored that her love for you is so constant you know what she'll choose before you even offer her the choice."

The black lightened to gray, more like rain than tar. After observing his own hands for a while, Sascha said, "I guess that's love."

"Such love is rare even in an Eldritch's lifespan," Hirianthial said.

"If you say it, it must be true," the Harat-Shar with a flush of green humor. He twisted to look up at Hirianthial. "I hope you've known love."

Faced with such friendly eyes and the suffusion of warmth in the tigraine's aura, Hirianthial could no more remain silent than he could stop breathing. "Yes."

"Good," Sascha said. He took a long breath. "I guess some people are always the actors and some the followers."

"Sometimes," Hirianthial said.

"And I'm an actor," Sascha said.

"Yes."

"And you're a follower."

Hirianthial paused, which gave the tigraine time to fill in the space. "So I'm telling you to pay more attention to eating. And to sleep better. Just looking at you makes me ache. And no more hiding away from the two of us, because Reese wasn't kidding when she said she'd need us both. I get the feeling it's going to be even worse when we finally get to Mars."

Startled, Hirianthial said nothing.

"So start being more intrusive, okay?" Sascha said. "I don't know how someone six and a half feet tall and dressed like a foreign prince can disappear at will, but you've been doing it for days now and it's not helping. Not Reese, not me and not you. Will you promise?"

"To be more intrusive?" Hirianthial said, finding humor in it despite himself.

"Yes," Sascha said. "To be more helpful."

"My help is not always enough," Hirianthial said quietly.

"Is that any reason not to offer?" Sascha asked.

"No," Hirianthial said.

Sascha nodded. "Good. So promise. And I mean that. I want to hear it out loud."

Hirianthial found a short laugh. "You aren't going to give up, I see."

"No. And trust me, we might not be very patient as a race, but we're certainly obsessive. You don't want me to get obsessive about you giving me your word."

"I certainly don't," Hirianthial said. "Very well. I promise I'll be more intrusive."

"Good," Sascha said. He stood and shook his head. "I don't know where you get this idea that you're no good to anyone, you know. Only a few minutes of talking with you and I feel better about everything."

Hirianthial thought it best not to respond to that and was doing well on that course when Sascha threw a pillow at him.

"Stop that!"

"Stop what?" the Eldritch said, sitting up.

"Withdrawing. You think you've got all the answers and that you're always right. Well, you're not. Keep that in mind. And go drink some milk before your bones get too old to hold together anymore."

"Dubious science at best," Hirianthial said, but he stood anyway and straightened his clothes. "Where did you learn biology?"

"In school, like most people," Sascha said. "Unfortunately, the teacher was really really cute. I couldn't concentrate on what he was saying; I was too busy posing him in my fantasies."

"Harat-Shar," Hirianthial said.

"To the marrow," Sascha agreed cheerfully.

Staring at the smoldering orange surface of Mars, Re-

ese suppressed the urge to turn around and head right
back to Harat-Sharii. Once upon a time she'd looked upon
the polar ice cap and the vast plains and dry seas studded
with habitats and felt a thrill that made her body tremble
and her breath catch in her chest. Now she saw only a giant, red reminder of her own failure.

"I'm going to get this over with," she said, turning to the
two men. "Our shuttle leaves around midnight; check our
luggage into a locker and amuse yourself here on Deimos
Station. I should be back in a few hours."

"You're not seriously going to leave us up here, are
you?" Sascha asked. "We didn't come all this way just to
hang out on a glorified asteroid."

"Oh yes you did," Reese said. "Besides, what's wrong
with Deimos? If you stay here, there are restaurants,
shops, gardens . . . all the convenience of the Alliance. I bet
there's even a way to entertain a Harat-Shar, if you go to
the wrong places."

"Yeah, but you put a claw on the problem," Sascha said.
"We could go to restaurants, shops and gardens anywhere.
There's only one place to meet the boss's folks."

"Well the boss's folks aren't interested in meeting you,"
Reese said. "You'll just have to make do."

Sascha's ears fell. Even Hirianthial seemed uneasy,
though it was hard to tell—he moved so little you had to
examine his face, inch by inch, just to figure out how he
communicated any emotion at all.

"Let us accompany you," the Eldritch said, voice gentle.

"No," Reese said. The word came out harsher than she
intended. She sighed. "Look, they don't like off-worlders.
Having the two of you around will just make it harder for
me to do this so . . . just let me do it alone, okay? I promise nothing will happen to me. I'll be back before you two
agree on a place to eat lunch."

"But—"

"We'll be here," Hirianthial said, interrupting Sascha. For once, Reese was glad of him. Just this once, though. She had desperately wanted the escort to Mars—the thought of making this trip alone, the same way she'd made it when she'd left, had proved too much—but she couldn't bring them with her. She just couldn't.

The shuttle down to Landing One rattled just as noisily as it had the first time she'd taken this trip. Reese gripped the thick restraints that held her in place while staring out her pinhole window. Joining the Alliance hadn't inspired all that much change in Terra's solar system, and the humans she'd grown up with had fallen into two groups: the bitter isolationists who were glad there were so few reminders that the Pelted existed, and the star-eyed expansionists who wished the Alliance would come and renovate until all of Terra's colonies and stations glimmered with the same wealth and technology as the many starbases planted throughout the Neighborhood. There had been little room to walk in the middle. Reese herself had never wished for a complete overhaul . . . but she wouldn't have minded much if someone had found some way to replace the older ships in the civilian space fleet.

No, she hadn't wanted the Alliance to come to her. She'd wanted to go meet it. If it had already swept through Terra's system, what impetus would she have had to leave?

What excuse, more like.

Landing Port had never looked dingy until she'd left and seen what passed for a port in the Core. Now Reese stood in the milling rush of people and smelled their sweat and the acrid high note of poorly recycled air and thought the port looked especially small. Had any Alliance engineer seen the high ceilings crossed with gray girders, he would have hung banners from them. Or found trained vines to climb along the ceiling as combination decor and air freshener. Some enterprising Tam-illee would have spray-painted the place a neutral but friendly color . . . or knocked the entire ceiling down and replaced it with windows. But Landing had been built when humans had been lucky to reach Mars, much less cling there, and the war that had disordered the Martian economy had also given natives a certain fatalism about remodeling.

Melancholy made her angry. Already clenching her teeth, Reese forced her way through the crowds disembarking from the Earth and Deimos shuttles and headed for the blue-station people-mover that would take her home. The township that included her family residence was the sixth stop down the rail and it wasn't a quick ride. Reese hooked a hand through one of the overhead loops and stared out at the naked Martian landscape as the people-mover glided through its protective steel and plastic tunnel.

Reese stepped off the rail and squeezed her way out of the station into one of the planet's giant hemispherical habitats. Here at last there was at least some room to breathe; trees stretched tall and thin by the low gravity helped the air-recyclers handle the load of the one thousand people living beneath the dome. This township, barely larger than the crew complement on the Alliance's warships, had been Reese's childhood. It was the largest group of people in one place she could handle.

It still wasn't large enough to keep her from getting home too quickly.

The Eddings household looked like a cottage, but hid a basement in the dense red earth that was twice as long as the ground floor. The property abutted the Wall; as a child, Reese had tried climbing over the hedges to touch it but had found an electrified fence awaiting her. She remembered staring at a landscape distorted by the thick plexiglass that shielded the habitat from the not-quite-right conditions outside . . . feeling safe. She didn't trust the invisible glass walls of the Alliance.

The flowers that lined the walk to the door looked much the same, but the tree—the eucalyptus Reese had hidden in, had climbed nearly to its topmost branches, had hung her hammock from—was gone. When the door opened for her knock, the first thing she said to Auntie Mae was, "What happened to the tree?"

"Your mother got tired of it raining kernels on the roof," Auntie Mae said. "We cut it down. Good gracious, child! You've lost weight! What are you eating out there?"

"Who's at the door, Mae?"

"Oh, it's Reese."

"Well for the love of blood and planet, tell her to come in! No use letting in all the dust."

Reese set booted foot on the braided mat inside the door and reconciled herself to actually having come home. Mae led her down the hall over wooden floors to the break-fast room, where her grandmother, a hunched figure with skin pink as dry flowers, was knitting by the table.

Her mother was pounding bread dough on the kitchen counter. "Well, lookie here! She's come home at last. How about that, Mother? Here's your granddaughter, just as you said."

"I told you she'd be back," Gran said, knitting needles clicking.

Ma Eddings wiped her flour-dusted hands on a purple apron and walked around the counter to clasp Reese's arms. She hadn't changed much: there were new creases around her mouth and the line between her brows had become more pronounced; perhaps her figure was rounder, or the gray in the short hedge of her hair a little paler. Reese couldn't tell. As her mother hugged her, Reese tried to unbend and hug back.

Auntie Mae took her place at the breakfast table. "You need some feeding, girl."

"I'm not hungry," Reese said.

"Of course you are," Gran said. "You just sit right down, Theresa, and let your mother make you breakfast."

"Nonsense," Ma said. "She's family, not a guest. You come over here and help."

So Reese donned the older battered apron, the white one that had faded to a soft apricot color, and helped her mother with the baking as the pink sky beyond the kitchen grew paler. Her aunt and grandmother fell into relaxed gossip about the neighbor's daughter, the mayor's new pet, how indecent behavior was yet again on the rise.

Butter on the table, glistening and warm; apple preserves and fresh honey; new eggs, cracked and sizzling. Within an hour, a hearty meal appeared on the table and Reese had heard more than she wanted to know about how her schoolmates had fared in her absence. She asked after Aunt Mabel and Great-Aunt Charla, discovered what had become of some of her cousins and heard that Gran had survived another routine heart operation.

They waited until the end of the meal to begin the real discussion. It had always been that way: difficult topics waited on the food.

"I don't know why you've chosen to come home," Gran said. "But I'm glad you finally have. You're getting old, Theresa, and your body won't be good for anything much longer."

"Gran, I'm only thirty-two."

"Yes, yes. You've only got three years."

"The operation takes better if you're thirty-five or younger," Auntie Mae said. "You know that."

She hadn't, but it didn't seem like the time to volunteer. "I'm not here to have a baby."

"We wouldn't expect you to start the moment you came home!" Gran exclaimed. "You need to settle down. Find the rhythm of Mars again."

"I'm not here to settle down," Reese said. Her stomach clenched at the ensuing silence. "I'm here to ask for a loan."

Another few moments of quiet. Then her mother: "What?"

"I need money," Reese said. "For repairs."

"You came here for a hand-out?" Auntie Mae said.

Reese flinched, but said, "Yes."

"You already have your inheritance, girl," Mae said. "Why are you coming back here for more?"

"I'll pay the family back," Reese said.

Gran lifted her head and squinted past Reese at Ma. "This is out of hand."

"What am I supposed to do?" Ma said. "I can't make her stay home. She's an adult now."

"She's not acting like one," Gran said.

"Not proper at all," Auntie Mae said, eyeing Reese. Unlike Gran and Reese's mother, Aunt Mae had brown eyes to go with her caramel-colored skin. They were all different colors, the Eddings, thanks to the traditions of Mars. "Haven't you been listening, child? You need to settle down. Send away for a baby."

"I don't want a baby," Reese said, stunning them all into speechlessness. She'd never had the courage to say those words out loud before. Recklessly, Reese went on. "I've never wanted a baby. And even if I did want one, I wouldn't want a . . . a mail-order baby by some man I don't even know the name of!"

"And how else are you supposed to have a daughter?" Gran asked.

"That's another thing," Reese said. "What's so wrong with having a son?"

Their stares had lost their unfocused shocky quality; one by one, starting with her grandmother, they hardened with suspicion and anger. After weeks of reading Hirianthial's restrained body language, her family's disapproval radiated with the subtlety of a dropped atomic bomb.

"The Eddings family doesn't have sons," Gran said frostily. "We have daughters. We don't need any meddling men."

"Obviously she's picked up some off-world notion about marriage and family," Auntie Mae said with a sniff. "Disgusting. Next she'll be telling us she's found herself some man. How on earth can you insure a child of fine quality when you mix it up with some man? Who knows where he's been?"

"Or when he'll leave," Gran said with a curled lip.

Which was, in the end, the crux of the matter. The men of Mars had softened its soil with their blood in the civil war with Earth . . . and most of the families that had remained had never recovered from the loss. The Eddings clan wasn't the only one to have made tradition out of necessity when it came to artificial insemination.

"I'm not mixed up with any man," Reese said. "I just need a loan."

"You're not home to stay," her mother said quietly.

Reese turned. "No, Ma. I'm still working."

"You could work here," her mother said.

Reese shook her head. "I've got a good lead on some things," she said. Which she did, if one counted a mysterious Eldritch patron. "I just need to do some repairs and I'll pay you back."

"And then, when you've succeeded, when you've made all the money you want . . . you'll come home?" Ma asked.

Reese hesitated.

"I thought she said she was going off to be a wealthy merchant," Auntie Mae said. "She was supposed to bring home more money for us. Not take it away."

Reese flushed. "I will bring you more money. One day I'll buy you a new house. A nicer one. And you'll have everything you need."

"We've got everything we need, Theresa," Gran said. "Everything but you. You think money's going to replace a daughter to take care of us when we get old? You going to shovel us into one of those living graves where other children without a bit of gratitude put their aging family?"

"Your duty's here," Auntie Mae said. "You stay here, have yourself a baby. Then you'll have someone to take care of you when you get old, and you'll be here to take care of us. We don't need money. We need you, child."

"I'm not staying," Reese said.

"You'd be welcome," Ma said, distracting her. Reese turned to her. Her mother was wiping her hands on her apron . . . slowly, very slowly. "We could use your help around the house."

"I can't," Reese said. "I'm not done living yet." She ignored the hostile quiet that descended after that statement and hurried on. "I just need to borrow money. I promise this will be the last time."

"You're right about that," Ma said. "Walk on out of here, girl."

"Ma?" Reese said, startled.

Her mother's eyes were cold. Blue eyes could be incredibly distant. "You leave now, girl. Don't come back either. Don't ask me for money. Don't you come calling. Don't bring us back some man-bred baby, either, if you settle down. This isn't your house. We aren't your family."

Reese's lips parted. "Ma . . ."

"I'm not that to you either. Go on, now. You don't belong here and you never did."

Her mother turned to the kitchen table and began
clearing the dishes. Auntie Mae helped; Gran returned to
her knitting. They all ignored her, as if she'd become part
of the peeling wallpaper, the furniture, the red sky. Reese
turned, shaking, and made her way up the short hallway
to the door. She let herself out, carefully closing the door
behind her and barely hearing the soft click of the lock.

She stood on the welcome mat for a few minutes. There
were no passersby: nothing but the still air and the distant,
distorted sky. Her bones knew the planet's drag, but everything else had changed, even the smell of things. Without
the eucalyptus, it had lost its richness, its spice.

Reese couldn't summon any anger, and anger had always been her best shield. She judged it best to leave
quickly before she had time to examine the notion of never coming back. The trip to the station took far too long;
Reese used it to work on figures, though she had to force
herself to concentrate on the blurry numbers. By the time
the shuttle docked at Deimos, she'd decided to take the job
offer from the man in the bar. The first half of the payment
would take care of repairs; the remainder would pay her
crew and give her some room for upgrades and cargo after
the assignment. It would get them off Harat-Sharii. The
man had assured her it was legal; that was good enough.

Reese arrived on Deimos Station after lunch and decided against finding Hirianthial and Sascha. Instead she
located the locker and sat on the bench outside it. She
tried reading some of the romance novels she'd bought before the trip, but the words moved, drifted, wobbled.

It was no use not thinking about what had happened.
Her mother had disinherited her . . . disinherited. Reese
rubbed her forehead. A pretty word she'd lifted from books

about princesses and royalty. What little she would have inherited from the Eddings family had already gone into buying the *Earthrise*. What more did she have to look forward to? A catalog featuring photos of smiling men with their vital statistics listed alongside? A mail-order daughter? A life without testosterone? Not that men weren't annoying, but things started to feel lopsided without them. Reese flicked to the cover of the latest novel and stared at the Tam-illee girl swooning in the arms of the Eldritch prince.

No, she still had a home: the *Earthrise*. Even if she could never come back to Mars, she had a place to go back to. She'd never really planned to come here, settle down and have a fatherless baby . . . had she?

Maybe she'd merely never planned that far ahead.

Reese spent several hours sitting in front of the lockers, trying to sort it out and failing.

"Hey, boss . . . how'd it go?"

"Sascha, do you have the ticket for our baggage claim?" Hirianthial interrupted. "I can't seem to find it."

"I thought you—no, wait." Sascha checked his vest and pant pockets, came up with a plastic chip. "I have the ticket after all. I'll be right back."

Reese watched Sascha disappear into the building, then squinted at Hirianthial. "You sent him away."

"You needed a moment to compose yourself," the Eldritch said, stopping in front of her.

She stared at his square-tipped boots. "I don't need you reading my mind—"

"Lady," Hirianthial said, "I don't need to read your mind when your body fair screams your dejection."

Reese straightened, squared her shoulders. "I don't look dejected."

He simply looked at her. It was one of his most disarm-

ing, infuriating habits: actually looking at people, instead
of glossing over them. She grew more and more uncomfortable until the absurdity of the situation stuck her. Her
family had kicked her out for good and she was worrying
about having an Eldritch stare her down. Reese managed a
weak laugh. "Okay, I am dejected—woah!"

Hirianthial kneeled in front of her—not quite kneeling,
but one knee down and the other up. It put his face on eye
level. He looked comfortable there, posing like a knight
for a book cover . . . except in the book covers, the fragile
Eldritch princes had always looked effeminate. Reese reflected on how badly they'd messed that up. Long hair and
long bones alone did not feminize a man. The fussy lace
cuffs, the camellias on the tunic, the blood-sparkle ring
on his finger, none of it mattered. It was all in the carriage.

"It will pass," he said.

"I . . . I guess I know that," Reese said, looking away.
The silence that fell was so comfortable she couldn't stand
it. Without deciding to, she glanced at him and asked, "Do
you have a home?"

"My lady?" He looked as startled as he ever did.

"A home," Reese said. "Like the *Earthrise* is mine."

"I hadn't really given the matter much thought," he said.

"Isn't it a hard thing not to know?" Reese asked, and
was rewarded by his eyes . . . closing. She wasn't sure how
he did it, but their warmth drained away. The result wasn't
hostile, like her mother's blue stare, just distant. Formal.
She hurried on. "Because everyone should have one."

"Of course," he said.

"Look, I want to give you an employment contract. Instead of you just . . . you know. Hanging around until you
get bored or I get frustrated."

This time she expected the stillness. She'd hit a nerve.
Maybe. "You don't have to take it. But everyone else in the

crew's got one and you deserve one too. If you want one."

The warmth returned to his gaze, as slowly as a spring replenishing. For once his smile was neither cautious nor tired, merely small. He never seemed to do anything large or loud; it made Reese wonder how he bore her. "I would be honored."

"Yeah, okay. Then get up, all right? Last thing we need is Sascha coming in on you like this and getting all sorts of ideas—"

"What sorts of ideas?" Sascha asked, dragging their bags behind him as Hirianthial stood.

"The wrong ones," Reese said. Hirianthial brushed the dust from his pants.

"Curse it all!" Sascha said, shaking a fist at the ceiling. "Why do I always miss all the juicy bits?"

"Oh, hush," Reese said. "Let's get the hell out of here."

"Aye aye, ma'am."

PART THREE: ICE

"I'd like to meet your boss," Reese said.

The man on the other side of the screen grinned. "You've decided to take the job?"

"If no one else has taken it yet, sure," Reese said. "The climate here doesn't agree with me."

The man guffawed. "Yeah. Harat-Sharii: you either like it or you don't. I'm zapping you a contract. You sign it, I'll connect you with the boss and he'll explain what you need to do."

"All right," Reese said.

Her mail chirped a moment later, and Reese spread the contract. Excepting the clauses about the acceptable delivery of cargo, it didn't resemble anything she'd ever signed before. Granted, she hadn't signed many contracts in her life; most of the time she bought up what looked cheap but profitable and tried to sell it elsewhere. This document had clauses about whether she could talk about what they were doing, whether she could question what she was asked to do, who she was allowed to contact after signing it for more details . . . it even included encryption keys for later information drops. Reese groped for her glass of water and read. And read.

After half an hour she decided the document sounded like the work of a paranoid merchant but not a pirate, so she signed it and sent it back.

Within minutes, the man reappeared. "I'll build the call for you."

"Thanks," Reese said.

The screen blanked for a sector map with a connection status bar; some kind of encryption protocol, but Reese didn't recognize it. The Riggins scheme dominated the high-security real-time transmission market. No one with any money or power used anything else. Reese suspected that most of the successes claimed by the lesser schemes were the result of no one being interested enough in the contents of their calls to intercept them. Which, in itself, was a form of security.

The man now facing her was human, corpulent with sallow skin and dark eyes rimmed in a webbing of flesh and shadows. Reese disliked him on sight.

"Captain Eddings," he said in a thin tenor. "So glad to have you on board. Now that we have your signature, please proceed to Sector Tau, to the solar system designated in the file I'm sending you now. Once you've arrived, you'll go to the planet there to fetch no less than two hundred pounds of crystals and no more than two hundred twenty. Use the instructions in the file to properly remove and store the crystals, then send a call to inform us that you have completed the objective. We will transmit a location for your drop-off. Is that clear?"

Startled by the recitation, Reese said, "Fairly."

"If you have questions, you may use the contact address specified in the contract."

"I won't be able to lift off immediately," Reese said. "I have repairs to finish on Harat-Sharii."

"We don't care when you leave so long as you deliver the crystals within the contract window."

"Right," Reese said. "Who am I talking to?"

"Pardon?"

"Your name," Reese said. "In case I need to talk to you again."

"Your contract is with Surapinet Industries," the man said. "That should be sufficient. We look forward to seeing you within three months."

Before Reese could object, the screen blanked and her mail chirped again. She grumbled as she flipped to the box and spread the message: a bank statement. A bank statement now much, much larger than she anticipated. She stared at it for several minutes, trying to grasp it, then shook herself out of her trance.

"Nothing talks like money," Reese muttered, and placed a call to the repair shop on Harat-Sharii. By the time the shuttle brought them back to the crew she'd have good news for them.

Returning to Harat-Sharii did not disturb Hirianthial's re-won equilibrium until Zhemala found him in his borrowed chamber.

"Would you mind seeing me in the Moon Patio? I'd like to discuss a possible single-service contract with you and Captain Eddings."

"Of course," Hirianthial said, when what he wanted to do was to send her away. Still, it was not his to do, so he found his way to the Moon Patio and set himself on a stool to wait. Slaves brought meat-and-cheese rolls and milk; not long after, Zhemala appeared with Reese.

"Have a seat," the Harat-Shar said.

Reese sat on the bench, her aura a suspicious green.

"A drink?" Zhemala asked, pouring herself a cup.

"What is it?" Reese asked.

"Milk," Zhemala said. "A morning drink."

Reese eyed the spiraled rolls. "And you usually eat this heavily for breakfast?"

She laughed, showing off pointed eyeteeth. "We are part carnivore. And we work hard. We need the food. Now you," she said, turning to Hirianthial. "There's a loose end here that we'd appreciate you tying."

"What do you mean?" Reese interrupted. When Zhemala glanced at her, she said, "I'm in charge, right? So I'm asking the question. What loose end?"

Zhemala stroked the top of her nose, wrinkling the fabric of her veil. "I asked your doctor to look over a pregnant co-wife."

"And she miscarried. I heard the story," Reese said, and the sudden spikes of scarlet anger leaping from her aura made her scowl seem mild in comparison. "You're not pinning that on him, are you?"

"Should I?" Zhemala asked.

"You only hired him for three hours a day!" Reese exclaimed.

"He could have prevented it," Zhemala replied.

"He may be as arrogant as a god but he doesn't have magical powers," Reese said acerbically. "If he's not there, he can't help."

"A good doctor would have seen the signs," Zhemala said.

Reese turned to him, and through his numbness he wondered at the indignant prickles that traveled her aura. Why was she defending him? His negligence was indefensible.

"Well?" Reese asked. "Were there signs you could have

seen a day in advance?"

"Often," Hirianthial replied.

Reese's eyes narrowed. "How often? And what kind of signs?"

"Often enough," Hirianthial said. "Bleeding accompanied by cramping and pain. A cervical examination would have demonstrated whether a miscarriage was pending."

"So either it happened very suddenly, someone forgot to inform you about all these symptoms . . . or there were other factors," Reese said, aura flattening. She looked at Zhemala. "You wouldn't happen to know about other factors, would you?"

Zhemala's ears pressed against her head. "I assure you I have no idea what you're talking about, Captain . . . but your point is taken. You would agree that the situation is irregular?"

"Only if you agree that a doctor on call for only three hours out of a day can't perform miracles if no one tells him there's something wrong," Reese said.

Zhemala turned her cup. "I suppose we might agree."

Reese folded her arms. "Fine. Now tell me why you called us here."

"We'd like your doctor to perform an operation for us."

"What kind of operation?" Reese asked.

Zhemala glanced at Hirianthial, her eyes sly. "We'd like him to sterilize Salaena."

Hirianthial's hands began to tremble. He clasped them tightly in his lap. "My oath does not allow me to perform permanent operations on individuals without their consent."

She laughed. "You've absorbed the culture well, if you've assumed that I made the decision for her. You'd even be right. But I'm not the only one who wants it to be done. Salaena wants it as well. Miscarrying the baby has only convinced her that she'll die if she has another. Everyone will be happier if you ensure that for us."

"I don't have a specialization in gynecology," Hirianthial said.

Zhemala nodded. "Nicely said. Quite true. But a dodge. You do have a specialization in surgery which would be more than adequate for the task. We're not asking you to do something difficult. A few twitches with a medical laser and you'll take care of a very difficult situation for us. We'll pay you well for the service."

"I am not moved by money," Hirianthial said.

"Then be moved by pity," Zhemala said, exasperation tingeing her aura orange. "Salaena needs your help."

"No," Reese said.

They both looked at her.

"It's my decision to make, right? I'm the only one who can release him to employment in town. Well, I'm making the decision. He's not going to do it."

Zhemala paused. "Captain—"

"I'm sorry," Reese said. "That was a little abrupt. It's just that I have too much for him to do before we leave. I can't spare him."

The Harat-Shar looked at Hirianthial again, eyes half-lidded, with an expression of such cloying sweetness he didn't need to read the steel-gray resolve around her to feel its falsehood. "That's too bad. I thought you'd like the opportunity to make up for what happened."

Hirianthial stared at her.

"You would, wouldn't you? You feel responsible. Salaena would be glad of your help. It would answer nicely for you not being there for her in her need."

"*That's enough.*"

Hirianthial hadn't heard that tone from Reese . . . ever. Her aura had expanded to twice its size and blazed fire as

she stood. "Zhemala, the answer is no. And if you're looking to pin the blame on someone, choose someone else.
But don't you go sticking it on my crew because it's more
convenient to point fingers at someone who'll be gone in
a few weeks."

The Harat-Shar's ears slicked back. "You can't blame
me for trying, Captain."

Reese's halo sizzled. "I most certainly can. Hirianthial,
we're leaving."

Struggling with ambivalence and guilt, he followed
her into the hall and all the way to her chamber. There she
turned, still seething.

"Did you unpack?"

"Lady?" Hirianthial asked, distracted by the roil of her
aura.

"From our trip to Mars. Is there anything in your
chambers that belongs to you."

"A few things, yes," he said.

"Go pack them and meet me at the cafe when you're
done. We'll bunk at an overnight house until they're done
with the *Earthrise*."

"Lady?" Hirianthial asked.

"You think I'm leaving you here? You're crazy. I'm not
staying either. This might be a fine place for the twins and
maybe Bryer and Kis'eh't are just too unflappable for it to
get to them, but we're not staying here a minute longer
than we have to. Get moving."

"Irine and Sascha will be disappointed," Hirianthial
said.

"Then they can yell at me when I arrange the crew
meeting later today," Reese said. "They're going to anyway
when they find out we're leaving."

He said softly, "She was right."

Reese squinted at him. "About what part?"

"About being there. I should have been there."

Reese growled. "If she'd wanted you there twenty-four hours a day she should have hired you for them. I'm not going to let her blame you for not being precognitive. Unless that's a secret ability you haven't let me in on."

He looked away.

"Damn it all, Hirianthial. Could you have known? Under the circumstances?"

"No," he said after a moment, voice hoarse. "Up until I left her, there were no signs."

"And no one called you to tell you she'd started cramping and bleeding?"

He shook his head, his hair barely brushing his jaw with the motion.

"So how the bleeding soil is this your fault?" She waved a hand. "Don't even answer that. It's obvious. It's not. They have no business putting it on you and you have no business taking it. Pack up your things and meet me at the cafe, and don't waste a single minute doing it. Go."

Hirianthial took the first few steps down the hall, propelled by the force of her command. When it dissipated, he stopped, staring at the corridor and realizing some part of him had responded to the conviction of her words . . . her absolute belief in his innocence. He looked over his shoulder at her.

"What?" Reese asked, aura crackling.

What to ask? How to quantify the tangled confusion? It made no sense to him that she would believe in him. "Why?"

Something in his stare unnerved her: the wreath of anger deflated and was replaced with an embarrassed wrinkle of brown and something mysterious and iridescent. With a shrug, Reese said, "Because you didn't deserve it. Because you didn't want to do the operation. Because it was the right thing to do." She glared at him from beneath lowered brow. "I'd have done the same for any of my people."

The spikes that popped through her crinkled aura during her final words boded no further information and certainly no good if he remained, but habits older than any of the people in the building stopped him. He turned completely and bowed. Without the speech of his people and its delicate mood-modifiers, he could not impart the grace and gratitude he had always in his words with his Queen, his first and current liege, but he willed them into his voice anyway.

"Thank you, lady."

"Just go pack your stuff." But she blushed pink all the way into the air around her.

"We're leaving?" Irine said, grasping her ears. "But we just got here!"

"Just got here?" Reese asked. "We've been here for a month and a half, Irine!"

"That's nothing," the Harat-Shar said.

Reese hadn't been able to find a room she trusted for privacy in the entirety of Irine and Sascha's family house, so she'd arranged for the crew to meet her on the cafe patio. Kis'eh't lounged along the sunlit table, relaxed; Bryer seemed neither surprised nor disappointed by her announcement. Allacazam was all-too-pleased in Hirianthial's arms, and Sascha wore a resigned expression Reese was certain had more to do with forthcoming troubles with his twin than with her decision.

"Look, we got a contract," Reese said. "A really, really good one. I'm getting our repairs done at one of the better shops in the port . . . I'm even making some upgrades! And for once you all have pay in your accounts. Isn't that the point of being traders?"

"But what about what the Fleet captain said?" Irine wrung her tail. "About staying out of the way of pirates?"

"That shouldn't be hard," Reese said. "We'll be going past the system where we ran into them. Way past."

"How past?" Irine asked.

"Sector Tau."

"Sector Tau! We'll be stuck on the ship for weeks!"

"Maybe the upgrades will be entertaining," Kis'eh't offered.

"You actually have money for once," Reese said. "I suggest stocking up on things to keep yourselves busy." She folded her arms. "Why is it that when we go on a short hop, everyone complains about the work, but when we go on a long hop it's suddenly all about having nothing to do?"

"Not complaining," Bryer said.

"Of course you're not," Irine said. "You barely talk."

Bryer canted his beak and looked down it at Irine.

"The decision's made," Reese said. "We're lifting off in a week and a half. Unless you object, I'll be terminating everyone's temporary contracts four days before we leave. Hopefully that's enough time to make your good-byes. Okay?"

They murmured their assent.

"Good," Reese said. "One thing before you wander. Our assignment's in cold weather, on what looks like to me to be nothing better than a glorified asteroid. We need to play Seek in very cold weather. I'd like you all to pick up winter gear."

"How cold?" Kis'eh't asked.

"Negative two hundred degrees, about," Reese said.

"Gah!" Irine exclaimed.

"She finally found some place colder than the ship to put you two," Kis'eh't said with a laugh.

"I'm not going into any negative two hundred degree

weather!" Irine said. "I'll freeze harder than a statue!"

"We all will without thermal bodysuits and masks," Kis'eh't said, amused.

"I want everyone to get one," Reese said.

"But . . . but they'll be expensive!" Irine said.

"There's extra in your pay-drops for it," Reese said. "Humor me, okay? We might not need everyone to go, but I do want everyone to be able to. Just in case."

"Good plan," Bryer said.

Reese looked around. "That should be it. I've already made the deposit, so go enjoy your pay."

That perked Bryer and Kis'eh't, at least. They headed for the portside shops, with the latter drawing away Hirianthial. Leaving the kitties with her, of course. Reese steeled herself.

"Was it something the family did?" Irine asked, turning a thin sugar wafer in her fingers.

"No," Reese said. "It's exactly what I said. A good deal dropped into our lap. I'm not going to turn down an offer that earns us enough to make the ship spaceworthy again."

"I thought you were going off-planet to take care of our funding problems," Irine said.

Reese shrugged. "And I did. Not exactly the way I planned, but it worked."

Sascha tugged on Irine's tail, which was looped in his lap. "It's okay, little sister."

"No, it's not," Irine said. She sighed. "I just wanted it to last a little longer. Just a little. It's the last time I'll be back here and—"

"The what?" Reese asked, just as Sascha said, "The last time?"

Irine's laugh was halting. "I know this might be hard for you to believe, but I've always felt like . . . I don't know. I had a destiny. Me and Sascha." Her ears drooped. "You don't usually earn those by staying home."

"But all this time!" Sascha said. "I thought you wanted us to stay here!"

"Of course I did!" Irine said. "I want to stay here! But it's not Destiny if it doesn't make it impossible for you to do what you want. If you could just choose to not do it and that *worked*, well . . . that wouldn't be very Destiny-like, would it?"

Sascha gaped at her. Irine touched his open mouth. "It was a test, I guess. And now we're leaving . . . and we won't be back. Not to stay. I was right."

"Oh, don't be silly," Reese said. "You won't be working for me forever and then you can come back."

But Irine didn't answer. Sascha tried to smile at Reese. "What do you mean we won't be working for you forever?"

"Well, I certainly hope I'm not working forever!" Reese said, though the joke didn't sound as funny as it had in her head. "I want to make enough at this to retire. At some point. In the far, far future."

"I wish I could see there from here," Sascha said.

"Me too," Reese said.

They were silent, then, and the world filled in for their conversation with the calls of birds and the chunks of conversation released by the door as it snapped open and shut on the cafe's patio.

"I'll miss it here," Irine said. "But that . . . that's okay."

"Blood and freedom," Reese muttered, and thought of Mars and wherever Hirianthial'd come from and now Ha-rat-Sharii. If none of them had a home, where would any of them go when it was all over?

"I was hoping you could help me," Kis'eh't said.

"If I can," Hirianthial said.

"There's a chemical synthesizer upgrade I'd been eye-

ing for a few weeks that I didn't have money to buy. Now
that I've got the money . . . it's just that it's a little awkward
to carry. If it were a single piece I might have towed it myself, but it's a handful of strangely-shaped pieces."

"Lead the way," Hirianthial said.

As usual, she didn't take him literally—few out-
worlders did. He wondered whether the egalitarian Alliance philosophy had been so deeply internalized in most
of its members that they simply couldn't interpret a request that subordinated the speaker . . . or if most of them
simply chose to ignore the words. For a moment, very
brief moment, Hirianthial longed for the precision of his
own kind; or at very least, for the social habits that simpli-
fied their lives.

Kis'eh't walked alongside him and in this way poorly
steered him through the stores along the dockside. Avoiding her body when she refused to walk sufficiently in front
of him to warn him of impending turns occupied most of
his attention, until she decided to talk.

"You don't say much."

"No."

"Is that because you like to listen to people or because
you don't like people to know about you?"

He glanced down at the top of her head; she was looking for the next turn.

"Does it matter?" he asked.

"You're evading," the Glaseah said. "I know the
technique."

"It's an honest question," Hirianthial said.

"I'm sure you'd really like to know," Kis'eh't said. "That
way you'll know how you're supposed to answer me: with
what I want to hear, based on your seemingly innocuous
question."

He chuckled. "Is 'both' an acceptable response?"

"Yes," she said, radiating yellow cheer. He was close enough to her to feel it as soft as a towel on damp skin. After a moment, she added, "Quiet people make me curious."

"Because you're so talkative," he said, indulging in amusement.

"Because I'm also quiet," she replied, missing the humor. She peeked at him through the strands of her forelock. "I know what I'm hiding inside. How can anyone else be less interesting?" Then she grinned. "And now, because you're polite, you won't ask me any personal questions."

"Of course not," Hirianthial said, allowing her to see his smile. "That would be uncouth."

She laughed. "And if I wanted to talk about myself?"

"I would listen," Hirianthial said.

She shook her head, still grinning. "Of course you would. And I know you'd actually care about everything I said. But not a word will I hear from you about yourself."

"I am far less interested in myself than I am in others. Why then would I discuss myself?"

Kis'eh't laughed. "Good question! Because everyone wants to know the particulars?"

"The particulars of a life as long as mine are quite tedious," Hirianthial said. "It's why we take up so many hobbies."

"And is medicine a hobby?" Kis'eh't asked, aura a friendly fuzz of gold, like the down on a baby chicken. "Or is it your calling?"

"It is work worth doing," Hirianthial replied, amused.

"That describes a lot of things. Is there any other work worth doing? For you?" Kis'eh't persisted.

"I'm sure of it."

She waited for more, and when it was not forthcoming white sparks frolicked over her aura as she laughed aloud. "I can see where this is going . . . today anyway. Fortunately, you'll live a long time and I have plenty of patience. Ten or eleven years of questions will eventually wear you down, right?"

"I'd be delighted to attempt the experiment, if it means in ten or eleven years I'll still be with the *Earthrise*," Hirianthial said.

Kis'eh't glanced at him sharply, then grinned and shook her head. "Finally, something interesting and just as we arrive. I'm sure by the time I come out you'll have hidden that piece of you again." She chortled. "Ah well. You can come inside or wait here, as you prefer."

Hirianthial glanced into the shop and saw immediately why she'd offered the choice. The tiny store had been crammed full of used electronics and machinery, and the corridors separating the shelves were so miniscule he wasn't sure how she'd managed to squeeze her bulky body through them.

"I'll wait here."

She grinned again, then vanished into the shop with her good humor. Hirianthial folded his arms and leaned against the wall. The stores nearest the dock had appeared gracious enough, large buildings standing alone, each with an eccentric facade. The rows behind them, where this store was located, became increasingly small and twined in maze-like confusion. The breeze barely found its way between the buildings, and when it came it carried conflicting scents: fried pastries, machine oil, sweat, hot dust. For the most part, everyone hurried through the warren as if chasing errands through the alleys. Their auras blurred into a sense of motion and purpose, and Hirianthial closed his eyes to the visual noise.

Perhaps it was the hiccup in that tapestry that alerted him, or perhaps it was the waking of older senses, honed long before he lifted his hand and swore never to take another life or allow another to be taken. One of the two lifted gooseflesh along his arms and on either side of his spine. His cautious scan snagged on a man standing at a corner. Hirianthial had never seen him before, but he was unmistakably watching the Eldritch . . . and the moment Hirianthial caught his eyes, the man wandered away, seeming to drift though his aura reported steadier purpose.

"Ready?" Kis'eh't asked at the door.

Without taking his eyes from the man's receding back, Hirianthial said, "Surely."

"Something wrong?" Kis'eh't asked.

He shook back his hair and picked up one of the boxes at the Glaseah's feet. "No."

She squinted at him. "You sure? You're no longer aimless-looking."

"Just a passerby," Hirianthial said.

"Probably curious," she said, picking up the remaining box. The others were already strapped to her second back. "How often do you get to see an Eldritch in person, after all?"

"Too true," Hirianthial said, though over fifty years in alien space had inured him to such stares.

After buying the requisite cold weather gear, Reese stocked up on more important things: books, bath lotion and scented candles. Lift-off day found her crew milling at the *Earthrise's* pad with boxes and bundles of their own.

"Did they actually wash her?" Sascha asked, ears akimbo.

"Maybe by accident," Reese said. "I didn't pay for it." She stared at the bulky freighter. "It certainly does look shinier. Come on. Let's get out of here."

They filed into the ship; Bryer closed the lock and they all dispersed to their stations. Reese eyed the corridors as she headed to the bridge, hunting for any signs the ship had been mishandled, but it presented an innocuous facade from its clean deck plating to the Harat-Shariin freshness of its air. Satisfied, Reese joined the Harat-Shar and Kis'eh't.

"New sensors," Sascha said. "Very nice. And a better power plant! We might get an extra kick out of those."

"I wanted a little extra to run amenities in-flight," Reese said. "If we're going to be in transit for a few weeks I don't want us to notice."

"And it's nice and warm, too!" Irine said.

"Enjoy it while it lasts," Reese said. "I had them overhaul the air handlers." Irine's whine was so piteous, Reese patted her on the shoulder. "I'll give you a few hours after we get underway."

"Way too kind," Sascha said. "I think she's happy to be leaving."

"I'm happy to be making money," Reese corrected. "Get us off the ground, fuzzy."

"Aye, Captain!"

"The environmentals are nice," Kis'eh't said, feathered ears perking. "You must have made quite a bit."

"Hopefully for not too much effort," Reese said as the engines began to hum. As it rose through the deck the sound massaged her heels, and a tension she hadn't even noticed released between her shoulder-blades, down her spine and into her hips. Wherever home was, it wasn't on Harat-Sharii . . . or Mars. Or maybe any planet. This little bubble of air and sanity, controlled by her: this was where she belonged. It even had enough people on it to keep her from feeling too lonely.

Irine's soft, continuous patter with ground control faded into the background as Sascha lifted the *Earthrise* into the blue and then the black. As the stars steadied through the tiny windows, Reese smiled.

"Where to, boss?"

"Sector Tau, and the solar system around Demini Star."

"Sector Middle-of-Nowhere, on our way. ETA, three weeks, about."

Reese fuzzled the top of his head and strolled into the lift, hands in her vest pockets. She felt like whistling. Maybe she'd try learning during their downtime. Her state of cheer remained until she stepped into her quarters and realized there was a bit of business she'd been putting off. Usually she didn't take the time to use the computer locator to find someone—hitting the all-call and just asking was faster—but in this case she consulted the diagram and hit the mess hall pattern on the intercom.

"Hirianthial, can I see you in my quarters, please?"

"On my way."

Without a "lady," even. Reese eyed the intercom grate uncomfortably, then shook her head and shuffled through files until she found the one she wanted. She was ready with it when the Eldritch appeared at her door, wearing a mildly curious look.

"I promised you a contract," Reese said. "If you wanted one."

He stepped inside; she noticed for the first time that he had to duck his head to do so. Bryer did too, but the Phoenix was almost seven feet tall and crowned with a crest of spiky metallic feathers. Having someone humanoid doing it unsettled her more.

If she sat at the desk her back would be to him. Reese lit on the bed instead and slid her data tablet onto the stool. She watched him, struggling with her feelings all the while. She did want him to stay . . . but she had no idea how to treat him. He was a nuisance . . . he also did *something* to the crew. They were all more content since they'd found him. She'd wondered if this was some solidarity forged by their adventure re-capturing him, but it seemed to include him. She thought. Maybe she was imagining things.

As he perched on the stool and read the contract, Reese suppressed the urge to touch him, just to see what would happen. His doublet had roses on it this time: cardinal red with white vines on a saltwater-blue field. Where did he find such finery?

Hirianthial let the tablet sag. "I could sign this."

"But?" Reese asked warily.

"But when I take on work in my professional capacity, I must re-swear my ethical oath to my new employer, who must find it acceptable."

"That sounds reasonable," Reese said.

He closed his eyes and shook his head, just enough to make the hair framing it sway. "You must read it and its alternatives first, Captain."

"Then let me read them," Reese said, holding out her hand. To her surprise he handed the tablet to her directly after tapping an address on it for her: a page of the Alliance's most common medical oaths and their implications. It was laid out so simply she checked the u-bank source descriptor: "For potential employers," in the category of medical information. Figured.

She read and grew more and more dismayed, but did her best to hide it. Once she finished the entire page, she set the tablet down. "You hold to the Kelienne Oath."

"While I am engaged as a doctor, that is correct," Hirianthial replied.

"Which is the most extremely non-violent oath on the list," Reese said.

"It is quite controversial," the Eldritch said, and if his expressions and mannerisms before had been subtle, now they were impossible to read at all.

"If I understand this correctly," Reese continued, "Not only can you not kill, you can't allow anyone to die."

"You have understood the Oath, lady."

"Isn't that unrealistic?" Reese said. "Patients die. You've said so yourself."

"They do. Kelienne doctors are tasked to prevent death at any cost, but they fail. Death is a practiced opponent."

Reese squinted at him. "So you have to give aid to your enemies."

"Yes."

"And if the choice is between, say, Sascha and a slaver?"

"The most grievously wounded gets the first attention," Hirianthial said.

Reese shook her head. "I don't like that at all. You have some dangerous people on your tail, or you did anyway. If you swear this, you can't protect yourself from them."

"It is the oath I swore," Hirianthial replied.

She looked at him. He was breathing, but she had to watch the patterned brocade near the crease of his arm to see the rise and fall of his chest. His stillness wasn't merely patient, it was attentive, somehow. Did he care about the outcome of this? Was it her imagination, or did talking about it bother him?

"You said at the beginning that if you took work in your professional capacity, you'd have to swear this oath," Reese said. "What if I offered you a contract as a general crewman? Would you have to swear then?"

"I need only renew my oath—and hold to it—if I am practicing," Hirianthial said.

"A technicality," Reese said, looking at the oaths. "I bet one no one thought of, because no one in the Alliance lives as long as Eldritch do."

His brows lifted.

Reese sighed and scrubbed the back of her neck. "Can

you do something else? Pilot? Navigation? Mechanics?"

"I have not turned my hand to those endeavors, I'm afraid."

Her roving eyes snagged on his outfit. "Trade much?"

He paused. How she noticed it when he wasn't moving, she had no idea—a rasp of breath, maybe. A slight pursing of his lips. "I have some understanding of business."

"And a lot of understanding of luxury items, I bet," Reese said. "If I signed you on as supercargo and Sascha broke his other leg, would you fix it?"

"Of course," the Eldritch said.

"All right then," Reese said, blanking out the job description on her contract and filling it with new boilerplate. "That's what we'll do. Understand there are no officers on this ship, so don't be getting ideas . . . we're all equals except me. I'm more equal than everyone else."

A flicker of a smile then. "Understood, Captain."

"Good," Reese said and handed him the tablet, holding onto its edge with as little of her fingertips as she could. "Here's the new contract." As the tablet slid from her grasp and he began to read, she said, "Isn't it a little extreme? Tending to your enemies . . . that doesn't sound good for self-preservation."

"It wasn't intended to preserve me," he said.

That casual moment, as nearly unguarded as she'd caught him ever, revealed a depth of disregard for himself that made her stomach clench and her mouth go dry. Did he really hate himself so much? And if he did go in for self-destruction, would he pull the rest of them down with them?

Hirianthial signed the contract and handed her back the tablet. Now his face was gentle and his demeanor courtly, his smile genuinely grateful. Taking the tablet, Reese wondered whether to be concerned or really, really worried.

A few days into their journey, the twins surprised Hirianthial by appearing at his door and then standing in it, the very picture of Harat-Shariin remorse. Irine twisted her tail in her hands; Sascha's shoulders slumped and he stood unnaturally straight, without a carefree tilt of the hip or spine.

"*Alet-sen?*" Hirianthial said.

They blinked owlishly into the dark almost in unison, and the flame off Hirianthial's candle reflected into their lambent eyes.

"Can we come in?" Sascha asked.

"Of course," he said.

They advanced just far enough to allow the door to close behind them and no further, and while Hirianthial was glad of the distance, the fact that they observed it was worrisome.

"Do you always sit in the dark?" Irine asked, her voice timid.

"Only when I'm meditating," he said.

"Oh, we're bothering you!" she said and began to back away.

"It's no trouble," Hirianthial said. "I would not have let you in otherwise. I would not have heard you."

"Oh." They grew silent, restive. Finally, Sascha said, "We've come to apologize."

Hirianthial canted his head. "For what?"

"For the way Mamer treated you at home," Irine said. "Sascha explained it to me and then I called home to find out what she was thinking, saying such things. And acting as if you were a slave instead of a guest."

"Your laws aren't always clear on such things," Hirianthial said. "Perhaps she had cause."

"Oh, no! No I don't think so," Irine said.

"She put you in charge of one of our most annoying mothers," Sascha said. "Not even a mother yet, as we would call her, but still a concubine. Sort of. The language doesn't work well for this."

"An annoying concubine," Irine said, taking up the thread. "Everyone knew she was a hypochondriac, and no one wanted her to get pregnant and everyone was relieved that she didn't manage it, but . . . "

"I admit I do not understand," Hirianthial said. "Gentletwins, your mother hired me to take care of your . . . her co-wife. While under my care, sorrow befell her. Her behavior was understandable."

"No it wasn't," Sascha said. "She tried to make you feel guilty for something you didn't have any control over. Something that everyone was secretly glad happened anyway."

"She agreed with the Captain that the situation was unfortunate and there was nothing that could have been done," Hirianthial said cautiously. "I am not sure what there is to forgive."

"The way she treated you!" Irine exclaimed.

Hirianthial wasn't sure whether to be suspicious or perplexed: their gray distress was too intense for something that would have been business to anyone in the medical profession. "She did not treat me badly. The woman I cared for miscarried, which she did not blame me for."

"The thing with the operation," Irine said.

"Was merely a request for another service she judged I would be able to provide," Hirianthial said. "She needed something done. There was someone adjacent she could ask to perform it. She did as one would expect."

They didn't do anything as obvious as look at one another, but his explanations weren't enough to send them away. After waiting for them to explain, Hirianthial finally said, "What truly is the matter?"

"You were distressed," Sascha said.

"Few people would fail to be distressed by such a sad affair," Hirianthial said, feeling his way carefully around the hole in his heart.

This time they did look at one another. "We don't know why it upset you so much," Sascha said. "But we know it did. You don't have to tell us why, but at least let us make amends."

He looked at their faces, first one, then the other. "It would soothe your hearts."

Irine nodded vigorously.

"It was an . . . unsettling thing," Hirianthial said, and pitying their unhappy silence said, "Children are so rare for Eldritch. The thought of destroying someone's ability to have them is distasteful."

A rush of golden understanding then, and a deeper blue sympathy. "I don't like the idea much myself," Sascha said.

"I'm planning on having lots of babies!" Irine said.

Hirianthial laughed. "That would be apology enough."

"No, no, we want to do something for you now," Irine said. "But not, I think, what other Harat-Shar would do as apology. You wouldn't like that."

"Probably not," Hirianthial said, still smiling.

"What would you like?" Sascha asked.

"I don't know," Hirianthial said, and knew by their instant green grumpiness that the answer didn't suffice. "But whatever it is, you should make it yourself."

That cheered them. "We can do that."

"Then that would please me," Hirianthial said. "Even more than your empathy does."

"We'll be back," Irine said.

"Not soon, though," Sascha said. "We need to think about it."

"Do that," Hirianthial said, watching their auras touch and meld into a busy brilliant gold. He wondered if they knew how deeply they were intertwined . . . or how lucky they were to have such a bond, when shared parents did not guarantee such affection. Would that he had been so blessed, and the swords beneath his bunk had slept.

"Ah-ha!" Reese said, stepping into the mess hall. "You are hiding something!"

The twins and Kis'eh't looked up with varying expressions of guilt; Bryer merely met her eyes, then continued scraping at a piece of wood he held in his clawed hands. The four were hunched over the table, which was obscured by a mound of colored thread and little odds and ends, none of which Reese could make sense of. Sascha had a pair of pliers and Irine's fingers were tangled in a braid of brightly colored floss being held straight by a long metal pin.

Reese pulled up a chair and straddled it. "So you've found yourselves something to do and not invited me?"

"We didn't think you'd be interested," Kis'eh't said when the twins didn't answer.

"Well, try it by me and see," Reese said, grinning. When none of them responded, she said, "Oh, come on. I'm getting bored of reading."

"We're making a dangle," Irine said and took a breath. "For Hirianthial."

Reese started laughing. "You're making him a present?"

Sascha nodded. "An apology-present."

"Instead of jumping him," Irine said, showing her teeth.

"What did you do to him?" Reese asked, picking up a piece of strangely shaped steel.

"He was upset by Mamer asking him to do that sterilization," Irine said. "We wanted to apologize on behalf of the family."

"Oh," Reese said, her humor draining away. She set the bead down.

"She's gone all quiet," Kis'eh't said. "That could be bad."

Reese shook her head. "No, no. I'm just wondering how you people found out he was so upset."

"You forgot I saw him when he was covered in blood," Sascha said. "It doesn't take a genius."

"I'm sure he sees things like that all the time," Reese said. "He's a doctor. People die."

"But not babies!" Irine said. "Besides, he said his people are infertile."

"He didn't say that," Sascha said. "He just said they have trouble having children, and that it makes him sad when people choose not to have them."

"He didn't say that either," Irine said. "He said—"

"They've been like this the entire time they've been working on it," Kis'eh't said.

"Minds too busy," Bryer agreed.

"You're involved in this too?" Reese asked him.

"The work is diverting," Bryer said. He unfolded his hands so she could see the wood in his fingers: a tiny bird with narrow wings, barely an inch long.

"I didn't know you could carve," Reese said.

The Phoenix wriggled his fingers. "Good exercise."

She didn't want to think of how sharp those claws had to be to carve wood. Instead she turned back to the twins. "How hard is it to make a bead dangle?" Reese asked. "You can't have been at this long."

"A week already," Sascha said.

"Have you seen how much hair he's got?" Irine added.

"I can't imagine how long it must have taken to grow it

all," Kis'eh't said, musing.

"And what are you doing?" Reese asked the Glaseah.

"Mostly synthesizing pretty baubles when the twins ask," Kis'eh't said. "It gives me a chance to use my new toy. Though I did contribute a bell off the edge of my prayer blanket."

"I've never seen you use a prayer blanket," Reese said as the Glaseah passed her the bell.

Kis'eh't chuckled. "I don't use it as often as I should. But that's okay. My work is a kind of prayer. The goddess who made the universe by thinking it into being likes scientists."

Reese looked through the pile. "How can you find anything in this mess? What's this?"

"That's a washer from a brace in the Well Drive bracket," Sascha said. "I thought it would be nice to have a part of the ship in it."

"I hope you replaced it!" Reese said.

Kis'eh't snickered; Sascha merely gave her a withering look.

"Will you add something?" Bryer asked.

Startled, Reese looked at him. "What?"

The Phoenix pointed his bill at the jumble on the table. "Will you add something?"

"Everyone else is," Kis'eh't said.

"Even Allacazam?" Reese asked.

"He offered to sit on it when it's done," Irine said. In response to Reese's look, the tigraine said, "Well, he doesn't exactly have any things to contribute."

Reese leaned over and looked at the experiment: a combination of beads, strange ornaments and braided floss, it existed in several pieces; already woven into the strands were several tiny flexglass spheres filled with rosy liquid, a silver toe-ring with an inset garnet, and four incised spirals of steel. The dangle gave the impression of rose and silver and steel and glass, and for all its chaotic assembly had its own harmony. She could imagine it working with his dark wine eyes.

"So I'm supposed to be part of the apology?" Reese asked with a chuckle she didn't entirely feel.

"Not exactly," Irine said. "I think the fact that we're making it is the apology, but the things that are going into it are gifts from everyone. You could be part of it too."

"Just think," Kis'eh't said. "He could still be wearing it centuries after we're all dead."

"Bleh!" Irine said.

Reese privately agreed.

"Do you want us to save you a space?" Sascha asked casually, bending a fitting around a diamond-shaped charm.

"Maybe," Reese said.

"Scared," Bryer said.

"I am not," Reese said. "I just think it's a little silly, is all."

Irine frowned. "Our apology is silly?"

"No, no, not that," Reese said. "It's just... well, when have you ever seen him wearing something like that?"

"All the more reason to make him one," Irine said.

"Scared," Bryer said again, shaving another miniature curl from his bird.

"I am not," Reese said, then waved her hands. "I'll go get something."

"Yay!" Irine said.

"I'll be back," Reese said, pushing away from the table.

"Make it something good," Sascha called.

Reese snorted and left them in the mess hall. She reached her quarters before she realized she was stomping and grumbled about that. Nor was Allacazam in her hammock, which irritated her more. In the end, she dropped onto her unused bunk and stared at the laundry she hadn't yet put away.

She should just bring back one of the chalk tablets she'd eaten like candy before the man had replaced her esophagus. It would serve him right. And the peppermint ones were pink, which would match. What did they think they were doing, making him jewelry? As if he could care about them... one day, they'd all be dead and he'd still be around, forgetting them.

Reese was still on the bunk when the door chime rung.

"Come in," she said.

Irine padded inside and sat next to her without asking permission.

"Don't be mad," the tigraine said.

"Why would I be mad?" Reese asked.

"Because we've never given you a gift like this," Irine said.

"I wasn't thinking anything like that," Reese said.

"Oh yes you were," Irine replied. "It was on your face when you left."

"You must have mistaken me," Reese said.

Irine snorted. "Are you jesting? You think a Harat-Shar doesn't recognize jealousy? You're crazy. You must have forgotten how many people I grew up with."

Reese folded her arms across her chest and ignored the tail that wrapped around her waist from behind. After a moment she said, "Well, why haven't you given me something like that?"

"You won't like the answer," Irine said.

"I'm not surprised," Reese said.

"You didn't seem like you'd want it."

"And an Eldritch would?" Reese asked, incredulous. "Has he given you a reason to think he'd care more about you than I would?"

"It's more like he's given us fewer reasons to think he wouldn't," Irine said.

Reese scowled. "Try that one again."

Irine sighed. "Hirianthial is just mysterious. You're prickly."

"You're saying I push people away."

"See? You knew exactly what I meant," Irine said. Her tail tip twitched against Reese's ribs until finally Reese had to pet it, just a little.

"I don't mean to be prickly," Reese said.

"We know. And we like you too. We're just not quite sure if you like us. All the time."

Reese stroked the orange fur a few more times, then unwrapped herself from the tigraine's tail. She walked to the bathroom and opened one of the drawers, picking through the contents until she found a plain wooden box in the back. Maybe petting Harat-Shar tails gave a person supernatural sensitivity... or maybe the wood simply seemed finer than usual because she hadn't touched it for years. Reese opened it and selected one of the blonde beads in it, rolling it between her fingertips and savoring the wood's cool, spicy fragrance.

Irine approached, stood in the bathroom door.

Reese gave her the bead. "Here."

"I've never seen you wear these," Irine said quietly.

"I stopped wearing them long before I hired you and Sascha," Reese said.

"Why'd you stop?" Irine asked.

"I didn't want them to lose their smell," Reese said. "They were special."

The tigraine's ear flicked forward. "Something changed?"

"I thought those were better times," Reese said and patted Irine's fingers closed over the bead. "I was wrong."

The tigraine engulfed her in a sudden hug, all fur and musk and swift Harat-Shariin heartbeat. Reese was so surprised by it she almost forgot to hug back. But then she did and she thought she could get used to it.

The raspy lick up her cheek, though, was too much. "Irine!" Reese said, laughing.

The Harat-Shar beamed. "I couldn't resist."

After the girl had left, Reese studied the box with the remaining beads. She wondered what to do with them. As remnants of Mars, she supposed she should burn them as unnecessary reminders of life before the *Earthrise...* but they smelled too good, and their tree would never grow another branch to replace the one she'd used to make these. It seemed like a waste to destroy the far-flung remnants of an uprooted tree. Reese closed the box and hid it back in the drawer.

"We have your apology ready," Irine said at the door. "Can we come in?"

Hirianthial set his book aside. "Of course."

Sascha followed Irine inside, carrying a thin case . . . and then Kis'eh't entered, holding Allacazam, with Bryer trailing. His room could barely hold them all at one end, and yet he was so surprised to see them that he couldn't quite concentrate on the mental noise of their presence.

"This is quite an entourage," he said.

"Everyone helped," Sascha said. "So everyone wanted to see you receive it."

"Except Reese," Kis'eh't said, settling onto her haunches with Allacazam between her forepaws.

"Scared," Bryer said.

"She's not scared," Irine said. "She helped too."

Hirianthial's brows rose.

"It's our apology to make, so we made it," Sascha said. "But everyone contributed materials." He opened the case, brought it to the opposite edge of the bunk and turned it so that its contents caught the light.

"Jewelry?" Hirianthial asked, reaching for it.

"Hand-made!" Irine said proudly, just as his fingertips brushed it—

—and his eyes lost the room in a wave of good will and contentment. His fingers caught on a square token, and he saw Bryer accept it in exchange for an offering in a temple. Beneath it, a ring Irine had bought at a bazaar to fight a heartache that had seemed eternal at the time. The hum of a Well Drive; the creak of a tree in the breeze and a sense of loneliness and determination; each sensation building on the next from the thinnest crystal at the top to the dusty bell at the bottom, perched on a long braided pin and vibrating with a chorus's soaring song in a Glaseahn siv't.

Never in his life had an object spoken to him, nor had he ever heard of an Eldritch having such an ability. And yet the feelings were there: the taste of herbs steeped in wine, the wail of a far-ranging ocean tern, the imbued warmth of Allacazam's crumpled neural fur.

He was so shocked he almost dropped it.

"Is it okay?" Sascha asked with a hint of worry.

"I am . . . I am overwhelmed," Hirianthial said. "I have never received such a generous gift."

They all smiled then, save Bryer who mantled his feathers and leaned back against the wall. Looking at them while holding the flashes of their lives in his hands, he knew he owed them the trust they had unknowingly given him.

"Would you do aught else for me?" Hirianthial asked.

"More!" Kis'eh't said with a laugh. "We should go into business."

"This you will not be able to sell," Hirianthial said, allowing laughter to touch his eyes.

"Of course," Sascha said. "Just ask."

"Braid it in."

Silence fell, along with Irine's jaw. Only Allacazam seemed to find the situation as humorous as he did, blooming a bright magenta in patches across his body.

"You want us to touch you?" Irine said with a squeak in her voice.

"If you're careful you need not," Hirianthial said.

"But we'd have to get very close to you," Sascha said, eyes wide.

Hirianthial nodded. "Would you be willing?"

The twins looked at one another, then at Kis'eh't. "You do it."

"Me?" Kis'eh't laughed. "No, no."

"But you're not . . . you know."

"Not hormonal?" Kis'eh't said. She snickered. "No. It's your apology to make, remember?"

The twins looked to Bryer, who clicked his claws together. "Hair too soft."

"Surely I'm not so frightening," Hirianthial said.

The twins looked at one another. "You braid," Sascha said. "You have better fingers."

Irine looked her hands, which trembled even when viewed at a distance. She whimpered.

Sascha approached, one cautious step at a time, as if stalking a skittish animal. Hirianthial watched him come, hiding a laugh.

"Where do you want it?" Sascha asked. "Near the top of your head?"

"Oh no," Hirianthial said, distracted from the task of putting them at ease by the wrongness of the idea. He shook his hair off to one side and said. "Here, behind the ear."

"Near your skin?" Irine said, aghast.

He did laugh this time. "Come," he said. "I'll make it easy for you." Bracing himself against the bunk, he leaned back until the lowest layer of hair, still warm, stood apart from his back.

Neither of them rushed to his side. He sensed from their auras that they were staring; Irine's thought was so loud it broke past his careful ignorance of people's thoughts: *Oh-my-I-want-some-of-that!*

When the silence dragged on too long, Hirianthial said, "Gentlefolk, I am no longer so young that I can hold this shape indefinitely."

Sascha shook himself, then swooped behind the Eldritch. A moment later the weight of his hair, so habitual, lifted from his skull.

"Wow," Sascha said. His gulp was audible. "I'm actually touching you!"

"My hair isn't exactly my body," Hirianthial said.

"No, but it's attached to it!" Sascha said. "This is the closest I've even been allowed to an Eldritch."

"Does he feel any different from a human?" Kis'eh't asked.

The grip on his hair shifted. "I don't know. I mean . . . oh, I don't know." After a moment, "This is really heavy."

"One becomes accustomed to it," Hirianthial said.

"Come on, Irine!" A thin happy thought behind it, run together: *Oh-you-have-to-feel-this!*

Irine hovered at his side, wiggling her fingers. She picked a lock so carefully he couldn't bear to tell her how loud her aura was despite her efforts. "Is this okay?"

When the dangle fell it would run along his neck and down near the center of his spine. "Yes."

She leaned over and plucked the dangle from the box in his hands, pressing in against his aura with her own densely packed one: so many feelings and thoughts, most of which would be wildly inappropriate if mentioned aloud. But she spoke none of them and the nervous gloss over her space shouted how much she feared discomfiting him.

It had been a very long time since someone had done this service for him; very long indeed since he'd allowed anyone this close to him by choice, rather than from necessity or in the course of his duties. With his eyes half-closed, Hirianthial experimented, allowing himself to sink into the sensual pleasure of it . . . and each time the end of the strand brushed against his body it tingled against his senses, mental and physical.

"How do you brush all this?" Sascha wondered.

He roused from reverie. "With a comb."

Kis'eh't chuckled.

"It's too straight to tangle," he finished.

"You must have been growing it forever," Sascha said.

"It would have been inappropriate to cut it," Hirianthial said, thinking of customs older than any of the species in the room.

Irine tugged on it, setting the bell to singing. "There. You'll have to take a knife to it to get it out."

The rest of his hair slid through Sascha's fingers until it pressed on the dangle, hiding it from view.

"Umm . . . I hope that's what you wanted, at least," Irine said, coming around in front of him.

"Yes," Hirianthial said. "That's just as I'd have it. I can feel it now." He lifted his head. "It is a magnificent gift. A kingly thing."

"Are you sure we can't apologize properly?" Irine asked with a glimmer of pornographic hope.

Sascha elbowed her. "We're glad you like it. We had a lot of fun putting it together."

"Show's over," Bryer said, straightening from the wall. Kis'eh't picked up the still pink Allacazam as the Phoenix walked out into the corridor.

On the way out, Irine said, "Even Reese added

something."

"I know," Hirianthial said, feeling it between his shoulder-blades.

"We already said that," Sascha said, chivvying her out.

"Gentle-twins," Hirianthial said just before they left. When they paused and looked back, he said, "The apology has far exceeded the sorrow that inspired it."

They grinned and left, tails twined together.

Once the darkness and quiet of his room seeped into the spaces the aliens had been and filled in their outlines, Hirianthial pulled the strand over his shoulder and turned it, watching the light glint off the bits of metal and glass, play over the wood and thread. At home he had worn the Eldritch equivalent as custom dictated, ornate, gem-encrusted things as heavy as the silver belts worn by women around their corseted waists. Each day a body-servant would select a new one and weave it in, using a long-handled brush and a hand so deft no part of his aura ever contacted his master's; the experience was the opposite of what had just happened in every way.

The Alliance had similar ornaments; he'd seen them braided into the hair of humans and Pelted alike. He'd never felt the urge to imitate them. This, though . . . Hirianthial turned off the light, then stretched himself flat on his stomach and felt the wave of affection shift across his back, edged with flashes of smell and sound and sight like falling glitter.

Fifty-odd years he'd spent wandering without purpose or plan, stumbling onto each succeeding course of action without building toward anything. He'd become a doctor because he couldn't bear the guilt of his own failure with Laiselin and then later the blood he'd spent justly but in too much passion. After that, he'd tended the sick because doctors did that, but all of the deaths he'd prevented had never taken away the deaths he hadn't been able to or had himself caused, the ones that had driven him away.

And then allowing the Queen to send him on her errands, not caring if he died in the process, since life had seemed long enough. His joints had already stiffened . . . the days had grown harder and longer.

He'd drifted, who'd always loved the hearth.

The twinkle of a Flitzbe's amusement scratched against the back of his neck as he shifted. Irine laughed; the bell tinkled.

Had these people opened his heart? Or had his heart merely been ready to be open?

Did it matter?

At last, he was no longer anyplace but there. Now he was here. A place in itself. A place worth staying.

Hirianthial closed his eyes and let the sensations of a half-dozen minds and hearts anchor him in place as he fell asleep.

"We've been rising out of the Well for a few hours," Sascha said. "It shouldn't be long before we coast to a stop. Maybe fifteen minutes now."

"Good," Reese said, leaning over his chair.

"Sick of us already?" he said with a grin.

"I didn't say that," Reese said.

"She was just thinking it," Kis'eh't said from her station. Reese sighed.

"Don't worry, Boss. A couple days harvesting whatsits and we can go collect your chest of treasure."

"Maybe we can buy something fun to sell finally," Reese said. "Exotics. Hand-woven textiles. Religious items. Art."

"We could check the latest colonies," Kis'eh't said. "I've been reading the bulletins and a couple of new ones have popped up. Neither of them have dedicated shipping or

Pads yet."

"That sounds promising," Reese said. "Maybe our drop-
off point won't be too far up-Core. Then it won't be quite
as long to get to the edge of settled space."

"Coming out of the Well," Sascha said, then cursed and
yanked the *Earthrise* so hard to starboard Reese staggered
against the wall.

"Sascha!"

"Pirates!"

Reese grabbed the back of the pilot's chair. "Where?
How many? Have they seen us?"

"Two," Sascha said. "They're near the first asteroid belt."

"What are they doing in the middle of nowhere?"
Kis'eh't asked.

"Maybe they're after our crystals," Reese said. "Have
they seen us?"

"I don't think so," Sascha said. "I sent us onto a new
insert. One pretty distant from where they're drifting. If
we coast—"

"Let's do that," Reese said. "At least until we figure out
where they're heading. Maybe they're on their way out of
the system."

"Let's hope," Sascha said.

"Trying to break the new engines?" Bryer asked
through the intercom.

Reese leaned on the button. "Pirates, Bryer."

"Unexpected."

"So say we all." Reese switched to the all ship and repeated, "We've got pirates. If Sascha starts twisting the
ship into knots, you know why. Sit tight, we're going to try
to slip past them to our destination."

"Gee, get them all hopeful, why don't you?" Sascha
muttered.

"You can do it, fuzzy," Reese said. "If I have to I'll pet

your arm myself to help you concentrate."

Sascha laughed. "No, no, don't do that. I'd be too distracted by the novelty. Just let me work."

In the following half hour, Reese glared at the plot on the station next to Kis'eh't's, waiting for the red blips of the ships to do anything more threatening than glide in place. They never changed course, riding herd on their cluster of asteroids.

"Have they missed us?" Reese wondered. "Or do they just not care?"

"They might not be able to see us," Sascha said. "You just upgraded our scanners, remember? And pirates aren't typically that well equipped."

"Maybe cleaning the hull made it so sparkly it burned out their sensors," Kis'eh't said.

"I don't think the ship was that shiny even when it was new," Sascha said.

The *Earthrise* continued its approach to their destination, an unprepossessing planet on an irregular and distant orbit from Demini Star. The plot showing their trajectory and the assumed paths of the pirates continued to bore, though there were points Reese thought would give the pirates a full view of them.

"I knew I was forgetting something," Reese said.

"What's that?"

"Guns," Reese said with a scowl.

"No use now," Kis'eh't said. "They don't look too hostile, though."

"They might be waiting for us to do all the work," Reese said. "How long before we grab orbit?"

"Three hours, twenty minutes. And it'll seem a lot longer if you don't start blinking occasionally."

"Yeah, why don't you go get something to eat?" Kis'eh't said.

"Food's the last thing on my mind," Reese said. "I'll go organize our landing party. Maybe we'll get lucky."

"With all the bad luck we've had lately we're bound to have some happy soon," Sascha said.

"We've had bad luck?" Kis'eh't asked.

"Don't answer that," Reese said. "I don't want to tempt anything that might be listening. Call me if something changes."

"Don't worry," Sascha said. "If something changes, you'll know."

The instructions she'd received after signing the contract had been specific to the point of monotony. In accordance with the exhaustive requirements, Reese had purchased three five-foot by three foot by three foot boxes made of steel, each with a cushioned layer and five layers of insulation. They looked like coffins and handled just as clumsily on the mechanical dollies the contract specified, probably out of a paranoid fear that anti-gravity sleds dropped their loads if their power failed. Reese leaned on the intercom.

"Bryer? Could you come by Bay 2?"

"Coming."

While she waited, Reese flipped through the maps supplied with her information packet. The areas that had been designated as "harvest sites" were on plateaus too small for the *Earthrise* to land. They'd have to set down on one of the lower stretches and climb to the top. She'd bought block and tackle to lift the boxes to the harvest site, but the entire task struck her as more manual labor than she liked. She hadn't picked her crew based on how many pounds they could lift or how severe a climate they could survive.

The Phoenix arrived and eyed the boxes.

"I need them moved," Reese said. "Out to Bay 5."

He eyed the boxes. "Five?"

"It's got the biggest airlock," Reese said. "The less we jostle these things, the better."

Bryer flexed his coverts, something Reese usually interpreted as a shrug. "Fine."

They approached the first box together. Bryer took one end and she braced herself at the other. "Ready? Now!"

They lifted it with barely enough clearance to make it onto the dolly bed, a maneuver that required them to shift their feet and pivot together. Reese's shoulders and arms were shaking, and before they could begin the turn Bryer set his end down.

"Hey!" Reese said.

"You will break something," the Phoenix said.

"I will not," Reese said, annoyed. "It's only a few seconds while we get the things onto the dolly and that's it. I can do it."

"You will break something," Bryer repeated. "Get the man."

"Sascha is busy," Reese said. "I'm not taking him out of the pilot's chair while we're sneaking around a system full of pirates."

"The other man," Bryer said.

Reese snorted. "You want me to believe an Eldritch is stronger than me? If we need help, I'll call Irine."

"Irine is too small."

Reese glared at Bryer. "We can do this. We will do this."

"I will not."

She frowned and straightened, folding her arms. "What's wrong? You're never this obstinate."

"You require this."

"Excuse me?"

He canted his head and studied her with one eye. Phoenixae had blind spots directly in front of their faces, but she'd never quite grown accustomed to having Bryer look at her sideways. Kis'eh't had more legs. Irine and Sascha shared unmentionable acts. Bryer staring her down like a real bird somehow struck her as more viscerally alien.

"You require this," Bryer said again. "Your sight is clouded."

"Clouded," Reese repeated.

"By the Eldritch," Bryer said. "He closes you to the Eye in the Center of the Void."

Reese opened her mouth to argue and then stopped. It was useless to argue with someone whose religion considered visible emotion evidence of sin. "I don't see it that way."

"That matters less than how it causes you to act."

Full sentences out of Bryer were rarely a good sign. "I don't see that I'm acting much differently."

"You wouldn't. You are closed to the Eye and its omniscient truth."

Her head started to throb in time with her shoulders. "And if I call him down here to help you, everything will be better?"

"A start," Bryer said.

Anything was better than discussing her fitness as a practitioner of an alien religion. Reese went to the intercom with alacrity and called for the Eldritch. She stood next to the wall and fidgeted until he showed up . . . which he did. Dressed in a brown leather jerkin and pants, with a wool shirt and leather gloves tucked into his belt.

"Captain?"

At least he was using the right title. "I'm not sure if you can help, but Bryer requested you," Reese said. "We need to get these boxes to Bay 5."

He eyed them.

"They're heavier than they look," Reese said.

"They have a sinister mien," Hirianthial said.

"I noticed," Reese said as he walked around to the end of one of the boxes and glanced at Bryer. The Phoenix stationed himself at the opposite end. "Look, you don't have to do this. I know about surgeon's hands and all that—"

They lifted the box onto the dolly. A few moments to synchronize and the thing was replanted. Reese gaped.

"A surgeon's hands are useless if they can't be used," Hirianthial said. He wheeled the dolly through the door and vanished down the corridor until even the click of his boots on the deck plates faded.

"How exactly is this unclouding thing supposed to work?" Reese asked.

Bryer directed his eye at her. "You must look more closely."

So she slouched against the wall with her arms folded over her ribs and did her best to observe everything. She was used to the sight of Bryer's body in motion, a strange collection of feathers and scales and muscles moving at unexpected angles and with a choppy abruptness that surprised the eye. She'd never seen him in full flight and her attempts to imagine his wings outstretched had never yielded a coherent image, but at least his stiff metallic feathers were familiar, sprouting all the way from the base of his smallest finger to his arm near the pit. She supposed he had muscles like everyone else, but watching him on his end of the box she had to guess: she couldn't see anything past the scales.

Hirianthial moved enough like a human that his grace disconcerted her. No one should disturb the air so little. As he gripped the edge of the second box, his hair swirled against a shoulder but didn't foul his grip or his legs; somehow, knee-length hair never got in his way, and that was the most apt way to describe him moving. Every part of him ended up exactly where it should, no matter how difficult or how much strength or focus it required. She expected him to show strain but he didn't. She expected him to act weak but he never did. Eldritch were supposed to mince. They were supposed to be weak and fragile and fussy. All the books said they were!

Bryer took the next box down the hall. Reese wished she'd bought another dolly.

"You sure this isn't bad for you?" she asked the Eldritch despite her better judgment.

He shook his head, and for a moment she saw the dangle; it was indeed in the unlikely location the twins had reported when they'd told her in detail about its presentation. Several times over. The entire crew had glee about the twins' having petted an Eldritch. "What will we do when we land?"

"We'll all exit through the Bay 5 airlock with the boxes. I'll take Bryer and Sascha up the cliff to pack them. I'd like you and Kis'eh't to remain at the base of the cliff to steady the boxes on their way down, and then get them inside; don't wait for us, the sooner you get the things put away, the better. Then we'll head out of here as fast as the refits will take us." She glanced at the leather. "You're wearing that under a thermal suit? It'll be warm enough without layers."

"It's barely warm enough in the ship," Hirianthial said with a laugh, and turned the lapel to reveal a fuzzy white layer. "Even lined with fleece. Don't worry, Captain. I'll be comfortable enough."

"You laughed," Reese said.

He looked at her and cocked an eyebrow, but even that expression seemed different, a little looser somehow. "I didn't laugh before?"

"Not like that," Reese said.

"Ah," he said. "I suppose not."

It wasn't fair of him to go changing. She wanted him to stay aloof and old. Laughing made him too accessible. How could she stay irritated at him that way? He looked almost merry.

Bryer returned and they loaded the remaining box. Hirianthial toted this one away, leaving Bryer to glance at Reese. "Did you look?"

"Yes," Reese said. "He looks happier."

The Phoenix's wings mantled, a ripple of motion and hissing sound that flowed all the way through his long tail. "Not look *at him*. Look *in you*."

She'd annoyed a Phoenix—truly an accomplishment. "You didn't say that."

"Truly," Bryer said, "You are occluded."

Two hours later Sascha set the *Earthrise* down on a world marked as "Selebra" on their star charts with no more fanfare than, Reese imagined, a puff of frost at the landing struts.

"I guess the pirates weren't interested in us," the Harat-Shar said on his way to suit up.

"I still think they're waiting for us to do all the heavy lifting," Reese said. "Meet us in Bay Five."

"Right."

Bryer had already opened the interior airlock door when she arrived, revealing a world of ice through the window . . . ice and bleak darkness.

"We've got lamps, don't we?" Kis'eh't asked, rummaging through their supplies.

"The *Earthrise* has emergency lighting, yes," Reese said, standing on the airlock ledge and staring at the frozen world.

The Glaseah padded up next to her. After glancing at Reese, she peered through the window. "There," she said, pointing. "That dot is Demini."

Reese said nothing.

"You forgot to buy us lanterns," Kis'eh't said.

"Think of it as a challenge," Reese said.

The Glaseah shook her head and headed back into the bay, calling, "If you've got lamps or lanterns or personal lights, you'll want to go get them."

Reese rubbed her forehead. She should have realized Selebra was far enough away from Demini Star to not have a day but celestial mechanics wasn't her strongest subject. She hated planets. Give her the clean, broad plane of space any day. Or even the calm nothingness of folded Well-space. At least the blood-cursed rock didn't have a grabby hold . . . gravity here was even lighter than Mars.

"Rock-climbing ice cliffs in the dark," Sascha said cheerfully. He had already pulled his thermal suit's hood over his head and ears. "It's the newest frontier in sports!"

"We'll be fine," Reese said, turning from the forbidding vista and joining them at the piles of backpacks and sup-plies. She hunted through them until she found the ship's single telegem, which she affixed to her ear before drop-ping her mask around her neck. "We'll just have to take it slowly."

"I'm all for slow," Sascha said, shouldering his pack and brandishing an ice pick. "Ready when you are!"

"Stop waving that before you put out someone's eye," Reese said.

"Awww."

"Don't mind her," Kis'eh't said. "She's just grumpy be-cause she forgot that planets don't automatically have day and night just because they're planets."

"Wouldn't that be convenient?"

Bryer rumbled.

"Is he laughing?" Sascha asked.

"Augh!" Reese exclaimed. "Let's just get going. Bryer, wheel the boxes out to the base of the cliff. Sascha, you and I are following him. We'll call when it's time to lower the boxes."

"Understood," Hirianthial said.

Reese pulled the suit up over the back of her head, catching a few of her beaded braids in the collar and headed into the airlock. Sascha and Bryer followed her. They did suit checks and mask seal checks before closing the interior door. Once outside, Reese paused to let Bryer pass her, pulling the boxes on sleds. She waited for her agoraphobia to erupt, but having a bubble of air of her own and a suit that hugged her with her own body warmth, she couldn't quite believe she was outside. She couldn't even hear the crunch of her footsteps on the ice. With a shrug, Reese followed Sascha and Bryer to the base of the cliff, where she and the Harat-Shar performed safety checks on the climbing harness and ropes.

Bryer stopped beside them and ruffled his feathers. Unlike the suits made for the rest of the bipedals, the arms on his suit only hugged the bare parts. Long spars stretched from the edges into the feathers, warming them within some kind of shield Reese wasn't enough of an engineer to understand. It looked like magic to her and was probably as astronomically expensive.

"Ready?" she asked him through the suit intercoms after double-checking his harness.

He nodded and took the end of the rope, flexing knife-like talons on the end of his feet that the suit only barely sheathed. She waited for him to trudge away—surely he needed a running start?—but he simply stood between her and Sascha, staring at a fixed point near the top of the cliff.

Then with a muffled rattle of feathers, he simply leaped into the air, wings flaring bright gold just before they passed out of range of their lanterns.

"Wow," Sascha said, the intercom placing him much closer than he was actually standing.

They could no longer see the Phoenix, only hear his wings beating the air, great metallic thrashes that penetrated the suit's insulated cover. Reese had never heard anything like it.

The rope tumbled into view. Reese tugged on it, then yanked as hard as she could. It held.

"Looks good. Let's go."

Halfway up the cliff, Sascha asked, "Captain?"

"What?"

"What do you think's so valuable about these crystals anyway?"

"They're art objects? I don't know. I didn't ask any questions. I just took the money."

"Rich people are strange."

"Yeah," Reese said. "I hope that's all it is."

At the top of the cliff they stopped to rub feeling back into aching muscles before hauling up the boxes. It wasn't until all three boxes had safely arrived that Reese turned toward their goal, set a-fire by the light of their lanterns. The top of the rise was encrusted with long columnar spikes, faceted so sharply they seemed to cut wounds that bled bright red onto their planes. Eye-watering blues and shocking purples flickered in the corners of the crystals, broken beams of light fractured against their edges . . . hundreds of them, some as high as her own waist.

"Blood and Freedom," Reese whispered.

"Nice," Bryer agreed, an observation that caused both Reese and Sascha to start.

"Seems a pity to have to hack at them," Sascha said.

"Yeah, well, that's why we're here," Reese said. "Let's get to it."

Bryer opened one of the boxes, withdrawing the three pairs of tongs. He took one and applied himself to the nearest specimen with his customary detachment.

Reese shrugged, took up the second pair and went to work. It took her several tries to figure out how to use them to apply enough pressure on the narrow bases of the crystals to separate them from the ground, and her muscles ached by the time she'd cut a half dozen.

"We should have brought lunch," Sascha muttered.

"Fill the boxes and you can eat," Reese said, bringing her armload to the first and setting them carefully inside. The instructions had included a stacking diagram and a scale to weigh each specimen. There was nothing her employer hadn't thought of . . . excepting the pirates.

The day—night?—wore on and her arms and hands throbbed from her labors, but the boxes filled until at last Bryer closed the last one. Reese tapped her ship telegem.

"All right. We're ready."

"On our way," Kis'eh't said to the intercom and set aside her cards. "She's just in time to save me. You're too good at this game."

"It's luck," Hirianthial said.

The Glaseah snorted and gathered the brightly colored cards before sliding them into the box. "You never say that about playing Pantheon."

He laughed and stood. "Right. Iley might show up and laugh at you."

"Better the Tam-illee deities than the Harat-Shariin," Kis'eh't said, sealing her parka. "I notice there's no Eldritch god or goddess in the deck."

"Of course not," Hirianthial said, grinning at her. "That would be telling."

She laughed. "Let's go take care of Reese's boxes."

They suited up and trotted to the base of the cliff and squinted up into the dark. Kis'eh't shone her lantern up the wall and spotted the bottom of the first box. "I've got the rope. You steady the box when it gets in reach. Your reach, not mine."

He chuckled.

Inch by inch the box lowered into view until finally he could stretch up and tickle the corner with a gloved finger. A few moments later and he could flatten his palm against the bottom, so he did.

The hair along his neck rose. He shivered.

"Cold?" Kis'eh't asked.

"No," Hirianthial said. "Just a reaction." He steadied the box as Kis'eh't position the sled under it, then guided it onto the bed. "I'll just take this to the lock."

"All right."

He pushed the box back to the *Earthrise*, leaving it just outside the airlock, before going back for the second. By the time the third hove into view and settled onto the sled, he had dismissed the chill.

"I'll wait for Reese to get down," Kis'eh't said. "I know you want to get back to where it's warm."

"I wouldn't mind it," Hirianthial said with a smile.

All three boxes fit in the airlock, though there was little room to spare. Hirianthial sealed the external door and watched what little atmosphere existed on Selebra flush out and the *Earthrise's* warm air fill it. The sigh of relief escaped him before he could stop it, and it was nice to be able to hear it properly with the mask off.

He dragged all three boxes into the bay before stripping off his gloves, then crouched in front of the first to check the seal.

The moment his fingers lit on the box's edge the shivering returned. He observed the symptoms in himself with

clinical interest—no fever, no dizziness, no doubled vision
. . . nausea, though. And the shaking wouldn't stop.

He lifted his hand. The shivering stopped. He rested
it on the top of the box again. The nausea re-doubled. He
leaned on the dolly as a wave of sweat broke through his
skin. Was it covered with some toxin? Surely not, but his
medical equipment wasn't distant. He could fetch it. Hirianthial turned and took a step, and the world spun. Looking back, the boxes doubled in his vision, and then rose
into the air—no, that was himself, sliding to the ground.

He fumbled for something to help him stand, and his
hand caught on the box seals. The nausea nearly overpowered him. What could possibly be the problem? Something
inside the boxes? He had to look. He had to know. The seal
clicked open beneath his fingers and he looked inside.

Corpses. The boxes were full of corpses—no, dying
bodies. Their screams crowded out the world in his ears
and smeared his vision with a kaleidoscope of ragged black
and searing red.

"Where are the boxes?" Reese asked as Bryer spiraled
to the ground beside them.

"Already inside," Kis'eh't said. "Hirianthial took care of
them."

"Good. Inside sounds good, too." Reese switched to the
telegem. "Irine? We're on our way back in."

"Yay! I'll have hot chocolate for everyone when you get
back."

They chatted companionably on the way to the airlock.
The boxes were inside the bay as promised. Reese was still
peeling out of her suit when Kis'eh't stopped alongside one
of them.

"Aksivaht'h! Reese, *help!*"

"Help what?" Reese said as Sascha darted past her to

the Glaseah's side. She joined them and stared at the body of the Eldritch, having a flashback to that moment she'd imagined him, graceless and vulnerable at the feet of a slaver. Of course, in reality he couldn't even sprawl without grace. She managed to get angry with him for that.

"What the—?"

"One of the boxes is open. Maybe he touched one. Are they poisonous?"

"Of course not!" Reese said testily. "If they had been, my tome of instructions on completing this job would have mentioned something about that."

"He's out cold," Sascha said. "I mean, really cold."

Bryer scooped up the unconscious Eldritch, pausing as Sascha lifted the man's hair and tucked it into Bryer's arms so the Phoenix wouldn't trip on it. He had just finished when Irine appeared in the door with a tray of steaming mugs. Her mouth gaped open at the sight.

"Angels! What happened? Will he be okay?"

"Of course he'll be okay," Reese said. "Since obviously his sole reason for being in my life is to be a victim we have to constantly rescue."

Irine set the tray down and hovered, blocking Bryer from carrying the Eldritch any further into the *Earthrise*. As she watched the Harat-Shar coo, Reese's initial surge of anger faded. She *looked* as Bryer had insisted. The Phoenix seemed comfortable with the Eldritch's weight but Hirianthial was far too tall to be easily held that way. His legs and arms draped over Bryer's feathered arms, and strands of his hair had fallen over his slack face and glided over Bryer's wings. Irine was shifting from foot to foot, her hands a few inches away from Hirianthial's body, as if she was desperate to touch him and afraid to. Did one touch an unconscious Eldritch? Was it okay because they weren't awake to notice? Or worse because their minds weren't on guard against you?

The tableau was haunting because of its very wrong-ness. People didn't carry Eldritch in their arms. Forcing normal people to fight between wanting to stroke them and not wanting to touch them was just as bad.

"Irine," Reese called. The Harat-Shar looked at her guiltily. "You and Bryer get him to the clinic, okay? Bundle him up in something."

The Harat-Shar nodded and pulled Bryer after her.

She, Kis'eh't and Sascha worked in grim silence. When every last crystal had been checked for damage and the final box secured to the cargo axle, Reese straightened and pressed her hands against her back.

"Should we lift off now?" Sascha asked.

"Check on Hirianthial first," she said. "I need you to be able to concentrate in case those pirates come after us and I'm sure you want to know what's wrong with him."

Kis'eh't was already through the door. Sascha paused at it. "What about you, boss?"

"I need to call to find out where we're going," Reese said. "Go on."

Sascha nodded and left her alone in the bay. Finally. Reese dropped onto the floor and pressed the base of her palms against her closed eyes. Her stomach no longer felt like it was being etched with acid when she was un-der stress, but it could still tie into uncomfortable knots. It wasn't just the pirates. It was having someone be sick when they were so far from known space and its hospitals.

Reese took a long breath through her nose and let it es-cape slowly through her lips. Then she picked up the tray of mugs Irine had forgotten and stopped by the galley to drop them off before heading for the nearest comm unit, in her quarters. After entering the code from her instruc-tions and waiting, a thin, almost cadaverous man appeared on her screen.

"I have the delivery," Reese said.

"I am sending you the drop-off coordinates in a coded packet. Use the encryption key attached to the contract to unlock it," the man said so brusquely she knew he was about to cut off contact.

Before he could, she said, "There are pirates in this system. Are they after this stuff?"

"Don't bother us with your problems," he said. "Just make the delivery." The screen blanked.

Reese stared at it, eyes unfocused, until the machine pinged and an encoded packet popped up in the corner.

"Reese?"

She leaned to the intercom. "Yes?"

Kis'eh't sounded fretful. "You'd better come down here."

Reese sighed. "All right."

As she stood, she caught movement in her peripheral vision: her hammock shifting where she'd left Allacazam to sleep. She detoured there and pulled him into her arms.

A muzzy veil of lavender drifted past her eyes.

"Not quite awake, are you?" she said. "You will by the time we get to where I'm going."

A bruised peach aroma: not quite a question, but close. "You'll see."

She headed for the makeshift clinic-lab and found it crowded with everyone else. The bunk had been folded out of sight and Hirianthial swaddled with blankets and then tucked into a nest of comforters on the ground; he was covered in so many of them she couldn't see his face. When Reese stopped at the door, Irine said, "He was too long for the bunk."

Kis'eh't was the closest, tucked into a tight loaf-shape with her hands pressed onto her ankles. "I ran the diagnostic from the first aid kit over him, but it doesn't come up with anything. He's barely breathing."

"And I loosened his collar, but it hasn't seemed to help," Irine added, wringing her hands.

Reese joined them at the Eldritch's side and set Allacazam down on the ground before leaning over and folding an edge of fabric down. Her breath hissed through her teeth.

"Is that—he's crying," Irine said, eyes wide.

"While unconscious," Sascha said from the stool, sounding uneasy.

"He looks awful," Kis'eh't said.

Allacazam rolled past Reese and attempted to scale the ziggurat of blankets. When she noticed him trying, she picked him up and set him on top near Hirianthial's chest. The Flitzbe rolled over it and nestled against Hirianthial's ribcage, tucked against the armpit like a second heart. The Flitzbe's colors flared through orange and yellow to a dull, ugly maroon.

"What does that mean?" Irine whispered.

"I don't know."

"He's still not breathing well," Kis'eh't said, "And he's too cold. What do we do, Reese?"

"How do I know?" Reese replied, her irritation erupting out of nowhere. "I'm not the doctor . . . he's the doctor! The doctor's not supposed to be the unconscious one!"

They stared at her with wide eyes and she sighed. "Sorry."

She reached to the Flitzbe instead, rested her hands on the soft fur of neural fibers. She swallowed and composed herself. *Allacazam?*

The faintest sense of reassurance.

What's wrong?

Her eyes opened and settled on Hirianthial, saw a gaping wound the size of her joined hands over his breastbone pulsing the same dull maroon as Allacazam's fur. She snatched her hand back.

"Reese?" Sascha said from behind her.

"I . . . I don't know. Kis'eh't, you and Irine can watch over him while the rest of us get out of this system."

"This isn't the time to be thinking about business!" Irine said.

"I'm not thinking about business," Reese said, balling her fists. "I'm thinking about the fact that there are pirates crawling around this system and we're a weaponless freighter. I'm also thinking that the faster we get out from under their guns, the faster we'll get to the Core and a real hospital and a real doctor."

Irine's ears fell. "I'm sorry. It's just . . . how can you fix something when you don't know what's wrong?"

"I wish I knew," Reese said. "Sascha, Bryer, come on. Let's get the bleeding soil out of here."

Anxiety. Fear. Sickening fear, bright as acid, pulling breath after breath until—

Anger. Confusion, no concentrating, taste and smell twining.

Will I ever live to have my children?

Pirates—I had forgotten about the pirates—have to focus—

—lived so long, nothing that lives so long should die—

So many "I"s. So many selves. Surely there was a single one in the middle, something to hold onto in the wave. But every "I" turned out to be the wrong one. Sorrow, gray as too many days without sunlight. Worry as corrosive as centuries of water wearing at stone. Flashes of panic like memories of knives parting flesh. Hirianthial shredded like wet paper and vanished into the maelstrom.

A sight now of a body. Familiar, even concealed by

covers. That ankle still had twinges after he'd fallen on it poorly, dismounting a horse. Those twin aches were his knees, a whine that had grown so gradually he'd never realized how stressed the joints had become. That scar: a visceral memory of the armsmaster catching him on the side, cutting a divot of flesh from between the two ribs. Those scars, thin ridges crossing his back and stomach, perfidy's mementos. His chest, which no longer flexed with the ease of youth; his wrists, broadened by the House swords.

His body. And Allacazam on top of it, building shields around his mind to replace the ones he had no energy to lift. When he tried, his faculties failed him entirely, and he almost lost touch with his own body.

A twinkle of stars and a gentle wind blew past him, as if to counsel patience. As he grappled with that, it also offered him the image of a patient convalescing.

That was before he examined the extent of the damage. His entire mental apparatus, that part of him that sensed the unseen energies and shaped them, was in tatters.

A fluting curiosity asked while holding him apart from the wound.

"I've never seen the like," Hirianthial said to the Flitzbe's presence. "I've heard that we can be hurt in these areas, but I've never . . ." He stopped, sinking into a blank despair.

The crystals.

The screams.

The star-sprinkled sky returned and dropped around him, sealing it away. He wanted to protest that the screams were important, but Allacazam was adamant. There would be time for the screams after the wound had closed a little further. Healing came first.

"You have *got* to be crazy," Sascha said. "This is a joke,

isn't it?"

Reese stared at the opened packet, then leaned forward and checked the encryption key. Twice. Then the packet. Twice.

"Angels on the battlefields," Sascha said. "It's *not* a joke. Our drop-off point is in Sector Andeka, the place we're supposed to be avoiding."

"It's not the same solar system," Reese said in a small voice.

"Yeah, well, let me tell you, Boss, a couple of solar systems is not enough distance between me and slavers."

"Fleet cleaned out that nest," Reese said.

"Fleet also told you to stay far-clear of it for a year!" Sascha said.

"So what are we supposed to do, renege on the contract?" Reese snapped. "We're supposed to drop off the shipment. We're expected. We'll just sneak in, deliver and leave."

Sascha's reluctantly slid into the pilot's seat and took the controls. "I think this is crazy."

"I think this is the last time I'm signing a contract this mysterious," Reese said. "But we can't just break off because we think someone might be left to shoot at us. Come on, Sascha. You got past slavers in that system, and now pirates in this one on the way in."

The engines woke beneath the Harat-Shar's touch. "We're not out of this yet."

Reese ignored him and sat at Kis'eh't station, belting herself in. "It's going to work out. It can't not work out, because I'm not planning to die here."

The *Earthrise* shuddered, then vaulted upward, bursting loose from the ice that had formed over its landing feet. Reese lapsed into the silence of her checklists as Sascha pulled them out of the thin atmosphere and out into the dark, the dark that was supposed to be so vast the chances of being found in it were laughable. The dark that was supposed to be safe.

The dark that wasn't. Two red triangles popped up on her sensors the moment they spiraled out from behind Selebra's shadow.

"Sascha—"

"I see them," Sascha said, voice tight.

Reese hunted for something to hide behind. The nearest asteroid belt was too far. The planet itself—no, they'd be target practice if they landed. The red blots were no longer ignoring them . . . they were approaching. "We're going to have to out-run them."

"We're going to have to try," Sascha said, and something about the word "try" made the muscles in Reese's gut clench.

She tapped the intercom. "Bryer, pet the engines. We're going to haul tail. Even if it means leaving some tail behind."

"Understood."

The pirates coasted closer. They weren't even burning their engines, from the sensor data. Were they so certain of themselves that they were being careless?

"Hang on," Sascha said, and for once Reese gripped the chair's battered plastic edges in time to save herself from being thrown across the bridge as the ship twisted back on its own course and flung itself in the opposite direction. The safety belt kept her in her chair, but it bit into her neck so hard she smelled blood. When she blinked the spots out of her eyes, Reese found them lengthening the intercept cone. If the pirates had the kind of engines the slavers in Andeka had mounted, Sascha's strategy wouldn't work. . . .

But the pirates didn't accelerate. They didn't even fire their in-systems.

"What the—?"

One of the ships flickered on her screen and Sascha yelled, "Evading!"

The *Earthrise* jerked to port, flinging Reese forward so hard she gagged on the safety harness. She rubbed her throat and checked the instruments for damage. "They missed?"

Sascha was scowling. "I'm not even sure they fired!"

"But the plot—" Reese double-checked the data. "They had an energy surge. No, it only looks like a surge. They flashed their lights."

"Why would they do that?" Sascha asked.

"No idea," Reese said. "And as long as they're not chasing us, I don't care either."

"I just hope they don't think of us as friends," Sascha said.

Reese glanced at him askance.

"You know. Sending code. Why would you change your running lights for an enemy? Maybe they think we're on their side."

Reese laughed. "If thinking that keeps them off our backs, it's fine with me."

"Dropping into the Well in ten minutes."

"Not a minute too soon," Reese said.

Under Allacazam's care, Hirianthial felt divorced from the outside world, even the parts of it his physical body would typically report. He floated in a sensory deprivation that would have alarmed him had he not been so tired. Instead, he sank into the exhausted unconsciousness of healing and woke only infrequently to "feel" the Flitzbe's mental touch. On one occasion he remained aware long enough to wonder at the sutures one bound an invisible wound with. Instead of floss, did one use sunlight? Was the needle a memory of a mother's touch? What kind of antibiotics did one use on a person's mind?

The Flitzbe healed the way he talked—invisibly, using mechanisms that seemed as natural as the waves on a pebbled beach. Hirianthial had no idea how long it would take, only that it wanted all his strength.

The memories began to seep back into him. This time, Allacazam let them filter through. The touch of the boxes, the sense of unease, the nausea . . . the screams.

Screams.

"I need to wake up," he said.

Allacazam showed him the barely stitched bits of his mental center. To shield with it would be impossible. Waking would mean subjecting himself to everyone's thoughts and wishes and feelings, and though he would now remain centered in his body the experience would undo some of the Flitzbe's work.

But the screams rang in his ears. "It's that important."

Unease, like seeing shadows in an empty house when walking alone to bed. Warning, as well, this time pulled directly from Hirianthial's own memories of a halo-arch monitor emitting a piecing siren as its patient attempted to break free. Hirianthial ignored it and rose toward the light.

Riding through the Well would have proven pleasantly monotonous had it not been for Hirianthial's state. He remained unconscious, so deeply so that Kis'eh't had had only marginal success hydrating him and they were now all worrying about him drinking. With the ship guiding itself on its pre-determined course, each of the crew took a shift at his side, sometimes doubling up if fear overcame other considerations.

Reese arrived for her shift to find Kis'eh't facing the

door, hands clenched on her paw's wrists. Some of the medical supplies Hirianthial had brought with him were laid out on her lap on a clean towel. There was a needle there. And a tube. And a bag of some fluid Reese couldn't identify.

"Is that what I think it is?" Reese asked, stopping at the door.

"It's been five days," Kis'eh't said. "We have to do something about this or he's going to die."

"We're not doctors," Reese said.

"No," the Glaseah agreed. "We're just going to have to follow the instructions in the manual and hope we get it right."

"But we might puncture something!"

Kis'eh't bent forward and examined the needle's tip. "I hope not. Or at least, I hope we puncture the right thing." She covered her face. "Aksivah't hear me, Reese. I don't want to. But I can't think of anything better to do."

"I thought . . . isn't there some other way to keep him alive?" Reese asked. "Something besides needles? One of those pumps?"

"Pumps require vials full of something to be pumped," Kis'eh't said. "I found plenty of anti-toxins, antibiotics, anti-virals, vaccines and anti-fungals, but I didn't find anything we could use to sustain him. Only this. And before you ask, no I can't break open the bag, or it won't be sterile anymore. And even if I did I have no idea if the hydration formula for the pump is different from the one for the needle. The pump is pushing through tissue, the needle isn't... I have no idea if that makes a difference, but I don't want to be wrong."

Reese waved a hand at the mysterious-looking machine Kis'eh't had brought with her from Harat-Sharii. "You synthesized glass beads . . . can't you synthesize whatever the pump needs?"

The Glaseah choked on a laugh, then covered her eyes with a hand. "No. I need a formula to make something I'm not familiar with and appropriate supplies to make it out of. My specialty is inorganic chemistry, Reese, not medicine and not pharmaceuticals. I can identify drugs but I don't know how to make them. And I certainly don't know what you inject directly into someone's bloodstream to hydrate them, beyond it not being plain water." She sighed and dropped her hands onto her wrists. "Look, all we have that we know will work is this bag. I looked and looked, but the u-banks all say if you don't have a halo-arch and you don't have medical facilities and you don't have what you need for the AAP and you do have one of these . . . this is what you use."

Reese sat next to Kis'eh't before her shaky limbs dumped her there. "I can't stick a needle in him. What if we do it wrong?"

"Then I guess he'll die," Kis'eh't said. "He'll certainly die if I can't get more water into him somehow. The health monitor in his own pack says so."

Reese stared at the limp body and its cocoon of blankets. "Someone should get first aid training."

"What a good idea," Kis'eh't said. "Too bad we didn't think of it, oh, say, several years ago."

Reese eyed the Glaseah, ready with a retort of her own, then let it die in her mouth. She'd never seen Kis'eh't so exhausted. Embarrassed, Reese looked away and found Hirianthial's face among the blankets. "I guess we should get it over with."

"Yes," Kis'eh't said.

But neither of them moved.

They remained that way for a while. Long enough for Irine to show up for her shift and pause at the door, as startled by the tableau as Reese had been when she'd entered.

"Are you sticking him with that thing?" Irine asked.

"We've come to the conclusion that we should," Reese said.

Kis'eh't nodded. "Definitely."

Irine looked from one to the other. "And that's where you stopped."

"Do you know how to do it?" Reese asked hopefully.

Irine sat between them and shook her head. "No." She looked clear-eyed but her coat was dull. Had any of them been resting well? "Maybe Bryer knows."

"We could consult Allacazam," Kis'eh't suggested.

Reese started laughing. "Consult Allacazam. I like that." It continued to seem funny until it stopped. "Wait a minute. That might actually work."

Both women stared at her.

"Allacazam knows the things that are in your mind," Reese said, working it out as she spoke, "that's how he communicates with you. He's hung in Hirianthial's arms long enough to pick up something of what's in his mind. Maybe he'll have a memory of putting a needle like this in!"

"I'm not sure I followed that," Kis'eh't admitted.

"Me neither," Irine said. "Try it anyway!"

Reese reached for the Flitzbe's mottled fur, patched in magenta and deeper purple. Her hand creased the fibers. "Allacazam?"

A distracted bobble made her close her eyes and brace herself. She hadn't realized the Flitzbe could make her doubt her senses.

Please, she said. *We need help—*

A wall this time. Not slammed before her, but just there. Was the Flitzbe actually turning her away? She listened carefully and heard a low buzz, like an annoyed insect. It didn't seem directed at her. She caught edges of images that made no sense: a monitor above a patient, maybe. A distant alarm.

Is this a bad time? Reese asked.

"Reese! Come back!"

Reese blinked a few times to clear her vision; as she pulled her hand away she saw the wound again, a translucent hole barely pulled together with brilliant white stitches. Allacazam's fur wriggled as it released her fingers, and the vision vanished.   The thick white lashes lining Hirianthial's nearest eye trembled, then parted to reveal something mostly pupil, a great black hole with the slimmest rim of dried-blood red.

"He's awake!" Irine squeaked.

"Hirianthial?" Reese said, hesitant with the name. She couldn't quite believe his open eye above the taut gray skin of his cheek. He couldn't possibly be conscious.

"Reese," he whispered, and she bent lower to hear, low enough that his breath warmed her ear and lifted the hair along her arms. A few moments later, he finished, "They were alive. They *thought*."

Her stomach clenched tighter. "I don't understand."

"The crystals. They were alive."

"No," Reese said.

Hirianthial's eye closed, and Allacazam's brilliant plum-purple faded to dark red.

"Reese!" Irine's head lifted, golden eyes rounder than ten-fin coins. "He can't be right . . . can he?"

"Crystal people?" Kis'eh't mused. "That would be new. Not impossible, though."

Reese could only look at Allacazam. How long had it taken the first humans to understand that the Flitzbe were sentient? A species that ate like plants, looked like furry volleyballs, reproduced by budding and talked in a way that could be mistaken for a brain disorder? Reese reached again for the soft fur, fingers trembling. She let her hand sink on top of the rippling fibers, closed her eyes again.

Is it true? She asked the Flitzbe. She'd only known Hirianthial a few months, but Allacazam had been her companion for years. She trusted him. *Did we kill them?*

A complicated mesh of color and sound resulted, blacks and lurid reds, blood and void, hues translated from the Flitzbe's discordant electrical signals into ones with the proper associations. From the back of her mind, the crash of a thousand cymbals, like ice shattering against a stone floor.

Reese yanked her hand away.

"Reese," Kis'eh't said, touching her arm. "Keep him awake. He can talk us through the IV."

"I think it's too late," Irine said.

It was too much at once, and anger had never been one of her easier masters. Reese grabbed Hirianthial's shoulder and shook him, ignoring the jangled alarms Allacazam sent through her other hand. "Wake up! You need to drink something."

Lashes parted again. The lines beneath his eyes were so deep they almost convinced her to let him die in peace. Instead, she said to Kis'eh't, "Get the water. Real water, not whatever's in that bag."

The tools on the blanket scattered as the Glaseah lurched to her feet and grabbed a bowl.

"You," Reese said to the eye. "You will stay awake until you finish whatever Kis'eh't gives you. And you," to Allacazam, "will only let him sleep once his body has what it needs, and not one moment earlier. Understood?"

Muted unease and an unexpected surge of dry humor. She imagined him saying 'Yes, lady' and added, "And stop calling me lady!"

"He didn't say anything," Irine said in a small voice as Kis'eh't rejoined them.

Reese ignored her. "Watch him," she said curtly to them both as she rose to her feet. "Keep him warm."

Before the arrival of the crew, Reese had preferred to brood in the *Earthrise's* vast cargo bays, perched on one of the horizontal spindles that would ordinarily have hung swollen with bins had she made a normal run. Instead she'd opted for a long flight to an icy middle-of-nowhere and ended up killing three boxfuls of crystal people. Same amount of money, but now she had blood on her hands. Water. Whatever.

Reese sighed and cupped her chin in small dark hands. One booted foot against the docking clamp braced her on her perch. The floor hung fifteen feet below her, but she had no fear of heights, particularly in the lighter gravity of the bay. The childhood she'd spent dashing across the branches of the eucalyptus that had grown unexpectedly tall on Mars had prepared her so well for her chosen profession. She'd climbed more than one tree, of course, but mostly the eucalyptus. And now those were trees she could no longer return to. Maybe it bothered her more than she let herself accept. She was very good at not looking at things she couldn't let herself accept.

A shadow painted itself against the cool gray floor, bristling with feathers. Reese frowned, sliding her hands onto the spindle and leaning over.

"Bryer."

He stopped under her and met her gaze.

"I came here to be alone."

The Phoenix spread his wings and leaped easily onto the spindle alongside hers. Great clawed feet grasped the cylindrical axle as he crouched, tail fanned.

Reese sighed. "Look, I don't want to talk."

He trained that impenetrable eye on her, too much iris for his eye socket. One eye ridge twitched in a credible imitation of a raised brow.

She looked away, dropping her head. If he wasn't going to leave until she talked, then she might as well get it over with. "Bryer . . . we're murderers."

He canted his head.

"The crystals," Reese said. "They were living beings."

He considered that for a few beats. Then, "A mistake."

"Fine. So it's manslaughter. It doesn't matter if it was an mistake or not. Those things . . . we killed them."

"Certain?"

Reese glanced at him so sharply her braids whipped her neck. "Hirianthial said so." She looked down. "Besides, Allacazam agreed."

"So now what?"

She twisted around to face him. "Now what?" she asked, incredulous. "Now what? Bryer! We're killers!"

"That's past now. Cannot be changed. Now what? What will you do?"

"I . . . I hadn't really thought about it."

The Phoenix mantled his wings. He looked alarmingly like a real bird in the heavy shadows of the cavernous bay. "Think now."

Reese rubbed her forehead. "I guess I'll call our buyer and tell him we can't sell these things. Corpses. Whatever. Then contact the sector authorities and inform them of our findings."

Bryer's crest slicked back. "Better. You focus now on what needs to be done." He straightened, leaped lightly off the spindle. "Do not lose focus, Captain."

"No, Bryer," Reese said softly.

His shadow receded. She strained her ears in the following silence until she heard the soft hiss of the door.

Reese hugged the axle and let her feet slide off so that she dangled above the ground. She landed lightly and headed toward her quarters with so little enthusiasm it surprised her that she even arrived. How should she tell her employers that she was backing out of the contract? They'd be upset, though perhaps they'd understand once she explained why. They might even be upset themselves. There was the cachet of having discovered a new alien species, even by accident . . . surely that was something to celebrate?

Of course, making first formal contact with aliens by presenting them with over a hundred corpses wasn't ideal.

Reese dropped in front of her terminal with a sigh and entered the contact code the contract had stipulated for emergency use. The screen glowed blue and a status indicator in the lower left corner scrolled through the connection and handshake messages. The Alliance sigil popped up on the screen seconds later as the *Earthrise* punched the call through the loopholes some Tam-illee engineers had found in Well space. It took a few minutes to reach their destination and the screen de-pixellated on a pale weed of a human man whose narrow limbs and hunched posture made him look harmless . . . until one spotted his cold eyes.

"Captain Eddings? We weren't expecting you."

"Mm. Yes. I'm afraid we've run into a problem."

The man leaned toward the screen. "I'm afraid you'll have to solve your own problems, Captain. Just get to the delivery point within the specified time frame."

"I can't deliver," Reese said.

He stopped. "Pardon me?"

"The crystals you asked us to get? Well," Reese paused, then rushed on, "They're living things. Or they were before our harvest killed them."

The man's mouth stretched into a grim smile. "And you discovered this how?"

"Our on-board esper evaluated them," Reese said, alarmed by the glint of curiosity in his eyes.

"Your on-board esper? Curious, Captain. I had no idea you had one."

"He's a recent addition," Reese said.

"Ah. Not your Glaseah, then," the man said. "Perhaps this is the Eldritch."

"How did you—" Reese stopped and composed herself. What did it matter if they knew about Hirianthial anyway? "It doesn't matter, sir. What matters is that I can't give you these people."

"Corpses, Eddings. Not people. When will you be arriving?"

"You misunderstand me," Reese said. "I can't give you these things. They're bodies! Of a new alien species! They need to be reported!"

She knew instantly she'd done something wrong, though the man's voice remained calm and measured. "The contract you signed holds you to silence, Captain Eddings."

"Silence about something like this? You must be making a joke," Reese said and then stopped as a cold wave passed through her body. "Unless you knew."

"A pity you didn't read the paperwork more carefully," the man said. "We would encourage you not to renege on the contract, Captain. We would hate to have to send someone to enforce it."

Reese stared at him.

"You'll be along, won't you?" he said.

"Yes," Reese said, and then galvanized by the threat, "Of course. They're bodies right now . . . there's nothing we can do about that. Why raise a fuss?"

He smiled again, though the smile never made it to his eyes. "We love a reasonable woman, Captain. We'll see you soon."

As soon as the screen blanked, Reese ran to the bathroom and dropped over the toilet, not trusting her stomach to remain calm. With her fingers clutched on the rim, she thought of the boxes full of dead people and the cold in the man's eyes. It was no mistake that they were heading back to Sector Andeka, where Fleet had been trying to clean out the pirate and slaver activity. Somehow she'd signed up to do the dirty work for a criminal. The question was why?

"Why?" Reese asked. She wanted to pace; she wanted to shout, wave her hands, something. But Hirianthial's body remained coiled on the floor and she couldn't bring herself to wake him. So instead she sat, hands folded so tightly her knuckles hurt, on the stool just vacated by Sascha. "That's what I want to know. The client's given us enough money to make three boxes worth all the cargo we could stuff into the bays. He knows they were living—" her voice quivered, "So my question is . . . why?"

Kis'eh't sighed as she rubbed her lower back. Then she removed the specimen and traced its flaws and cracks with delicate fingers. "I'm not sure. I've been examining them for several hours and all the tests I've run have been inconclusive . . . but that might be completely meaningless. This isn't my specialty, but on the other hand, this isn't exactly organic chemistry, either." The Glaseah studied the read-outs scrolling across the screen. "Maybe he just thinks they're pretty."

"Somehow I doubt that," Reese said.

The Glaseah nodded. "I do too. This . . . this is a body,

correct?"

Reese nodded.

"And we were not contracted for a specific amount of bodies, were we?"

Put that way, Reese couldn't help but flinch. Nevertheless, she said, "No. Just to fill the boxes."

"Then this specimen won't be missed," Kis'eh't said and pulled a set of goggles over her eyes.

"Uh, Kis'eh't—"

"Stand back, Reese."

"What are you—"

The Glaseah whacked the crystal with chisel, shattering its base with a sound like claws on glass. Most of the column remained unmarred but from the broken middle oozed a translucent sludge. Kis'eh't captured it in a vial and slid it with practiced motions into the sample station. She started a test running and washed her hands while waiting. "Let's see what that wins us."

"Was that a good idea?" Reese asked, stunned. Somehow the ruined remains of the crystal evoked a body far better than it had as a whole.

"It was a hunch," Kis'eh't said. "We look different on the inside than we do on the outside, and only our most advanced medical equipment can fully itemize those differences."

The test ended with a high-pitched ping. Kis'eh't examined the resulting list and touched the top-most entry. A holograph of a molecule appeared and rotated. "Well how about that. Nudge it just the tiniest bit and you could roll in the money."

"I don't understand," Reese said. "What is it?"

"Wet, Captain," Kis'eh't said. "You can use its innards to make wet, far more quickly than you could piece it together in a lab."

"You must be kidding," Reese said. Her heart faltered. "We don't have three trunks full of dead aliens because if you break their bodies up you can make braindead from them."

"It's either that or he really is looking for *objets d'art*," Kis'eh't said.

There were very few illegal drugs in the Alliance, given the number of member cultures that either believed in the responsible use of recreational substances or used them in religious ceremonies. The few outlawed drugs had earned their places on the blacklist. Wet had a slew of other nicknames: 'braindead', 'zombie', 'mindmelt'. Users didn't live long, but they paid well for their final days of addiction.

"How much of it can you make with that sample?" Reese whispered.

Kis'eh't squinted at the read-out. "Mmm. Dose per person is what . . . less than a milligram? Maybe two hundred doses from what I have here." She glanced at the shattered crystal. "That's probably only three-quarters of what's in the body."

She was carrying almost a quarter of a million doses of one of the deadliest street drugs in the Alliance in her cargo holds, acquired by the murder of unresisting aliens because she had been willing to sign anything to get herself and the *Earthrise* solvent and off Harat-Sharii. Her own thoughtlessness had brought her here . . . and now centered her in the sights of some of the worst criminal elements in the Alliance. She was in danger. Her crew was in danger. And a crime lord who'd wanted to drag money out of people dying in the worst ways possible had used her to do his dirty work. Reese had spent much of her adulthood angry, but this . . . this rage was so consuming, so towering her entire body trembled and her vision bled crimson.

"Reese?" Kis'eh't asked softly, touching her shoulder.

"Just go," Reese said, not seeing anything, not even the wall on the other side of her eyes.

The door slid shut on the Glaseah, leaving Reese shaking on the stool. What did one do with so much anger? Where could you put it? She slid carefully from her perch and bent over the remains of the crystal corpse, counted the shards around its body, tried to imagine what it was like to think, to grow, to live life beneath a sky without a day.

She would have to tell the crew. They'd have to tell Fleet. They'd have to find a way to tell Fleet without bringing down her employer's enforcement.

A little more of the crystal's inner fluid pooled from the break.

She'd tell Fleet even if it did bring the enforcement down on them. And if Fleet gave her a chance, she'd kill her employers herself with her bare hands, for dragging her and so many innocent lives into their sordid crimes.

The meeting first. Then they'd figure out how to call down help. Everyone could make it . . . except the person who'd warned her in the first place. Reese walked over to the blankets and dropped down beside them. The Eldritch was unconscious, as he'd remained since imparting the information. The skin around his eyes was delicate, almost translucent; tiny creases wove a fine gray net at the edges of his eyelids. He still looked unhealthy despite the water, and against his side Allacazam remained stubbornly pressed, refusing to leave even to eat. Sascha had brought his sunlamp from the mess hall.

Reese brushed the Flitzbe first, long enough to see that the wound appeared to be held closed, though its puffy, angry edges disturbed her. She wasn't well-versed in wounds, so she wasn't sure where Allacazam was drawing these images from . . . perhaps Hirianthial's mind. She hadn't really thought through the implications of the Flitzbe being able to bridge minds by selecting images from someone else's and overlaying them.

It didn't matter. What mattered was that he was unconscious but better and only likely to wake if she touched him . . . so she did, resting a hand on his shoulder.

That listless eye opened, but this time she could see more wine than black.

"Our employers," Reese said, and the anger rose anew. "Our employers knew, Hirianthial. They knew, but the insides of the crystals can be used to make wet, so they didn't care."

His pupil dilated visibly, and he tried to lift his head. She stopped him with a hand hovering in front of his face. "Don't. You're too weak." She bared her teeth. "We're going after them. We're calling the Fleet and by the time we're done with them that fire you set to the slaver's house will look like someone playing with a candle."

He closed his eye and at his side Allacazam's colors flowed to a muted, pulsing blue. Warmth and pleasure radiated up her arm from the hand that still rested on the Flitzbe's body.

He's getting better, isn't he? she asked him.

A swell of blue clouds, of rain and the smell of wildflowers.

And knowing we're going to kill our enemies makes him happy, she said. To that, Allacazam did not respond. Perhaps it was the notion of bringing their employers to justice that pleased the Eldritch, and it was her bloodlust that she felt in her mind.

But she remembered the look in his eyes when she'd first met him in that cell. She remembered how clearly he'd indicated that he held to the Kelienne Oath only while employed as a doctor. It made her wonder what he was hiding.

It made her think that gentleness and weakness were not the same things.

Reese pulled herself to her feet and tapped the intercom. "Everyone to the mess hall. We've got some things to discuss."

The silence in the mess hall after her explanation was so uncharacteristic that Reese would have worried had all her emotional energy not already been taken up by anger.

Finally, Irine squeaked. Sascha petted her tail and spoke for her, his voice so brisk and sober Reese suddenly wondered just what she'd hired when she'd bought herself the twins. "So we're breaking the law and we've been threatened if we tattle. That's the marrow of it."

"Yes," Reese said.

"What are we going to do?" Kis'eh't asked.

"We have to tell Fleet," Reese said. "There's no way we can let these people get away with what they're doing. If we don't say anything, they'll just mow the entire planet down to make wet. What if that's the only planet with the crystal people? We can't let them commit genocide."

"But if we just broadcast a message, they'll know we told on them," Irine said, quivering. "I bet they find us before Fleet does."

"We could divert," Kis'eh't said. "Head for a starbase."

"How much you want to bet they're watching us now that Reese's sent that message?" Sascha said.

"Then what do we do?" Kis'eh't said.

"Fail," Bryer said.

Reese glanced at him. "What?"

"Fail," Bryer said. "Distress call."

"You mean fake an engine failure?" Sascha asked. He plucked his lower lip. "That might work. If we send a generalized distress call, we could get Fleet's attention without broadcasting to them directly."

"What if they don't respond?" Irine asked. "What if some other ship finds us first?"

"Then maybe they can carry a message for us," Reese said. "I like it. It's better than just yelling for Fleet and hoping they get to us before the drug baron sends someone to smear us against the nearest asteroid." She nodded. "Bryer, you and Sascha get to fake our drop out of Well. And if you can put us somewhere closer to Fleet than to the pirates, that would be wonderful."

Bryer stood. "Done."

Everyone left except Irine.

"Let me guess," Reese said. "You'd rather be a drug lord's slave than dead."

Irine shook her head. "Belonging to someone I can handle. Being drugged with something like wet . . . " She shivered.

Reese surprised herself by hugging the Harat-Shar. "We'll get out of this one just like we've gotten out of all the others."

"Are we ever going to make money in a boring way?" Irine asked in a small voice.

"I don't know," Reese said. "But if we don't start, I'm going to think seriously about an early retirement."

"Dropping out of Well in five-four-three-two-one—"

The engine noise cut off abruptly, followed by a dwindling high-pitched whine that faded to complete silence.

"You're sure it's not actually dead?" Reese asked.

From the intercom came a Phoenixae huff. "Pretending."

"I hope so," Reese said. "We spent a lot of blood money on those engines." She leaned over and cupped a hand over the broadcast panel.

"Take a deep breath, Boss," Sascha said.

Reese nodded, then tapped the panel and spoke. "This is an all-call from the TMS *Earthrise*, Captain Theresa Eddings commanding. We have suffered a catastrophic Well failure and request immediate assistance. Repeat, we have had a Well failure and request the assistance of any nearby friendly."

"Sending," Irine said.

"Put it on repeat until someone hails us," Reese said. "Let's see if we can't attract a nice, studly warcruiser."

Sascha laughed. "Since there's only a handful of those in the whole Alliance, we might be waiting a long time."

"I'll settle for a battlecruiser, then. Or any Fleet ship with more guns than we've got."

"That would be all of them," Sascha said, unbuckling his harness and stretching his arms above his head.

"Then it shouldn't take long," Reese said, pleased. "Maybe a nice hour eating in the mess hall, a nap and we'll have lunch with the sector commander and make him understand."

"What was his name again?" Irine asked.

"Jonah NotAgain, of the UAV *StarCounter*," Reese said.

"NotAgain," Sascha said. "I wonder why he chose that for a Foundname?"

"I don't know," Reese said. "But right now "Not Again" is about what I'm feeling with this whole pirate thing. Care to join me for lunch?"

"Yay!" Irine said, and bounced to her feet.

"Lead the way," Sascha said, standing.

They reached the lift when the hail alert sounded.

"Already?" Irine said.

Reese quashed the sense of foreboding and said with forced cheer, "Maybe their galley will serve better food than ours."

Sascha dropped into the pilot's chair again. His ears

flattened immediately. "Angels damn it all! It's the pirates!"

"Which pirates?" Reese said, joining him.

"The ones from Selebra!" Sascha said.

"Were they following us?" Irine asked.

"They must have been," Sascha said. "There's no way they could be right on top of our tails like that otherwise. Which means . . . "

"Which means you were right when you said they thought of us as friends," Reese said. "Back in Demini System when they flashed their lights at us. They were guarding the planet for our employers. And then they tailed us . . . for insurance."

"ARTV *Crawler* to TMS *Earthrise*. We are responding to your request for assistance."

An Alliance Registered Trade Vessel could be from anywhere. Reese leaned forward and opened the channel. "*Earthrise* to Trade Vessel *Crawler*. We're glad to see you."

"We're happy to help," a man's jaunty tenor replied. "We've got a great Well engineering team we'd be happy to lend you."

"We appreciate the offer, *Crawler*, but we'd hate to inconvenience you. All we need is a few spare parts and we'll be good to travel. We'll repay you, if you've got what we need."

"I'm sure we do, *Earthrise*."

"Great," Reese said. "If you could just net them and push them out an airlock we'll haul them in."

"No need for the trouble . . . we've got a Pad."

Irine and Sascha were staring at the panel with flattened ears. Reese would have rathered having ears to flatten than the cold sweat she got instead. She separated her collar from the damp skin at her neck. "We'd hate to put you through the trouble," she said.

"It's no trouble at all. Just give us coordinates in a cargo bay and we'll drop them off ourselves. We can send our engineering team over to help with the install. It's really no trouble."

Reese said, "*Crawler*, we appreciate your help but we're not too fond of outsiders. We'd prefer to do the work ourselves. Engineers get superstitious around machines."

"And captains get superstitious around cargo," the man said, his tenor hardening. "We're here to help, *Earthrise*. We wouldn't want you failing to fulfill your contracts."

Reese dropped her head. They were threatening her. If they suspected her of bluffing, what would they do to her and the crew? They might just kill them and leave with the crystals. They might do that anyway. "Any help you could give us would be greatly appreciated," she said finally. "Just don't step on my engineer's talons."

The man's cheer magically returned. "We'll do nothing of the sort. Send us your needs and the coordinates and we'll take care of business."

"Will do. Thanks, *Crawler*. *Earthrise* away."

Reese slammed the channel closed and said, "Blood and *death*, arii'sen, we're in trouble now." She turned and punched the intercom. "All hands to the mess hall, and fast."

"We need to sabotage the engines," Reese said. "So that it looks real."

"Are you crazy?" Irine asked. "We won't be able to run!"

"But they're coming to the ship," Kis'eh't said. "If they arrive and discover our engines aren't broken, they'll figure out our real reason for sending the distress call."

"So it has to be real," Reese said. "Bryer, can you do it?"

"Yes," he said.

"Good," Reese said. "Go make it happen."

The Phoenix loped out of the room. To the rest of

them, Reese said, "We're going to have boarders. What I'm worried about is that they'll just shoot us all and haul the cargo away."

"We'll have to hide it," Sascha said.

"Somewhere that's locked," Kis'eh't said. "As locked as we can. Voice, at least."

"More than voice," Reese said. "Voice prints can be forced."

A moment's tense silence.

Irine said, "There's a cabin that's DNA-lockable."

"There's *what*?" Reese asked, incredulous. DNA-locking required voice prints, blood matches and iris checks, all from a conscious individual within a pre-set stress index. "I didn't install a DNA lock anywhere."

"I know," Irine said. "I had it put in." Her tail swished. "I leave it open almost all the time. But for an hour or two it's nice to know you won't run into us."

Reese stared at her. "You have sex in it?"

"Where you can't find us by accident," Irine said. "I did it for you."

And in a twisted Harat-Shariin way, it was a great gift, one that would have required the twins to float above their own acculturation long enough to realize just how deeply it disturbed Reese to know about typical Harat-Shariin family relationships.

"How big is it?" Reese asked.

"It's the storage closet across from our room," Irine said. "It's big enough."

"And it's locked to . . . "

"Me or Sascha."

Reese set her hands on the table. "You or Sascha."

"What are we waiting for?" Kis'eh't said, getting to her feet. "We don't have much time."

"Go start moving the boxes," Reese said to her.

"I know what you're thinking," Irine said once the door closed on the Glaseah. "You're worried that I'll give under pressure. Well, I won't."

Reese shook her head, but the Harat-Shar kept talking. "I'm not as soft as I act, I know. I might not be good with other people's blood, but I'm pretty good with my own, I can handle it—"

"I'm not worried that you can't handle it," Reese said quietly. "I'm upset that you might have to. Are you sure you want to do this?"

Irine stopped, glanced at Sascha. They turned two sets of golden eyes to her. "We're sure."

Reese nodded. "Let's get the boxes moved, then. Kis'eh't was right about not having much time."

The urgent fear infesting the *Earthrise* grew so intense Hirianthial could no longer remain asleep. He found himself staring at the cabinet while panicked thoughts careened against him, passing too swiftly for him to assign them to the appropriate person. They were so distracting it took him several minutes to understand that the reason he was staring at the cabinet was that he was on the clinic/lab floor, and the edges of the door weren't furry, but blurred from tired eyes.

Allacazam didn't object to him being awake, which was well; there was no way he'd fall back asleep with the ship in such turmoil. It was like closing one's eyes while a hurricane tried to strip away the bedroom walls and windows. Instead, he tried gaining his feet and making his way to the sink to drink something. Bent over the water stream, Hirianthial wondered how long he'd been out. His entire body throbbed from the effort of remaining upright, and his limbs felt drenched with fatigue, too heavy to lift without tremendous effort. And his mental centers . . .

He couldn't block the tumult out. He couldn't even re-
liably distinguish between his own thoughts and the feelings rushing outside him, save by the mixed blessing that
he was likely to be too tired for such emotional furor. He
no longer felt shattered, but his emotional body was in
the same state as his physical: too drained to respond to
emergencies.

Perhaps it would be better to crawl back into the blankets and trust that no one would need him.

The door slid open for Kis'eh't, who stopped abruptly
at the sight of him.

"Oh . . . oh-no-no-no-REESE! *WE FORGOT ABOUT
HIRIANTHIAL!*"

Hirianthial wobbled as the shout rang through him on
every level, driving the thoughts from his head.

Reese popped up behind the Glaseah, the warm chocolate hue of her skin draining to a grayish brown. He wondered if she would faint. "Blood and death! Where are we
going to put him? If they find him—"

'They' was accompanied by crisply imagined silhou-
ettes, bulky shoulders, towering weapons, and then white
teeth set in menacing grins.

"Can he walk?" Reese asked, then shook herself and
said, "Can you walk? No, you have to run. We have to
get you . . . *IRINE! CAN YOU FIT SOMEONE IN THAT
CLOSET?*"

Distantly, "Are you crazy? We've barely fit in the boxes!"

Panic in waves now. Kis'eh't said, "We could leave one
of the boxes out and get him in there instead . . . "

"No," Reese said. "If they can get even one of the boxes,
why would they bother to keep us alive for the rest?"

"I wish I had a better idea what you were discussing,"
Hirianthial managed.

Their minds focused on him, though unfortunately not

on the same tangent: Kis'eh't thought he looked terrifying-
ly weak, too weak to stand up to pirates and slavers, and
Reese was busy being angry that he wasn't either not there
at all or not invisible. She pointed a finger at him. "If I have
to rescue you again, I will throw a sack of rooderberries at
your queen! Do you have a weapon?"

"I thought you didn't want us to carry weapons!"
Kis'eh't said.

"I have a knife," Hirianthial said.

For once, both of them had a unanimous thought: a
knife was totally inadequate, ridiculous, insane.

"That'll have to do," Reese said. "Kis'eh't, you stay here
with him. Maybe they won't think to look for him."

"Don't leave me here!" Kis'eh't exclaimed. "I can't de-
fend him!"

"I'll stay," Sascha said, showing up. "If Irine and I stay
split up—" *They can't use us against one another.*

Did he finish that sentence? Reese acted as if he did.
"Good idea. Stay here—"

The ship bucked beneath their feet, tossing Reese
against Kis'eh't's lower back. Anger, adrenaline, panic,
distress—he couldn't sort it out from the feel of the floor
moving and slid down next to the cabinet.

"Bryer's done the engines," Sascha said. "It won't be
long now. Go on, Boss!"

Reese nodded. "There's a small chance we'll be able to
bluff our way out of this."

"Ha," Sascha said.

"But if not—" Reese eyed them, then said, "Come on,
Kis'eh't. Come be steady for me."

"Aye, Captain," Kis'eh't said, and leaped after the human.

Sascha turned to him and squatted a fair enough distance that Hirianthial almost thought he could tell the difference between their ideas.

"You're in a bad way," Sascha said. "Can I help? Or at least not make it worse?"

"Explain what's going on," Hirianthial said. "I need to focus."

"Turns out we accidentally signed up to be drug-runners for mob bosses," Sascha said, backing away as Hirianthial forced himself to his feet again. "We decided to call Fleet by sending a fake distress call, but guess who answered it first."

"I'd guess someone on the wrong payroll," Hirianthial said.

"Worst part, it's in Sector Andeka," Sascha said. "We're kind of thinking it's all connected . . . the ring you busted up, this drug business. And they know that we've got an Eldritch on board."

"So they want . . . the crystals. And me."

Sascha nodded.

"More," Hirianthial began and lost his breath. He gathered it again and said, "More excitement than I planned for. This late in my life."

"I'm just glad you're alive so far," Sascha said after his uncertainty solidified around the words. "We really thought you were going to die of whatever those crystals did to you."

"They didn't do anything to me," Hirianthial said. "They merely died where I could feel it." Water helped. He drank another handful from the tap. Had he even turned it off since staggering here? Probably not.

"Are you . . . are you going to be okay?"

"Yes," Hirianthial said. "But I'm not yet." He sighed and splashed his face.

"This is the first time I've ever been this scared," Sascha said.

Hirianthial glanced at him and could barely see his features for the cold, compressed black lining around him. He recognized it: not the fluorescent spikes of panic or the mindless explosions of adrenaline-fueled terror, but the bitter stillness of facing one's own mortality.

"I sympathize," Hirianthial said after a moment. "But we'll survive this."

"And if we don't?" Sascha asked.

"Then we'll die," Hirianthial replied.

"And that doesn't bother you?"

It did, strangely—was that Sascha's response?—no, truly, it was his own. "Surprisingly, yes." Hirianthial double-checked, then nodded. "It does." He laughed haltingly, fighting his ribs for every breath. "I never thought the sun would dawn again on that day."

"But you're not afraid," Sascha said, his own black cold loosening.

"No," Hirianthial said, and found that as surprising as the first. "No, if I must, I could die here."

Sascha did not understand, but the puzzle distracted him from his fears. Well enough . . . the puzzle distracted Hirianthial as well—until the terror on the ship crested, carrying with it a set of new presences, hard, violent and cruel.

"They've arrived," Hirianthial said.

Twelve men appeared out of the nauseous nowhere that filled a Pad tunnel. All of them human. All of them carrying themselves like muscle. The one at point had a short amber beard and changeable eyes, the kind that could be any light color, the kind that got most of their character from their owner's expression.

The man was grinning, but Reese hated him on sight. She hardened herself and prepared her bluff.

"So, Captain," he said. "Having a little extra trouble? Or

was that explosion an attempt to weasel your way out of a tight spot?"

"I have no idea what you're talking about," Reese said. Beside her Irine and Kis'eh't remained very quiet.

"I don't like dawdling, Captain, so let's just lay things out, shall we? You're carrying special cargo for our mutual employer. Either you've actually had engine trouble, which we'll fix, or you were trying to get out of your contract . . . which we'll also fix. Either way we're here to do the job. You can either help us or we'll make sure you don't make any more mistakes."

"Are you suggesting that I'd bust up my own engines just to yell for help?" Reese asked. "You must be kidding. You know how much money I spent *fixing* my engines?"

"I can imagine," he said, still showing teeth.

"Just give us the parts so we can fix the blood-cursed things and get the shipment to the boss," Reese said. "I don't want your help and I certainly don't need you playing nursemaid. The money's talked. I'm not missing out on it."

"Tough words," he said. "But we're not leaving until we're sure you're not going to sneak away when we turn our backs."

"I signed a contract," Reese said hotly. "That might not mean anything to you people, but keeping my word is what keeps me in business."

"Nice speech," he said. "You should be glad I'm not one of those types what gets angry at being called names." He nodded to the men behind him. "Move."

They spread out. More than half headed down the corridor. Two started setting up a portable Pad, one that would allow them to return to the *Crawler*. The others stood at their leader's back.

"Should I offer you coffee or are we going to just stand here until your people finish their survey?" Reese asked, exasperated.

"I was about to escort you to your engine room," he said and grinned. "If your problems are real, I'll have that coffee with you later and maybe we'll . . . talk."

She was so accustomed to ignoring the twins that it took her several heart-beats to realize that he wasn't interested in talking. "You're not my type."

"You might change your mind," he said.

"I doubt it," Reese said.

He laughed.

"Don't even say 'I like them with fire,'" Reese said. "I'll vomit."

"I was thinking more 'I like them spunky,' but that might be improper language in front of a lady." He drew the last word out until it passed the realm of insult and entered the realm of threat. "Move along then, Captain. I'm sure you know the way. And take your two pretty minions with you, slowly."

"Go in front," Reese said to the two, and was glad when they didn't object. She wanted to be between them and their boarders; they couldn't fit in the corridor abreast and she couldn't bear the image of them so close to the men. It made the trip to the engines the longest ever. She could hear their breathing and the creak of their leather vests, and the smell of metal and animal musk made the hair along the back of her neck rise.

They entered the engine compartment to find six of the men crawling over the Well drive. Bryer was being held by an additional two.

"So?"

One of them dropped to the ground next to the joint attachment. "We're still looking."

"Take your time," the leader said. "Wouldn't want any mistakes."

The other guffawed and ducked back into the housing. Reese had been hoping they would shuffle or sound
drugged or act like undisciplined thugs, but though they
weren't saluting or marching in formation their motions
were crisp and their gazes alert and their patter, alas, indicated they had a good understanding of mechanics.

Bryer worked magic, as far as Reese was concerned.
But he'd always worked it to fix the engines, not to take
them apart. She stared at a fixed point on the wall and
tried not to think about what would happen if—no. She
just wouldn't think.

One, two, four men appeared. A fifth.

"Well?"

"Looks legit," the fifth said.

"Can you fix it?"

He shrugged. "Sure. It's a basic repair."

The leader prodded Reese between the shoulder-
blades. "And you don't have equipment for a basic repair?"

"I'm not exactly swimming in money," Reese said.

"Get to it, then," the leader said.

"Right."

They turned back to the Well drive and their leader
said, "About that cup of coffee, then—"

"Wait!"

Reese's heart thudded so hard she shook.

"Damn, this is clever! And it almost worked!" The sixth
man laughed. "Don't kill the Phoenix. I want his secrets."

"It's a fake?" the leader asked, his voice hardening.

"Sabotage," the last man said, sliding off one of the bars
and wiping his forehead with the back of a grease-streaked
hand. "But subtle as a snake. They stressed the parts themselves so they'd fail exactly the way they would with time. I
almost missed it, but a good screening of the parts showed
the metal's not as old as it would have to be to have built

up that much pressure."

The smack the leader delivered to the back of Reese's head was so abrupt she bit her own tongue. "You're going to be so sorry."

Reese swallowed blood and said, "I wasn't looking forward to our 'date' anyway."

The men laughed and their leader's humiliation bought her another blow. This one set her ears ringing.

"Ooh, I'm so scared," Reese said.

The leader's glare transformed into a rictus. He spun around and struck Irine so hard she cried out and crumpled, grasping at her shoulder. Reese froze.

"Now that I have your attention," he said. "Here's the story. You give us the cargo and the spy and we'll leave you alone. Very simple. We'll even leave you enough scrap metal to fix your engines . . . if you're smart enough to figure it out."

"And the alternative?" Reese asked. "Let me guess, something original. You'll kill us all and take what you want anyway."

The man stamped on Irine's instep and the Harat-Shar's shriek shattered Reese's bravado. "Something like that. We might have a little fun with you first, just to put the living fear of God into you."

Reese said, "Fine. I'll take you to the cargo."

"And the spy," the man said.

"I have no idea what you're talking about," Reese said. "And no, I'm not being obstinate. What bleeding spy would we have on board? Besides an incompetent one incapable of warning us you were on our tails?"

"The Eldritch," the man said.

"He's dead," Reese said.

"Then I'll take his corpse along."

Reese clenched her fists. "I want to keep it."

"You want to keep a lot of things," the man observed. "I want to take them. Guess who's got the guns?" He smiled thinly. "First the cargo."

"Fine," Reese said. "This way."

This time they forced her to take the lead and separated her from Irine and Kis'eh't with several men. As she walked, she raced through her options . . . so few. Most of them involved bargaining, but there was nothing she had that the pirates couldn't simply take given enough time. What thing of value could she possibly distract them with?

They reached the closet too soon. Reese stopped and nodded toward it. "They're in there."

"Unlock it," Blond said. "I assume it's locked."

"She can't," Irine said. "Only I can . . . and you'll have to fix me to make it work."

He looked her over and said, "Awww, poor tiger-girl. Did I break a bone?"

"The door won't open unless I'm within a certain stress range," Irine said. "That's not going to happen when I'm in pain."

"Whatever," the man said. He waved a hand. "Bring the torches."

"You can't do that!" Irine squeaked. "It'll explode!"

"You bought a detonating DNA lock?" Reese asked incredulously.

Irine's ears flattened, but not before the blush showed. "We really, really didn't want you walking in on us."

"She's right," one of the men said. "It's got the manufacturer's label."

Blond shrugged. "Those things blow inward, not out. Get the torches."

"Are you crazy?" Reese asked. "You'll destroy the cargo!"

"Did you read your instructions, chocolate? That entire

room could go up in flames and those boxes you bought will come out whole." He nodded to the men. "Get moving. You two, find the spy and bring him to . . . oh, let's say the mess hall. Somehow I doubt he's a corpse. Besides, that cup of coffee's sounding better and better."

"They're coming for me," Hirianthial said.

Sascha said, "Reese and the others?"

"Already in their hands," Hirianthial said.

"Then it's up to us," Sascha said, flexing his hands. "How many?"

"Two right now," Hirianthial said. "Another ten on-board. They're armed."

Sascha growled. "We'd have to be lucky."

Hirianthial leaned against the wall. The texture of the air around them had become too dense, too interwoven with violence and anger. "There's only one guarding the bridge."

"The bridge," Sascha said. He straightened. "The distress call. They probably shut it off. We could get new a signal out . . . if they haven't destroyed our comm facility."

Hirianthial pulled the knife from his boot and tossed it to the Harat-Shar, who caught it with a frisson of silver-cold surprise.

"I can't make it that far," Hirianthial said. "The only way I can help is by distracting them."

"Will that work?" Sascha asked, eyes wide.

"They're looking for me," Hirianthial said and managed a thin smile. "If they find me, they won't have a reason to search the room. Good luck."

"Hirianthial, wait!"

He stepped out into the corridor; the searchers were still four doors down.

"Down here," he said.

They stopped and aimed their rifles at him.

"Presumably your employers prefer me alive to dead," Hirianthial said. "Which suits me fine, since I'm not up to running."

—set us on fire like he did that building—heard he can read your mind from fifty paces—looks like if you pushed him he'd fall over—

"Poor mortals," Hirianthial said. "Any more afraid and you'd miss me if you shot."

That sent sparks of anger shooting from them both. That the sparks were more real to him than the men gave Hirianthial cause for concern. Fortunately his tenuous hold on consciousness required so much energy he had none to spare for worry.

"You just come quietly," one of them said.

"I had no other intention," Hirianthial said. "Lead the way."

"You first."

He shrugged and started down the corridor, concentrating on setting his feet on the approximate location of the floor and bracing himself with a hand against the wall. The river of suspicion and resentment flowing past him felt so solid he kept trying to lean on it and surprising himself by beginning to fall.

"Are you drunk?" one of them asked abruptly.

"No," Hirianthial said. "Just very, very sick."

That gave them both unwelcome images of him vomiting. *—shouldn't rush him—boss'll kill me if he keels over on our watch—yuck—*

Hirianthial smiled grimly and kept going.

"Here," one of them said finally. "In the mess hall."

The Eldritch stopped at the door, barred by the miasma of black and sickened yellow, the smell of gagging bile and the sound of wailing. The distress was so real he couldn't even see the door.

"Come on, pastehead, we don't have all day."

He grasped along the wall until he found the edge of the door. Even then he questioned his senses. Was that ridge the rounded molding on the wall or the softened edge of a haloarch?

"Oh for—" The man behind him shoved an elbow into the small of his back with all the violence of a spear. His thoughts, edged like razors and raw as wounds, punched through the slight grip Hirianthial held on reality and shattered it. Was he on the floor? Standing up? Was the man looking down at him real or a construct formed out of Reese's anger and Irine's fear and Kis'eh't's numb horror?

He was fairly certain the blow to his ribs was real. Booted foot, his training supplied. He'd have a contusion, but the bone was fine.

"What did you do to him?"

"Nothing!" a voice exclaimed.

"You didn't do nothing. You pushed him."

"Well, he was just standing there at the door like he couldn't find it! What was I supposed to do? Let him hang there?"

The voice above him hissed like water on hot metal. "You touched him? Are you an idiot?"

"It was just my elbow."

"Get out of my sight before I show you what I can do with an elbow."

The hot voice and monstrous presence hove near. Hirianthial tried to see it past the phantasmagoric mask painted on the face and failed.

"Still with us, spy?"

To talk would only give the man ammunition . . . but beyond his spiked body Hirianthial saw the huddled shapes of the others. His friends. When had they become friends? That didn't matter. What did was how their shapes had been distorted by a terrible dread. Their thoughts wove them glittering halos, made of partial phrases: *what-did-they-do-to-him* and *he's-going-to-die-for-certain* and *better-dead-than-tortured.*

Instead of talking to the demon, Hirianthial addressed those rattled thoughts. "Nothing is certain."

Consternation shot through their auras. *Maybe-he's-already-dying—this-wasn't-how-it-was-supposed-to-work-out*

"It hasn't finished working out yet," he continued, and then added reflectively, "I could die here."

He meant that to reassure them, but it failed. It also aroused the incredulity of his captor, who said, "You absolutely will not die. I'm scheduled to deliver you in one piece, still breathing."

"You're doing a poor job," Hirianthial said conversationally. He simply could not take a satyr with a demon's face seriously, even though his rational mind insisted that he was simply re-interpreting the detail he was receiving into images he could understand. Strange how that worked—like most Eldritch, he'd been controlling his mental talents since the moment of manifestation. He'd never experienced them unfettered. He'd never allowed himself. Particularly given how much stronger his talents had been than those of the average Eldritch, who needed touch to evoke the ability to sense thought and feeling. Perhaps this is how the fabled mind-mage Corel had always felt, and that was why he'd gone insane.

More likely this was the danger of his own broader-than-average ability, untrammeled. His brain could not process the wealth of information and began blurring the line between truth and hallucination. He'd never heard of esper synaesthesia. Someone should commission a medical study.

"Are you even listening to me?" the demon demanded, kicking him again. A new bruise. Too close to the fragile bones near the center of his chest, though. Hirianthial imagined the xiphoid process cowering.

The demon actually wanted an answer. Hirianthial said, "When you say something interesting, I'll be sure to listen."

Exasperation grew like twin horns from the man's head. "Here's something interesting, then. If you tell me what I want to know, I might let you go."

"You're lying," Hirianthial said.

A blank stare. The halo of thoughts from the others started spreading, bouncing off the walls. *he-shouldn't-do-that-he'll-incite-violence, what-can-he-possibly-know, oh-angels-if-he-hits-him-I'll-scream*

"If he's going to be violent I won't stop him," Hirianthial said to the voices outside his head. "He's not allowed to break me into actual pieces anyway. His employer was adamant on that point."

Fury showered sparks from the demon, who straightened. "Think you know everything, do you, witch? Think I'm stupid? I'm not. I know exactly how to hurt you." He motioned to two of the guards. "Put him in a closet."

that's-not-so-bad

"And dump him in with the rest of the prisoners. Let's see how he likes being crammed in with them, skin to skin."

The wince he heard as a strange combination of a violin squeal and a door creaking must have been visible, because the demon laughed. "Oh, that bothers you, fine Captain? I didn't mean it literally—"

Don't relax, Hirianthial thought.

"Until now. Strip them and get it done. The hour it'll take us to get through to the cargo should reduce him to eager compliance."

How little he understood. An hour in this state in close proximity to other people would reduce him to complete insanity.

Reese fought for every square inch of her clothes until it became obvious how much the pirates were enjoying her struggles. Then she took off the last few bits herself and handed them over. Irine had foiled their darker thoughts by writhing out of her clothing so provocatively they'd had trouble keeping their hands to themselves. And of course, Kis'eh't wore only a vest, which she took off without fanfare, and Bryer's pants were mostly about providing pockets. Why was it that the only person with a decent nudity taboo was herself?

Well, herself and Hirianthial. Except she highly doubted he was in any condition to care. And he was a doctor, anyway.

The pirates chose the smallest closet they could find, which was far too small for Reese's taste. Bryer went in first, flattening against the back wall. Then Kis'eh't, making herself as small as possible but still taking up more than two people's floor-space. Irine solved that problem by straddling the Glaseah's back.

"Come on, Captain," Irine said, patting the space in front of her. "There's room for you here."

Reese eyed the remaining space. If they scrunched up enough, they might be able to give Hirianthial a little clearance. She sighed and wedged herself in front of Irine, arms crossed in front of her chest. The air on her body didn't just embarrass her . . . it gave her the uncomfortable feeling that every part of her body was now vulnerable. How could she possibly protect it when every inch was exposed?

The guards didn't seem to know where to start with Hirianthial's elaborate clothes. As one of them plucked at his buttoned collar, Reese couldn't contain herself any longer. "I wouldn't."

"I'm sure you wouldn't," the one holding the Eldritch up said.

"I don't think you understand," Reese said. "If you strip him and shove him in here with us, he's going to go crazy."

They eyed her suspiciously. She couldn't blame them. She had no idea where her conviction came from, but she was certain. To be trapped in here skin-to-skin with so many off-worlders would drive Hirianthial's mind away, permanently.

"The boss said . . . "

"Your boss said he was supposed to deliver him alive and capable of answering questions. Look at him," Reese said. "He's already half-gone. You want to be the reason why he ends up all gone?"

"We have orders."

"Fine," Reese said. "Follow them. But Blond and Nasty's not going to get the axe when the Eldritch dies because you stripped him naked and shoved him in a closet . . . you are, for doing it."

That gave them both pause. As they exchanged nervous glances, Reese hid her clenched hands behind Kis'eh't's back. Irine's body trembled behind her.

"Don't want him drooling crazy when they come for him," one of the men said finally.

"Just chuck him in," the other said.

A nod. They were agreed. They deposited Hirianthial in the closet fully-dressed and shut the door.

Irine hugged her tightly from behind. "They listened to you! I can't believe they listened to you!"

"Well, I was right," Reese said. "Kis'eh't, can you arrange him so he has a layer of air between us?"

A hoarse whisper. "I can. Arrange myself."

Reese ducked behind Kis'eh't's upper body. "I thought you were unconscious!"

"I'm not?" Hirianthial asked. He sounded curious, distracted. His eyes when she chanced a look at them failed to focus on any one person or point in space. Still, when he folded his limbs up, knees to chest and arms around them, Reese let out a relieved breath.

"Now what?" Kis'eh't asked.

"We wait," Hirianthial said. "For Sascha."

"I miss him," Irine said.

"Sascha," Reese said, puzzled. "Where is he, anyway? Hirianthial?"

But the Eldritch had closed his eyes again, forehead lowering until it touched his knees.

"Hey, no, don't do that. Hirianthial! Stay focused!"

He didn't move.

"This is ridiculous," Reese said, covering her face. "Ridiculous. I'm trapped in a storage closet while pirates ransack my ship."

"Naked," Irine added.

"You're not helping," Reese growled.

"Sorry," Irine said. "If it helps, you have nothing to be ashamed of."

"Nothing to be ashamed of!"

Kis'eh't fanned her feathered ears. "You could have phrased that better, Irine."

"If I tell her she's attractive in any other way she'll decide I'm flirting," Irine said.

"Are you?" Kis'eh't asked.

"No," Irine said. "Well, not yet."

Reese scowled.

"Clear your minds," Bryer said suddenly. "Or you will

tax the healer."

"Right. Easy for you to say," Irine said.

Hirianthial mumbled something. Kis'eh't bent closer, carefully. "Speak again?"

"Take the tabard. For the lady."

"I don't need your clothes," Reese said, frowning.

"That's just what I was saying!" Irine said.

Long white fingers unclasped one of the brooches, then the other. The tabard dropped forward into Hirianthial's lap, crumpling between his knees and his stomach.

"He's still dressed under it," Kis'eh't said, pinching one of the tabard's edges and pulling it free before drawing the opposite side from behind the Eldritch.

"Why me?" Reese asked.

"Because you make more of it than we do," Bryer said. "That disorders your mind more."

"Well, your nakedness disorders me as much as mine does!" Reese exclaimed.

"Yeah, but he's only got enough clothes for one more person," Kis'eh't said, twisting toward her. "Besides, we've got fur. And, er, scales. You don't. Here, put it on."

Grumbling, Reese accepted the fabric. Her fingers began petting it before she stopped being angry. It was very soft. She wouldn't have called it velvet, but it had pile and it felt good on both sides. Irine helped her with the brooches, which were surprisingly heavy. Similar pins she'd handled in jewelry stores were usually hollow or alloyed with something lighter. These pressed on her shoulders like stones.

"Better," Bryer said.

"I guess so," Reese said. "How are we going to get out of this, though?"

"Sascha's still free," Irine said.

Or dead. Reese didn't voice that thought. Instead, she

asked, "Can we break out of the closet?"

"I can check," Irine said.

"Do that."

Irine sidled past her, skirting as far around Hirianthial as she was able—which was only a half-inch or so. She ran her hands over the door frame, sticking a claw-tip into the seam between the door and the pocket and checking the join and the corners. She ran her claws under the bottom, tapped along the opening edge, finally kicked it.

"No good," Reese guessed.

"Closets aren't meant to be opened from the inside," Irine said. "Standard Alliance construction wouldn't allow a closet to lock at all, but the *Earthrise* was built to a Terran spec that keeps doors on rooms under a certain size open while someone's inside."

"Except this door is closed," Kis'eh't said.

"If you short the circuit, the door will close and stay that way," Irine said. "Actively. It's supposed to be a response to possible decompression." She flattened her hands on the inside of the door and dragged. "This would usually work, but the door's holding itself closed."

"If we could get enough leverage on it could we get it open?" Reese asked.

"Possibly," Irine said. "But we'd need a door hook. If I had my clothes with me we could do it . . . " She scanned the cramped walls. "Is there anything in here made of wire?"

"There's nothing in here but us," Reese said. "I didn't use this closet for anything. I didn't even bother with shelves." She squinted. "You always carry lock-picks on your clothes?"

Irine shrugged. "Or things that can be made into picks. You never know when you're going to be locked in a closet."

"Nude," Reese finished.

"I'll have to start hiding them in my—"

"Don't finish that sentence," Reese said, covering her eyes. "I don't want to know." She rubbed her aching brows. "Look, are you sure we can't use something? A pin?"

Irine eyed the door. "You can't make a door hook out of a pin. You need at least an arm's length of heavy gauge wire. The short of the matter is we're not getting out of here by forcing the door."

Reese stared at her. "And you were hiding that kind of thing on your clothes?"

Irine shrugged, still pressing on the door frame. "I wasn't wearing those outfits because I needed lift. You'd be surprised what you can do with steel-sprung boning." She backed away from the door and snuggled back in behind Reese. "No go on the door. Not that way, anyway."

"Maybe we could talk our way out? The way we did in the slaver prison?" Kis'eh't said.

"Can they even hear us?" Reese asked.

"No," Irine said. When Reese eyed her askance, Irine blushed at the ears. "Well, what good are empty closets if you can hear through the doors?"

"We could yell," Reese said. "Or is yelling also not enough?"

"No, if you yell it's audible," Kis'eh't said, and added, "And I have my own cause to know that."

Irine blushed harder. "Sorry."

Kis'eh't waved a hand. "You have a nice voice at that octave."

"Ack!" Reese said. "Moving on from this topic. So if we yell we'll be heard. We need a plan."

"We could just say that Hirianthial needs medical attention," Kis'eh't said. "That would be true enough."

Reese tried not to look at the man slumped against the wall. "And then what? We jump them? They're still armed and we're not only not armed, we're naked."

"Bryer's always armed," Irine said. "And I've got claws, too."

"There's only room for one of you to jump out at a time," Reese said.

"Bryer then," Kis'eh't said. "He's more likely to succeed."

"So we jump the guards," Reese said. "Disarm them. Then what? Kill them all? How do we keep the *Crawler* and that second ship from sending more people? We can't escape them with a dead Well drive."

The door opened, flushing in a wave of cooler, fresher air. Stunned, they all looked out just as Sascha tumbled in, then fell over Kis'eh't's paws and landed in the narrow space between Hirianthial's calves, Bryer's claws and Reese's thigh. The door swooped shut again.

"Sascha!" Irine said and grabbed him. "Angels! I thought you were dead!"

"Did you?" Sascha asked. "Silly sib."

"Ungh," Kis'eh't said. "I love you all but three of you pressing on my spine is too much. And you're stepping on my wing, Sascha."

"Sorry!" Sascha said, wiggling down onto the ground and pressing his back against the wall opposite the door.

"You're hurt," Irine said. "What did they do to you?"

"Nothing serious."

"Contusions," Hirianthial said without looking up. "Two broken ribs. Fractured radius. Bind the cut on his forehead."

Sascha touched the patch of red above his eye. "They just beat me up. It doesn't matter. I got a call out on the Fleet broadcast channels, and they didn't catch it until just now. It's been going out for fifteen minutes now."

"Will they come in time?" Irine asked.

"I hope so," Reese said.

⇛ ⫣ ⇚

Hirianthial had seen centuries pass—had spent those centuries in what he'd perceived as appropriate tasks. He'd bred horses through generations. He'd mastered many of the more genteel arts a lord of any rank should know. He'd become educated in several disciplines, traveled, and even taken up a profession when he'd left Jisiensire. Though he'd done more and learned more than the member of any other Alliance species could have in several lifetimes, he'd never felt old until he'd lost his Butterfly. His wanders through Alliance space had been an epilogue to a life he'd decided was over until the *Earthrise's* crew reminded him that there was still joy in the world, still surprises. When remembering that hadn't chased away all the aches and pains in his limbs, he'd realized he actually was old, but hadn't minded.

Some part of his mind had always equated age with death.

That part of him was wrong.

He was currently trapped in a closet surrounded by people, but he could feel neither the floor beneath his flesh nor the touch of their bodies. He couldn't tell where the walls stopped and his hallucinations began. He couldn't hear his own heart beating . . . couldn't hold a thought about anything long enough to freight it with meaning.

He was standing across from death, and his knees were weakening. Too much longer and they'd crumple, and he would fall at the mercy of that shade and be gone. And to leave so soon in such an ignominious fashion after discovering relationships worth tending was too much to bear. He had to stay alive, somehow. That the disconnected thoughts of the people in the closet with him were hastening his demise was obvious. Out of well-meaning concern for him they remained silent, as if stilling their voices would likewise still their minds. Instead it allowed each of them to descend into a private storm of thoughts, all on different topics with crazed tangents. He had to stop them. He had to get them thinking down the same path.

"Story."

Their attention focused on him, though he couldn't see their lifted faces. His voice sounded hoarse and too far away. He cleared it. "Tell us a story."

"Are you sure?" Sascha asked.

"Please," Hirianthial said.

"It would pass the time," Kis'eh't said.

"What story, though?" Reese asked.

"Tell us what happened on Mars," Sascha said.

Reese's denial fractured the fog in the room. "That's not a story."

"You went to Mars?" Irine asked.

"I want to hear about this," Kis'eh't said, her thoughts narrowing to a pinprick of curiosity.

"It's not your business what I did on Mars," Reese said. "I don't want to talk about it."

"Is it all that important compared to us dying in an hour or two?" Sascha asked.

"We're not going to die!" Reese said testily.

"I hope we're not," Kis'eh't said, "but odds aren't good."

The silence grew top-heavy with Reese's wariness and fear.

"Tell us, Reese," Irine said. An arabesque of humor that dissipated like incense smoke, softening the air: "What could be worse than sitting naked in a closet with a bunch of Harat-Shar?"

Reese's voice lost its taut pressure. "Fine. Fine. Mars." A sigh. "A long, long time ago, Mars was a colony. It was a productive colony. Lots of cities under bubbles, tourism, mining, very exciting stuff. We were humanity's first major colony in space, the first self-sustaining one . . . would you believe the Moon didn't get a permanent colony until after Mars was established? Yeah, really."

With the words came pictures: rolling landscapes, red and pink and dusty. The approach from space, with the long curve of the planet seeded with Reese's affection. This place was home. All the thoughts of the listeners aligned, caught up in Reese's words. Hirianthial began to breathe again—no, to notice his breathing.

"We were just heading into space, really into space. Those were really special times," Reese said. "It wasn't as easy for us as it was for you in the Alliance. You left and . . . I don't know. You just had it easier. We had to fight our own instincts to get out into the solar system. It was expensive. There was so much to do on Earth . . . how could we justify spending the money on pie-in-the-sky projects like space? If we hadn't started getting scared about asteroid hits, we might have never gone." An introspective pause, full of apprehension over something that had never happened. "But we did go. And we prospered. Humans need to be pioneers, you understand? They need to get out. I think we must have given that to you Pelted, and I'm glad, since it's one of our better qualities.

"Anyway, we were a colony under a strange charter. Earth had a united world government then, if a sort of rickety one made up of all the nations agreeing to a superbody above them. It wasn't a very effective world government, but it worked for a while. Mars was established under their charter, so they're the ones Mars went to when it decided it was done being a colony and was ready to be a real nation. Except they didn't want to be governed by Earth's global government because it was, well, Earth's global government. Mars was a different planet. We had different needs. And since Earth needed so much more than we did . . . and we had so much to give, we didn't want to end up indentured servants for life. We thought it was reasonable, anyway."

Reese stopped for a moment. The dense cloud of thoughts and emotions in the room had clarified to the point where he could see again; she was picking at her nails.

"This is ancient history, but it feels like it happened to me because in a way it did," Reese said. "The short of it is that there was a war. The nations on Earth couldn't even agree on whether to attack us or not, so they separated and started fighting one another at the same time half of them were fighting us. It was a very long, vicious war, and by the time it was done Earth was in shambles and Mars had lost most of its fighters. Most of them men. The women got by and had families by ordering sperm and getting artificially fertilized.

"That was ancestors ago for me," Reese said. "Most Martian families now are normal, but some insist on keeping tradition. My family's been an unbroken line of girls born to fatherless women for generations. We stay home, eke out a living doing something appropriately homey, have a nice baby daughter and then that daughter takes care of us when we get old."

"And you're out here," Irine said—Hirianthial was fairly certain, at least. Their thoughts were so loud it was sometimes hard to tell when they were being said or being nursed in silence.

Reese nodded. "I'm out here. Spending the family money on something not very homey at all. And very definitely not settling down to take care of my mother and grandmother and having a girl of my own." *No, instead, I'm looking for the father my mother never picked because she was afraid of real partnerships. Of love. Love like in romance novels. Love that lasts until you die and maybe after that.*

"You can't give your mother a husband," Hirianthial said.

Utter shock, so bright he realized Reese's last thoughts had been just that.

"Excuse me?" Reese asked.

So long as he was damned, he should give her the antidote in its entirety. "Nor can you prove to your family that not all masculine endeavors are unworthy and not all marriages are travesties. You cannot give them the happiness and balance they have denounced. You can only seek it yourself."

All the doors in her mind slammed shut, demonstrating that non-espers could in fact shield their thoughts—they just didn't know how to do so consciously and rarely had cause. The last thing that leaked from her before the lock-down completed was a wrath at his betrayal so towering it nearly branded the words into his heart: *HE ROBBED MY MIND. HE INVADED ME!*

"My deepest apologies," he said, though he knew the words would fall on closed ears.

"It's okay, Boss," Sascha said. "We're all looking for something we can't find."

"What's that?" Reese asked.

"Home," Sascha said.

"Purpose," Irine said.

"A garden," Bryer said, surprising them all.

Kis'eh't nodded. "All of those things. And peace."

Reese eyed Hirianthial. "And you?"

Surrounded on all sides by the purity of their longing and the clean light of their candor, Hirianthial thought of how lucky he'd been to have had all those things for a short time . . . and how unlikely it seemed that he could hope for them again after so much destruction and pain.

And you? What do you want?

"A second chance."

The intensity of their married thoughts helped keep Hirianthial focused, so focused he could prepare for the door opening.

"Time to go," the guard said. "Pastehead first. Then the rest of you." He grinned and waved several pairs of cuffs. "This time, no tricks."

"You could just leave us in the closet," Sascha said cheerfully. "We might even look the other way about you stealing our cargo."

"No go, furry," the guard said. "The boss wants you all now that you've become so much trouble." He grinned. "White and skinny first."

The guard was not alone, and using what remained of his strength in an attempt to win free of the tangle of limbs and escape the men lined up in the hall would be a waste. If there was a path leading to freedom from this place it didn't diverge now. Best they thought him weak—it wasn't far from the truth anyway. "I can't get up alone."

The guard snorted and grabbed his arm, stabbing him with irritation and the smog of an unexamined mind. With the help of a comrade, they cuffed his hands behind his back. His knuckles rested over his hair and against something hard that filled his eyes with the sight of Irine's mischievous smile. The dangle, probably.

Shaking his head, Hirianthial waited in the corridor as the guards marched each of the crew out of the closet. His tabard fell to the floor on Reese, and Irine hadn't found the side clips that held it closed at his waist; on Reese, those clips hung near the upper thighs. As they started down the hall, she tripped on the tabard's edge twice.

"Cut it," the guard said. "We don't need her making an excuse for any sudden movements."

"No!" Reese said, twisting away. "I don't know where

Blond and Nasty picked you people up, but don't you have any decency at all?"

"The lady says decent," the guard said with a grin and grabbed the front end of the tabard. Before Reese could object, he burned it off at the knees and left it hanging, ragged. "There. Nice and modest for the queen here."

"Do you like destroying beautiful things or is it just part of the job?" Reese asked with a knotted asperity.

"Just keep moving, chocolate."

Throughout the trip to the cargo bay, Hirianthial forced himself to narrow his thoughts to the future, to finding a solution to their impending capture. His knife was gone. His hands were locked behind his back. And if Irine's laughing in his ears was an indication, he was still going insane. He could sense all five of the crew's anxieties separately, like burrs under his skin, dragging his attention from one direction to the next.

They were in the cargo bay. The pad station's status lights were on, including the blue one that signified the stable tunnel. The boxes were already arrayed beside it, each one crowded with carrion birds and crowned with a cold black shadow.

The blond leader awaited them near the pad. "First the spy," he said. "Then the boxes. Then the rest of the riffraff."

"You're calling us riffraff?" Reese asked. "You must be kidding."

"No kidding, Captain," Blond said. "I note you're finely dressed for someone I sent to a closet naked." He glanced at the guards. "Our spy is prettily dressed as well."

The guards shrugged. "He was going to die."

"I highly doubt that," Blond said.

"Why are we going across?" Kis'eh't asked.

"I don't ask questions, four-foot, and neither will you." The leader grabbed Hirianthial's wrists, pressing them

against his back, and the Eldritch lost the sight of the cargo
bay entirely.

*You're not seriously going to put that into the dangle,
are you? Sascha, grinning.*

*Why not? Irine's fingers, braiding the floss, hiding it
from view. We need something stiff at the bottom so the bell
will have something to move against. Besides, remember
how we met him?*

In a cell? Sascha laughing this time.

*Irine grinned. You never know when he might need one.
Her fingers tucked the final knot around the base of the lock
pick, concealing its metal gleam.*

I have a weapon, Hirianthial thought, stunned. His
mind flashed back to the hospital on Harat-Sharii and the
hours he'd spent toiling on the Medimage platform; he saw
the diagram he wanted, right down to the page number.

"A couple more steps," Blond said. "You can make it."

Hirianthial twined his fingers through his hair . . . and
stumbled. His captor cursed as they fell and Hirianthial
rolled onto his side, yanking at the base of the dangle
where Irine's clever fingers had left a loop.

"What are you doing?" Blond said.

Push me back—and the man did, kicking him in the
stomach. Hirianthial flopped onto the pin he held out in
his clenched fingers . . . driving it through the winking
lights on the Pad. If it really was as much like the Medimage platform as the manual had claimed . . . and it was. An
innocuous click, too small for the magnitude of its meaning. The lights on the Pad died.

"What the—" Their leader grabbed his shoulder and
jerked him forward, then exploded into red flame, seething. He turned to the guards that had escorted them into
the closet and killed them, two bursts from his rifle.

"Next time when I say naked, I mean naked," Blond said

to the remaining pirates. "Not dressed and *NOT ARMED*."

The brutal murder of humans should have scarred him, defenseless and open . . . but it had been so quick Hirianthial didn't have time to feel them passing before another wave crested against his mind, alien and unexpected. He smiled and closed his eyes as the cavalry charged.

Dozens of people erupted into the cargo bay out of Pad nothingness, black and blue uniforms sprinting past, beams of light appearing out of nowhere. A voice barked orders: "Keep them alive!"

And then Jonah NotAgain of the UAV *StarCounter* and his very welcome crew immobilized every single pirate, disarmed them and pressed them flat onto the deck with their hands behind their backs and their legs cuffed. With quiet competence, the Fleet men and women stripped the fetters off her crew and Reese found herself catapulted from abject fear and hopelessness to a profound joy.

"I could hug you," she said to the craggy-faced captain of the *StarCounter*. "In fact, I will." And she did. The Tamillee held his arms out from her, then chuckled.

"You called, Captain Eddings? I wish we could have arrived sooner."

"You're here now," Reese said. "And am I glad. But there's another ship—"

"We've already impounded both ships," NotAgain said. "The first's not much good anymore; we had to poke too many holes in it. The second didn't put up much of a fight, so we figured most of them were here. Turns out that part's true."

"So all the pirates," Reese started.

"Dead or in the brig," NotAgain said. His gaze caught on the captives on the floor. "Or they will be soon." He nodded to his people. "Take them back for questioning."

"Captain," Reese said. "We've got to talk. And our Eldritch needs a real Medplex, if you've got one. And the twins, they broke some of their bones."

"Our medical staff's at your disposal," NotAgain said. "Shandy, see to the injured, please."

The medic checked the twins over and said, "The woman's fine, but we'll have to take the man back." She looked up at Irine. "You're going to have some pretty ugly bruises, though."

"Bruises I can handle," Irine said.

NotAgain looked down at Reese. "Perhaps we can meet in two marks? That should give you time to assess the damage to your vessel."

Reese wondered if that was a polite way of giving her the time to get dressed. The shorn tabard suddenly felt draftier. "Two marks sounds fine, Captain. We'll have coffee."

"And pie," Kis'eh't said weakly.

"You have pie?" NotAgain asked, amused.

"If you've got fruit, we do," Kis'eh't said. She ran her hands down her front legs, as if trying to keep them from trembling. "Anything for our saviors."

NotAgain laughed. "You don't have to trouble yourself."

"It's no trouble," Kis'eh't said.

"Let her," Reese said. "If you don't I'll never hear the end of it."

The Tam-illee shook his head. "All right," he said with a smile. "We'll send a bag over from stores. Pie and coffee in two marks . . . and we'll take care of your wounded."

"Thanks," Reese said and stepped back. In silence, she and the crew watched NotAgain's people rouse the prisoners, unfold their portable Pad, pick up the unconscious Eldritch, guide Sascha in front of them and vanish, all within minutes.

"They're fast," Kis'eh't said, eyes wide.

"They're good," Irine said, then started laughing. "I can't believe he used the pick!"

"What pick?" Reese asked, irritated.

"I put a pick in the dangle," Irine said. "I didn't think he'd have to use it so quickly! Now we'll have to repair it."

"With another pick?" Kis'eh't asked, distracted.

"Of course!" Irine said. "At the rate he's going, he'll use more of them than I will!"

"If he survives," Bryer said suddenly.

The conversation stopped.

"You don't think—he's just unconscious—"

"Surely a Fleet ship will be able to heal him," Kis'eh't said. "They have real doctors."

The Pad's blue channel indicator flashed, then began to glow. A few moments later a sack appeared on the station.

"They really don't waste time, do they?" Irine said.

"And neither should we," Reese said. "We'll meet in the mess hall in two hours."

In her own quarters, Reese shucked off the tabard and hopped into the water shower. She'd read countless stories where heroines recently handled by evil villains felt "soiled" and longed to wash themselves clean of the psychic dirt of their captivity, but Reese couldn't identify any psychic dirt, only the real stuff. She felt grimy, but the shower put paid to that and dressing in her own clothing fixed the rest of her misgivings. The pirates were gone. Fleet was here. Sascha and Hirianthial had access to real doctors. Things were looking up. She spent some time hunting the ship for Allacazam and found him still in the clinic. A short nap with the Flitzbe and she was ready to present herself in the cargo bay to receive Captain NotAgain, who stepped through with Sascha behind him.

"Captain Eddings," NotAgain said, and though his voice remained confident and friendly, he held himself tensely. "I think you'll find your crewman in much better shape."

Reese glanced past him at Sascha. "That true?"

"Very," Sascha said. "Hirianthial's sleeping, too. Really sleeping, not just unconscious."

"I guess that's a good sign."

"My C-med tells me it's as good a sign as we can expect," NotAgain said.

Reese nodded. "If I can show you to the mess hall?"

"Thank you," he said, and as he fell into step behind her she was certain that her visitor was preoccupied. He made no attempt at idle conversation and his eyes seemed focused on something inside himself, not on where they were going.

When the door to the mess hall opened, the aroma of cinnamon and apples flooded Reese on a wave of escaping air. She stopped in the door.

"I see our supplies went to good use," NotAgain said at her heels.

"Don't just stand there, Reese," the Glaseah said. "Let Captain NotAgain in so I can get him a slice!" She stood in the kitchen, cleaning a couple of bowls and wearing an apron.

"What about me?" Reese asked, walking into the room.

"And me?" Sascha asked.

"There's enough for everyone," Kis'eh't said.

The Tam-illee took a seat at the table and folded his hands on it. "Captain Eddings, will your crew be attending this meeting?"

"I hadn't really thought about it," Reese said, startled. "Should I send them away?"

"It may be easiest," NotAgain said.

His words weren't met with the chorus of groans and

wheedling that hers would have been had she said some-thing similar. Instead, before Reese could turn to them and tell them to leave, Sascha took himself out and Kis'eh't brought the pie in silence. She served them each a slice and a cup of coffee, removed her apron and left it hanging on a chair on her way out.

"They're never that well-behaved," Reese said, eyes wide. "How did you do that?"

NotAgain laughed. "By being someone they don't deal with daily who's also wearing a uniform. I suspect."

"So much for learning that trick," Reese said. She cupped her mug with her hands. "I imagine you've heard an earful about this already."

"We convinced some of the pirates to talk to us," Not-Again. "And your man Sascha filled us in on some of your half. I'd like to hear the full story from you, though."

"All right," Reese said and took a long breath. She start-ed with the call from the Eldritch Queen that had sent her searching for Hirianthial and left nothing out from there, even the bits she didn't understand clearly, like how Hiri-anthial had known the crystal people were sapient. Not-Again ate his pie and listened without interruption until she reached the end of her story; his questions sent her back-tracking across events, clarifying parts of it, bring forth details that seemed unimportant.

At last he set his fork down and pushed the plate aside. "You've been through a lot in the past few months, Captain."

"I'm ready for things to calm down again," Reese said. "I didn't sign up to be pirate-bait."

He laughed. "I imagine not. You're not angry they keep coming after you?"

"Angry? Of course I'm angry!" Reese said. "They chased me around, wrecked my ship *twice*, if you count me having to sabotage myself to keep them from killing us, and they made me murder over a hundred aliens? Yes, I'm angry. I can't wait for you to drag their sorry tails into a maximum security facility. Preferably a human-run one on a dirty airless asteroid."

"And if I said in order to do that I'd need your help?" NotAgain said, and sipped from his mug.

"My help?" Reese stared at him. "You must be kidding me. You're Fleet."

"Yes," NotAgain said. "And your information and the pirates we just impounded have given us what we need to disband one of the largest pirate-slaver rings in the Alliance Crown. We've been hoping for the key to the organized activity in Sector Andeka for two years. Now we have it. But we can't reach it without your help."

"Keep talking," Reese said warily.

"Fleet's jurisdiction is interplanetary piracy," NotAgain said. "In order to claim criminals on planets, we need either permission from the planetary authorities or evidence of space piracy."

"I guess that makes sense," Reese said.

"We suspect the man who wants these crystals, the one you've signed a contract with, is the link between the pirates and the Andeka slavers," NotAgain continued. "But it's only a suspicion unless he does something obvious."

"He signed a contract with me for dead people," Reese pointed out.

"But you haven't delivered," NotAgain said. "Until he either says something ridiculous in our hearing or transfers the full amount to you in acceptance for the contraband with both of you knowing full well what you're delivering, we don't have enough evidence to demand extradition."

"This is crazy!" Reese said. "The man is a drug dealer! Isn't knowing that he wants to make drugs enough, that he paid for me to go get him raw materials?"

"He could say the materials were intended for something else," NotAgain said. "He could claim he didn't know what they were. We need to catch him full in the act to take him away." He looked at her. "We would like you to complete your mission, Captain. Take him the crystals. Deliver them in person."

"And try to get him to confess he's a drug lord?" Reese asked. "Why would he do that?"

"Why wouldn't he do that to a possible partner?" NotAgain said. "As far as he knows, not only did you do the work he asked for, but you wiped out two of his ships when they got in your way. If you sound motivated by money, he may want to employ you permanently. Once he finds out that the pirate ships are gone you become intriguing."

"And a Fleet ship being in the vicinity isn't enough reason for pirate ships to blow up?" Reese asked.

NotAgain smiled. "Not if that Fleet ship is Dusted."

Reese toyed with the handle of her mug. "This sounds very dangerous."

"It is," NotAgain said. "But we'll do everything we can to give you the back-up to get out safely."

The idea was patently ridiculous. Why would she want to go directly into the den of the bad guys? That was Fleet's job, not hers. And to do it pretending to be a bad guy herself . . . she wasn't sure she could pull off an acting job like that. She was definitely sure that if she succeeded she'd have to figure out how to wash off that famed "psychic dirt" she hadn't noticed after merely being handled by the bad guys.

"Captain Eddings," NotAgain said. "These people are killers. They prey on people like you who are trying to make an honest living. They strip their cargoes from them, destroy their livelihoods. They kill them if caprice moves them. They sell drugs that destroy people's minds and lives. And when they're done with that, they kidnap people and sell them to the Chatcaavan empire, to be abused by aliens: men. Women. Children barely tall enough to reach your hip. Help us shut them down, please."

Reese covered her face, rubbed it, looked at her untouched dessert. "I want to help, but knowing how bad they are doesn't make me feel any braver."

"It won't be easy and it won't be safe," NotAgain said. "I won't trick you into this by telling you we'll be able to insure you come out in one piece. But we'll do everything in our power, Captain Eddings. Everything."

She'd gotten them into this. She couldn't just step out and let someone else fix it. And even if she tried to step out of it there was no guarantee they wouldn't find her again. No one was going to be safe until Fleet cut the ring apart. She took a deep breath. "All right."

"Thank you," NotAgain said.

"Thank me when I walk out of this and after delivering what you need," Reese said. "It's not over until then."

"I'll thank you twice," NotAgain said, "because you'll have earned it." He grinned. "Don't dwell on the worst, Captain. In a few weeks you'll probably be on your way . . . and just think what a story you'll have to tell your children!"

"Yeah," Reese said, grimacing. If she decided to have any. If she *lived* to have any.

He stood. "I need to coordinate the plan. You don't mind remaining here?"

"It's not like I have a choice," Reese said. "My Well drive's down."

"We'll send some people over," NotAgain said. "Unlike your previous boarders, we'll actually fix the drive."

Reese managed a chuckle. "That would be greatly appreciated."

He nodded. "Expect some people in half a mark. I'll be in touch."

"I look forward to it," Reese said.

The moment the Tam-illee stepped out of the room, everyone else rushed in. Kis'eh't first, then the wriggling of the twins and finally Bryer, sauntering in last.

"Tell us all about it!" Irine said, Allacazam in her arms.

"I thought my quarters were locked," Reese said as the Harat-Shar presented the Flitzbe to her.

"Well, we had to find him!" Irine said. At Reese's expression, she said, "If it makes you feel better, your quarters were the last place I checked."

Reese stroked the Flitzbe's fur. "Well, get his lamp set up. We can all eat while we talk."

"Did the captain like the pie?" Kis'eh't asked while the twins went for the plates.

"He must have," Reese said. "He ate it."

"But he didn't say anything?" the Glaseah asked.

"We had other things on our minds," Reese said. She stuck a fork through the end of her slice and tried it. "I'll say it for him. It's really, really good."

Kis'eh't brightened. "Remind me to tell you about the recipe."

Once the Flitzbe had been set in the light and everyone had something to eat, Reese said, "We have a task."

"Uh-oh," Kis'eh't said.

"Isn't this how we started on the whole pirate adventure?" Sascha asked. "With a "task"?"

"I bet we're not getting paid for this one either," Irine said, grinning around her fork.

Reese eyed them. "This is not funny."

"Yes it is," Irine said.

"Let her finish," Kis'eh't said. "I want to hear about 'The Task.' "

Reese said, "We're going to deliver the crystals to the nasty people so that Fleet can catch them in the act of doing something illegal in an extra-planetary way."

"That sounds dangerous," Kis'eh't said.

"Last time we took jobs that sounded easy, they turned out to be dangerous," Sascha said. "That means the dangerous one should turn out to be easy."

"I'm not sure you're taking this seriously enough," Reese began.

"Give us the democracy speech!" Irine crowed.

"The what?" Reese said, staring at her.

"You know, the part when you tell us that you all hired us and if we don't agree then we can just have our severance pay in something useless," Irine said. "Like rooderberries."

"Or engine parts," Sascha said.

"Except this time it would be crystals," Kis'eh't said.

"Bleh," Irine said.

"We're even missing Hirianthial, just like the first time," Sascha said. "For the same reason, even . . . he got on the wrong end of a bunch of pirate-slavers."

Reese fought the sensation that she'd lost control of her own meeting. "Can we stay on target here? We're about to do something dangerous. I want to make sure everyone knows that."

"We're trying to tell you we're fine with it," Sascha said.

She looked at them all. "Without knowing more? After everything that's happened?"

"We're still breathing," Sascha said.

"To do this is to serve the Eye," Bryer said.

Kis'eh't nodded. "It's the right thing to do."

"That's it?" Reese asked, incredulous. "You're fine with it? Even though the pay is sporadic, we keep getting shot at and according to you I'm prickly as a potted cactus?"

"A steady paycheck we could get anywhere," Sascha

said. "Finding steady adventure is much harder."

Kis'eh't chortled.

"All right," Reese said, then laughed. "I don't know what I did to deserve you people, but thanks for coming along."

"Just don't forget Hirianthial," Kis'eh't said. "He's one of us too."

"He might not want to stick around," Reese said, trying not to sound as resentful as she felt.

"We'll see," Sascha said. "Do you need us to do anything, boss?"

"If you and Bryer could help the Fleet engineers with the Well Drive, that would be great," Reese said. "They're due in twenty minutes or so. I won't know more until we're up and running."

"Sounds good," Sascha said. He stood and stretched. "Twenty minutes. I wonder what happened to that DNA-lock?"

"It probably exploded all over the inside of the ship," Reese said.

Irine laughed. "Oh, Reese. Of course it didn't. It wasn't an exploding lock!"

Reese stopped in the act of setting down her fork. "But it had the manufacturer's seal!"

"Of course it did," Irine said. "It wouldn't have been a convincing fake otherwise." She reached for Sascha's hand. "Let's go have a look at it."

"Is it even a real DNA-lock?" Reese called after them. Irine's only answer was her trailing laugh. Bryer followed the twins out, leaving Kis'eh't to cover the pie and put away the dishes. The sound reminded Reese suddenly of her mother cleaning in the kitchen and a surge of melancholy overwhelmed her. It reacted poorly with her anxiety about the forthcoming Fleet mission, and for several minutes she listened to Kis'eh't's paw pads scraping on the floor and the sound of the tap running as the Glaseah washed off her hands.

Reese thought she'd be glad for a broken silence until Kis'eh't spoke.

"I don't know why you're mad at him, but you shouldn't be."

"What?" Reese asked, startled out of her contemplation of the dregs of her coffee.

"Hirianthial," Kis'eh't said. "He only irritated you before. Now when anyone mentions him you tighten up like drying twine."

"If you don't know why I'm mad at him, how can you say I shouldn't be?" Reese asked.

"Because he means well," Kis'eh't said.

Reese rolled her eyes. "And that excuses everything."

The Glaseah sighed and folded her apron, tucking it beneath the counter. "One day, Reese, you'll have to stop being so closed to other people."

"I'm not closed to other people," Reese said. "I'm just cautious. Besides, being closed is a courtesy. It keeps other people from having to know you in order to work with you."

Kis'eh't said, "That makes so little sense I can't even begin to address it."

"The point is that foisting your moods, opinions and ideas on other people is rude," Reese said. "And having other people being able to pluck them out of mid-air is worse."

Kis'eh't folded her arms. "So that's it. You're angry at him for reading your mind when he was so sick he could barely stand, much less do you the courtesy of not hearing the things you were shouting at the top of your mental lungs."

"Well he shouldn't have!" Reese said.

"He couldn't help it," Kis'eh't said. "Any more than you could help throwing up on him when your esophagus was tearing apart."

"How do you know?" Reese asked.

"Because I went through esper school like every Glaseah ever born," Kis'eh't said, exasperated. "Unlike ninety-nine percent of my race, I don't have the faculties needed to become an esper, but I had plenty of theory classes. And I definitely know this: if you're absolutely shredded, you can't stop yourself from hearing other thoughts."

"How do they know?" Reese asked. "There's no testing it. It might as well be magic."

"It's not magic," Kis'eh't said. "It's the facts as we know them, unless you're willing to accept so many bizarre co-incidences that you'd have to rewrite some of the laws of the universe to make them possible. It's not magic just because we can't see it and we haven't codified the math that explains it."

"He should have stayed out of my head," Reese muttered.

"You should have stayed out of his," Kis'eh't replied.

"I'm not the psychic one!" Reese exclaimed.

"That doesn't matter," Kis'eh't said, then threw up her hands. "You're so ignorant on this matter you don't even know how little basis you have for being upset. But there's plenty of literature in the u-banks. Why don't you actually read something about esper abilities before you decide to be upset about them?"

"Because it's not about him being able to read my mind and doing it," Reese said. "It's about him having done it and now knowing what's in my head!"

Kis'eh't's round-eyed stare was so shocked Reese fumbled to a halt. The Glaseah shook her head slowly. "Oh, Reese."

That was it. Nothing else. The Glaseah headed for the door and was out of it before Reese could get up a good head of anger about being pitied. She ran to the door and looked out it. "Oh Reese what?"

But Kis'eh't had already gone around the bend, leaving her to stand in the door and fume.

The first thing Hirianthial noticed on attaining consciousness was the familiar symphony of a Medplex: the hum of generators, the assorted musical status sounds of halo-arches, the occasional hiss of an AAP. From the range of the alerts, Hirianthial guessed he was in a high-end facility—he hadn't heard some of the musical combinations since leaving one of the more impressive teaching hospitals on Tam-ley.

"Welcome back," Sascha said.

Opening his eyes, Hirianthial found himself trapped beneath a halo-arch in a streamlined room. The electronics he'd identified by ear were so tightly arranged he had to be on a ship.

All of which mattered less than the fact that he was within touching distance of a Harat-Shar on a stool and he couldn't hear the tigraine's thoughts at all.

"You're on the UAV *StarCounter*," Sascha said.

"How's your arm?" Hirianthial asked, noting the tape.

"Good," Sascha said. "The doctors told me when they wrapped it that I didn't really need to keep it on for a week, but we were in Wellspace so I couldn't transfer over for them to have a look at it until now."

"You didn't break it again, then," Hirianthial said.

Sascha grinned. "Not for want of trying!" He shook his head. "Seriously, I'm fine. They said they were just going to take it off and get a cursory look under my skin to make sure their quick-heal went well."

"Good," Hirianthial said. "Everyone else . . .?"

"They're good," Sascha said. "Preparing for the grand adventure, which you haven't heard about yet."

Hirianthial cocked a brow.

"We get to help Fleet crack open the multiple crime rings in Andeka by delivering the cargo as planned . . . in person. And Reese has to act like a cold-hearted mercenary to convince them that they shouldn't bother killing her when she shows up," Sascha said. "When she gets them to give her the rest of the money in exchange for the cargo, that'll give Fleet what they need to clean up. We just dropped out of Well, and we're planning the approach for tomorrow."

"And this will allow Fleet to finish what they began a few months ago," Hirianthial said.

Sascha nodded. "The rumor in the corridors is that it's going to lead to hundreds of arrests throughout the sector. Of course, that's just rumor. What their captain told Reese he's certain of is that it'll shut down this sector's link to the slave trade. The dragons will have to find their toys somewhere else."

The anger that had prompted him to set fire to a slave lord's house had only been sleeping; Hirianthial felt it flare anew when presented with the opportunity to help bring Fleet into the nest of criminals Liolesa had sent him to investigate.

"You're lucky you woke up in time," Sascha said. "We'd have hated to see you sleep through the fun."

"I would have hated to sleep through it," Hirianthial said.

"Sascha," said a voice just out of Hirianthial's eyeshot, "I see you've arrived. Doctor Endalish will see you in conference two . . . that's the second door down that hall there, on the right."

Sascha hopped off the stool. "Thanks."

"Sascha," Hirianthial said.

The Harat-Shar paused.

"Thank Irine for her prescient gift when you get back."

Sascha laughed. "I'll do that."

The Harat-Shar vanished, and the man who replaced him on the stool was an older Tam-illee in the stark blue and black of the Fleet uniform. Unlike his captain, the doctor looked more like a fox, with soft auburn fur, black arms and ears and a demi-muzzle. He had the composed demeanor only experience seemed to grant to doctors, and folded his hands as he sat, showing no haste.

"Lord Sarel Jisiensire," the man said. "My name is Doctor Brit SorrowsEase. I'm the Chief Medical Officer of the UAV *StarCounter*." He shifted on his chair. "You are a peer in the profession, so perhaps you'll appreciate that in my thirty-seven years of practice, twenty-two of which were spent treating what I believe to be the most accident-prone people in the Alliance, I have never seen a case as peculiar as yours."

"I believe you," Hirianthial said.

"Fortunately I had access to several other specialists elsewhere in Fleet," SorrowsEase continued. "Between the four of us we restored you. Or we think we did. Frankly, I believe rest, fluids and an environment free of stimulus did most of the work. How do you feel?"

"Normal," Hirianthial said, testing as he spoke. His shields were intact. The room remained comfortable and the Tam-illee's presence merely decorated with his aura, not drowned out by it. With concentration Hirianthial could feel the ship's personnel, but they did not swamp him with their feelings. "Remarkably so. May I ask how I presented?"

"Unconscious, dehydrated and showing signs of muscle cannibalization," SorrowsEase said. "We could detect no external actor on your body at all: no pathogen, no physical injury. The electrical activity in your brain was depressed."

"Depressed," Hirianthial mused. "I would have expected the opposite."

"So did we when your crewmate described your symptoms previous to your arrival here," the Tam-illee said. "Our theory was that while in that state your brain was overactive and your body reacted as if you had a severe fever or infection."

"The metabolic signs," Hirianthial said.

SorrowsEase nodded. "We could see nothing to treat, so after conferring we isolated you here. One week later, you're awake and seem cogent."

"Curious," Hirianthial said.

"Very," SorrowsEase agreed. "I have never treated an esper for overload before. I'm not sure the experience has clarified any of the questions I had." He smiled. "But you've recuperated, which was our intent. I won't argue with results."

"Are you releasing me?" Hirianthial asked, thinking of the crystals.

"I can," SorrowsEase said. "I'm not entirely comfortable with it. If as far as you can ascertain your mind is working as it should, I must take your word for it . . . but you've just woken from the equivalent of a bad bout with the flu. You need bed-rest and nourishment. And you need to work your way back to your prior condition. Which reminds me . . . you have significant arthritis in your knees, elbows and wrists. I have no idea how old you are, but you seem in good health. Given that your organs aren't going to fail you soon, you should be taking more conscious steps to prevent wear on your joints."

Hirianthial said, "Therapeutic exercise hasn't been on my mind, I admit."

"Consider it prescribed," SorrowsEase said. His eyes traveled over the Eldritch's body with a detached curiosity. Then he reached over and tapped the halo-arch, causing it to withdraw with a descending arpeggio. As Hirianthial gingerly sat up, the Tam-illee said, "A final note, Lord. Fleet medical procedure is strict on the matter of patient confidentiality and rigorous in particular with allied species. I am required to ask your permission to release the medical information I obtained while treating you. If you decline, all data gathered and shared with my colleagues will be purged."

That would have been Maraesa's doing. Liolesa's aunt had decided to take Jerisa's Veil even further and re-negotiated the treaty with the Alliance during her reign, pushing for more stringent privacy laws . . . all wasted, as far as Hirianthial had been able to tell, since Maraesa's policies had fueled xenophobia among the Eldritch to a point where not a single one would have stepped off-world, even at sword-point. Nothing in Hirianthial's medical ethics code addressed whether he should honor the Eldritch Veil or add to the Alliance's biological knowledge base.

"Am I the first Eldritch you've ever treated?" Hirianthial asked.

"Yes," SorrowsEase said, then smiled. "You'll decide based on whether I'm likely to treat another Eldritch, won't you."

"Out of respect to the laws of my people, I can't release data merely for scientific curiosity," Hirianthial said.

"In fairness I must say that I'm not likely to have another Eldritch in my Medplex . . . unless your people are planning to become less isolationist?"

Hirianthial shook his head, the minute motion twist of

the chin he'd learned as a child, not the full head turn he'd learned in the Alliance. "Not likely. I'm afraid I cannot give permission, Doctor SorrowsEase . . . though I hope having had the experience will be some consolation."

This time the Tam-illee grinned, a look so unexpectedly gleeful Hirianthial almost laughed. "I will much enjoy trotting you out at dinner parties in the future, Lord."

Hirianthial chuckled. "You've richly earned it. Other than rest, food and judicious exercise, you have no other recommendations?"

SorrowsEase shook his head. "None."

"Then perhaps you can tell me where I could find Captain NotAgain," Hirianthial said.

"So I set down here," Reese said, tapping the map, "then take the crystals into this compound, where you believe the man in charge of it all is waiting."

"Marlane Surapinet," NotAgain confirmed. They were sitting in one of the *StarCounter's* luxurious but small conference rooms, having extremely fresh shipboard coffee. Reese had never been aboard a Fleet ship, though she'd seen pictures of their interiors. Nothing prepared her for the visceral reality. The *StarCounter* smelled fresh, was clean and well-appointed; its corridors seemed designed for comfort and yet nothing struck her as overdone. And the technology level was simply astonishing. The appliances in this conference room alone would have cost her as much as employing the twins for a couple of months.

Back to the plan. "I convince him to personally sign over the money for the crystals and then you have your evidence," Reese said. "And then I leave."

"That's the plan under best circumstances," NotAgain said.

Reese eyed him. "What are the worst circumstances?"

"That they know you're coming and that you're working for us, and they imprison you. At which point we'll come after you, since they'll have no legal reason to kidnap you."

"Okay, I like that option a lot less than option number one," Reese said, shivering.

"There's worse," NotAgain said. "We have cause to believe they base a lot of their operations out of the Barris, where you'll be landing. If they have ships there and they realize what you're doing, your arrival might inspire them to flee."

"Why's that bad?" Reese asked.

"Because I'd be required to stop them," NotAgain said.

Reese shook her head. "I'm so glad I don't have your job."

He laughed. "It's rewarding work. It's just not easy." He tapped the map. "What I'd like you to do is to stay on-planet after you make your drop-off until you receive word that local-space is clear."

"That sounds straightforward enough."

"We'll also loan you some men to help secure the area around your landing site," NotAgain said. "Unfortunately I don't have a lot to spare, but I can get you at least two, possibly four."

"Every extra hand will help," Reese said. "Thanks. When do you want me to make my final approach?"

"I've called in some help," NotAgain said. "We should be ready in a couple of hours. Speaking of which, I hope you've evolved a cover?"

Reese nodded. "I think I've created a persona I could actually believe." She smiled wryly. "I'm not exactly the most dangerous person in the world, but I have a good imagination."

"Good," NotAgain said. "I hope your persona wears

a button-down shirt." He set a pin topped with a round black seed on the table between them.

"What is it?" Reese asked, picking it up. The pin was barely the length of one of her nails.

"A remote 3deo capture," NotAgain said.

Reese started. "This thing? It's microscopic! I've never seen a camera this small on the market!"

He laughed. "And you won't find one there."

"I guess there are benefits to being Fleet," Reese said. "Aren't they going to detect it, though?"

"They shouldn't," NotAgain said. At her look, he said, "We do our best to stay ahead of the curve, captain, but that doesn't mean we always succeed. That's the latest in surveillance equipment but you should never assume the advantage. If they find it at all, it will probably be in the same check that finds the weapons we're lending your crew for verisimilitude. Shrug it off as something any mercenary would have and they shouldn't think twice about it."

"Unless they recognize it as Fleet issue," Reese said.

"They won't," NotAgain said. "Nor the weapons. We're careful about clandestine operations."

Reese sighed. "I guess I can't hope for more than that."

He shook his head. "No. I've already sent the weapons to the Pad room, where your crewman should be waiting—" The meeting room door chimed. NotAgain glanced at the ceiling. "Yes?"

"Captain, one of the *Earthrise* crew to see his captain."

NotAgain looked at her. "Are we done here?"

Reese nodded. "It's probably Sascha."

The Tam-illee said, "Thank you, Ensign. Let him in."

The door opened on a young human who acknowledged his captain before stepping aside for Hirianthial. For once, Reese allowed her frustration full rein: doing that made it easier to ignore just how gaunt he looked. And was he listing to the side, just a touch?

"Lord Sarel Jisiensire," NotAgain said. "It's good to see you on your feet."

"Thank you, Captain," Hirianthial said. He looked at Reese. "I am given to understand you are following the pirates to their den?"

Reese had the feeling she'd regret any answer she gave. She scowled. "Yes."

"I'm going with you."

"You're crazy!" Reese exploded. "Look at you! You can barely stand straight and you want to waltz into a slaver junction? They'll tie you by your hair and cart you away before I even open my mouth! What exactly are you going to tell them you're there for?"

"I'm your bodyguard," Hirianthial said.

Reese gaped at him. No one spoke, so she had to. "You can't be serious."

"It might work," NotAgain said.

Reese composed herself. "I already chose someone to act as my heavy," she said. "Bryer. He's tall, he's impossible to read and he's got talons an inch long."

"Having more than one isn't unusual," NotAgain said.

"But him? Look at him!" Reese said. "You could knock him over with a feather!"

"What exactly would you be doing to protect her?" NotAgain asked.

"Reading the minds of her enemies," Hirianthial said.

"That's not funny," Reese growled.

NotAgain ignored her, rubbing the edge of his chin. Then he said, "You should take him."

Reese looked from him to the Eldritch, then back. "Are you serious? Who would believe him as a bodyguard?"

"Believe him?" This time NotAgain met her stare with a

polite incredulity. "He wouldn't be pretending." He looked at Hirianthial. "Am I correct?"

Hirianthial said. "You have divined my intent, Captain."

The world had gone insane.

NotAgain continued, "If you're worried about them abducting him you'd have better luck having him in full view; if he hides on the *Earthrise* they could plan a raid while your back is turned and deny complicity when you found out. Taking him along, on the other hand, would fit the profile of a brazen, self-confident mercenary. I don't think they'll doubt his efficacy. And having along one of the men they dearly want to take for themselves would be a significant statement."

"Of what?" Reese asked, recovering the use of her tongue. "Stupidity?"

NotAgain squinted at her. "Captain Eddings, I confess I don't understand your misgivings. Your Phoenix will make an excellent combatant if negotiations come to blows . . . but an Eldritch mind-reader at your back will be a deterrent to violence that your enemies won't be able to equal or anticipate. And the man has volunteered to protect you."

"I'm more worried about protecting him," Reese said.

NotAgain nodded. "We've already covered that. If they want him, they'll do their best to kidnap him whether he's in plain view or not. Best to have it in the open."

Reese clenched her hands under the table. "If you think it's a good idea—"

"I think you should count yourself lucky to have such a resource," NotAgain said. "And I think you should guard yourself against dismissing his value."

Reese sighed. "Fine. He comes. But I hope everything works out as planned . . . and that's as planned for option one, not all the rest."

The Tam-illee smiled. "You and me both. Now unless

there's anything else . . .? No? The ensign outside can escort you both to the Pad room."

"Thanks," Reese said. "I'll be waiting for the signal." She stepped outside, paused to allow the ensign to gather them with his eyes, and then started after him. She had resolved to remain silent, but the dogged presence of the Eldritch at her back nagged at her until the words broke loose. "This is a bad idea."

"Chasing pirates, slavers, thieves and killers?" Hirianthial said. "I find no part of it objectionable."

"Not that part! The 'you coming along' part," Reese said. "You're barely out of bed! Not only that, but you're not a killer! What good is a pacifist bodyguard?"

"Be careful what you assume, lady," he said, and something in his voice, some hint of a husk, put the hair on the back of her neck up. Then, with a lighter tone he said, "I have more than one ability to apply to the situation."

"Yeah, let's talk about that," Reese said. "I thought you said you don't read people's minds."

"It is considered immoral," Hirianthial said.

"Doesn't seem to stop you," Reese said.

A whirl of white and the jingle of a prayer bell and he was standing in front of her, so abruptly she almost ran into him. Reese stopped only a few inches short of his stomach, and though at this angle she had to crane her neck to look at him she decided to do that rather than backpedal. She raised her head.

Long ago—far longer than the actual passage of the days—she'd sat beside him in a straw-filled cell and watched a look cross his face that had not belonged on a healer. She remembered being glad that look hadn't been directed at her. Faced fully with it now, she didn't stumble away because fear petrified every part of her but her hands, which started shaking. His habit of looking at someone completely was bad enough. She didn't want to know that his eyes could make her heart palpitate and sweat pop from her skin.

Before her knees could loosen and dump her to the floor, Hirianthial twisted his head aside and closed his eyes. He visibly composed himself; she could almost see the anger draining away. He straightened, stepped to one side and said, "I find myself unmoved by ethical arguments when they protect men I already know are criminals."

Just like that, he was Hirianthial again, the doctor who wouldn't kill anyone even seemingly in self-defense, the annoying Eldritch who'd fished around in her mind and pulled out her deepest secrets. That she had to force her shaking legs to propel her after the silent ensign only added to her rage. By the time they reached the Pad room, she was ready to throttle him.

The greeting Sascha started to voice died as he opened his mouth. "Err . . . do I want to know?"

"No," Reese snarled.

"Riiight," Sascha said.

"Are you sure no one's hailed us?" Reese asked, standing behind Sascha on the bridge of the *Earthrise.* In the portals space had given way to sky.

"Not a peep," Irine said from her chair.

"It doesn't make sense," Reese said. "They should have challenged us fifteen minutes ago."

"They don't know yet that we're not planning to dump the cargo out of the holds and lift off again," Sascha said. "My bet is they won't start complaining until we show up on their doorstep."

"I hope you're right," Reese said, gripping the back of the chair so hard her fingers ached. She had dressed in her normal jumpsuit and ribbed blue, orange and black vest, having decided that the stereotypical mercenary outfits depicted in movies couldn't possibly be accurate, and even if they were she couldn't have carried one off. Irine had wedged the pin with its bead into the rolled hem along the vest's collar and gotten Kis'eh't to synthesize a twin black bead for the opposite side. The goods Fleet had sent over with its three-person team had already been distributed: weapons for everyone, perimeter cordon kits for their landing site and DNA locks for the boxes that would give Reese an edge in negotiations—she hoped.

They set down without incident. For once, there was no landing chatter, no immediate unbuckling of safety harnesses, no movement at all. All four of them remained where they sat and stared out the windows.

"I guess this is it," Irine said.

"I guess it is," Reese said and reluctantly wiggled out of the harness. "Kis'eh't, you're in charge. Keep our Fleet visitors entertained."

"I'll do that," Kis'eh't said.

"Irine, Sascha . . . let's go."

In the cargo hold, the boxes had already been loaded onto their sledges. Bryer stood beside one of them, dressed in more clothing than she'd ever seen on him: not just crimson pants of tanned hide, but a matching vest laced at the sides instead of down the front, cut low enough to loop beneath the intersection of his wings and his body. Bright red feathers were interwoven throughout his crest and tail. The color and arrangement should have made the Phoenix resemble a puffed-up gaudy bird; instead it gave his spiked crest a menacing flare while reminding Reese pointedly of spilled blood.

Standing beside Bryer's riotous presentation, Hirianthial should have faded into the wall, but he didn't. He wore white from wrist to ankle: white blouse, white pants, white tabard, even white boots. His single colored accent was the hint of the dangle the crew had woven him, resting near skin revealed against the blouse as even paler than white cloth. Colors made Hirianthial seem, if not human, then at least not as alien. Seeing him in all white . . .

"Oh wow," Irine said.

Neither of them smiled. Or even moved.

"Oh, come on," Reese said, exasperated at her own reaction. "We know you're unsettling so you can stop trying now."

"Leave them alone," Sascha said. "They're doing their jobs. Don't ask them to joke about it."

Reese eyed him. "I'm not actually a mercenary ice princess, remember?"

"That's true, you're not," Sascha said, double-checking his palmer and then walking to the nearest pallet. "But they're actually your bodyguards."

"This is ridiculous," Reese said.

"Can we just get moving?" Irine asked. "The sooner we start, the sooner we'll get this over with." She grinned, though a little more wanly than her wont. "Some of those Fleet boys were too cute."

"Fine. Let's go."

They exited the cargo hold, walking past the Fleet officers who, dressed in mufti, were setting up the perimeter alarms. Their destination was ten minutes southeast of the *Earthrise's* site down a narrow paved path that connected one of the major settlements on-planet with some of its farms.

"So this is the Barris," Sascha said, pushing the dolly along while gazing at the scrubby fields bordering the street.

"It's ugly," Irine said. "And hot. There's not even a breeze. How come they always choose these ugly places?"

"Maybe because no one else wants them," Reese said, staring at Sascha's back. As the leader she should have been in the front but one look at the vast nothingness from horizon to horizon had given her a panic attack. She hated open spaces, and the barns she saw dotted across the landscape only emphasized the emptiness somehow. Staying near the middle of the group kept the anxiety at a manageable level, so she'd taken over the dolly-pushing duty from Bryer, who'd relinquished it without fuss. Nor had the twins objected. It made her suspicious of them all.

"It's not ugly," Sascha said. "It's just wild."

"Wild is bad," Reese said. "I'm all for the civilizing influence of concrete, steel and glass."

"That should make you feel better then," the Harat-Shar said, pointing.

NotAgain had warned them not to expect a city, but even so the collection of warehouses clustered around the office building looked ridiculous. The campus wouldn't have looked out-of-place on the fringe of a bustling port, but to have it in the middle of nowhere . . . they might as well have plastered "Pirate Hang-Out" signs on it.

"Where does everyone live?" Reese asked. "Underground in a bunker?"

"You never know," Sascha said.

"What's wrong with living underground?" Irine asked.

By the time they reached the office building, Reese's body ached from steering the box and her mind ached from listening to the twins' banter. The unrelenting silence from the two men following her had heightened her anxiety, and perhaps that was for the best. When they were stopped at the doors, Reese discovered all her fear had been transformed into belligerence.

"Thanks," the human woman at the door said. "If you'll leave the boxes here we'll have someone take them to the warehouses."

"Fine," Reese said. "I'll see your boss now."

She smiled a very unconvincing smile down at Reese. "I'm afraid he's busy."

Reese nodded. "I'm sure he is. So am I. This won't take long."

"Perhaps you misunderstood me," the woman said. "Mr. Surapinet doesn't see people without an appointment."

"And twenty thousand fin says I have an appointment with him," Reese said. "So be a nice secretary and let me in."

Her eyes grew icy. "In case you hadn't noticed, ma'am, your only currency with Mr. Surapinet is being wheeled away."

Reese chuckled. "Yes, and it's nice of them to do the work for us. But if your boss actually wants to open the boxes without reducing their contents to cinders, he'll see me before I start getting too hot and demanding a drink."

The woman glanced at the boxes sharply.

"Go ahead," Reese said. "Check for yourself. They're DNA-locked."

The woman followed the boxes, which by now were halfway to an adjacent warehouse. Reese leaned against the wall and watched.

"So far so good," Sascha said.

Reese shrugged.

When the woman returned her composed expression did not disguise the anger in her eyes. She forced a grin that showed more teeth than welcome and said, "If you'll step into the foyer I'll tell Mr. Surapinet you're here while our security guards examine you. You do know we don't allow people like you into our offices without a weapons search?"

"I'm not surprised," Reese said.

The woman nodded. "This way, please."

The first room inside the building turned out to be the foyer: a room decorated in monochrome with a gray carpet, lighter gray walls, and black leather couches facing steel and brushed metal coffee tables. A receptionist's desk repeated the theme, as did the two men guarding the hallway, dressed in gray uniforms with black accents. The woman whispered to them before vanishing down the hallway.

The men advanced on them. Before they could step up to her, Reese said, "I sincerely hope you're not going to pat us down like crime suspects."

They paused. The taller of the two cleared his throat and said. "We have a wand, ma'am."

"Good," Reese said. "I don't want either of you touching me."

They ignored her and went to work. Her heart pounded as the wand passed over her chest, but it didn't beep until it found the palmer on her belt. Reese handed it over. She had never fired a weapon but she wasn't comfortable with being unarmed either.

Irine and Sascha gave up their weapons as well. Waving the wand over Bryer came up with nothing—likewise over Hirianthial. The guards consulted, then said to Reese, "We'd like to check these two further."

Reese snorted. "Good work. You've identified the dangerous people in the group. Unfortunately, what makes them dangerous can't be taken away from them. Unless you want to de-claw the Phoenix and lobotomize the Eldritch."

"Our wand doesn't pick up all kinds of weapons. We'd like to search."

"Go ahead," Bryer said suddenly.

The guards patted him down, awkward around the

wings and tail as if not sure how to check the feathers without breaking them. Their search found nothing, so they turned to Hirianthial.

"No," Hirianthial said. "You will not touch me."

Reese almost said, "What a fine way to make them want to," but to her surprise one of the guards stepped back and the other hesitated, then said, "He looks clean."

"He could be hiding something," the other said.

The first guard looked at Hirianthial, then shrugged. "What's he going to have . . . a rifle? I don't want to touch him. I don't want him rummaging in my mind."

The second guard snorted and moved away. When the woman returned, he said, "They're clear to go."

"Thanks," she said. "Come with me, please."

Past the foyer the carpet switched to black and the walls to dark gray paint with steel ribs, giving Reese the uncomfortable impression of walking through a poorly lit ship's corridor. The elevator trip was even worse, since only half of them could squeeze in at a time: Irine and Sascha went first with their guide and Reese went up last with her "bodyguards." They exited at the top of the building, so Reese was not at all surprised to be led to a corner suite. It was twice the size of her mess hall; two of its walls were clear glass panels, and a minimum of clutter in the room gave onlookers an unparalleled view of the landscape. If only there had been something worth looking at.

The man behind the desk was human, tan with bleached hair. He didn't look old enough to be running a multi-planet crime ring until Reese met his eyes and felt the force of their appraisal.

"Captain Eddings," he said. "I'm Marlane Surapinet. Do step all the way inside so my men can close the door." He smiled. "For privacy."

"Of course," Reese said, glancing at the guards. These two

made the ones downstairs look like guard-impersonators.

"I'm glad to have the pleasure of meeting you in person," Surapinet said. "I admit I'm not sure why you insisted. The money will be in your account as soon as we verify the integrity of the goods you've delivered."

"I insisted because you irritated me," Reese said. "And I like to clear up irritations with people I work with."

He cocked his head. "An irritation."

"You sent people to check up on me," Reese said. "People I had to subsequently deal with." She folded her arms. "I don't like being tailed and I don't like having to waste time and energy dealing with tails."

His brows lifted. "You didn't expect me to leave you unwatched, Captain Eddings? I'd never hired you before."

"You bought my ship, my sweat and my silence," Reese said. "You asked for a lot, but you paid good money for it. And then you disrespected my integrity. I don't like that in an employer, Mr. Surapinet."

"I see," he replied. "So you put paid to the tail, is that your story?"

"Have they come round since they waylaid me?" Reese asked.

Surapinet said nothing. Then he leaned back in his chair and folded his hands behind his head. "You sound as if you'd like me to continue to be your employer."

"I might," Reese said. "It depends on how fair you're going to play."

He smiled. "I always play fair with my associates. My word is my bond, Captain Eddings."

"And that's why you set two vessels on me," Reese said. If she concentrated on her anger it made it easier to ignore her terror.

"I set those vessels on you precisely because I am a man of my word . . . living in a universe where few people keep theirs," he said. "Surely you've been burned yourself. We honest people are so few."

"I still feel disrespected," Reese said. "And the damage I sustained squashing your over-zealous heavies is going to bite into my profit margin."

He studied her. "And what would settle this between us?"

"You could give me a cut of the sales," Reese said. "Let's stop playing pretend, Mr. Surapinet. Even one of those crystals is going to net you more in wet sales than the lump sum you're paying me. I hardly think that's fair since I'm the one Fleet will be chasing if they hear even the faintest rumor that those crystals might be classified by a bleeding heart researcher as thinking beings."

"And now we're a chemist as well as a merchant?" Surapinet said.

"I have good people working for me," Reese said.

"Ah yes," Surapinet said, eyes flicking past her shoulder. "Good people." He leaned forward. "How's this deal, Captain. You get half my profits from the wet sales—"

Her brows lifted.

"—and I get the Eldritch."

"No." She said it before she could think about it.

"No?" the man said, and she didn't like his tone at all.

"He's my Eldritch, no matter how scrawny," Reese said. "He's not for sale."

"That's too bad," Surapinet said. "He's a wanted man in our organization." A thin smile. "I'll pass you some of the profit from his sale, if you like."

"It's not about the money," Reese said testily. Surapinet's sharpened gaze made her aware of just how close she was to breaking cover. She made herself relax, sigh, run a hand through her hair. "Look, I don't want to give him up . . . yet. I'm having too much fun with him, if you know what I mean."

Both his eyebrows arched. "Why, Captain, are you saying you and he are lovers?"

Reese didn't need to fake her derision. "Hardly. He's a toy, not a lover. But he's a very, very good toy. I guess being psychic means he always knows exactly what I want." She tried mimicking one of the lazy smiles she'd caught on the twins' faces. "I'll sell him when I get bored, but I'm not bored yet. If you want exclusive rights when I do decide to give him up, I'm amenable to that."

"It's so nice to talk with a fellow professional," Surapinet said. "Although you understand that I simply can't give you as much if I don't get the Eldritch immediately."

"That's fine," Reese said. "I'll settle for a quarter of the wet profits and a half-stake in the final sale if you exercise the option to buy him later."

"You want me to pay for him twice?" Surapinet asked.

Reese smiled. "He's that good."

Her smugness must have passed muster, because Surapinet leaned over and pressed a button next to his desk. "Ms. Deigle, please have someone from Legal meet us downstairs."

"Yes, sir."

"We'll draw up the contract before you leave," Surapinet said.

"Fine with me," Reese said. "But about the current contract. I'd like the money."

"And I'd like the locks opened," Surapinet said.

"Fair enough," Reese said. "Shall we go?"

"I'd be delighted, Captain Eddings. Or should I say Theresa?"

"Depends," Reese said. "Is this the beginning of a beautiful relationship, or are you just positioning me for disappointment?"

He laughed and walked around the desk. "I think it's a little early to make predictions. But I am intrigued."

As Surapinet reached for the door it swung open for the angry woman. Behind her the guards Reese had dismissed had multiplied from two people into fourteen, maybe fifteen.

"Mr. Surapinet," she said. "There's a transmission originating from this room."

"There is?" he asked, and the look on his face boded very badly. He turned slowly to her. "Would you know anything about this transmission, Captain Eddings?"

A moment to decide, and she chose to brazen it out. "That would be me," she said without any visible unease . . . or she hoped without any visible unease. "Or did you really expect me not to take out some insurance for myself? Having a record of the meeting is good business sense."

"Without informing me?"

Reese smiled. "You were the one telling me about how people of their word get burned, Mr. Surapinet. You sent pirates. I brought a camera."

He began to relax.

"And you regularly store your records in the middle of empty space?" the woman interrupted. "Because that's where the transmission's leading."

Surapinet's gaze hardened. "Not to the *Earthrise*?"

"No," she said. She sneered at Reese. "Of course, she's not going to tell us how many Dusted Fleet ships are waiting for her little recording, is she?"

"I have no idea what you're talking about," Reese said, but it was too late. Surapinet pinned her with a glare so intense her knees wobbled.

"Take care of them," he said brusquely. "Except the Eldritch. Him I want alive."

The guards lunged into the room, more than enough

of them to kill them all. Reese leaped behind the desk as one of the Harat-Shar yowled and she heard curses and the thick smacks of fists against flesh. A hand grabbed for her ankle and she kicked back until it let go, but someone had followed her behind the desk. Reese dropped beneath it.

They were going to kill her. She had no idea why they hadn't fired on her yet. A single shot with a palmer and she'd be dead. Instead they were trying to drag her out from beneath the desk. She bit the hand that grabbed her shoulder and writhed as several more tore at her arms and legs. Two people hauled her into the open . . . and then flew up over the desk. Dark gold talons gripped the edge just above Reese and then Bryer looked down at her.

"Hurry," he said.

Reese scrabbled out from her hiding hole and stared at the bodies on the ground.

"Come on, boss, they've got Hirianthial!" Sascha said as he strapped on one of the guard's weapons.

"What about Surapinet?" Reese said. "Which way did he go?"

"Who cares?" Irine said.

"I care!" Reese exclaimed. "If he goes free we'll be dead in a week! We have to go after him!"

"Fleet will take care of him," Sascha said, pointing out the windows. "See, they're already here."

Reese glanced behind her shoulder and saw smoke rising from one of the warehouses and a swiftly passing shadow on the ground, shaped like a fighter. A dozen smaller fighters were already in the air, but they didn't look like Fleet's. "Where did those come from?"

"Keep your eye on the prize, boss," Sascha said. "If they get off the ground with Hirianthial we might never see him again."

"Same goes for Surapinet," Reese said, then waved her

hands. "Oh for the love of freedom! We don't all have to go after them both! Bryer, go take care of Surapinet!"

The Phoenix huffed, then leaped off the table, leaving scratches on the metal. He whisked through the door.

Irine handed Reese a palmer. "Here. You might need it."

"Why didn't they fire on us?" Reese asked.

"Too close quarters, probably," Sascha said. "Doesn't matter. They went this way."

"I'd appreciate not having to rescue the man at least once," Reese said.

"Yeah, well, it took four people to drag him away and that was after he took care of five of them."

"And you saw that with your own eyes in the middle of a fist-fight," Reese said.

Sascha's ears flattened, but he turned to the nearest body. "I don't need to have looked during the fight," he said. With a grunt, he pulled at one of the bodies and then held up a gory dagger. "He didn't make the same kind of kills as Bryer did."

Reese stared at the dagger in shock.

"Come on," Irine said, grabbing Reese by the vest. "This way!"

The downstairs guards hadn't searched him, which meant when the first of his attackers lunged for him Hirianthial drew his dagger from the back of his boot and put it neatly through the man's carotid artery. The second man managed to get a hand on him and the talent Hirianthial had assumed would be a liability proved instead an unexpected asset, for that violent grasp conveyed flashes of all the man's previous crimes.

The very last time Hirianthial had been called upon to execute a criminal, he'd stayed his hand, out of sentiment, and from an exhaustion with killing. In retrospect, that mercy had been misplaced; some nagging feeling insisted that act would return to plague him, if he lived so long. This time, he let no such reservations fog his mind. He'd spent decades practicing in the profession of mercy, but before he'd taken up a doctor's caduceus he'd carried swords sworn to just service, and the sensibilities of both worlds mingled in his mind as he fought. Every man who attacked him forced on him knowledge of his perfidy, his cruelty, and like a doctor faced with the worst malignant tumor, Hirianthial destroyed them.

He was out of practice but the advantage they gave him by attempting only to disarm him rather than kill him would have evened the odds . . . had his body not suddenly stopped working. He barely had time to notice the fatigue before it overwhelmed him and he staggered. As his attackers rushed him en masse he reflected that engaging in combat was probably not Doctor SorrowsEase's idea of bed-rest, food and judicious exercise.

Hirianthial managed to wedge the knife into one more man before they overpowered him and dragged him into the hall.

"Where do we put him?" one of them asked.

"We need to get real restraints on him," the other said. "I don't trust him."

"Fleet's here."

"Yeah. We'll take care of him and bolt."

At the end of their exchange, Hirianthial ceased his struggles so abruptly the guards stumbled. When their grips eased he lurched away and started down the hall. He surprised himself by managing a sprint despite the dizziness that threatened to bring him crashing into unconsciousness, and when the guards caught up with him he surprised one with a knee between the legs.

That earned him a smack hard enough to throw his face against his shoulder.

"Don't hurt him! He's supposed to stay in one piece!"

"They didn't say he had to be pretty," the other snarled. Behind him the third guard was moaning. "Did you see what he did?"

"I'll go get something to tie him with."

"Are you crazy? We'll drag him to the supply room. We're going to need all of us to keep him down."

If only they knew just how exhausted he was. He was so weak he was sweating from the minor exertion of running a few feet down the hall.

"Just knock him out. We'll carry him."

Hirianthial twisted to avoid the first blow. They pinned him for the second but he wrenched away in time. Adrenaline gave him the surge he needed to climb to his feet and run again, but he stopped as four more guards came around the corner.

"Get him!" someone shouted from behind him.

They all rushed him, from behind and from the front. He couldn't fight them all, and the combined assault of mind and body loosened his limbs until he could barely stand.

"You have cuffs?"

"Yeah, sure, here."

The first guard took great pleasure in jerking his hands together behind his back and hooking them together. "We should do his feet too."

"I don't have ankle cuffs. He looks pretty weak. You think he could run far?"

"Who knows?"

"Hey, let go of our Eldritch!"

The sound of Sascha's voice galvanized Hirianthial. He thrust the point of his shoulder into the man on one side of him and kicked the one in front of him, then dropped to a crouch and rammed the legs between him and the sound of fighting. Palmers squeaked, filling the corridor with the smell of burnt fabric and blood.

"Hirianthial!"

"Here!" he called, hoarsely. A man grabbed him and began dragging him in the opposite direction, then fell beneath a palmer shot.

Lying on one arm, Hirianthial reflected that the looming twins were one of the finest sights he'd seen in at least the last decade. Certainly in the past year.

"That's all of them," Irine said as Sascha crouched next to him.

"You okay?"

"I need unlocking," Hirianthial said. "One of them should have a key."

Reese stomped up behind the twins. "A couple of them got away."

"No problem," Irine said, sliding a few picks from her hair and dropping behind Hirianthial's back. Furry fingers brushed at his wrists, accompanying the tiny clicking sounds of pick on metal and the mental brushes of concern, fear and a steady focus.

"You look beat-up," Sascha said, gaze traveling over Hirianthial's face.

"They barely handled me," Hirianthial said. "It's of no concern. Where's Bryer?"

"Following the primo bad guy," Sascha said.

"Done!" Irine said, flourishing the cuffs.

Hirianthial sat up and flexed his hands. The ache in his wrists worried him far less than the dizziness that sent spots rushing in front of his eyes. He pressed a hand to his forehead.

"Damn, you're not well yet," Sascha said. "Can you

make it to the *Earthrise*?"

"He'd better," Reese said, "This place is crazy with guards. If we don't get out of here while Fleet's distracting them, we might not get out at all."

Hirianthial forced himself to his feet with only a trace of a wobble. "Let's go."

Reese eyed him.

"Are you sure you don't need a hand? A shoulder?" Sascha asked.

"I'm sure," Hirianthial said, then smiled. "For now, at least."

Sascha nodded and pulled the Eldritch's dagger from his belt. "You'll want this back."

Hirianthial stared at it, then shook himself and took it. "Yes. Thank you."

The trip to the first floor proved uneventful, which was an unexpected hardship. Only the sense of imminent danger kept Hirianthial on his feet, and deprived of it, he began to list to one side, giving in to increasingly ardent demands from his body that he close his eyes and sleep.

Picking through the tumbled furniture and shattered glass tables in the lobby, Irine said, "Wow. We missed the party."

"Thank freedom," Reese said, peeking out the front door. People in and out of uniforms, pirates and Fleet, darted into view, firing all the while. "I wonder if we could steal a ride to the *Earthrise*? I don't like the idea of navigating through that at anything slower than an eagle's pace."

The thought of the long walk back almost stole Hirianthial's remaining energy.

"Hey, it's Bryer!" Irine exclaimed and waved.

The Phoenix wiggled into the foyer through one of the broken windows. Aside from a few missing red crest extensions and a lace of blood spatters, he looked hale.

"Did you get him?" Reese asked.

"Left on a ship," Bryer said.

"Curse it all!"

Bryer's maw gaped and this, Hirianthial divined from the sudden shot of sparkles that decorated the Phoenix's usually inscrutable aura, was amusement. "A ship tuned too high. Told Fleet. They will find him."

Reese deflated. "I hope so. I don't want to spend the rest of my life on the run."

"Look on the bright side," Irine said. "Being on the run is part of a merchant's job, so it won't be too much of an effort to disappear."

"That's what we thought last time," Reese said and peered out one of the windows at the sky. "We have got to get out of this place before Fleet decides to bomb it out of existence."

"That way," Bryer said, pointing, and jogged out of the foyer.

With a sigh, Reese followed him. Irine dogged her steps. Sascha looked at Hirianthial. "Can you make it?"

"The alternative doesn't appeal," Hirianthial said and took one step forward. The world sheared around him and he leaned against the wall. He felt the wave of matter-of-fact concern and the touch of Sascha's alien mind before he registered the pressure against his side.

"Steady there," Sascha said. "We still need you."

"Are you sure?" Hirianthial asked with a faint laugh.

Sascha broke into a toothy grin. "You and Bryer are our only fighters, sad to say. The rest of us don't have formal training."

"And Bryer and I do," Hirianthial said, letting the Harat-Shar help him out of the building, step by laborious step.

"I'll eat my tail if you don't," Sascha said. "So if I'm wrong, don't tell me so."

Hirianthial laughed. At the threshold of the building he sucked in a long breath and forced himself upright. The sight of people streaking past helped center him in the present. He let his mind yaw open, gathering the feel of the rest of the crew and their relation to the combatants still shooting nearby. He'd never thought to use his abilities so; he wasn't even sure if he could have in the past. But if by doing this he could get them out of harm's way—immediate harm's way—he would do it. He could collapse later, once they were safe.

His body ached. Breathing hurt. But he started after the others with Sascha at his side and caught up to them with a short jog. Ignoring Reese and Irine, he called to the Phoenix. "Bryer, I'll take point."

The Phoenix glanced over his shoulder, then dropped back to hold the rear. Hirianthial took his place.

"You sure you can do this?" Irine asked from behind him.

"I'm the only one who can," Hirianthial said, and led them forward.

Zigzagging across the campus, using some of the warehouses as cover, Hirianthial wondered how Fleet's end of the fight was going. From what little he could see and the less he allowed himself to sense, the numbers on the ground were about equivalent. He hoped Fleet's superior hardware would give them the edge they needed to prevail.

The first time he halted, Reese hissed, "Why are we stopping?"

"We're hiding," Hirianthial said.

"I don't see anyone!"

"Hush."

The minds he felt nearby dispersed. Ignoring Reese's agitation, he started moving again.

Each time they stopped, her disgruntlement grew. He

knew he should assuage her fears but staying upright while searching for holes in the fight to guide them through occupied all his attention. They were almost off the campus when a mass of angry minds clotted right around the corner of the wall they'd been hugging.

"Against the wall!" Hirianthial said.

The twins and Bryer flattened. Reese opened her mouth to object as their enemy reached the corner. Hirianthial grabbed her, covered her mouth and pressed her flush to his body. He barely noted the explosion of her feelings in his mind as she struggled against him. He tried to hold her without hurting her, but she had fewer compunctions about returning the favor.

The first of the pirates jogged into the open, followed by nine others. Only then did Reese stop fighting him, all her rage inverting into terror.

You don't see us, Hirianthial prayed.

Reese whimpered, a sound that moved her lips against his palm, wetting his skin with the heat of her breath.

You don't hear us, either, Hirianthial prayed.

They marched on. Only when they had passed the succeeding building entirely did Hirianthial release Reese and prepare for her outburst.

Irine beat her to it. "Rhacking *angels*, Reese! Are you trying to get us all killed?!"

"I didn't know!" Reese said.

"What did you think he was doing? Stopping to enjoy the scenery?" Irine shouted. "You want to pick a fight with him, do it on the ship, don't do it out here where you'll get us all killed!"

Reese deflated. "I thought—"

"Quiet," Bryer said.

"We're not safe yet," Sascha said. "Let's save all the fights for later."

Irine grabbed her ears, then forced herself to calm down.

"Let's go," Sascha said.

Hirianthial nodded, checked for enemies, and headed for the road. He kept the group moving at a steady pace until the campus dropped out of sight behind a hill, then stopped and concentrated. Nothing before them. Nothing behind them, though they weren't very far from town. Nothing around them.

"We're clear for now," he said, and tottered. Sascha caught him before he fell entirely.

"Battlehells," Sascha said. "Don't die on us yet."

Bryer stopped beside them both and met Hirianthial's eye with an alien one. "Point?"

"You take it," Hirianthial said. "I'll keep watch on the rear."

The Phoenix nodded and loped ahead.

"And you're in such condition to take any kind of guard position at all," Sascha said. "And no, don't you try to stop leaning on me. Let's just get through this together."

Hirianthial managed a faint smile. "Far be it from me to argue with a Harat-Shar."

"You got that right," Sascha said.

Together they limped after the others. The slower pace gave Hirianthial time to assess his condition and call himself lucky: other than the bruises and incidental slashes he'd gotten in the fight, he was intact. His biggest problem remained the weakness he'd inherited from his battle with the mental-wound, and that would resolve itself with enough sleep.

"You're so light," Sascha said. "You've got to eat more."

"It's on the agenda," Hirianthial said, glad enough of the warm density of the Harat-Shar and the softness of the fur that cushioned the edges of the man's body as they bumped together down the road. That Sascha's mind was relentlessly focused on their situation helped diffuse the impact of his thoughts; all things considered, it was the most comfortable way Hirianthial could imagine being half-dragged down a road.

"It's so quiet. You'd think there'd be someone around," Irine said.

"I'm just glad there aren't," Reese said. Her aura had a sullen gray flatness.

"You think Fleet destroyed all the barns?"

That piqued Sascha's interest strongly enough that Hirianthial ended up looking off the road with the Harat-Shar. He followed the tigraine's series of thoughts from the observation of the pattern of destruction to the memories of similar constructs.

"They were hangars," Sascha called forward.

"For planes?" Irine said.

"That would explain the overhead fight," Reese said. "I hope Fleet made out okay."

"I'm sure they did," Irine said.

The two continued to talk, the nervous chatter Hirianthial associated with the lingering effects of an extreme adrenal dump. He ignored it and concentrated on walking . . . until a whisper at the edge of his perceptions brought him fully alert.

"What is it?" Sascha said in a low voice.

"Get Bryer," Hirianthial replied, standing on his own.

Sascha trotted ahead. "Hey Bryer . . . you go be Long-Tall-and-White's leaning post for a while. I'll take the front."

The Phoenix padded back and stood beside Hirianthial as Sascha led the three on. Then he turned his head to the Eldritch. "Trouble."

"Feels like five people," Hirianthial said. "They're definitely looking for us."

Bryer stretched his fingers and the sun flashed off his claws. "Five. Easy kill." His crest flared. "You will kill, yes?"

"They want most of us dead and the rest of us in chains," Hirianthial said. "And they're armed to do it. Yes, I'll kill them."

Bryer nodded, then scanned the road. "Little cover."

"We can crouch behind the brush," Hirianthial said. "They're not expecting an ambush. If we let them pass us and keep going it shouldn't take long."

Bryer eyed him. "Sneaky."

Hirianthial smiled. "We'll be outnumbered at least two to one and I'm barely conscious. They'll have a fair enough fight."

The Phoenix dipped his head in assent and ducked behind the shrubs. Hirianthial joined him. The brushy vegetation lining the road was barely tall enough to hit his knee and its open branches seemed to invite investigation, but the land was sear and yellow, not far from the color of Bryer's feathers. By now Hirianthial imagined himself a grimy ivory. The gouges and rents in Bryer's clothing broke up the red hide, resulting in unanticipated camouflage.

Down the road came five pirates, looking far scruffier than the guards in the building they'd fled. They were armed with rifles and their own seething anger, and their certainty that their quarry ran before them blinded them. They strode past the shrubs.

"Now," Hirianthial said.

Bryer flung himself from the leaves and knocked down one man, ripping out his throat with a clawed foot before any of them even realized they'd been ambushed. Hirianthial followed the Phoenix, though he dispatched his first man with less drama. The second bashed him in the ribs with the butt of his rifle, but as Hirianthial fell he grabbed the strap and took the man down with him. Rolling onto him he employed the dagger, which by now had become glued into his hand.

Bryer whistled and Hirianthial ducked, pressing his head against the dead man's chest. The blow meant to knock him unconscious missed. The Phoenix's swipe snuffed that man from Hirianthial's senses, leaving all their attackers dead.

"I don't think I can get up," Hirianthial said hoarsely, propping himself on top of his last victim with both hands. The palm on the dusty ground stuck, but the one sealed to the dagger slid, dropping him onto the body.

Bryer chuffed and grasped his arm. "Done. Must move."

Except the world wasn't just distant now, it was rocking. Hirianthial tried to lift his head, which seemed heavier—perhaps the blood soaking through his hair? But he decided quickly that moving his head made the vertigo more intense.

"Did well," Bryer said. "Mind being carried?"

"I don't think I have a choice," Hirianthial said, and lost his grip on everything.

"Is he okay?" Reese asked, stunned.

"Fine," Bryer said.

"That's the first human thing I've heard you say about him," Irine said.

"Oh shut up," Reese snapped. Bryer came to a halt. Hirianthial was slung over one of his shoulders, unmoving. His sleeves and the lower half of his hair were drenched with darkening red. "Is he awake?"

"No," Bryer said.

"At least he waited until we were almost at the ship to need rescue," Reese said.

"For the sake of Angels, boss!" Sascha exclaimed.

"Well look at him!"

Bryer grunted, then flung something at Reese. She jumped back as the dagger bit into the ground, quivering at her feet. Blood slimed the hilt, the cross-guard and what she could see of the blade.

"Killed the people following us," Bryer said, then as if realizing the ambiguity of the statement, "He did."

"Damn," Irine said. "I thought he was about to topple over."

"He was," Sascha said.

"If there were people following us, we'd better get moving," Reese said.

"No more," Bryer said. "He's unconscious."

"Exactly," Reese said. "He won't be awake to tell us about any more of them."

"No," Bryer said. "He's unconscious *now.*"

"I noticed," Reese growled.

"I think he means Hirianthial would be awake if he thought we'd need him," Sascha said. "But you might be too stubborn to notice that, well, let's see, he's saved our tails continuously since he led us out of the building back there?"

"If it wasn't for him we wouldn't have needed saving!" Reese said. "In case you don't remember, it was breaking him out of jail that got us involved in this mess!"

Sascha stared at her, both ears flattened.

"Let's just keep going," Irine said. "We're almost to the ship."

Bryer huffed and strode past them. Reese started after him until Sascha moved into her way.

"What?"

"You're forgetting something," he said.

"I have no idea what you're talking about," Reese said.

"The dagger," Sascha said. "*His* dagger. The one he's

been using to cut people up to keep them from killing us. Reminder: 'us' includes 'you.' Go get it."

"I'm sure he has others," Reese said.

Sascha stepped forward until he was almost nose to nose with her. "Boss, I don't know what the battlehells is wrong with you. But you're not going to leave a man's weapon behind just because you feel put out by him dropping unconscious after spending himself to save our lives."

Reese stepped back, astonished, but Sascha had already turned his back on her and started after the others. When she didn't move, he said over his shoulder, "If you're feeling squeamish, use a blood-damned towel."

Reese grabbed her braids and suppressed her urge to scream. She didn't want to pick up any dagger. She didn't want to think about Hirianthial, or what they'd just been through, or the fact that she'd somehow hired two people who could cut through groups of armed bad guys like knives through butter. She was still in one piece, still moving and still functioning, and asking for more was asking for something she had no capacity for. But the look in Sascha's eyes . . . she couldn't go back to the ship and face that look again. She squinted at the dagger standing upright in the ground.

Forced herself to touch the sticky handle.

Forced herself to pull it from the earth, crumbs of dirt falling from the blade. A layer of soil coated the tacky parts of the metal, blunting the impact of the amount of blood on it.

So far she'd gotten him to haul boxes with his surgeon's hands and now kill people with them. It couldn't get much worse than that. If he could forgive this whole episode, maybe nothing else would faze him. Assuming, of course, that she even cared about his forgiveness. Assuming that he'd even stay around after all this.

If she wanted him to.

Could she be any more confused?

Shuddering, Reese stripped off her vest and wrapped it around the dagger, then ran after the others. She caught up with them as they reached the perimeter set up by the Fleet officers. One of them hailed her.

"Captain Eddings! You all made it back safely! We're glad to see it."

"Thanks," Reese said as they took down the section so they could cross. "What's the word from your side of the fight?"

"Things are really hot in the air right now," the man said. "Captain NotAgain recommends you remain on the ground until he sends a signal. Apparently the pirates used this place to repair and rebuild ships. We weren't expecting quite so many of them."

"I have absolutely no problem staying here," Reese said. "In fact, I'm sure we could all use a shower and a long nap."

"Sounds good," the man said. "We'll keep watch out here."

"Thanks," she said, and followed the rest of her crew into the cargo bay. She set the dagger down on one of the crates. Kis'eh't was already hugging the twins, but the Glaseah broke off to engulf Reese in an embrace of her own. "Aksivah't! When I saw those ships go by overhead I thought for sure—"

"We're okay," Reese said, and hugged Kis'eh't back. "We really are. I don't know how, but we are."

"The twins told me Bryer and Hirianthial saved the day," Kis'eh't said. "That was before Bryer took Hirianthial off to his quarters. Are you all really unscathed? I'm no doctor but bandaging scratches I can do."

With the Glaseah's arms looped around her waist and the smell of the woman's clean soft hair in Reese's nose, all the fear and tension suddenly broke loose. Reese quivered, then shocked herself by choking on a sob. Kis'eh't drew her into a tighter hug and said nothing as she started crying. Even the twins were silent as they approached and added their arms to the embrace until the space they enclosed grew humid and started smelling of wet fur.

"Ugh," Reese said, pulling back and rubbing her eyes. "I'm sorry. I don't know what got into me."

"I can't believe you, Boss," Sascha said gently. "You get threatened, manhandled, shot at and chased and you have no idea what got into you? I'd say mortal terror got into you."

"But it's over now," Reese said, fighting the return of the tightness in her chest. "I should be happy."

"And you are," Irine said. "Your body's just confused on how to show it." Her ears drooped. "I could use a good cry myself."

Reese dabbed at the inside corners of her eyes. "Let me guess. Harat-Shar cry by hiding in locked closets with their brothers."

Irine grinned. "Sex isn't our answer to every question."

"Just most of them," Sascha said.

Reese chuckled despite herself. "I need to wash my face. And my body."

"And sleep," Kis'eh't said, squeezing her shoulder. "Go rest, Reese. We'll take care of things."

After all this they were still willing to stick with her. Reese couldn't trust her voice, so she nodded and slipped into the quiet of the corridors. By the time she reached her room she'd calmed herself enough to feel the weight of the fatigue that dragged at her body. Washing her face and hands in her bathroom seemed a ridiculous luxury. Her wrists beneath the tap trembled.

Reese stripped. The bead camera had somehow remained affixed to her collar; she carefully removed it and set it aside. Then she examined herself for damage and found nothing more than a few tender bruises and one or two cuts—how she'd gone into a pirate lair and come out again with so little to show for it escaped her, but she gave fervent thanks for it and took a very long shower. If she cried with her hands full of soap, the steam did a good job of hiding it.

Not long after, she pulled herself into her hammock and snuggled into the blankets and pillows, expecting and finding Allacazam among them. The Flitzbe asked no questions, though she sensed him assessing her condition.

"I'm fine," she whispered. "Thanks for asking."

And then she snuffed the lights and slept.

"You awake, Reese?"

"I am now," she said groggily, twisting in her hammock to fumble for the intercom.

"Not awake enough, I guess," Irine said with a laugh. "I'm at the door."

Reese squinted into the light. "I see. Now. I see now. What is it?"

"Captain NotAgain asked to see you," Irine said. "He's at the campus. The Fleet folk are standing by to drive you there."

"Already?" Reese asked, scrubbing at her face.

"It's been five hours, believe it or not," Irine said. "Do you need help dressing?"

"From a Harat-Shar?" Reese asked. "I might not get there until tomorrow."

Irine laughed and wiggled her hips. "Why, Captain! Are you flirting with me?"

"Yes. No. I'm asleep. Get out!"

The tigraine chortled and let the door close. Reese

grumbled all the way out of her hammock, but as she zipped up her shirt she realized she was smiling. The smile persisted as she rummaged for the camera and tucked it into her pocket.

"Guess that's how they start getting under your skin," she said, petting Allacazam on the way out. The Flitzbe agreed with the image of a smug cat sprawled in the sun.

Outside the sun had set, obscuring the horizon Reese had found so distressing. She sat in the back of the kestrel the Fleet officers had waiting and stared at the twinkling stars scattered across the firmament. The wind blowing past her ears felt good for once, and the cool air reminded her of the temperature in the *Earthrise*, though with the novelty of being maintained outside without aid. She listened with partial attention to the banter of the men driving the ground-flier—something about whether the last alcohol they'd tried matched the superior product they'd found on some colony world—and relaxed into her own skin.

No one was shooting at her or threatening her and the sky on a planet was beautiful. She closed her eyes and let her head dip back against the rest and memorized the feel of the wind on her cheeks.

By night the pirate compound was an ugly place, and the giant lamps the Fleet personnel had erected didn't help. The glaring light exposed the debris from the fight. Walking around some of the shattered buildings, Reese was thankful they'd fled when they did. From the look of things it had gotten much worse after they'd gone.

"Ah, Captain Eddings!" NotAgain was standing near a landed fighter, a data tablet in hand. "I'm glad to see you well."

"I'm glad to be well, believe me," Reese said, taking his proffered hand and covering it with hers. "Did you get what you hoped for?"

"All that I hoped for and more," NotAgain said. "You and your crew did superb work, Captain. In fact, I think it's fairly likely you'll all receive a Copper Sickle for it."

"A what?" Reese asked.

He laughed. "You might not have heard of it. It's one of the few civilian citations given by Fleet. It's quite an honor."

"Wow," Reese said, cheeks warming. "That's . . . unexpected."

NotAgain grinned. "Don't look so pole-axed, Captain. You've all earned one several times over." He shook his head. "As it is, you'll be one of the few people to have earned one and still be upright afterwards. You were damned lucky to have such good back-up."

Reese nodded. "I meant to thank you for that. The weapons, the personnel—"

He laughed. "I wasn't talking about them. I meant your bodyguards. You should have told me you had an Eye-trained Phoenix. Though I doubt you could have known your Eldritch would hold his own so well either."

"An . . . Eye-trained Phoenix?" Reese asked.

"You didn't know?" NotAgain's brows lifted. "Count yourself lucky, then. As I understand it, most of the Phoenix you meet off-world are Eye-worshippers, but few of them get far enough 'long in their meditative practices to get to the physical training. I hear it's rigorous . . . takes a really well-placed palmer shot to the head to put them down, or significant injury. Maybe you could find out more about how they do it?"

"From Bryer?" Reese laughed. "Not likely."

NotAgain grinned. "They do tend to be quiet. Keep him around, though, Captain. He's the one who told us how to find Surapinet, though it took our engineers to de-code the information. He got a message to us that Surapinet was in a flier that sounded disharmonious in the high notes. Seems an overpowered engine emits an unpleasant combination of sounds in the ultrasonic range—once we sifted the data for that we found him easily."

"It sounds like something he'd say," Reese said. She shuddered. "I'm glad you caught him."

NotAgain's voice hardened. "Me too."

Reese watched the Fleet officers striding in and out of the light. She'd had enough of people talking in voices like that, but on the other hand she was grateful they existed. The contradiction was discomforting. "I guess Surapinet won't be paying out my contract."

"Mr. Surapinet won't be doing anything but sitting in a prison cell for quite some time," NotAgain said.

"And the crystals?"

The Tam-illee sighed. "We're not sure yet. That's a matter for the Alliance Diplomatic Corps, not us. But we're sending them the bodies and the information you provided, and hopefully they'll be able to salvage the situation. Speaking of which..." His ears perked. "I hope you don't mind that I'm having your salvage towed with ours to Starbase Kappa."

"My what?" Reese said, startled out of her contemplation of the work being done by the captain's personnel. "I don't have any salvage."

"Such modesty," NotAgain said. "Of course the pirate vessels we found alongside your ship when we answered your distress call were your wrecks. I took the liberty of registering them in your name since you were busy helping us conduct this operation."

"I was what?" Reese said, gaping at him.

"Busy," NotAgain said. She swore that with every word he grew more cheerful. "But don't worry. When you arrive at Starbase Kappa you can decide whether to cannibalize them for parts or sell them whole. The Fleet depot would certainly be interested, but I'm sure the civilian wreckers would be willing to bid for them as well."

"You're giving me the wrecks?" Reese asked, unable to believe him.

"Giving?" NotAgain shook his head and tsked. "You can't give someone something that's already theirs." He grinned.

"But you—they—doesn't Fleet need them?"

"With all the fighters they just threw at us? We've got plenty of our own, Captain Eddings. You don't have to give us yours."

"I . . . should stop arguing with you, shouldn't I," Reese said.

"It would be a waste," NotAgain said. "Fleet appreciates your generous desire to donate your profits, but we have more than enough for ourselves. Keep your rightful salvage, Captain . . . and with it, our thanks for your service to the Alliance."

"Yes, sir," Reese said.

NotAgain held out his hand. "If we don't meet again, it was a pleasure."

She clasped it and squeezed. "Me too." Remembering the Tam-leyan emphasis on families, she added, "I hope you have more grandchildren than you can hold in your arms."

He laughed. "May it be so for us both. Be well, Captain."

"Good night," Reese said.

A different Fleet officer drove her back to the *Earthrise*. Standing just inside the cargo bay, Reese watched the dwindling lights of the kestrel and leaned against the wall. Salvage from two wrecks was a windfall she could barely wrap her arms around. Had Fleet not already repaired her Well drive, she could have done so several times over. And while it wouldn't make her fabulously wealthy, she would certainly have enough to fund her merchant endeavor for several years . . . if, in fact, she wanted to.

Reese turned to the shadowed depths of the bay and her eyes fell on a crate and her crumpled vest. She had forgotten about the dagger. Without unwrapping it, she lifted it from the crate and took it with her to her room.

In the sink, the dagger tinted the water she dunked it in bright pink with oily whorls of brown soil. She ignored them. She ignored that the crust she was scrubbing at with a sponge was blood or something unnamable only a doctor would have been able to identify. She tried not to think too hard about anything while doing it—she just rinsed, scrubbed, drained the sink and refilled it until all the grime had come off. This was her responsibility, wasn't it? To face what had been done on her behalf. To acknowledge that as uncomfortable as it made her, Bryer's and Hirianthial's violence had kept her in one piece. The least she could do was stare at that until she stopped flinching at it so hard. She'd done harder things in her life... she could do this one, too.

Wiping the dagger dry with a cloth she finally allowed herself to examine it and see that it wasn't the one from the case, but something plainer and newer. She turned it in her hands, confused. Had Hirianthial bought it in the Alliance? Why not use the ones he had? In her curiosity she twisted the thing to one side and nicked herself on its edge, which was when the door chimed.

"Come in," Reese said around her thumb.

The twins appeared in the door, looking washed and perky.

"Feeling better?" Sascha asked as they entered.

"Much," Reese said. "You two look better too."

"What did you do to your hand?" Irine asked.

"It's nothing." Reese drained the sink and joined the Harat-Shar in her room. "Just a cut."

"We checked the ship from feet to sensors," Sascha said. "Fleet did everything but tap out the dents in the hull. We can leave whenever you're ready."

"Good," Reese said. She waved them to her bunk and sat on the chair. "Let's do that after everyone's gotten at least six hours' sleep."

"Do we have a destination?" Sascha asked as Irine settled at his feet.

Reese grinned. "Do we! Turns out we're civilian heroes and while Fleet doesn't do anything as crass as paying them for bravery, they do get generous with gifts."

Irine's ears perked. "This sounds good."

"The pirates that were tailing us? Their ships are ours now. Salvage waiting for us at Starbase Kappa."

Sascha whistled. "Not a small gift."

"No," Reese said. "So we'll head there, evaluate the wrecks and sell them to best advantage. After that . . . who knows? I guess we'll go wherever sounds most interesting."

"We could go anywhere," Irine said, eyes wide.

"We could," Reese said. "Just not back to Harat-Sharii."

Sascha chuckled.

"I'm guessing you're not here to check up on me," Reese said.

"You're wrong," Sascha said. "We are here to check up on you. We're just also here for one more thing."

Reese took a deep breath. "Which is?"

Irine said, "You know."

"Pretend I'm without clues," Reese said.

"You've been treating Hirianthial like the lowest form of dirt," Sascha said. "Since the rest of us like having him around, we're hoping you'll make it clear to him that you like having him around, too."

"What if I don't like having him around?" Reese asked, surprising herself with her own uncertainty.

Apparently her quiet tone surprised the twins as well. They exchanged glances. With furrowed brow, Irine said, "How can you not like having him around? You read more novels about Eldritch than any person I've ever met. Now you've got the real thing!"

"Sometimes the things you fantasize about aren't what you end up really wanting," Reese said, staring at her folded hands. She shook herself and smiled wanly. "Though I don't guess that's something Harat-Shar are familiar with."

Sascha was studying her. "Actually, that's the first thing you've said that makes sense."

Reese frowned. "Really?"

"Really," Sascha said. He sighed. "Look, if you really want him gone then send him away. But if you're not sure . . . then tell him he's welcome."

"Because if you don't expressly tell him," Irine said, anticipating Reese's question, "he'll go away. He won't stay if staying is going to make you miserable."

"He doesn't make me miserable," Reese said. "He just makes me . . . " She shifted in her chair, looking for the right word. "Uncomfortable."

Sascha nodded. "Of course he does. That's how all the best things start."

"Pardon?" Reese said.

He smiled. "The best things. Adventures. Destinations. Knowledge. Relationships. All of them start with uncomfortable moments. It's only when you're grappling with something new that you might uncover something wonderful . . . but unfortunately, that means grappling with something new."

"New things chafe," Irine said, plucking at her tail.

Reese stared at them.

"Promise you'll be decisive," Sascha said quietly. "Either tell him to go or tell him to stay, but make a decision."

She ran a hand over the top of her head. "Sascha—"

"Please, Reese," Irine said. "If we're going to lose the prettiest guy on the ship, let it be because you really don't want him around, not because he thought it would please you to leave."

"I promise," Reese said, then glared at them as best she could. It wasn't much of a glare—hadn't she been planning to work on that? "You two are such trouble. If I'd have known what I was in for when I hired you . . . "

"You would have done it anyway," Sascha said with a grin. "Because we've grown on you like flowers on an open field."

"Get out of here," Reese said, suppressing her laughter. "Before I throw you out. I have thinking to do."

"Aye, aye, ma'am!" Irine said, climbing to her feet. She added, "I learned that from the yummy Fleet people."

"Did you—oh, get moving. I don't want to know!"

Irine snickered. They headed for the door, where Sascha bent down and plucked up a crumpled cloth from beside the door. "You might want to return this, Boss."

Reese caught it as they left. She shook her head and started to stand when her fingers registered the caress of felt-soft fabric. Abruptly she sat again and looked at the tabard in her lap. Cleaning her room had been the last thing on her mind the past few days and she'd given little thought to the clothing she'd discarded on the way to the shower after Fleet had dragged the pirates off the *Earthrise*.

She petted the silky material. The pile was so thick it reminded her of Allacazam's neural fur, plush and soft. On the tabard's face, deep channels cut through the velvet, exposing the nap in an elegant but random pattern of swirls and spirals. Most of the books she'd read about Eldritch had only made passing references to their clothing . . . but the recent ones, the ones by the Harat-Shariin matron, had mentioned an expensive but beautiful tapestried cloth the Eldritch called meander. One of the novels had even described its laborious production, hand-made by artisans famed for the individuality of their patterns.

Reese bit her lip. If that part had been true, the tabard represented months of painstaking craftsmanship, unique and irreplaceable. Her fingers traced the tattered edge of the front panel, following the broken threads, the unraveling seams that connected the satin lining to the cloth. It suddenly seemed so senseless. She bent over it and hugged her knees.

The smell of perfume—no, cologne—clung to the fabric. Something rich with a touch of spice, a woodsy scent that reminded her of trees. She wondered if the twins had smelled it when they'd been braiding the crew's gift into Hirianthial's hair . . . and she was suddenly glad she'd added her own contribution to the dangle.

But he'd read her mind. And he could do it again. She'd seen the ease with which he'd guided them through the chaos in the pirate compound. Not only could he read minds, but he wasn't dumb. Simply hearing her thoughts wasn't scary enough alone. The fact that he could read them and then construct the secrets of her heart after knowing her for the briefest fraction of her life . . . and that didn't even begin to touch what he'd done with a single dagger. Not even one as impressive as the ones she'd glimpsed in the case.

Bad enough that he knew all her secrets. It was entirely unfair that he got to keep all his own. And she wasn't sure she knew what to do with the knowledge that someone knew her well enough to hurt her, without her having anything to use against him as a shield.

Even thinking of it that way hurt. Why did she always have to plan for the inevitable hurt?

Reese closed her eyes. The tabard pulled her in one direction. The dagger another.

"Good morning, sleepy," Kis'eh't said in a gentle voice. "Or rather, good night, since that's about the time. You've been sleeping for nine hours!"

Did he have a voice? He did. He used it. "I'm surprised. I expected to sleep for well over twenty."

The Glaseah, barely visible in the low light, shook her head. "Don't joke like that. We were all worried. How are you feeling?"

Hirianthial assessed his body. "Better than I probably look."

Kis'eh't winced. "That wouldn't be hard," she said. "We put an ice-pack on your face so you aren't swollen, but your skin's going to turn interesting colors."

"I'm sure," Hirianthial said. He tried sitting upright and surprised himself pleasantly by succeeding. Someone had delivered him to his quarters and tucked him into bed under a mound of blankets.

"I'm apologizing on behalf of the crew for taking off your boots and sponging off the worst of the dirt," Kis'eh't said. "Bryer's the one who did it, since we think he's the one who emotes the least. Did he wake you?"

"I doubt a falling meteor would have woken me," Hirianthial said, gingerly pressing on the back of his neck. The longer he remained conscious, the more aware he was of the wrenched muscles, deepening bruises and joint aches he'd incurred fleeing the pirates. It never ceased to amaze him how nothing serious could hurt so badly. "I thank you for the attention, though."

"It was the least we could do," Kis'eh't said. "Everyone

says you and Bryer are the only reason the whole mission came out okay."

"I wouldn't go so far," Hirianthial said. "The captain and the twins did excellent work."

She shook her head. "You can re-assign praise however you want if it makes you feel better. The rest of us . . . well, we're really grateful."

He couldn't help a laugh. "I hope this doesn't mean I'll have to fend off the twins."

"No," Kis'eh't said, grinning. "And I think we're all out of things we can make into jewelry. You'll probably have to settle for a party. Not just for you, mind you. For Bryer too. We're going to put a party cap on him."

A Phoenix at a party. It beggared the imagination. "That sounds like quite a challenge."

Kis'eh't nodded. "It figures that we're going to end up fêting the two people on the crew who like the least fuss," she said. "But we're going to do it anyway, once we get underway."

"And when is that?" Hirianthial asked.

"Soon," Kis'eh't replied. "As soon as the twins wake up, I think."

"And Fleet?"

"They're still cleaning up," Kis'eh't said.

"Ah."

"You're not thinking of leaving, are you?" Kis'eh't asked, feathered ears drooping.

"I'm in no condition to rush away," Hirianthial said carefully.

"Good," Kis'eh't said. "We were worried you'd want to leave."

He said nothing—it seemed safest. Kis'eh't continued. "If you like, I'll bring you food? The best cook is sleeping but I can make tea and toast."

"That sounds wonderful, thank you," Hirianthial said. "Perhaps after I've showered."

"Okay." She brightened: not the instant sunlit glee of the twins, but a slower, steadier glow. "We're really glad you're here, Hirianthial. Things wouldn't be the same without you."

He dipped his head. "Thank you."

Once she'd left, he remained on the bunk with the blankets cocooning his lower body and a prickly cool along his back and arms. He was too tired still to worry about whether he'd stay or go. There were more pressing concerns. His body would tolerate no more neglect. Cautiously he gathered clean clothes and went to shower. The sponge bath had removed the superficial layer of dirt from his exposed skin, but he remained grimy from head to ankle and his hair still bore a faint pink shadow. He scrubbed the blood off his body, out of his clothes, from beneath his fingernails. That last inspired visceral memories of home. Surgery as a doctor was done with gloves; it was only when he used a blade that he got blood running, hot and too fluid, and then sticky on his fingers. How many times had he washed his hands of it? And all he felt over the memories was a kind of exhausted acceptance.

He was what he was—all of it, from killer to healer. And, he thought, he was also alive... and at peace with that, and the years in front of him. While washing his hair for the second time, his fingers tangled in the beaded cord and he pulled it forward to examine it.

Beneath his fingers he could still sense the laughter and glitter-glimpses of memory each charm on the dangle represented. As needles of water struck the cord and washed it clean, Hirianthial rested the edge of a shoulder against the shower wall and read the chain again.

Had he been mind-blind, he would still have known

the dangle for an act of friendship. But he was not mind-blind. The ferocity of their affection transcended mere friendship. He couldn't imagine abandoning them.

If he had the choice, it wouldn't be a choice at all.

Hirianthial shut off the water, dried himself and returned to his quarters. He changed the sheets on the bed and put away the dirty linens. Doing so little had already made him drowsy, but showering had opened the multiple slashes traced across his body. He rolled back the sleeves of his nightdress and unpacked the necessary parts of his first aid kit.

The door's mellow chime caught him in the middle of the final bandage. "Come in."

The door opened not on Kis'eh't and the expected tea and toast, but on Reese. Hirianthial slowly lowered his arms into his lap.

"Sorry," Reese said after clearing her throat. "I have some of your things. Can I . . .?"

"Come in," Hirianthial said again.

Reese stepped inside. "I have your dagger," she said. "Should I . . .?"

"You can leave it on the table," Hirianthial said. "And thank you. I didn't expect to see it again."

"We thought we shouldn't leave it behind," Reese said. Her reticence bewildered him; it muted her aura to a soft brown and left him no hint as to her emotional state. "I've heard about . . . um, daggers and things. Being special."

"Some are," Hirianthial said. "That one not so much. But I'm glad I don't have to replace it."

Reese nodded. "I've also brought this back." She showed him a folded square, and the low light shone off the exposed nap of his tabard. "It's meander, isn't it?"

Surprised, Hirianthial said, "Yes."

"And they broke it," Reese said, crestfallen. "It can't be

fixed, can it?"

"I'm afraid not," Hirianthial said. "I will see if what remains can be salvaged."

She nodded and set it beside the dagger, petting it with a self-conscious hand. He watched her and knew not what to think.

Reese turned and rested her hands against the edge of the table. "I just want you to know that . . . I'm sorry. For things. Especially me, how I act sometimes. Well, a lot of the time." She looked away. "I'd like you to stay."

"Lady?" Hirianthial said, astonished.

She flexed her hands against the table, looking at the ground. "I haven't had time to figure things out yet," she said, more to herself than to him. She lifted her eyes. "I'd like you to stay. If you want to. Please."

He couldn't read her feelings past the blur in her aura, and lacking that he fell back on more visceral things: the swiftness of her breath. The trembling tension in her fingers. And the uncertainty in her unguarded blue eyes.

"I would be pleased to do so," Hirianthial said.

She took in a little breath, then nodded and left in surprising silence. Hirianthial stared at the door. He stared at it so long that when it chimed again he started.

"Come in."

This time the door slid open for Kis'eh't holding a tray. "Ready for food?"

"More than ready," Hirianthial said, putting aside the first aid kit.

As the Glaseah set the tray on the table, she said, "Was that Reese I saw walking down the hall?"

"Most probably," Hirianthial said.

"Did it . . . was she . . . "

"She came to ask after my health," Hirianthial said.

Kis'eh't let out a long sigh. "Thank the goddess. Reese

is good people, but sometimes she bites off her foot after the trap is open."

The truth of the words surprised Hirianthial into a laugh. "So do we all. But only sometimes."

"Thank goodness for that," Kis'eh't said, setting out the dish and a napkin. She peeked past her arm. "Are you really staying?"

Hirianthial closed his eyes. Between his shoulderblades, resting over his back where his heart kept time, he felt a warm breeze through high branches and smelled the cool spice of Martian wood. He rose slowly from that memory. "Yes. I am."

ROSE POINT
Book Two of
Her Instruments

AVAILABLE IN WINTER 2013

Reese is only just getting used to running the *Earthrise* in the black—and with an Eldritch in her crew—when a trip to a colony world gives rise to a whole new problem: Hirianthial is showing powers that even the Eldritch rarely have, and that only in legend. He badly needs training, support and advice, and the only place he can find them is . . . at home.

To see the world of the Eldritch is a once-in-a-lifetime opportunity, a thing of fantasies and rumor. And to finally meet the Eldritch Queen, the author of so many of Reese's windfalls! You'd have to twist her arm to get her to admit it, but Reese can't wait to go. But a court out of fantasy and a breathtaking land aren't enough compensation when they come packaged with a rabidly xenophobic species whose world is falling apart. The last thing they want any part of is some mortal interloper.

Is Reese ready for the Eldritch world? Better to ask: are they ready for her?

ABOUT THE AUTHOR

Daughter of two Cuban political exiles, M.C.A. Hogarth was born a foreigner in the American melting pot and has had a fascination for the gaps in cultures and the bridges that span them ever since. She has been many things—web database architect, product manager, technical writer and massage therapist—but is currently a full-time parent, artist, writer and anthropologist to aliens, both human and otherwise. She is the author of over fifty titles in the genres of science fiction, fantasy, humor and romance.

Earthrise is only one of the many stories set in the Paradox Pelted universe. For more information, visit the "Where Do I Start?" page on the author's website.

mcahogarth.org
www.twitter.com/mcahogarth

Made in the USA
Middletown, DE
06 March 2018